WHAT DREAMS MAY COME

OTHER COVENANT BOOKS AND AUDIOBOOKS BY DANA LeCHEMINANT

The Thief and the Noble

"A Twist of Christmas" in *The Holly and the Ivy*

WHAT DREAMS MAY COME

A Regency Romance

DANA LeCHEMINANT

Covenant

Covenant Communications, Inc.

Cover image credit line: *Woman in Red* © Monica Lazar, Arcangel

Published by Covenant Communications, Inc.
American Fork, Utah

Library of Congress Cataloging-in-Publication Data

Name: Dana LeCheminant
Title: What dreams may come / Dana LeCheminant
Description: American Fork, UT : Covenant Communications, Inc. [2023]
Identifiers: Library of Congress Control Number 2022944922 | ISBN 9781524423087
LC record available at https://lccn.loc.gov/2022944922

Printed in the United States of America
First Printing: May 2023

29 28 27 26 25 24 23   10 9 8 7 6 5 4 3 2 1

To my mom: the best unexpected brainstorm buddy
I'm starting to think you should write your own book.

Praise for Dana LeCheminant

What Dreams May Come

"*What Dreams May Come* is a really good historical romance that I truly enjoyed. This book meets all of the requirements for a Regency romance and more. I found myself reading whenever I could, hoping that Lucy would find peace and happiness. It was impossible not to love her and want a happily ever after ending. Dana LeCheminant created wonderful characters, each with a strong personality, and whether to love or hate them is an easy choice. I cannot praise this book enough. I really loved it and hated coming to the end and having to say goodbye to Lucy, Simon, William, and the rest of the Calloway family and friends. If you like good historical romance, this is one you can't pass up; it is a winner."

—Readers' Favorite Five-Star Review

The Thief and the Noble

"A delightful retelling of the Robin Hood tale . . . with some added Regency glitz!"

—*InD'tale Magazine*

The Holly and the Ivy

"This festive anthology of sweet historical romances overflows with Christmas cheer . . . In LeCheminant's standout 'A Twist of Christmas,' love blooms between Lord Graham Bartlett, future Earl of Greystone, and Lady Elizabeth Spencer, a duke's daughter, when they respectively swap identities with his brother and her lady's companion to see what it's like to live without the burden of their titles . . . All four stories [in this anthology] deliver witty exchanges, personal growth, and holiday goodness in spades. Readers looking for wholesome Christmas reading will be pleased."

—*Publishers Weekly*

"Historical romance is quickly becoming a genre I'm obsessed with, and I loved how heartwarming and wholesome the characters and plot in each story were. Sarah M. Eden, Esther Hatch, Dana LeCheminant, and Anneka R. Walker are very talented writers, and I'm glad I was able to discover them while reading this collection. I would recommend this anthology to readers who may be wanting to get into the historical romance genre but aren't quite sure where to start. This book has a little bit of everything—banter, love, deep themes of grief and loss, and many other elements that make for a great reading experience, especially around the holidays. I enjoyed it!"

—Readers' Favorite

"Dana's charming characters are real, witty, and oh so lovable! 'A Twist of Christmas' will leave you with a huge smile on your face."

—Anneka R. Walker, author of the Matchmaking Mamas series

Chapter One

Oxfordshire, June 1815

Under the circumstances, Lucy was grateful for the rain and the protection it gave her despite the grumblings of her traveling companions. While it made the roads slick and the air cold, it gave her an odd sense of security knowing only a fool would be out in this weather. Unfortunately for her, Mr. Jonathan Granger was one of the biggest fools she'd ever met.

Why else would he be so determined to marry her, a penniless governess?

As the public coach moved steadily farther from London, Lucy breathed more and more easily. After spending the last five years dodging her employer's younger brother and his professions of love, she was more than ready to move on to something new. Now that the Granger girls were too old to need her as their governess, she finally had both the freedom and the recommendation to start over in a quiet country estate, far from Mr. Granger's searing gaze.

Assuming she arrived in one piece, of course.

"I don't like this storm," Rebecca muttered next to her. The maid, a few years older than Lucy's twenty-two, had offered to accompany Lucy to her new home under the pretext of visiting family in the area, though Lucy suspected Rebecca had no such family. The young woman had taken Lucy under her wing five years past when Lucy had been forced to take up the governess position, and Rebecca had adamantly refused to let her undertake the journey on her own. Honestly, she wasn't sure why Rebecca feared the coach so much. Lucy had taken it alone once before, after her father had died, and while the experience hadn't been pleasant, neither had it been dangerous.

This journey was simply another in what she suspected would be a long line of them. With her father gone and no money or prospects to her name, she would likely never find somewhere to truly call home. She would never belong anywhere, and she had come to terms with that fact.

"We have only a few hours to go," Lucy said, though she knew nothing of the sort. The way Rebecca was staring out the window at the utter darkness was making her nervous.

"It's nearly pitch-black out there," the maid argued. "We're likely to stop soon."

Not thirty seconds later, the coach slowed until it came to a halt, and the other three passengers of the coach breathed a collective sigh of relief. The roads truly had been slippery, knocking them all about as the driver struggled to keep them from sliding off the road.

From her window, Lucy could see the lights of a little inn glowing through the rain, and she winced. She would not part easily with the money it would cost to pay for a room for the night, but what could she do? They couldn't very well keep driving through a storm so violent, and she wasn't due to meet the Winthrop family until late tomorrow. She had time yet.

"Let's get inside, then," she said to Rebecca, gratefully taking the water-logged coachman's hand as he helped her climb down.

The sooner she could go to sleep, the sooner tomorrow would come and her new future along with it, but that was only if she managed to fall asleep in the first place. She had always had a hard time sleeping anywhere but her home, and she had endured nearly a full week of sleepless nights at the Grangers' before finally settling in there when she'd first come to them. Tonight would likely be several hours of staring at the ceiling, but at least she would be out of the rain and in a warm bed.

Or perhaps not.

When she entered the inn, Lucy's stomach twisted at the sight of so many people inside. There must have been others caught in the storm, and the whole gathering room was full of soaked men and women. Standing out of the way with Rebecca, Lucy prayed there would be room for them.

"I don't like this either," Rebecca whispered, leaning in close. She had her eyes fixed on the crowd of weary travelers, and she jumped when the door opened behind them to let in even more.

Lucy frowned. Rebecca was supposed to be the brave one between them. She had, after all, been the only one to befriend the gentleman's daughter-turned-governess when the rest of the staff had turned their noses up at Lucy. Her father *had* been a gentleman, technically, but after a series of disasters destroyed most of the income from their land, he had taken up tailoring in order to keep food on the table, so Lucy was not unused to laboring for survival.

But then he had gotten sick, and Lucy had suddenly found herself alone and penniless at seventeen, with a mountain of debts to repay. The governess position with Mr. and Mrs. Granger had been a godsend, as had Rebecca, but Lucy had still spent the last five years feeling unsettled and lost.

Taking the maid's hand, she tried to ignore the sopping people behind them. Most likely, the two of them would end up stuck in the front room along with everyone else, and Lucy would not sleep for a moment. How could she with so many people around?

The door opened once again, and she looked over on instinct. She had grown accustomed to checking the door in case it might be Mr. Granger coming to propose yet again, as he had made it a habit to seek her out whenever he visited his brother. She almost thought she recognized him beneath the hat of the man who stepped in from the rain.

"Nonsense," she told herself. She had no reason to expect him so far from London, and she was only tired, imagining his face in her exhaustion and nervousness.

The new arrival pushed his way through the crowd to the harried innkeeper, who was deep in conversation with three people at once. "I'm in need of a room, good man!" he said loudly.

And Lucy's blood turned cold. She would recognize that voice anywhere, and she shrank back against the wall. It *was* Mr. Granger. But what was he doing here? He almost never left London.

"Lucy?"

Lucy clapped a hand over Rebecca's mouth and frantically searched for somewhere to hide. Mr. Granger hadn't noticed her yet, but it was only a matter of time before he turned around and found her.

"I'm afraid all my rooms are taken," the innkeeper said to Mr. Granger. "Everyone else will have to find a place down here."

Lucy felt dizzy. She had nowhere to go, but she couldn't stay where she was. If Mr. Granger found her here, he would take it as a sign that they were meant to be together and offer his hand in marriage yet again.

He likely wouldn't give her a choice.

Not knowing where to go, she released Rebecca and ducked behind the nearest person between her and Mr. Granger, a man of considerable height and enough bulk to keep her from view until she found a way to keep herself safe. Perhaps someone would be willing to shield her.

But who would protect a stranger all night?

"Er, good evening?" a deep voice said.

Lucy glanced up, eyes going wide as she realized her unwitting protector had noticed her. "Good evening, sir," she squeaked, ducking into a hasty curtsy. "I . . ." How could she explain?

The man frowned at her, as she was still bent over to hide. "Are you all right, miss?"

The truth came out of her before she could decide whether she could trust this man. "No." He looked kind enough, but so did Mr. Granger, and appearances could be deceiving. Lucy had made the mistake of trusting Mr. Granger and his outward goodness when she met him, and his hungry, roving eyes had quickly changed her opinion of the man. With no one else to turn to, she prayed she wouldn't repeat the mistake with this gentleman.

"Is there some way I can be of assistance?"

Mr. Granger had broken into an argument with the innkeeper, and Rebecca had finally noticed him, her face pale as she adopted Lucy's method and slipped behind a person waiting out the storm.

Lucy swallowed. The only way to ensure their safety was to seek help, and so far only this stranger had noticed her distress. "That man over there"—she nodded to Mr. Granger—"is someone I would very much like to avoid."

The man studied Mr. Granger for a moment, and thankfully he lowered his voice a bit as he asked, "Do you know him?"

"Too well."

"A relation?"

Lucy shuddered. "He would like to be my husband."

A smile played on the man's lips. He was quite young, likely only a year or two older than Lucy, and he dressed well enough to indicate he came from decent money. From all outward appearances, he had no reason to give her any notice, but he seemed to be studying her just as she studied him. "And you are not of the same mind," he surmised.

"Not particularly." Lucy had hoped she would never see Mr. Granger again.

Something akin to mischief entered her protector's eyes as he glanced between Lucy and Mr. Granger, as if a plan were forming in his mind, and Lucy wasn't sure she wanted to know what that plan was. She didn't know this man, and she had no reason to trust him. Surely there was a woman somewhere who could—

"Follow my lead," he said, straightening up and tucking Lucy's arm around his. Before she could protest, he steered her toward the stairs, pausing when they reached a woman who looked to be the innkeeper's wife. "Is our room ready, Mrs. Jones?" he asked.

The woman blinked in surprise, clearly unsure why Lucy was standing there. "Yes, of course, Mr. Calloway. Forgive me, but I didn't realize your wife was so close behind you."

Wife? Lucy was most certainly *not* his wife.

But the man—Mr. Calloway—smiled, looking all the more handsome with the expression. He truly was attractive, though there was a roguishness to him that Lucy did not much like, particularly because a gleam in his eyes told her he knew exactly what he was doing, as if he had done something similar before. "I am not keen on riding in carriages," he said, "so I was on horseback. I rode ahead when the storm hit so I might secure a room for us. My dear, we should get you warm." He said that last bit to Lucy.

Perhaps she did not know much of the world, but she knew enough to know that she should never, under any circumstances, go up to this man's room. If she put up enough of a fight, she was sure the woman would come to her rescue, if not others as well. She may have only been a governess, but she would ensure her reputation remained intact.

If she could keep Mr. Granger at bay for five years, she could certainly handle a strange gentleman in the middle of who knew where. As long as she didn't make enough of a scene that she caught Mr. Granger's attention. He would surely come to her "rescue" and find some way to bring her back to London against her will.

Mr. Calloway leaned in close, and all of Lucy's faculties failed her when his breath brushed her neck. Not even Mr. Granger had been so close before, and she had no idea how to respond to the sensation. "I mean you no harm," he whispered, as if he knew her thoughts. "I will explain everything, and you will have my room for your use. Without me in it."

She wanted to tell him she would never believe his lies, but there was something in his gaze that spoke of goodness, not only on the outside but on the inside as well. Was it possible to know a man's intentions simply by looking at him? Lucy had always thought so when it came to Mr. Granger and his staring, but could the same be true of the opposite sort of person?

It was Rebecca who answered the man before Lucy could, appearing at her side in an instant. "Yes, my lady, we must get you dry."

Only because Mr. Granger had lost his argument with the innkeeper and was heading their way did Lucy agree to follow Mr. Calloway up the stairs, though she had no intention of remaining in his room. When she had sought his help, this most certainly had not been what she meant.

When they reached Mr. Calloway's fire-warmed room upstairs, she prepared her defense. She would not be staying in his room, and she would tell him so just as soon as she found her voice.

Rebecca had no such problem. "Thank you, sir. I was most worried for Miss Hayes."

Mr. Calloway smiled, looking very charming as he did, and Lucy had to wonder how many women he had lured into his rooms with those lips of his. She shuddered at the thought. "I am happy to be of service," he said.

"Why?" The word slipped from Lucy's tongue, and she was certain the only reason she had found the courage to speak was because Mr. Calloway had left the door partially open. "Why would you help me? You do not know me."

Putting a few more logs onto the fire, he yet again flashed Lucy that handsome smile, the kind of smile that likely broke many hearts in London.

His clothing was fashionable enough to put him rather high in social status, and she wondered if he had ever interacted with the Grangers. Not that she had ever met any of their acquaintances. And she wondered again why such a man would help her. There had to be a reason he would risk both their reputations with his deception.

Once he deemed the fire big enough, he stood at his full height and gestured to a chair at the small table in the room, which was piled with far more food than a man could eat on his own. "You were in distress. Need I another reason? Please, eat. I am sure you are famished after your journey."

Lucy only sat because she was tired and hungry. Not because she trusted the man. She wanted to be anywhere but here, but she could no longer go downstairs without risking an encounter with Mr. Granger. "I cannot go along with this lie, sir."

"Of course you can," Rebecca replied. She had no qualms about loading up a plate with food and was quick to shove it into Lucy's hands.

"No, I cannot," Lucy repeated, trying to shove the plate back. "It was kind of you to offer, sir, but I refuse to share—"

"I will be sleeping in the stables." Mr. Calloway folded his arms and raised an eyebrow, as if daring Lucy to find fault with that statement. "Like I said, you may have the room without me in it."

She had plenty of arguments, even if his comment caught her off guard. "You can't sleep in the stables."

"Why not? Plenty of us will be out there."

"But you have a bed."

"Which I have already offered to you."

"Miss." Rebecca eyed Mr. Calloway for a moment, then leaned in close to whisper into Lucy's ear. "I don't feel right about staying here."

"Exactly." *Finally* some sense. Staying in a man's room—even being here in the first place—was dangerous.

"No, I mean, with Mr. Granger downstairs, we should find a horse or cart to keep moving," Rebecca said.

"In this rain?" Mr. Calloway's voice made them both jump. Apparently Rebecca had not been as quiet as she'd thought.

Lucy grimaced, torn between the growing fear in Rebecca's expression and the watchful look in Mr. Calloway's. She was too tired and unsettled to juggle them both. "Rebecca, I know Mr. Granger is downstairs, but we cannot—"

"I will not let you put yourself in danger!"

"Please," Mr. Calloway threw in. "I insist. I cannot in good conscience subject you to that man when you are clearly afraid of him. Remaining up here as my wife will give him no reason to think you might be in the same place."

"Remaining here as your wife when I am not will lead to my ruin, sir."

"Only if someone discovers the truth," Mr. Calloway countered, his voice growing softer. "Which they will not do if you stay. And in the morning, we will part ways as strangers, and you never have to see me again."

As Lucy struggled to know what she should do, something shifted in Mr. Calloway's countenance. Though it was subtle, Lucy recognized it easily enough. She had seen the looming pain in her father's face many times before he'd died, and her heart immediately picked up its speed.

Rising to her feet, she approached the man. Sure enough, a sheen of sweat had already beaded on his brow, and not from the heat of the fire behind him. "Are you well, sir?"

He nodded but slowly. "Perfectly. I need only a drink of water and . . ." His stance wavered at the same time his arms loosened in their fold.

Lucy swallowed. "Sit," she said, though she hardly had any right to command the man.

He did as directed, however, falling heavily into one of the armchairs by the fire. "Perhaps I . . ." Whatever he might have said was lost in a sigh.

Lucy's issue with the lie he had told downstairs was lost as well. She couldn't focus on the problems he had created when his eyes glazed over with delirium. The man needed help.

Rebecca leaped to her feet, turning pale. "What is wrong with him?"

Lucy grimaced even as she fumbled to grab her handkerchief. It was already soaked with rain, so she pressed it to Mr. Calloway's burning forehead. As she suspected, he hardly acknowledged her touch. "Fever," she said, though she had never seen one come on this quickly. "We must send for a doctor, but if I go downstairs . . ."

Thankfully, Rebecca was swift to listen and slipped out the door in search of the innkeeper. Hopefully without running into Mr. Granger. Rebecca was used to slipping around unnoticed and would be better able to avoid the man.

Mr. Calloway moaned a little, his eyes meeting Lucy's in the firelight. "Just wait until they meet you, my love," he muttered before slumping, unconscious, in the chair.

Lucy bit her lip. Perhaps she did not know the man, but she prayed he would make it through the night. He had shown her nothing but kindness and seemed to be of a good sort, and men like that were rare. He had been right when he'd said staying here was her best chance at remaining undetected, and she owed her safety to the man in front of her. Ensuring his own safety was the least she could do.

* * *

The night passed in a whirlwind. The doctor had already been on his way to the inn to help one of the coachmen who had also taken ill after being out in the storm, but he gave most of his attention to Mr. Calloway. According to him, it was the worst fever he'd ever seen.

Lucy did what she could to be helpful. Though a perfect stranger to the man—she had not even introduced herself—she felt indebted to him in a strange way. If he were to be believed, he had been about to go sleep in the stables, even though he had been in the rain far longer than she had, on horseback as he'd been.

When the rain finally let up sometime in the early-morning hours, the doctor decided Mr. Calloway needed to be sent home, where he could have better care.

Lucy was exhausted, and her worry over Mr. Calloway had left her in a state of anxiety and hardly aware of what was happening around her. Would the poor man survive? The physician did not seem hopeful, nor did the innkeeper's wife as she wrapped a blanket around Lucy's shoulders and helped her downstairs to a waiting carriage. That didn't stop the woman from trying to convince Lucy otherwise. "He will be right as rain once he gets home, mark my words, dear. You just keep on looking after him until you arrive, and all will be well."

Lucy chose not to argue, using the woman as a shield to avoid being seen by anyone in the main room downstairs, Rebecca following closely behind them.

When the carriage door closed and the driver called the horses to move, she finally breathed a small sigh. She had plenty of problems still to deal with, but at least Mr. Granger would no longer be one of them.

"Where do you suppose we are going?" she asked Rebecca, keeping her voice low to avoid waking Mr. Calloway slumped on the other seat. He likely wouldn't wake during their journey, considering he'd been unconscious all night, but she wanted to be courteous regardless. He had offered his assistance and was continuing to give it even without his knowledge.

Rebecca shrugged with a wide yawn. "Mr. Calloway's home, I suppose."

"But we're supposed to be in Lowbury tonight."

"We'll find a coach when we get there. From what I gathered talking to the driver, this one is taking us part of the way already, and it can't be much farther."

Rebecca yawned again, falling against Lucy's shoulder and snuggling up. She had never been very good at working without a good night's rest. Though Lucy had teased her about it over the years, now she wished she had taught her friend how to stay awake when faced with catastrophic circumstances, for surely that was what this was. Lucy was in a strange coach with a strange man, under the guise of being the man's wife. She had no idea where she was, and all her possessions, few though they were, were back at the inn because she had not had a chance to bring them up to the room she had unwillingly shared with Mr. Calloway. The fever had come on so quickly, and there had been no way to correct her mistaken identity without risking being found by Mr. Granger, and Lucy had no idea what to do now.

How would she explain this?

If she was lucky, Mr. Calloway lived alone. She could explain to the servants that she had been sent to look after their master, and then she would return to the inn and carry on her way. Would the driver find it strange that she was not staying with her supposed husband? She would explain to him as well and reveal the truth. It wasn't as if he knew her true name, and as long as the village of Lowbury was still a good distance away, no one need ever know of her involvement with Mr. Calloway, little though it may have been. If nothing else, she could have the man himself deny any rumors that might fly about.

Perhaps everything would be all right, assuming Mr. Calloway did not die on the journey. Though he shivered beneath the blankets that had been draped over him, he looked well enough under the circumstances.

With that thought, Lucy rested her head against Rebecca's and finally fell fast asleep.

Chapter Two

"Oh my goodness. William!"

Lucy woke with a start, Rebecca jumping awake beside her, and sunlight filled the coach as the door opened, though it was quickly blocked by a silhouette as someone peered inside. She felt as if she had only just fallen asleep, though she must have been out for at least an hour, judging by how brightly the sun shone. Mr. Calloway hadn't moved, but two young men were already reaching inside and pulling him up into their arms.

Had they arrived already? Lucy wasn't prepared to explain why she was in the coach with Mr. Calloway, and the elegant woman who watched over him soon fixed her gaze back into the coach where Lucy waited with Rebecca, bleary-eyed and exhausted.

"Come along, dears," the woman said, holding out a hand. "Let's get you inside before you are stuck in there a moment longer."

Only because she was so tired did Lucy choose not to argue. She would explain things as soon as she was asked, but for now, she could only follow where she was led.

The house—it was rather large, though Lucy didn't get a good look at it before she was inside—was a flurry of activity, servants rushing about and being most attentive to Mr. Calloway as they carried him inside. The woman who still held Lucy's hand was quick to give orders, asking for clean water, extra blankets, a bath drawn up, and the physician to be fetched from the drawing room, where he was already waiting.

"And where is Olivia?" she asked a passing maid.

"I am here," another gentle voice replied, preceding a young woman a few years younger than Lucy. "Oh goodness, he looks terrible, doesn't he?"

"Olivia," the older woman replied, "I need to see to William. If you would take—"

"Of course," Olivia replied and wrapped her arm through Lucy's. She offered a kind smile as the other woman—her mother, perhaps?—rushed off after Mr. Calloway. Everything about her was soft, from her chocolate-brown curls to her hazel eyes to her touch on Lucy's arm, and Lucy liked her immediately.

Perhaps she would not be too put out with Lucy once she explained everything. Just as she was about to offer up her explanation, however, Olivia spoke again. "You look absolutely exhausted." She pulled Lucy closer. "We're drawing up a bath for you, and your maid can—"

"She's not my—"

"Tell me how to get downstairs," Rebecca cut in, "and I'll be right happy to help with the preparations."

Lucy stared at her. They were practically equals now that Lucy had taken to working as a governess, so why would Rebecca be so eager to serve her? "You don't have to do that," she whispered.

Rebecca shook her head. "Yes, I do. It's better for everyone." She had whispered as quietly as Lucy had, glancing at Olivia with wary eyes. What on earth was she thinking? They were perfectly safe now.

With a warm smile, Olivia nodded at Rebecca. "I think most things are ready, but you could assist upstairs. I'm sure your mistress would prefer a friendly face before we overwhelm her."

Lucy was *already* overwhelmed. She had no idea what was going on.

"Do you mind if I call you by your Christian name?" Olivia asked as she led the two of them up the wide staircase. "It seems so silly to call you anything otherwise, all things considered."

As they reached the top of the staircase, they walked down a grand corridor full of more doors than Lucy could count, and her heart picked up its pace. This family was more than just a wealthy family, and the longer she was inside the house, the more trouble she realized she was in. As soon as someone figured out who she was, they would run her out of town with their influence alone. Whoever the Calloways were, they were not a family to be crossed.

The girl's question suddenly registered, and Lucy faltered in her step. "Er, I'm Lucy," she whispered as a shiver ran through her. She shouldn't have said that. This was absolutely not the place she should be right now, and she had no business sharing her name. Wherever this was, it was far from her actual destination, and she had no connection to this family.

"I'm Olivia," Olivia replied, as warm as ever. "Though, I'm sure you knew that already."

A nervousness beyond what Lucy was already feeling started to creep up into her stomach. The way she spoke, Olivia seemed to think Lucy should know all about the family. But why would she think that? Just who did she think Lucy was?

As she led Lucy into an exquisitely elegant bedchamber with a blazing fire, Olivia answered that unspoken question for her. "You can't imagine our surprise when we received that note from the innkeeper," she said. "William was coming home—and with a wife, no less!"

Lucy felt near to fainting, and she sank onto the softest mattress she had ever felt. How was she supposed to come out of this unscathed if the whole family thought she was married to Mr. Calloway? They would hate her, no question, and they would ensure anyone they knew would hate her. She would be ruined. "I am not Mr. Calloway's wife," she breathed. No point in prolonging her downfall.

Olivia's hazel eyes opened wide, her mouth forming a little *O*, and she looked to Rebecca, as if hoping for clarification.

For some reason, Rebecca chose to respond to her silent question. "Not his wife *yet*, that is."

Lucy's jaw dropped. What in heaven's name was Rebecca thinking? "No, that's not—"

"Oh, that makes so much more sense!" Olivia said, and her smile returned even wider. "William has always enjoyed surprises, but I hardly thought he could get married without telling us about it. Oh, but we cannot have you in this room! It connects to William's, and that is entirely inappropriate until you are actually married. I will have this fixed immediately."

She was out of the room before Lucy could get a word in to correct her.

The instant they were alone, Lucy grabbed Rebecca's wrist and pulled her down onto the bed so they were at the same level. "Why would you say that?" she hissed. "I have no understanding with him! I hardly know the man!"

Though she turned a little pink, Rebecca set her jaw and looked determined to stick to her lie. "I told you, Lucy. This is better. It might be the only way to keep you safe."

That caught her off guard, and Lucy leaned back a little. "Safe? From what? Mr. Granger?"

"Yes."

"But he did not find me. I'm already safe."

"For now."

"*Rebecca.* I cannot marry a man I met at an inn!"

The maid scoffed and got back to her feet, looking around the room as if searching for something to do. "No one said you had to marry him. I only think you should keep the mistake going for a little while, just in case."

A headache was building in the front of Lucy's head, and she rubbed her temples, trying to dispel the pain. Surely she would be better off finding a way to Lowbury so she could begin her new employment, but Rebecca was so afraid; there had to be more to this. "In case of what? Rebecca, what aren't you telling me?"

Cringing, Rebecca shook her head. "Oh, miss, if you'd but heard what I did."

That was all she said before Olivia returned, as bright and happy as ever. "Never fear," the girl said. "We've got a different room all prepared for you, and the bath is almost ready to go. You must be frozen after that storm!"

Lucy opened her mouth to yet again attempt to set things right, but Olivia cut her off with a sudden embrace.

"You have no idea how happy we are that you are here," she said into Lucy's ear. "You've brought my brother back. Mother was afraid he would never return, and I think this is the best thing to ever happen to her. You're the best thing to ever happen."

Tears pooled in Lucy's eyes, and she had no idea what to feel. She was both terrified and excited, and she couldn't remember the last time she'd been held so tightly. The deception could never last, and her guilt would bring out the truth sooner or later no matter what Rebecca was hiding from her, but for this moment, she just let Olivia hold her as her exhaustion practically overwhelmed her. She pretended she had come home.

Chapter Three

When Lucy woke after her bath, though she couldn't remember falling asleep, she was in the softest bed she had ever felt. The room they had given her was no less elegant than the first, and she knew without a doubt that the Calloway family was wealthier than she could imagine. She had tried multiple times to tell Olivia the truth before the girl left her to her bath, but Rebecca had kept up a steady stream of conversation until finally Lucy had given up. Whatever reasons the maid had, they were enough to make her a formidable opponent.

Lucy would simply have to wait until she was alone with one of the family to explain everything.

She found Rebecca asleep on the chaise longue at the other end of the large room and wondered if she could sneak out, but it took her only a moment to realize she was dressed in a nightgown and could hardly walk around a stranger's house in such disarray. Even worse, she realized she had absolutely nothing to wear, as all her things were still at the inn. What was she to do? Would she have to suffer humiliation as well as guilt? Perhaps if she rang the bell pull, a servant would arrive and fetch one of the family members, preferably Olivia.

"Oh, you're awake!" Rebecca shot up so fast that Lucy jumped, nearly stumbling into the wall where the bell pull hung. "You should have woken me."

Though she should have marveled at the fact that she had slept so soundly in a strange place, Lucy was still too tired to feel at all capable of addressing the mess she was in in being mistaken as Mr. Calloway's intended. She could focus on only one thing at a time.

"Rebecca, I need to find something to wear. Do you—where did you get that dress?"

Rebecca glanced down. "One of the other maids lent it to me. The housekeeper said she would find me some spares to use while we're here."

The way she'd worded that, it sounded as if Rebecca planned to stay for a good deal of time. Lucy couldn't condone that. She was due to meet the Winthrops in Lowbury that evening. She would do well to write to them in case it took longer to arrive than she hoped.

First things first. "You and I are about the same size, aren't we? Do you think you could procure me another—"

The maid's wicked grin cut Lucy off. "I have something much better," she said and hurried to the wardrobe. From within, she pulled an exquisite gown of pale green that made Lucy's jaw drop. "Isn't it beautiful?" Rebecca asked. "Miss Calloway said she never wears it, so she'll hardly miss it."

"I could never," Lucy whispered, even as she tiptoed forward so she could feel the silk. Even with a tailor for a father, she'd never seen such fine fabric. Her heart ached to wear such a thing, but her guilt grew stronger with each passing second. "Rebecca, we cannot stay here."

"But it isn't—"

"Safe? Will you not tell me what you mean?"

Hanging her head, Rebecca sank onto the chaise. "Mr. Granger."

An involuntary shudder ran through Lucy, and she glanced at the door, as if he might step into the room even here. Whenever he had visited his brother's family, he had always sought Lucy out, even when she was with the girls in their chambers. Luckily, he had never broken any rules of propriety such as being alone with her, but Lucy was certain that was only by luck. Had they been anywhere but his brother's home . . .

She frowned. "Mr. Jonathan Granger has continued on to wherever he was going. I'll never have to see him again, though I am sorry you will." Her eyes went wide as realization hit her. "Rebecca! You need to get back to London! You were supposed to be gone for only a few days."

"I came to make sure you arrived at your final destination safely," the maid replied, though her voice had gone quiet. "The missus will understand, or if she doesn't . . . I can find work somewhere else. Maybe that would be better, after Mr. Granger . . ."

Lucy's stomach clenched. She didn't miss how pale Rebecca had gone. "After Mr. Granger what?"

The maid bit her lip. "I really don't want to say."

"Rebecca."

"I overheard him telling one of the footmen that if he couldn't stop you from leaving, he planned to waylay our journey before we ever arrived at the Winthrops'," Rebecca whispered. "He wants to carry you off back to London so he can finally marry you. The only reason he didn't catch us leaving London was because I arranged for us to leave while he had business dealings."

Lucy had wondered why Mr. Granger had not been at his brother's house the morning she left, when he had certainly known she was leaving soon. She had expected a final attempt at persuading her to take his hand, but she had said her goodbyes to the rest of the family with ease and left without any strife.

At least, that was what she had thought until she saw him at the inn.

"Wait," Lucy said, her stomach dropping. "Did you say *'carry me off*?"

Rebecca nodded slowly, her face still pale as she smoothed a nonexistent wrinkle in the green dress. "You saw him at the inn, sure as I did."

"He wouldn't dare something as brash as dragging me away," Lucy argued. Would he? She honestly didn't know, and the thought of the man forcing her into a marriage that would only bring her grief made her sick to her stomach.

Her father had always talked of how deeply he'd loved her mother even years after she was gone, and Lucy had always dreamed of finding a love that strong for herself. After his death, it was the only hope she'd had left, and she could never love Mr. Granger. Not even with time. The last five years had only made her detest him more with each moment of knowing him.

She had never known anyone to look at women the way Mr. Granger did. It was the same look he gave his favorite dog and his stacks of banknotes when he and his brother made a good business deal.

"This is why you need to be engaged to Mr. Calloway," Rebecca said, pulling Lucy out of her thoughts.

That made no sense whatsoever. "Rebecca, I—"

"Mr. Granger will never think to look in a place like this," the maid said, as if Lucy had agreed to her scheme. "And if, by chance, he does come, all anyone will be able to tell him is you are already to be married. What could he do then?"

"Carry me off anyway," Lucy argued. "Because I am *not* engaged to Mr. Calloway, and I never will be. He will admit to as much as soon as he wakes."

"*If* he wakes, you mean."

"Rebecca!"

"No disrespect to the man, only he doesn't look well. But Mr. Calloway helped you at the inn, so maybe he would help you now. Besides, you need pretend just long enough for Granger to give up the hunt."

Folding her arms with a huff, Lucy wished she were dressed so she could avoid this ridiculous conversation. As it was, she was tempted to leave the chamber anyway and suffer humiliation. Anything would be better than entertaining the idea of lying to such a wealthy family. "And how long will that be?" she asked. "The man has been trying to win my hand for five years. I would not be surprised if he kept at it for another five. He's an idiot, but he's a stubborn one."

Rebecca wrinkled her nose. "You know as well as I do he's got no sense of industry. He's earned his wealth through easy trades and tricking weaker minds. You were only his target because you were an easy one."

"Thank you."

"I didn't mean it as an insult to you, my lady."

"Don't call me that, Rebecca. I'm not anyone's lady. And I will not deceive this family any further than I already have."

"Even if it would keep you safe?"

As much as Lucy wanted to keep up her end of the argument, the thought of Mr. Granger finding her made her cringe. Rebecca was correct in thinking the man would likely never find her here at the Calloway estate. Wherever here was. Even a day or two with the Calloways might delay his search long enough that she could arrive at her new place of employment after he had already been there, leaving her free to continue forward without him causing problems.

But could she really use the Calloway family like that? They had only shown her kindness and didn't deserve to be thrown unknowingly into her sad little life.

"Please think on it," Rebecca said, grasping Lucy's hand in a very sisterly way. It was similar to how Olivia had held her arm the day before. "You deserve better than the likes of Jonathan Granger. Maybe this family can help you. Now, let's get you dressed."

Lucy stared at the young woman, unsure how to proceed. She must take things one step at a time, starting with the most important. "I am not letting you risk your position for me, Rebecca. You need to go back, and I will find my own way."

"I don't want to go back."

"Why wouldn't you—"

"You need to get dressed, miss."

"I am not wearing that gown!"

The next thing she knew, Lucy was standing in the corridor in the loveliest dress she had ever worn and wishing she was better at wrestling. But Rebecca had put up quite a fight, and Lucy had stopped struggling only for fear of tearing the gown that didn't belong to her.

This was as far as she would go, however. Rebecca could force her to dress, but she could not force her down to luncheon.

"Oh, my dear, that color is lovely on you."

Lucy spun around with a gasp, dipping into a curtsy out of reflex at the sight of the family matron. Without knowing more about the family or how highly they were ranked, she wasn't sure how to address Mr. Calloway's mother, and she hated that, but she had to say *something*. "Mrs. Calloway, I—"

"Oh, come now." The elegant woman waved her hand at Lucy before she'd even gotten halfway through her curtsy. "None of that. We are to be family."

Now was as good a time as any to explain the truth. "Um, actually, I'm not—"

"You forgot this, miss!" Rebecca dashed out of the room behind Lucy and stuffed a pin of some sort into Lucy's dark hair. "Oh, beg your pardon, ma'am. I didn't see you." She sank into a curtsy of her own, but there wasn't even a hint of surprise in her expression.

Mrs. Calloway, or whatever she was called, smiled at the maid before reaching out and taking Lucy's hand. "That's quite all right," she said warmly. Then she turned back to Lucy and smiled even wider, though she looked as weary as Lucy felt. "Now, would you like to see William before we go down for luncheon?"

No, she did not want to see the man she hardly knew. "I am not sure that would be appropriate," she said, "seeing as I'm not—"

"Nonsense. You'll be his wife soon enough, so there could hardly be anything untoward in visiting his sickbed. If we can get him to wake, I am sure he would be most eager to see you."

Eager? Hardly. Confused? Most certainly.

Mrs. Calloway talked almost nonstop as she led Lucy down the corridor, leaving her no room to speak the truth. The woman spoke of her son's long absences, how he was so often traveling and rarely at home. But when they entered the room where a doctor still attended to an unconscious Mr. Calloway, Lucy could feel the woman's energy dim until it was almost entirely gone. Perhaps the one-sided conversation had been to distract herself more than anything else.

"Has there been any change?" Mrs. Calloway asked the physician.

Lucy retreated to the corner, resting a hand on a bureau and wondering when she would get a chance to tell the family who she really was. At least now she did not have Rebecca interrupting her, but she could not drop such a surprise in a sickroom, of all places. The room was dreary enough already.

The physician sighed after feeling the pulse of Mr. Calloway's heart. "I'm afraid not, Lady Calloway."

Lucy's hand slipped from the bureau, and she nearly tumbled to the ground. *Lady?*

"Are you all right, dear?" Lady Calloway asked. Her voice had lost its strength, leaving her words airy and thin.

As much as she wanted to tell the truth, Lucy could not do so now. Not here. "Will he survive?" she asked instead, staring at Mr. Calloway's ashen complexion. What if the man was so ill that he died? Lucy's presence would only make things worse, and the family would likely hate her for bringing their son and brother home in such a state. It wouldn't matter if she was at fault for his fever or not.

She wanted to run, but she wasn't sure that was the best course of action. Oh, why had Rebecca told that lie in the first place? They could have avoided all of this and been well on their way to Lowbury.

To Mr. Granger.

Lucy tucked her arms around her middle, trying to dispel the discomfort churning in her stomach.

With tears in her eyes, Lady Calloway approached and pulled Lucy into an embrace that caught her off guard, enough that she stood frozen. "William has been in worse states than this, my dear. I am sure he will pull through."

Lucy hoped he did. Then maybe he could correct Rebecca's misguided deception since Lucy was having a hard time of it on her own. Horrified by such a selfish thought about a man who might be dying of fever, Lucy wrapped her arms around Lady Calloway's waist in search of comfort and was surprised by how familiar the embrace felt.

For the smallest of flickering moments, she entertained the idea of this woman becoming her mother-in-law and couldn't help but smile a little. To live in such a grand home alongside ladies like Olivia and her mother would be a dream. Simply having a *family* would be a dream. Lucy had never known her own mother, and she wondered what her life might have been like if her mother hadn't died when Lucy was so young.

"Is Lord Calloway at home?" the doctor asked, interrupting the moment.

Lucy gulped. Of course there was a Lord Calloway, and she had little hope that he would be as gracious as his female family members. Whatever his rank, he was so far above Lucy that he would hardly give her notice. Unless . . . She bit her lip. Unless he thought she was to be his daughter-in-law, in which case he would want to know everything about her.

He would certainly be the one to learn the truth, and he would be furious.

Leaving Lucy to her wild and fearful thoughts, Lady Calloway returned to her son's side. "Simon is not due to return until tomorrow, I'm afraid."

Lucy breathed a sigh of relief. If he was not going to be at home until tomorrow, that gave her plenty of time to explain the situation to the kind ladies of the house. Away from the sickroom.

"Well, there is not much more I can do for young William today," the physician replied. "I would like to discuss his condition with Lord Calloway when he returns, so I will return tomorrow as well."

Lady Calloway took the man's hand between both of hers, tears shining in her eyes. "You are a godsend, Mr. Pritchard. I will keep him under constant care until you arrive, and I will alert you to any changes."

"Very good. I will see myself out." He nodded to Lucy as he passed, though she couldn't do much more than attempt a smile. There must have been someone out in the corridor, because muffled voices came through the open door, and then a maid slipped inside with some rags and a bowl of water.

"Come, Lucy," Lady Calloway said, linking her arm with Lucy's. "I am sure you are famished after the night you had."

Lucy tried to respond, but she made the mistake of glancing back at poor Mr. Calloway, unconscious but clearly suffering from his fever. He was not doing well; even she could see that. And though Lady Calloway smiled, her expression only partially masked the worry she must have been feeling over the safety of her child.

Lucy could easily tell this woman the truth as they walked alone down the corridor, but was it really the best thing to do? Perhaps she should wait until Mr. Calloway's future was less uncertain. At the very least, she should wait until Lady Calloway was stronger than she was now. Otherwise, the truth might injure her more than the lie.

Or was that simply her selfishness talking? Yes, maybe lying about who she was would keep her protected from Mr. Granger. But even more than that, Lucy had never been in a house this grand nor worn a dress this fine, and she had never even spoken to a lady, let alone embraced one. Lady Calloway and her daughter had treated her like family, and she hadn't felt so wanted since before her father had died.

Five years was a long time to go without a family, and she felt safe for the first time in years. She'd thought she would never feel this way again.

"Are you crying, dear?" Lady Calloway stopped just short of what Lucy guessed was a dining room of sorts, a wrinkle on her brow as she brushed a soft finger across Lucy's cheeks. "You must be so overwhelmed, in a new place with William indisposed and you knowing no one. I cannot imagine what you've been through these last couple of days."

I'm not who you think I am, Lucy wanted to say, but she couldn't bring herself to do it.

Not yet.

Chapter Four

Simon Calloway was not keen on traveling, and he considered it quite the ordeal every time he had to go anywhere beyond the estate boundaries. There was always so much to plan: horses to rest, carriages to maintain, inns to secure. He would do away with all of it if he could. Still, it was part of his role as baron, and he was not about to shirk his duty after his father had always done it so well. There were few things Simon did well, but he hoped filling his father's shoes in this regard was one of them.

He was never so glad to be on the road than when he knew he was on his way back home.

This time, he had opted to ride his horse rather than take the carriage, which would follow him with his valet, as riding on his own would bring him back half a day early. He had already been delayed by a massive rainstorm, so he was eager to keep the rest of the journey as short as possible.

Calloway Park came into sight none too soon, and Simon's horse, Hermes, seemed as eager to finish the ride as he was, picking up his pace and seeming to fly down the road.

Both man and beast were breathing hard when they came to a halt outside the stables, and Simon rubbed the steed's sweaty neck in appreciation. It had been a while since they'd had a good bruising ride like that, and they had probably both needed it. Hermes spent far too much time being walked by the stablehands while his master was away on business.

Just as Simon was slipping from the saddle, the estate's head of stables, Jed, stepped out and called, "Master Simon! We didn't expect you until tomorrow." Taking hold of Hermes's reins, he gave Simon an examining look and smiled. Jed was barely thirty, only a year older than Simon, but he had taken to guessing Simon's mood simply by looking at him, and more often than not, he was right. The two had developed a friendship since the Calloways had taken the stablemaster on.

"Eager to be back, I see," Jed said, rubbing the horse's neck as Simon pulled out his few belongings he had brought with him in the saddlebag.

"More than ever." Simon threw his bag over one shoulder and took a good long look at Calloway Park. He had always loved this house and the wild grounds around it, and the sight of it never grew tiresome. There was something special about the place, no doubt about it, and he felt like he could breathe again for the first time in weeks.

"William has come from London," Jed said, and Simon could have hugged the man. As much as he loved his family, he did not much like surprises. At least, not ones that concerned him. It was hard enough to keep up with the estate and all the business ventures his father had begun without his family doing anything unexpected. Jed's ability to decipher Simon's mood wasn't a particularly useful skill for a stablehand, but it certainly made life at home far more steady for Simon, exactly as he liked it. He fully intended to sneak into the house the back way and let one of his family members stumble upon him as if he had been home for days.

"Anything else I should know about?" he asked.

"He arrived just this morning, but I haven't been up to the house today."

That meant there could potentially be some new disaster for Simon to fix, though he would give his brother the benefit of the doubt. Perhaps William really had come for a visit instead of asking for something or causing trouble. "Olivia bring in any more strays?" There always seemed to be some new animal or other after Simon was away.

"None that I know of," Jed replied, and he had a strange grin on his face as he started leading Hermes into the stables to brush him down. "It's not Miss Calloway you need to worry about anyhow."

Simon frowned. He hardly expected his mother to do anything out of the ordinary. She was the most predictable person he knew. "What is that supposed to mean?" What had William done this time?

But the stablemaster waved a hand and disappeared, leaving Simon with a nervousness in the pit of his stomach as he made his way toward the house. Perhaps he should rethink his friendship with a man who spent more time with animals than he did with people.

As far as Simon could tell as he slipped into the kitchens to take the servants' staircase to his room, the house was just as he'd left it three weeks ago. Cook was far too busy preparing luncheon to notice him sneak past, and none of the lower servants were willing to make eye contact with him.

He would work on that with them later, but it wasn't anything out of the ordinary. Nothing looked in disrepair, and outside of the usual hustle and bustle of the servants, the house was quiet and calm, as it should be. So what had Jed been referring to?

Most likely he had said it simply to sport with Simon's head and make him fret over nothing. He had done that before and had been monumentally amused when Simon figured out the ruse. Today seemed to be another of the same game. At least, Simon very much hoped so. His heart had been aching so much for home that he wasn't sure he could handle throwing anything else into the mix until he had settled in again.

That was a lot to hope for if William was in Oxfordshire.

Washing and changing as best as he could without calling up one of the footmen to help him until his valet arrived with the carriage, Simon ignored the temptation to take a quick nap before he sought out his mother and sister to make sure they had fared well without him, though they always did. Checking with them could wait, though, and there was likely work to be done here after such a long absence. The work was never finished, it seemed, and as much as he wished he could ignore everything calling his attention, he knew there was far too much to do.

There always was.

One of these days he would need to find himself a distraction. Nothing too ridiculous—just something that could take his mind off the growing pile of work looming ahead of him, if only for a moment.

Mostly clean and decently dressed, he let out a sigh and paused in front of his mirror. He looked exhausted, and he was surprised Jed hadn't commented on it. Perhaps that had been an act of mercy and he looked so terrible that Jed had decided it was best to leave it alone. Either way, a nap was sounding more and more inviting.

Perhaps he ought to go to the library and catch up on some work. If he happened to doze off, so much the better. Olivia would likely find him before long, and her squeal of delight would be a nice thing to wake to should his exhaustion overtake him. Yes, the library would work. Rubbing his weariness from his eyes, he quickly made his way through the house until he reached his favorite room, and he was more than pleased to see his chair by the window untouched. That had not changed. Good.

He settled in, opening a book on sheep husbandry and putting his feet up on the windowsill like he always did when spending a considerable length of time here. As he attempted to learn more about selective breeding, his eyes already drooping, he reminded himself that everything was as it should be with the house and his family and Jed had simply been pulling his leg.

There was absolutely no reason to expect any surprises when he opened his eyes. And with that thought, he settled a little more deeply into the chair and promptly fell asleep.

Chapter Five

Lucy escaped as soon as she could. Luncheon had been only the three of them—Lucy and the Calloway ladies—and the other two had spent every minute talking, leaving her to be a silent addition to their conversation. She suspected both were eager to distract themselves from the fevered man upstairs.

While overwhelmed by her growing guilt, Lucy could at least thank her time with the women for giving her a few more important details about the family.

Lord Calloway was a baron, a member of the aristocracy but the lowest rank within the peerage, which made him slightly less intimidating than he could be. He was also Olivia's brother, not her father, and therefore Mr. Calloway's elder brother as well. Though that did little to ease Lucy's worry over his reaction should she somehow be here long enough to meet him, at least she knew to expect someone younger. Perhaps slightly more sympathetic.

She had also learned that Olivia was seventeen and not yet out in Society, though she was due to be presented when the next Season began. She was a delightful girl, though perhaps a bit dramatic, and she cared deeply about her older brothers.

And William? Lucy's supposed betrothed almost never came home to Calloway Park. He had his own estate only a few miles away, but he spent most of his time in London or abroad, only returning to his childhood home once or twice a year. Both Lady and Miss Calloway were thrilled to have William home so unexpectedly, even if it wasn't under the best of circumstances.

"You are the reason we have him back," Lady Calloway had told Lucy, sealing her opinion with a bout of tears.

That was the point when Lucy had escaped, claiming a headache so she could formulate her plan for how to proceed. The house was much larger than she'd realized, though, and now she was undeniably lost. In search of the bedrooms, she had somehow stumbled upon the library, and suddenly she did not want to leave.

The Calloway library was incredible, filled to the brim with more books than any person could read in a lifetime. Oh, the things she could learn if she only had a genuine reason to be in this house in the first place. She would take a moment to dream about what might have been under different circumstances, and then she would hunt down her old gown and convince Rebecca to help her find a way to Lowbury. They had trespassed on the Calloways long enough. Perhaps if she wrote them a letter, she could avoid breaking their hearts so directly when she told them the truth about her relationship with William. Namely that there wasn't one. She needn't face them ever again if she so chose, and that would be easier than seeing the hurt in their eyes. Yes, perhaps a letter.

Running her fingers along the first shelf of books, she wondered if the whole family enjoyed these books or if it was only one or two of them. From the looks of things, it had been a while since anyone had truly taken the time to appreciate them. They were clean and free of dust, but they still looked untouched. A few stood out, though, like they had constantly been pulled out by the same hand: books about travel, languages, and politics—things Lucy had always wondered about but had never had the chance to explore.

Pulling one well-worn book from the shelf, she flipped through the pages and felt she was sharing something with the person who loved it. Father had always talked of traveling, and Lucy had always wished she had the means to do so. Everything she'd earned had gone to paying off her father's debts, and she had only recently become free to keep her earnings a few months prior. Perhaps if she saved everything she made while working for the Winthrop family, she could afford a sojourn to the Continent and get to see some of the places Father had once dreamed of visiting before his wife died.

After Lucy's mother passed away, Father had never been the same.

"Italy is nice," a voice said.

Lucy jumped so high she dropped the book, though she immediately leaned down to grab it before the pages became too bent. "I'm sorry," she gasped and turned toward the window. She had thought she was alone, but a man sat stretched out in a large armchair, his hazel eyes showing signs of sleepiness as he watched her, as if he had only just woken. "I did not realize anyone was in here."

He cocked his head to one side, studying her carefully. "No, the fault is mine. I should have announced myself."

Though she had never seen him before, parts of his features looked familiar enough that she could guess his name. He must be Simon, William's older brother. He had the same strong jaw as his brother, and his dark hair was just as thick, though a little more unruly, as if it didn't often behave. His eyes were far darker than William's blue ones, and much warmer. He did not dress nearly as well, though, and Lucy did her best to ignore his poorly tied cravat, even though she was tempted to tell him he needed to find himself a new valet if he was to be taken seriously in London. Mr. Granger had spoken of such things often, declaring himself an expert in the latest fashions.

"Lord Calloway?" she said. When had he arrived? He was not due until the morning.

Rising to his feet—he was tall, like William, but far broader—he straightened his clothing and bowed a little. "Either I do not remember meeting you," he said, "or you are more knowledgeable than I am."

He spoke with a lightness that immediately brought a smile to Lucy's lips, which she thought impressive, considering how on edge she had been since leaving London and that he was the person who would inevitably decide her fate once the truth came out. She should have been quaking where she stood, but she felt as calm as she had when she woke this afternoon.

There was some sort of magic to this place, this home, that quelled her fears in a way nothing ever had.

"Well," she said and carefully replaced the book on the shelf before offering a curtsy, "I can say with certainty that we have not met. I think I would remember a man who sleeps in a library instead of a bedchamber."

"Yes, well . . ." He glanced at the chair behind him, as if searching for a good excuse because the truth would not be in his favor. "I arrived early."

"I noticed," Lucy replied.

When Lord Calloway smiled, Lucy recognized the same broad happiness that she had seen in Olivia, though it had to filter through a less welcome emotion. The man looked weary to the bone.

"And I thought I might surprise the family," he added.

Lucy raised an eyebrow. "You and your brother seem to share that tendency." Then she bit her lip because she had no right to speak so boldly with a peer. She needed to keep her head down until she could explain things. Besides, she could only guess at Mr. Calloway being fond of surprises. Being in the same area as his family home without his family knowing did not necessarily mean he had intended to surprise them with his visit. Maybe he hadn't meant to come home at all and had been on his way to his own estate.

Lord Calloway's smile shifted into confusion again as he looked her over. "Forgive me my rudeness," he said, "but who are you?"

"I'm—" She stopped herself before she said her name, Rebecca's warnings repeating in her mind. Though she still wondered if it was the best idea to use the family to shield herself, using her real name would only do more harm than good. Adding another lie to the one the ladies already believed wouldn't necessarily do her any good either, but perhaps it would appease Rebecca a bit until Lucy figured out what to do. "Miss Lucy Staley," she said, using her mother's maiden name in place of her own.

Just in case.

Lord Calloway cocked his head to the other side, still confused as he studied her. He had to have recognized his sister's dress or, at the very least, realized Lucy was not a new servant. "Miss Staley," he repeated. "Are you a friend of Olivia's?"

"No, not quite. I—"

"Lucy!"

Lucy's heart skittered as Miss Calloway bounded into the library and took her by the hand. She hadn't known what to say, and the girl's timing had saved her from fumbling.

"There you are. Mother sent your maid up to assist you, but when you weren't in your room, we got so worried. I thought—Simon!" Practically shrieking, she threw her arms around her brother and laughed as he lifted her into the air. "What are you doing back early?"

"I missed you far too much," Lord Calloway replied as he set Miss Calloway back on her feet. "What news do I need to learn?"

That was the question Lucy didn't want him to ask, because now he would be led to believe the lie like his family had. But she had no idea how to avoid the answer.

Miss Calloway wasted no time, however. "Well, you've already met William's betrothed."

Lord Calloway's eyes went wide. "William's betrothed? Surely you're joking."

This was it. Lucy's unwitting lie would unravel right here in the library, and she would be run out of the house and forced to pick up the pieces of her failed journey. That was assuming the Winthrops even took her in after such a delay, as she could not possibly arrive until tomorrow. Only one day's delay would not convince them to turn her away, would it? She hardly dared think on the idea except to remind herself she needed to send them a letter before the day got too late.

Slapping a hand on her brother's arm, Miss Calloway took up Lucy's hand again and said, "Don't be rude, Simon. Lucy is amazing."

Though she wished she hadn't, Lucy looked up and met Lord Calloway's gaze. She had no idea what his expression meant, but he was undoubtedly studying her again, likely trying to understand how his brother would choose someone like her. The easy answer? *He wouldn't.*

After what felt like minutes, Lord Calloway said, "I was unaware my brother had formed an attachment. Where did he find you?"

The way he said it made Lucy feel like some trinket William had picked up while abroad, and she did not like the implied comparison. She said the first thing that came to mind. "We met while traveling, and I knew in an instant he was a good man." It was only halfway a lie.

"Of course he is," Miss Calloway agreed.

But Lord Calloway made a face, as if he disagreed. His reply confirmed it. "You knew that for certain, did you?"

Why did Lucy get the feeling he had seen through the ruse and was simply playing along now? But there was no way he could possibly know otherwise, unless he and his brother were closer than she had been led to believe.

According to Olivia, her brothers had never gotten along very well.

"Where is William anyway?" Lord Calloway asked his sister. "Surely he would not leave his beloved alone for long." He must have caught something in Miss Calloway's expression, because he immediately frowned. "What happened?" he asked, standing straighter. Suddenly he seemed to fit his role as baron much better than he had before, though Lucy had never interacted with anyone higher than a baronet before and hardly knew how a baron should act.

Miss Calloway bit her lip, and it seemed she couldn't find the words to explain her feverish brother upstairs. Based on the way Lord Calloway was growing tenser by the second, Lucy decided it would be best to answer for her and said, "He caught a fever in a storm on the way here."

Her response did nothing to ease the tension in Lord Calloway's shoulders. "How many days since?" he demanded, his full attention now on Lucy.

She did her best not to cower under his intense stare. Where William had been kind and good-natured, his elder brother had a sense of confidence in him, enough so that he was almost frightening. But Lucy held her ground as much as she could. It was the only way she would be strong enough to tell the truth as soon as she had given Mr. Granger time to arrive at the Winthrops' and leave again.

"We arrived early this morning," she told him. "He took fever last night after riding through a storm."

Lord Calloway folded his arms, clearly not pleased by her response, and it made him look bigger. More intimidating. This was not a man easily cowed by opposition. "I was caught in the same storm," he said. "But what in the blazes was he doing on a horse instead of inside a coach with you?"

"We were not traveling together," Lucy said, her heart pounding. How would she explain that? This was exactly why she had to make a plan. She wasn't sure she could risk telling him the truth until she could be more certain Mr. Granger would not find her in the village. Perhaps Lord Calloway would be as gracious as his female relations and help her, but could she trust in that possibility? She would have to try. "Mr. Calloway is not—"

"You know how he hates being stuck inside," Miss Calloway interrupted, scowling at her eldest brother. "What does it matter why he was riding?"

Narrowing his eyes, Lord Calloway pierced Lucy with a hard stare. "Because if I were coming home with a fiancée in tow, I wouldn't want to leave her side. So why did he?"

For some reason, Lucy had the sudden burning desire to defend Mr. Calloway. Though she knew little of the man, she knew he had offered up his room for two women far below his station after protecting her without hesitation. He most certainly did not deserve this odd suspicion from his brother. "Because he wanted to secure a room at the inn before they were all taken," she said, standing as tall as she could. "Your brother was thinking of everyone but himself, and I owe him a world of debt for seeing to my comfort before his own."

To her immense surprise, Lord Calloway smiled again, ducking his head as if genuinely embarrassed by the harsh way he had addressed her. The sudden change in demeanor had Lucy feeling slightly dizzy. Mr. Granger had never smiled like that, in a way that made her feel welcome and wanted.

"It seems William chose well for himself," Lord Calloway muttered, and then he kissed the top of his sister's head and disappeared through the library door.

Lucy was dumbfounded. Did that mean he had appreciated her comment? He should have taken offense, and rightly so, and she should have been forced to apologize profusely and then probably would have confessed everything at the same time because the secrets were weighing on her heart to a painful degree.

And he shouldn't have been so exceptionally handsome when he smiled at her like that.

"He must be tired," Miss Calloway said, wrapping her arm around Lucy's waist as she frowned at the door. "He's rarely in a bad mood like that."

Lucy had seen men in bad moods, and that was not a bad mood. In fact, she rather liked how honest he had been throughout the whole conversation, no matter how short it had been. She sincerely hoped William was similar to his brother. Not that she would be in the man's life once she told the truth. She merely hoped there were more good men in the world, like her father.

"Come," Miss Calloway said, tugging Lucy toward the door. "You look exhausted, and I would imagine another nap would do you a world of good."

Lucy didn't want to sleep. She wanted to tell the family who she really was, and she wanted to get out of their lives as quickly as possible. But she *was* tired, and she wasn't sure she had the heart to speak out just yet. Or if she even could. Perhaps she would after she slept, when she had figured out exactly how to explain everything.

Chapter Six

When Lucy woke, the sky outside was dark. She must have slept right through dinner. She felt entirely disoriented, and not just because she had slept most of the day away. Somehow she had become a man's betrothed in the course of a day. And not just any man! The brother of a baron. A wealthy baron at that. The kind of man who could ruin what little life Lucy had, no matter how warm his smiles.

This was such a mess.

Though she would eventually have to find one of the Calloway family—preferably Lady Calloway or her daughter—Lucy decided that for now she would simply see how Mr. Calloway fared. Perhaps he was awake and recovering by now so she could ask him for advice and he would still be the kind and thoughtful man she had met at the inn yesterday.

Had it been only yesterday? The day had felt like an eternity.

Slipping from beneath the covers, she wrapped a blanket around her shoulders and crept toward the door. The house was quiet around her, making her think perhaps it was later than she'd realized, and she hoped that meant everyone was asleep. She would be able to slip into Mr. Calloway's room and ensure he was improving, and then she would try to find something to wear so she could get to the nearest town, Downingham, and find a conveyance to Lowbury. If she did everything under the cover of night, perhaps she could avoid the risk of running into Granger again.

She had just about reached the door when she tripped over something and landed in a heap on top of a person lying on the floor.

"Lucy!"

"Rebecca!"

Rebecca clapped a hand over Lucy's mouth, even though she'd been the first to shout, and then she untangled herself and sat up. "Where are you going?" the maid demanded.

Lucy rubbed the sore spot on her elbow where it had hit the floor. "Why are you sleeping in front of the door?"

"To make sure you don't go tell the Calloways who you are."

Groaning, Lucy wrapped her blanket a little tighter around her shoulders. Goodness, this blanket was soft. "I can't keep lying to them, no matter what you say."

"But you have to!"

Now that she was a little more awake, Lucy could see the fear in Rebecca's eyes, even though it was dark. If the woman was willing to sleep on the cold, hard floor, perhaps her fears were not unwarranted. Rebecca truly believed what she had heard Mr. Granger say about carrying Lucy off and forcing her into marriage.

Lucy could hardly stomach the idea. "You said Mr. Granger was hoping to intercept us," she said. "Perhaps he was simply conducting business in the area and you were mistaken."

Rebecca shook her head, helping Lucy to her feet. "He never leaves Town this time of year."

That was true. Over the years, Jonathan Granger had waxed long about his business ventures, and he was always particularly adamant about remaining in London during the summers even though most of the *ton* tended to gravitate back toward their country estates until the next Season. Or perhaps he'd simply remained in Town because that was where Lucy had been.

"What was he planning to do if we reached the Winthrops' before he found us?" Lucy asked, trying not to picture the man dragging her from a coach in the middle of nowhere. She failed, and the thought made her shudder again.

Rebecca shrugged. "I didn't hear anything about that, but . . . you know Mr. Granger. What he wants, he gets."

As much as Lucy wanted to disregard that thought, she couldn't find an argument. Yes, he had remained within propriety over the years, but that had been when she was employed in his brother's house. In his business boastings, he had made it clear he was a man who didn't often take no for an answer. If she finally found her way to the Winthrops' home, would he be there waiting for her?

"Are you sure?" she whispered.

Rebecca nodded. "Robert Granger and his wife are decent people, but his brother . . . none of us belowstairs liked him. Us maids, in particular. He always looked at us like . . ."

Lucy didn't want to know how he looked at them; she had been on the receiving end of plenty of his looks, and she didn't like it at all. "What am I to do?" she asked. "Without a recommendation, finding employment anywhere else will be difficult, if not impossible. You know that."

Rebecca took hold of her hand. "We can stay here a while longer."

Jaw dropping, Lucy tore her hand free. "We can't—"

"Only until Mr. Granger has tried finding you, as I know he will. It shouldn't take him more than a day or two to arrive at the Winthrops' and find you missing. Then he'll move on."

"But—"

"Where else can you go?"

As harsh as the question sounded, Lucy knew it was a good one. Rebecca knew well the difficulties of living without money, and seeing as Lucy had little, she couldn't afford a journey of any considerable length. Remaining nearby without some sort of place to hide, like here with the Calloways, would make it easier for Mr. Granger to find her. She didn't want to believe she was in as much danger as Rebecca said she was, but she had little proof to back an argument. She had never felt safe around Mr. Granger.

But could she really lie to this family? They had been so kind to her so far, and perhaps if she told them the truth, they might help her.

As if she knew what Lucy was thinking, Rebecca shook her head. "I don't think you can tell them, miss. Everyone downstairs says the Calloways don't like trouble; they'd sooner throw you out than get mixed up with something of this sort."

Well, that couldn't possibly be true, but Lucy didn't know the family well enough to say with confidence how they might react if she told them she was being pursued, particularly because she would have to admit to her lie in doing so. What reason would they have to trust her at that point? They didn't have any reason *now*, and surely Lord Calloway would care more about his family's station than the liar who had infiltrated his estate. He would be the one she had to convince if she wanted assistance, and he rather frightened her. She had never seen the same intensity she had seen in his eyes.

"I think we shouldn't be too hasty," Rebecca said. "You don't have to decide right this minute. Besides, imagine if you really were engaged to that Mr. Calloway. You could live like this every day. You could be a part of his family. Wouldn't that be nice?"

Lucy couldn't keep herself from nodding. Every girl dreamed of living an elegant life, being swept up in the romance and extravagance of the upper class. But surely she could never be comfortable being a part of this world only because of a lie.

"At least think about it," Rebecca said, wrapping her hand around Lucy's. "There's talk downstairs about Mr. Calloway being sick like this before, and he might not even wake up. Lady Calloway is beside herself with worry, and her lady's maid is right anxious for her health. I don't know if she could take a blow like losing her son and his intended all at the same time. What if you just wait a few days before you tell the Calloways? Give them a chance to get stronger. Let them get to know you and love you like I do, and they'll be right happy to help you. They can't do that if Lady Calloway dies of heartbreak."

Lucy groaned. Leave it to Rebecca to find something even more guilt-inducing. "You're saying the truth might kill Lady Calloway?" When Rebecca shrugged, Lucy pressed the palms of her hands into her eyes. "I can't take this pressure, Rebecca. Why couldn't it have been you who was mistaken for his betrothed?"

"Because I wasn't raised by a gentleman. And you deserve this life, Lucy. Even if it's just for a few days."

As she folded her arms around herself, Lucy looked around the room that already felt more familiar than her little bedchamber back with the Grangers. How was that possible? "What time is it anyway?"

"Nighttime."

Lucy scowled, but she was glad Rebecca was here with her. Without a friend, she might have fallen to pieces hours ago. "How can I possibly go along with this? Pretend I am Mr. Calloway's intended? I could never act like a lady."

"You spent the last five years turning those horrible Granger girls into respectable ladies," Rebecca argued. "And your father was a gentleman, even if he was poor. You simply have to be yourself, and the family will love you."

"I don't want them to love me," Lucy argued. "I just don't want them to hate me when they inevitably figure it out. I want them to help me if they can." And they would never do that if they thought she was a stranger who had lied to them. But if they knew her? Knew she had no intention of causing them harm? Perhaps, given some time, they would trust her enough to protect her. Surely no harm would come to the family from sheltering her.

Was she really considering Rebecca's plan? She was, and she felt awful about it. But a few lies here and there were certainly preferable to being the cause of Lady Calloway dying of heartbreak. And if it would keep her away from Mr. Granger's obsession with her . . . it could be her only way to keep herself safe from the man.

Sighing, Lucy rose to her feet and wrapped her blanket around her shoulders once more. "We are going to visit Mr. Calloway," she announced. She might as well practice giving Rebecca orders; she would need the help of a lady's maid if she was going to convince anyone that she belonged there. She hadn't made any decisions yet, but it would be better to be prepared. "You will come with me to prevent any scandal."

Rebecca's eyes went wide. "But it is far too late!"

"Indeed. Come along."

By the time they found the right room, Lucy's nerves had risen to an almost unbearable degree. Pretending or no, a man's sickroom was hardly the sort of place she should be in the middle of the night. But she wanted to gain Mr. Calloway's opinion of her plan to deceive his family, even if he was not awake to reply. It would make her feel better about the whole thing if she went through with it.

Mr. Calloway was fast asleep, though Lucy suspected the physician had given him a good deal of laudanum to keep him so while his fever raged. The maid who had been attending him earlier was gone, leaving the room empty and almost eerie. Lucy was especially glad she had forced Rebecca to come with her as she took a seat by the man's bedside.

Now that she was here, though, she wasn't certain what to say to him. Could he even hear her?

"Good evening, Mr. Calloway," she said, feeling rather foolish when he didn't stir. "Or perhaps good morning." She still wasn't sure how late it really was, though it didn't matter much. "I thought perhaps I should explain the situation to you before things go too far."

She glanced at Rebecca, who took a seat in the corner and had the decency to bow her head in apology. Lucy knew the maid wouldn't have fought to keep the secret if she didn't have a good reason for it, though that helped lessen the sting of lying by only a small degree.

"Your family thinks you and I are engaged," Lucy said with a sigh. "And I'm not sure I'll be able to tell them otherwise. If you were awake, we probably wouldn't be in this mess, but—oh goodness, I'm not blaming you. Not in the slightest." So who was she blaming? Rebecca? Mr. Granger?

Fate?

"You have an amazing family," she continued. For some reason, talking to the unconscious man seemed to be calming her down far more than she would have expected. "And I feel terrible about lying to them. But . . ." She took hold of the man's warm hand, as if he could offer up some strength despite his illness. Lucy simply wanted the human contact. "But I think Rebecca may be right. I need to hide from Mr. Granger, and your family needs this bit of happiness in thinking you are engaged. Until they know you will survive this, I'm not sure I can tell them the truth. It would break their hearts, knowing you are not here to stay."

Perhaps he *was* planning to stay. Miss Calloway had told Lucy all about her older brother's estate not far from Calloway Park and how he was rarely at home. Though Lucy had no way of knowing whether William had been returning for a visit or for a more extended stay or for any time at all, there was the chance he had intended to take up a more permanent residence at his estate before the storm and subsequent fever had derailed his plans.

None of that would matter if he never woke up.

"Please wake up," she whispered, gripping his hand a little tighter. If anyone would help her, surely he would. He had done it before. "I need you to wake up and help me fix all of this. Please."

Chapter Seven

"Blast your inability to stay whole through a rainstorm, William!" Simon paced the corridor near his brother's chamber, trying to work up the courage to go inside and try to wake him enough to have a conversation. Just a tiny little conversation. Enough for the man to explain how he could have spent five years in London with no plans to settle down and then show up out of the blue—and engaged, no less, to a woman as charming as Miss Staley.

Two minutes of talking to the woman, and Simon already knew she was too good for William.

He had honestly thought he was dreaming when he woke in the library and found her perusing his books. Her dark hair had caught his eye immediately, contrasting the green dress she wore, and her eyes were even darker. He'd never seen a more handsome woman, and Olivia's declaration of who she was had only made the belief that he was trapped in a dream stronger. But no, Mother had confirmed it, and Mother never lied.

William was engaged to be married, and Simon needed to know why.

"There has to be a reason," he muttered to himself as he paced.

Miss Staley was too sensible to have fallen into some sort of trap. True, Simon knew nothing about her, but he was skilled at recognizing a person's values, and he could tell she had a good character. And William may have been wild at times and had been in plenty of scrapes, but he was not a *total* fool. With how lightly he'd always treated the idea of settling down, he would never get himself into a situation in which a marriage was necessary.

This was exactly why Simon needed to talk to William. What had changed to convince him to take a wife when doing so would force him to adapt to a new lifestyle? Sure, he could keep roaming the country and hop over to France or Spain whenever he was feeling trapped at home, but people would talk. A bachelor acting that way was commonplace; a married man never at home was not. Not without certain implications, and William would not compromise his family that way.

Simon groaned, running a hand through his hair despite the fact that his valet would get angry with him for ruining his coiffure so early in the day. He usually lasted a few hours longer than this.

William wouldn't hurt his family. Would he? It had been so long since he had spent any length of time in Oxfordshire that Simon couldn't really say what kind of man his brother was. At this point, all he knew were the rumors that circulated around Town, and he had no idea whether any of them were true. He had never put much stock in rumor if he could help it, but when it came to William Calloway, there was plenty of it to go around.

He couldn't wait any longer. Taking a deep breath, he pushed William's ajar door open wider and stepped inside, ready to force him awake and get him to talk. But he froze the moment he set eyes on the room because Miss Staley was there, gazing down at her fiancé with tired eyes.

He cursed under his breath, but thankfully she didn't hear him. She didn't notice him at all, in fact, so focused was she on William.

Simon's eyes jumped around the room on instinct, and he relaxed somewhat when he found a maid dozing lightly in the corner. Though he wasn't sure he approved of the familiarity between his brother and his intended, at least she had considered propriety and was not alone in the room with him. But at this early hour?

Simon's stomach twisted in his gut. So it was not to be a marriage of convenience, then, if she was so enamored of the man. There was one reason for the marriage disproved. Clearly it was a love match, and for some reason that made Simon's uneasiness worse. Nothing about this made sense, and he hardly had control over his life to begin with. He did not need William making things even more difficult.

At the moment, though, it didn't matter why his brother and Miss Staley had gotten engaged. What mattered was Simon leaving before he was discovered; this was far from the sort of scene he should be witnessing. He took only one step back toward the door, however, when Miss Staley jumped and looked over at him.

"Oh dear," she whispered, as if she were the one in the wrong. "I thought no one else would be awake."

"You can be at your betrothed's side if you choose," Simon replied, which sounded ridiculous. Surely there was some sort of rule about being in a man's room, particularly with a sleeping chaperone. To be honest, he had no idea, and though he was glad Miss Staley wasn't alone, he hated that Society cared so much about following rules. He hated more that this was the sort of thing he should know and didn't. "Forgive me," he said. "I hoped to find William in better health this morning. How is he?" Even more ridiculous. She was no doctor, unless she had many talents hidden underneath that timid smile of hers.

Glancing at William, Miss Staley gently put his hand back at his side and rubbed sleep from her eyes. "He hasn't woken, but he does not seem to be in as much pain as yesterday," she said softly. "Perhaps his fever is ebbing."

Simon hoped so, because he would not rest easy until he learned the full truth of this relationship in front of him. "That's good to hear," he said, and suddenly he had no idea how to stand. Where did he put his hands? He clasped them behind his back and felt absolutely ridiculous, like a schoolboy awaiting punishment.

Miss Staley rose slowly to her feet, taking a moment to smooth the hair off William's forehead, though she didn't seem to realize she was doing it—as if she had done it many times before. How long had they been engaged, anyway? Mother hadn't known, which was as suspect as the engagement itself. Had none of them asked Miss Staley, with William clearly unable to offer any clarity?

"I must beg your forgiveness," he said and sounded so stiff that he thought he might do better to turn around and walk away. "Yesterday I was just off a long spell of traveling, and I was not prepared for any surprises."

"Yet you were willing to offer up your own," she replied without hesitation.

Simon almost smiled, though he was far too uncomfortable to do so. No one beyond his family and closest friends had ever dared speak to him like that, and he found he rather liked it. "A truth indeed," he agreed. "But I had no reason to make light of the news of you joining our family. For that I apologize."

She opened her mouth to speak, but a little moan from the sleeping maid pulled her attention to the corner. "I should have her go downstairs," she said, though she didn't seem certain of her own thoughts.

Simon didn't recognize the young woman, though that didn't necessarily surprise him. He was hardly home enough to know all of the lower staff. Perhaps that was why they never looked him in the eye. "Is she yours?" he asked, then winced when Miss Staley threw him a rather sharp glare. "Forgive me. I didn't mean it like . . . she doesn't belong to anyone, of course. I only meant to ask if she is under your employ or mine. Or . . ." He glanced at William, unsure whether a man would offer up a lady's maid to his intended or whether that was as ridiculous as the way Simon held his hands behind his back.

"She came with me," Miss Staley said. Though she didn't fully smile, a grin played at her lips as she looked him over, like she had only just realized he was there. She must have been truly tired. "You're better dressed today," she said, and then she immediately turned pink. "Oh, I'm sorry, I should not have—"

"You're not wrong," he interrupted, and this time he did smile, if only because she had noted his attire both yesterday and today. That did not happen often, at least not as often as it did with the dandies he had the misfortune of interacting with when he was stuck in Town. "My valet was half a day behind me and is far better at knots than I am. He is never missed more than when I have to dress myself."

Miss Staley smiled as well, apparently warming up to him as he continued to make a fool of himself. "Did you know," she said, her voice light, "there are men in the world who manage to dress themselves without issue every day?"

"Well, that I simply cannot believe," Simon replied.

"It's true. They tie their own cravats and everything."

Simon bit back a laugh, only because he didn't want to wake William. The man needed his rest, after all, and there was no reason to bother him. "I simply cannot believe it until I see it for myself," he said. "Next you'll be telling me you did your hair all on your own this morning."

Miss Staley's hand flew to her hair, which was rather a mess from the course of the night. How long had she been at William's bedside anyway? Simon did not need an answer to that question. "I cannot claim credit for this," she said, though her smile had faded slightly, as if she knew what Simon was wondering. "I come by these tangles naturally."

"I have never seen more beautiful tangles." Simon frowned. Why had he said something like that? He hardly found the courage to compliment women he might actually have a chance with, so saying such a thing to his future sister-in-law was quite, well, *ridiculous*. At least it was better than telling her his own hair often shared the same fate, which had been the first thought to come into his head. "Are you planning to be a constant watchman?" he asked, if only to change the subject. "I doubt William has ever had a more dutiful companion."

Pulling her eyebrows together, Miss Staley looked back down at her betrothed as she said, "I worry for him. It's been two nights already, and—"

"He's had worse than this," Simon said. He didn't like the sight of her being anxious like that. "He caught a terrible fever when he was a boy, and he has been more susceptible to them ever since. But he always makes it through, and this time around will be no different."

"You think so?"

Simon had to resist the urge to step forward and take her hand in an effort to comfort her. He gripped his wrist tight behind him instead, and he knew it would be best to leave the room as soon as he found a good opening to end the conversation. "I know so," he told her, and the smile she gave him was worth lingering a moment longer for. Honestly, how had William managed to find himself someone with a smile as warm as that? It hardly seemed possible. Simon had met every woman in Town—the curse of being a particularly wealthy member of the aristocracy—but he had not met anyone the likes of Miss Staley.

Where had she come from?

As if realizing she had let the conversation lull, Miss Staley cleared her throat and searched around her. Finding nothing she might need, she roused the maid, muttered, "Good morning, Lord Calloway," then slipped out into the corridor with the other young woman in tow.

Simon watched them go, and he could not for the life of him remember why he had come into the room in the first place.

Chapter Eight

Once Rebecca had repaired the damage done to Lucy's hair during the night, Lucy crept down to the breakfast room, hoping most of the family had not woken yet. After that encounter with Lord Calloway, she needed a moment to gather her thoughts and come up with a plan for how she was going to proceed. If the way she had spoken to William's brother was any indication, she was not going to be able to last long unless she knew exactly what her goal was.

Did she mean to keep up with the lie until someone discovered the truth? Rebecca would like that. Or would she reveal everything herself as she had originally intended? If she stuck with the false story and took advantage of the Calloways' hospitality, well, Lucy hoped she could endear herself to them just enough to gain their assistance in dealing with Mr. Granger if he discovered her whereabouts.

Considering she had no idea where he was or whether he was still looking for her, she was leaning toward that second option.

Voices filtered through the doors of the breakfast room as Lucy approached, and she hesitated in the corridor. One of the voices was male, which meant Lord Calloway must be inside. She had been rather bold with him this morning, and though he hadn't censured her for speaking out of turn—he had almost seemed to appreciate her measure of him—surely he would not allow her to speak her mind again.

She had to keep her thoughts to herself, for everyone's sake.

"It isn't going to happen," Lord Calloway was saying when Lucy finally worked up the courage to step into the room thanks to her hunger; missing supper the night before had left her rather famished.

The baron, who sat at the head of the breakfast table, was far more animated than he had been in the sickroom, his hazel eyes alight with amusement and a crooked grin pulling at his lips.

Miss Calloway looked especially smug as she gazed at her brother. "You'd best believe it, Brother."

"I will not," he replied with a laugh, but then he caught sight of Lucy and froze. No doubt he was remembering how he had caught her in Mr. Calloway's room this morning, a place she had no right to be. Even as William's betrothed, it was quite improper to be in his bedchamber. Thank the heavens Rebecca had gone with her, but Lucy shouldn't have gone in the first place. It wasn't like Mr. Calloway had been able to offer up any advice, like she'd hoped.

"Miss Staley," Lord Calloway said, and he bowed his head a little after standing. "I trust you slept well last night."

Was Lucy imagining it, or was there a twinkle in the man's eyes? He was teasing her! She didn't understand him at all. But that didn't mean she didn't know how to respond to him, and playing along with his game might be just the way to convince him to help her. "I have never had a better night's rest," she replied and gave him her sweetest smile, the sort of smile that could get her father to give her anything.

As he sat in his place at the head of the table, Lord Calloway's eyes flicked up to Lucy's hair, and the sparkle in his eyes grew. "Your hair seems to tell a different story," he said.

"I happen to have an incredibly skilled maid at my disposal."

"So it would seem. You must be an excellent judge of character."

Though Lucy couldn't explain it, she was suddenly warm, and she hurried over to the sideboard to fill her plate with the barest amount of food before either of the Calloways noticed how flushed she had become. She wished she could eat more, but she felt guilty enough taking from the family when they had no reason to give to her.

"What is Miss Calloway upset about?" she asked, hoping the change in subject would make her feel less under scrutiny. Lord Calloway had a way of gazing at her so directly that Lucy was sure he would discover the truth simply by looking at her.

"She seems to think she can outride me," the man said, his voice light. "I heartily disagree."

"But I have Cordelia now," Miss Calloway argued. "She is remarkably quick on her feet and could easily outpace Hermes."

"No animal can outpace Hermes."

Lucy took her seat across from Miss Calloway, all too aware of Lord Calloway's eyes on her from her left. "I cannot say, as I have not seen either of you ride," she said, "but Miss Calloway does seem rather determined. Perhaps you should not underestimate her, my lord."

"And I've been practicing every day since you left the last time," Miss Calloway added, her head bobbing up and down. "I am sure I can win this time."

Lord Calloway let out a low chuckle, and suddenly Lucy shivered. Was there something odd happening with the temperature of the room? "You say that every time, Olivia," he said. "And I beat you every time."

"Not this time. Even Lucy thinks so; you heard her."

Turning to Lucy, Lord Calloway lifted one dark eyebrow. She could not deny he was a handsome man, but his gaze unnerved her. He was far too powerful and intimidating for her to be comfortable with him studying her. "What makes you doubt my ability to ride?" he asked her.

Lucy swallowed her bite of toast. It was as if he was tempting her to speak out again, hoping for her frankness on a subject she had no business speaking of. "It is not doubt in you, my lord," she said slowly, "but faith in Miss Calloway."

Miss Calloway beamed, but then she pointed at Lucy as if accusing her of something. "Do you hear her, Simon?" she said, sighing deeply. "She simply refuses to call me Olivia, even though we are practically sisters now."

Not technically, Lucy thought, trying not to frown. Miss Calloway had requested Lucy call her by her Christian name yesterday, but that would be pushing things too far beyond a safe boundary. She would pretend to be engaged to Mr. Calloway for a time, but she would not deign to act as if she would ever become a part of this family. As soon as Lady Calloway was stronger of heart or Mr. Calloway woke and helped her explain the mistake, Lucy would be gone.

Lord Calloway cocked his head, still studying her with far more interest than she liked. "You're right, Olivia," he said, a gleam of amusement back in his eyes. "I can't have my sister-in-law *my lording* me all day long, now, can I? What would the neighbors think?"

Lucy had been sound asleep when she'd arrived at Calloway Park and had seen nothing of the surrounding lands, but she was almost certain there were no neighbors within hearing distance of any part of the estate. "I expect the neighbors are clever enough to keep to their own business," she said and couldn't help but smirk at Lord Calloway. "Besides, I am not your sister-in-law."

He matched her smirk with his own and looked all the more handsome for it. These Calloway men certainly knew how to smile, though she had seen the younger's only once. "Perhaps," he replied. "But I must insist you call Olivia by her name."

Lucy could hardly continue arguing against that when she felt like a sister to Miss Calloway—Olivia—already. She knew their friendship would be short-lived, but she had felt welcomed by the girl from the first moment she'd stepped into the house. She hated to destroy their friendship before she could find a way to avoid Mr. Granger. She hated to destroy their friendship *at all.* "Very well."

"And me by mine."

That one was harder to agree to. Lord Calloway was part of the peerage, far above Lucy in every way. Calling him by his Christian name when she was not actually related to him seemed to be tempting fate.

"My lord," she said, "I couldn't possibly—"

"I insist, Miss Staley. Either you call me Simon, or you call me nothing at all." Though he spoke with authority in his words, amusement danced in his hazel eyes, as if he knew exactly how uncomfortable he made her. He hadn't been this confident in the sickroom this morning, so what had changed? And a better question: why did Lucy like this side of him far more?

Well, he did not know her as well as he seemed to think he did, and she sat up straighter in her seat. If Lord Calloway could sit there so unconcerned and thinking he had the upper hand, he was entirely wrong. She had spent all her adult life training young girls to be good and proper, and she would not back down now. "It seems you are to remain nameless, my good man. It will be a mouthful, I am sure, but you've left me no choice. From now on, you shall be called Lord Nothing-at-All."

Lord Calloway's expression shifted. He still looked amused, but there was something more to it. Some deeper emotion that seemed to linger beneath the surface, like he was missing something. "You are a stubborn one, aren't you?" he asked quietly.

"And she's far more intelligent than you, dear brother," Olivia added with a grin. "I think I'll start calling you Nothing-at-All as well, just for the fun of it. Now,"—she took Lucy's hand and squeezed it—"what shall we do today?"

That question caught Lucy off guard. Surely she would be expected to look after Mr. Calloway, seeing as she was supposed to be his intended. She could hardly go off and find entertainment for the whole of the day when her betrothed was ill with fever. Besides, she wasn't sure if she had the energy to match Olivia's exuberance. "I don't think I should—"

"Olivia, Miss Staley is likely too anxious about William to be running about the Park," Lord Calloway said, much to Lucy's relief.

Olivia scoffed. "I was hardly going to suggest *running about*, Simon. Just how old do you think I am?"

He pretended to think for a moment. "Twelve? Or are you thirteen now?"

"I am seventeen, and you know it. You promised me a Season next year! Surely you don't still see me as a child."

"Seventeen? Truly?" His frown was more theatrical than believable, but Lucy suspected there was some real misery behind his jesting. Looking after his family at so young an age—he couldn't be more than thirty—likely weighed heavily on the man. When had Lady Calloway said she lost her husband? Only a couple of years ago, if Lucy remembered right. Lord Calloway had been thrust into his role as baron unexpectedly, and she could well understand his reluctance to have his sister grow up and move on.

"Of course I don't see you as a child," he said eventually. "But, as I said, I think Miss Staley would prefer to stay in today. Perhaps you should practice, if you really want to win our race. And while you do that, Miss Staley and I will check on William."

Heat spread across Lucy's face, though she wasn't sure why. Perhaps it was the fact that Lord Calloway knew very well she had already been to see his brother, but she wondered if maybe it had something to do with the phrase *Miss Staley and I*. Even if that wasn't her real name, a thrill ran through her at the thought of being even remotely connected to someone like Simon Calloway.

"Yes, I would like that," she said, though she'd had half a mind to contradict the man. It was his gaze that stopped her, with one eyebrow a little lower than the other and a tightness in his mouth that told her to lie.

Why did everyone expect her to be so dishonest?

"You don't mind riding with Jed, do you?" Lord Calloway asked his sister. "You need all the practice you can get."

Olivia deflated a bit, glancing between the pair of them, but she must have felt the challenge enough to recognize the need to practice while she still could. She threw her brother a glare as she said, "Only because your loss will be more acute if you aren't aware of how fast Cordelia and I have gotten," and then she leaped to her feet and strode from the room with a determination that made Lord Calloway laugh.

Lucy couldn't help but join in, and she was amazed to realize she was becoming more relaxed the longer she spent at Calloway Park. By all accounts, her nerves should have been growing, but they were not. It was truly a strange sensation. Perhaps it was simply being away from Mr. Granger that had given her such a feeling of safety.

"Is she really as fast as she says?" Lord Calloway asked as soon as Olivia's footsteps died away. He leaned on the arm of his chair, toward Lucy, and that sparkle in his eyes had returned.

As she had not expected a playful side to Lord Calloway, Lucy wasn't entirely sure how to respond. Mr. Granger had often spoken of the loftiness of the upper class and how they saw anyone beneath them as worthless. "They don't bother with the working class like us," he had said more than once, though Lucy had never considered herself on the same level as him. He was a merchant like his brother and quite wealthy, but he had no land to grant him the status of gentleman and therefore disliked anyone who held that title or beyond.

Lord Calloway didn't seem to fit that prejudicial mold, though Lucy wondered if he would treat her the same way as Mr. Granger claimed if he knew she was merely a governess. Even without all her lies, was he a good enough man that he would help someone so far beneath him when she needed him most? That question terrified her, and she wasn't sure she was brave enough to put it to the test. Not yet.

For now, she wanted to play along with his teasing. Her father had always teased her, and she knew it was love that had fueled his jests. It had made their home a happy one, even if it was small, and she had been missing that in her life.

"Well, Lord Nothing-at-All," Lucy said, and she grinned when Lord Calloway scowled at the ridiculous moniker. "I would imagine Olivia is quite fast, though she has the benefit of a quick horse, so she says. Without knowing firsthand how either of you rides, it is simply impossible to make a comparison."

"Then, I suppose I will have to take you riding to allow you adequate information to pass judgment."

Lucy knew that would be a terrible idea; spending time alone with any of the family would inevitably lead to her spilling her secret too soon if put under pressure. With the whole family around, she could hide behind their conversations and hope to only skim the surface of their chats. She couldn't fathom why he would want to ride with her in the first place, and she knew it would be best to avoid as much interaction as she could. She needed him to like her, and she doubted he would appreciate her true, lying self.

But though she told herself to skirt around the invitation—for it surely was an invitation, if his smile were to be believed—the words that came from her mouth were, "I suppose you are right."

"Of course I am," he replied. "I am always right."

Goodness, that smile of his brightened the whole room. And despite his outward display of confidence, Lucy was positive it was a charade. Simon Calloway didn't seem arrogant in the least, and she very much liked that about him.

"Well," Lord Calloway said, pushing himself slowly to his feet, "shall we?"

Lucy frowned. "Shall we what?" They couldn't very well go riding now when that was what Olivia was planning to do.

Lifting a dark eyebrow, Lord Calloway looked at her like she should know. "See to William," he said.

"But we were there this morning."

"Olivia doesn't know that. Unless you want her to know about your delightful hair this morning, it would be best to follow through with the idea, in case she gets it into her head that she should remain indoors."

Without meaning to, Lucy touched a hand to her hair, just to make sure it wasn't an absolute mess. She had gotten so used to wearing it in a simple bun at the base of her skull that she had forgotten how it felt to have it lighter and looser, and Rebecca had remarkable talent with hair. She should have been made a lady's maid long before now, and Lucy wondered if perhaps that was part of the reason Rebecca was so insistent on going with her. Mrs. Granger's stubborn and rather terrifying abigail would hold the position until the day she died.

"I suppose." As much as she did want to make sure Mr. Calloway was recovering, she did not like the idea of being in the same room alone with Lord Calloway. Not again. *But how is that different from being alone with him now?* she wondered to herself.

The breakfast room was not a bedchamber. That was how it was different.

"Join me, Miss Staley," he said and held out his arm to her.

If she refused, Lord Calloway would wonder why, and Lucy already suspected he didn't fully believe the news of the engagement. Out of everyone, he had the most power to ruin her life, and she had already continued too far into this ruse to court more catastrophe. At this point, she would simply be doing everything in her power to salvage what she could of her life.

"Lord Calloway, I—"

"I seem to recall asking you to use my name, Miss Staley."

She groaned in frustration. "It would hardly be appropriate, given the circumstances. I am not your family, nor your friend."

"But we could become friends, could we not?" This time he reached out his hand, which Lucy took without meaning to. His fingers wrapped around hers with a gentle strength. "And would you give me leave to call you Lucy?"

The only people who had called her Lucy in the last five years were Rebecca and now the Calloway family. She had practically forgotten her own name, and hearing it on Lord Calloway's lips felt like a healing balm on her heart. It made her feel like she was home.

"Very well. You may call me Lucy because we are friends," she agreed, no matter how dangerous that could become. How desperate she was to have friends.

Helping her to her feet, he linked her arm through his and led the way out. Though he said nothing, he pulled his eyebrows together as he gazed down at her while they walked. Whatever he saw, it seemed to confuse him, but he said nothing about it until they were halfway up to Mr. Calloway's chamber.

"Will you really not call me Simon?" he asked. His arm tensed beneath her fingers, though he walked easily enough and with a bit of a confident swagger in his step.

Her decision truly bothered him? Lucy would not have guessed it. He was influential enough that he could have required civility and deference at all times. But she could not back down, at least not yet. Unless by some miracle she remained a friend to this family after everything, calling Lord Calloway by his Christian name was dangerous.

"I suppose you need to earn that right," she said, though it was a bit too impertinent for her own good.

Raising an eyebrow, Lord Calloway pushed his brother's door open and gestured for her to enter first. "Earn it?" he repeated. "How am I to do such a thing?"

Mr. Calloway looked just as she'd left him earlier that morning. Lucy sank into the chair beside the man, her heart aching for him. Surely he should have improved at least a little.

"You are a clever man, it seems," she muttered, though her focus was more on Mr. Calloway than his brother. "You'll think of something."

Lord Calloway took up a seat on the foot of the bed, and despite his reassurances earlier that Mr. Calloway would make a full recovery, concern pulled his thick eyebrows low. "He hasn't changed, has he?" he said and reached for his brother's hand. "He's still burning."

Lucy did not like sitting there feeling useless, so she took up a rag and dipped it into the bowl of water that had been left there last night. The water was blessedly cool despite the warmth of the room, and she pressed the rag to Mr. Calloway's forehead. "He does not seem quite as pale as yesterday, but perhaps we should send for the physician again." Mr. Pritchard had said he wanted to speak to Lord Calloway, and she hoped he would return before long.

"But he has such a dutiful nurse already."

Lucy managed a small smile at the compliment, but it was short-lived. Now was as good a time as any to test Lord Calloway's geniality. "I've spent the last several years as a governess for a family in London, and when the girls were younger, they took fever a few times. I spent a good deal of time at their side."

"That seems beyond the duty of a governess." Lord Calloway sat in silence for a while, leaving Lucy to her ministrations, but he could not stay silent forever, it seemed, and his next question was almost too quiet for her to hear. "How does a governess meet someone like William Calloway?"

Lucy wasn't sure how to answer that. "We met while tra—"

"While traveling, yes. You've said." He frowned down at his brother. "William is always traveling and meeting new people, so what made this time different?"

As his eyes rose to meet Lucy's, his gaze sharp and intense, she shivered, wondering what he saw.

"What made *you* different?" he added.

Mr. Calloway had simply happened to be in the right place at the right time. Or the very wrong place. "I could hardly say," she said, hoping she came across as coy, not suspicious. As it was, he watched her with a focus that made her nervous. "Mr. Calloway could tell you any number of things about what he saw in me." Oh goodness, she probably would have used his Christian name if they were truly engaged, and she couldn't decide whether she wanted Lord Calloway to question her or simply think she used surnames with everyone she knew.

The half-closed door opened before Lord Calloway could respond either way, bringing Lady Calloway and the physician.

"Oh!" Lady Calloway said as soon as she saw the two of them near the bed. "I am not interrupting, am I?"

"Of course not," Lucy said as she jumped to her feet.

It almost looked like Lord Calloway meant to say otherwise, but he shut his mouth tight and frowned as soon as she spoke. "How is he?" Lucy asked the doctor.

She offered the chair to Lady Calloway, which she took gratefully as the doctor accepted Lord Calloway's place on the bed.

Mr. Pritchard bent over Mr. Calloway, testing the skin on his forehead and checking the beat of his heart. "His fever hasn't broken yet, but as far as I can tell, he has not gotten any worse. That is a good sign."

"Is it?" Lady Calloway stroked her son's hair as she gazed down at him. "He is so pale."

"Lucy thinks he is in less pain today," Lord Calloway said. He had retreated to the corner, leaning his shoulder against the wall, but at least he had a spark of humor in his eyes. His worry for his brother did not run too deep, then.

Lady Calloway's eyes went wide. "Yes, I think you're right, Lucy!" she said, and a smile played on her lips. "He does seem to be resting a little easier, doesn't he?"

"We've been through this before, Mother," Lord Calloway said. "Do not lose sleep over him."

"That is not something you should say to a mother," Lucy chided him, though she had meant to keep her mouth shut. It was not her place to interfere in family affairs when she was not actually part of the family.

But Lord Calloway grinned at her, clearly appreciating her censure. "You are quite right," he said. "Mother, I am sorry. I know I don't know what it's like to have children, so I cannot understand."

Lady Calloway managed an even better smile than before, and she almost looked happy. "Oh, Simon, you certainly keep me on my toes," she said, but when she reached out a hand, it was toward Lucy.

Confused, Lucy took hold of the woman's fingers and let her pull her closer to the bed.

"What would we have done without you, Lucy?" Lady Calloway asked as she gazed down at William. "He might not have returned this time."

Was the fever as bad as that? Or was she talking about how much time Mr. Calloway—William—had spent away from home? Lucy had no idea, but she certainly was not brave enough to ask. No, she kept silent and glanced at Lord Calloway, who seemed to have lost some of his light as he stood there in his corner.

When he caught her gaze, however, he sent her a crooked smile and stood straight. "Well," he said, "I should be getting to work. Father's accounts are not going to sort themselves out."

"Is there something wrong with the businesses?" Lady Calloway asked, clearly alarmed by the idea.

But Lord Calloway waved the question away. "Of course not, Mother. He taught me well. When you are finished, Pritchard, I would like to know what should be done to help my brother's recovery. I will be in the library." He stepped out of the room before waiting for a response.

The doctor spent a few more minutes looking over William, but then he declared him at the very least stable, if not recovering, and excused himself to go find Lord Calloway.

Lady Calloway took hold of William's hand in both of her own. "Where is Olivia?" she asked Lucy. "I did not see her this morning."

"She's out riding." Lucy lowered herself slowly onto the bed, where Lord Calloway had been sitting earlier. She could tell Lady Calloway needed something to distract her, and she fully understood why. Gazing down at William's pale face was enough to tie Lucy's stomach in knots, and she barely knew the man. She could only imagine how worried his mother was, particularly if he had been through something like this before.

"No doubt she is trying to beat Simon," Lady Calloway said with a smile. "She'll never manage it, no matter how fast her horse is. I have never seen a beast that flies like Simon's Hermes, nor a master who rides as if weightless like he does."

"Olivia is quite determined to put him in his place."

"I wish her all the luck. Since the day he took over for his father, Simon has never lost a race."

A soft moan came from the bed, and both women turned to William in surprise. Lucy's heart kicked up a notch as she wondered if her moment of truth was suddenly here. Was he going to wake up and tell his mother everything?

"William?" Lady Calloway whispered, pushing his hair from his forehead with trembling fingers. "Can you hear me, William?"

But, despite his mother's fervent words, William remained motionless. If he truly had woken, it had been for only a moment.

Lucy let out the breath she'd been holding. She was not supposed to be glad he was asleep, but the longer he slept, the longer she would be able to stay with the Calloways and give them a reason to help her. "Maybe he will wake soon," she told Lady Calloway and put a comforting hand on the woman's arm.

Or maybe all of this would turn disastrous, and Lucy would be only one heartbreak among many in the Calloway home.

Chapter Nine

Simon had to admit it; Olivia was getting good. Her horse had run with the wind at its tail, and their upcoming race—whenever he actually found the time for it—would be far more interesting than any had been in the past. There was even a chance, however slight, that she might win, and Simon knew he would never hear the end of it if she did. She'd been trying to beat him for three years.

He fully planned to extend that time. Indefinitely.

He wished he could have been out on the grounds to tease her when she returned to the stables, but he'd had to watch from the window of the library while he and Mr. North, his man of business, had been going through a detailed report of how much Father's sugar farm was costing them. It was terribly dull work, but it was important.

And far better than discussing William's perilous health with Mr. Pritchard. According to the doctor, there was more to William's state than simply a fever, and Simon did not have the capacity to wonder why his brother had a half-healed scar from what looked like a pistol ball.

"You're saying he was shot?" Simon had asked incredulously.

"I'm saying he was lucky to be alive before this fever ever hit," the physician had replied.

None of the rumors Simon had heard in Town had involved William being shot, so the injury was simply another mystery—one Simon wasn't sure he had the energy to solve. Whatever William did with his free time, Simon was inclined to let his brother deal with the consequences himself so he could focus on the businesses that kept him far too busy. Particularly this failing one.

Thank the heavens he had not had to travel to the West Indies to see to the affairs himself. He had had the foresight to convince his father to hire a steward, who kept up regular correspondence and seemed open to being managed from afar. Simon knew the chance was great that the man was lying with every word he wrote and that every pound that came out of the crops went straight to his pocket, but he hoped for the best. Father had loved this venture in particular, and Simon would hate to see it fail.

"Assuming everything reported is correct," North was saying—Simon reluctantly pulled himself away from the window to pay attention—"I still don't see how keeping the farm will do anything but drain the full allotment we've given this business. It is barely breaking even as it is, what with you paying such high wages to the workers."

Simon was afraid of that, but he refused to treat those who worked the farm as anything less than they deserved as productive employees. "You wrote to Mr. Wyndham, didn't you?" The man owned land near Simon's and paid similar wages, and his farm had been thriving for the last two years.

North nodded. "I did. He agreed to take on your workers if you sell the land to him for three quarters of what you offered it for."

Settling heavy in his chair, Simon thought that over. Father had not bought a large farm, thankfully, but if they kept trying to keep the place alive, other ventures would suffer. Wyndham had more resources and could easily make Simon's land profitable. But for such a low selling price? Simon wasn't worried about going poor—his position had its perks, and the family had assets to spare—but admitting defeat and selling at three quarters of what the land was worth, like North was sure to suggest he do, meant he had failed and had not been able to keep everything flourishing like his father had.

"What options do we have?" he asked.

North said nothing, which was as telling as if he had laid out the hopelessness of this particular situation in vivid detail. He was not a man who liked giving bad news.

Simon sighed. "Sell it." Those two words seemed to draw out the last of his energy, and he dropped his head against the back of his chair. "And for all that is good and holy, do not tell my mother." He would have to hope Wyndham treated the laborers well, but at least they would have jobs. If Simon continued running the place to the ground, as he'd been doing, they would all inevitably be out of work. Anything was better than losing the livelihoods of so many people.

"Making a logical decision to protect your estate is not a failure, my lord," North said, though his hesitation made it clear he didn't fully believe his own words. He had worked for Simon's father as well and had seen the late Lord Calloway's endless success.

Simon had never understood why his father loved owning and operating so many businesses. Not only did the estate bring in plenty of money to keep the family well beyond comfortable, but he was a baron and had enough to occupy him in London alone. Yet, for as long as Simon could remember, Father had delighted in acting the part of a businessman as well as the nobility, as if Society would not consider him an oddity of the worst sort for doing so.

The only reason their family had not been shunned, Simon was sure, was because his father had been well-liked and altogether successful in his ventures. Simon did not have the same luxury on either account, which put him in a precarious position.

"I will see to the sale and alert you as soon as everything is finalized," North said, and he bowed slightly before slipping out of the room.

Simon sighed. What was he going to tell Mother? She had told him many times that she had full confidence in his ability to manage his father's affairs. Losing the farm would disappoint not only one parent but the other as well, and Simon knew he would not be able to forgive himself easily. If only Father had stuck around a little longer and taught him better. Maybe then . . .

He slammed his hand onto the table, breaking himself out of that thought before he finished it. "Be grateful for how long you had him," he chided out loud, then rose to go back to the window. Perhaps Olivia was still out training and he could search her technique for any weaknesses he might exploit in their race.

Looking out the window was a bad idea.

Miss Staley was out there, and Simon instantly froze in place as he watched his future sister-in-law wander the grounds as if deep in thought. *Lucy*, he told himself. It fit her much better than her surname, which didn't seem to fit her at all. Olivia was indeed riding still, but he hardly paid his sister any attention. Not when the summer breeze tugged at Lucy's raven hair and the folds of her dress. Unlike with her name, she somehow fit Calloway Park, like they had been tailored to match.

Where had she said she'd come from? She hadn't, because Simon hadn't bothered to ask her. But wherever she was from, that woman was born to live in the country.

William, on the other hand? He was not.

At what point of knowing Lucy had William decided he could overlook their differences? Surely he didn't intend to spend the rest of his life at his little country home, particularly not in its current state, but Simon could hardly imagine Lucy enjoying most of her time spent in Town.

He may not have known much about his brother's intended, but he was quite sure she did not love London. No one of her cheerful disposition and wit could truly enjoy the masked ridiculousness that was London Society, and she was so different from the lot of them.

"Deep in thought, are we?" a gentle voice behind him asked.

Simon's first instinct was to jump away from the window and pretend he hadn't been looking out, but Mother was far too intelligent to be deceived so easily, so he held his ground, though his feet itched to run like Olivia's horse.

Olivia. *Perfect.* "She is getting faster," Simon said with mock thoughtfulness. "She could beat me this time if I don't give it my all."

Mother came up beside him to look out the window as well, but her eyes did not follow the racing horse. She instead watched Lucy, a smile playing at the corners of her lips. "She is a good woman, is she not?"

Simon resisted the urge to agree without pause. "It seems that way," he said, though he had to count to ten first to check the words that might have come out of his mouth instead. "Have you learned much about her?"

Perhaps Mother could offer some insight into the strange circumstances of William and his betrothed.

"She is a shy thing," Mother replied. "Perhaps a bit overwhelmed. But we will have plenty of time to get to know her, now that we know we get to keep her."

Keep her. Lucy would go with William to Penworth as soon as he was well again. Though the distance was not particularly far, it was enough. Simon would not be able to watch her from the window when she was at Penworth. How long before they were set to be married? Perhaps they would have the banns read as soon as William recovered. Given a week for him to be strong enough, that left only a month before they could be wed.

Simon cleared his throat and stepped away from the window. He would do better to stop thinking about Lucy and the mystery she presented. The challenge. She was not his to decipher.

"We have decided to sell the farm," he said, then cringed. He hadn't meant to tell Mother that. What was it about Helena Calloway that made him give up all his secrets without any sort of prompting? She had had the skill for as long as Simon could remember, and it had gotten him into trouble more than a few times.

At least he wasn't William. Compared to William, Simon was a saint.

"Have you?" Mother said, though she kept her focus out the window. "Well, I suppose it is for the best."

"Is it?" He let all his breath out at once. That hadn't been anything close to the reaction he'd expected. How on earth was she not disappointed by his failure?

Mother smiled and slipped her arm through his. "You would know better than I, dear. Now, I assume you are done with business?"

For now, he thought bitterly. With all of Father's ventures, he had plenty to keep him occupied for the rest of his life. Plenty of other ways to fail. "Why?" he asked as Mother gently directed him toward the door.

"Because I want you to take a walk with me."

"I don't have time for—"

"You certainly have time to take a turn about the garden with your poor, ailing mother, Simon Calloway."

He gritted his teeth as her censure hit him right in the heart. Father had always had time to walk with his wife, though Simon had no idea how. With all the traveling and financial discussions and seeing to the hundreds of affairs around the estate, time was not on Simon's side.

"Of course, Mother," he said, though he could think of four things already that needed his immediate attention. But he knew better than to contradict the woman who had given him life. "And you are neither poor nor ailing."

Thank the heavens for that.

By the time they got outside, Lucy had disappeared. He tried not to be disappointed, but he was. There was something about that woman that intrigued him, particularly because she had agreed to William's hand when she could have found someone better suited to her. In truth, her acceptance of him confused Simon just as much as William's willingness to finally settle down and stop roaming the world like it all belonged to him.

"Why the sour face this morning, Simon?" Mother asked as they set out into the gardens. "It was only a farm, and your father would have understood."

"I suppose," Simon muttered. But Father wouldn't have let the farm fail in the first place. He would have ensured jobs for all of the laborers without having to trust someone else.

It would be best to change the subject before she launched into a lecture on cutting one's losses. He had no idea whether she even knew what that meant, but he could imagine such a lecture quite easily.

"I see the roses are doing well this year," he said, trying to sound cheery and unaffected by his failures. Would she believe him? Probably not. But it was worth trying.

"Those are tulips, dear."

Well, how was he supposed to know something like that? Father had never taken up gardening as one of his many ventures. Huffing out a sigh, Simon did his best not to scowl as he and Mother wandered the many flowers that grew at Calloway Park. She hated when he was grumpy, and keeping Lady Calloway happy had been as much a business of Father's as anything else. More so.

Father had loved his wife more than anything, and Simon wished he could find a love match even half as exquisite. Or a love match of any kind. He was not so foolish as to think he would find someone as perfect for him as Mother had been for the late Lord Calloway, but he hoped he could at least find affection.

William certainly had. Lucy had thus far spent half her time at the Park at his bedside. Simon hoped William cared for her as much as she did for him, though he had a hard time imagining it. William cared for no one but himself.

Mother squeezed his arm gently, pulling him to a stop at a low stone bench nestled in a copse of beech trees. "Simon, what is bothering you?" she asked as she lowered herself onto the seat. She patted the bench next to her like she had when Simon was a boy, and he scoffed.

"I am not six years old, Mother," he said as he joined her. "And nothing is bothering me. I am perfectly content."

"One of the things I love about you, Simon, is your inability to tell a lie. You have never had your brother's talent."

That was certainly true. William was, for the most part, harmless, but his tongue had a way of stretching the truth to his advantage. As much as he hated to think it, Simon wondered if his brother's silver tongue had come into play with his engagement to Lucy. What had he promised her? What was he getting in return?

"William will recover, as he always does," his mother said.

Taking up Mother's hand in both of his, Simon refused to look at her in case she saw too much in his face. "I'm not worried about William." That was only sort of true, but he had no way to explain what was going through his head. He would have to try though. "He can take care of himself and make his own choices, and he will wake up and go about his life as he always does."

"Now with a darling wife-to-be."

"He doesn't deserve her."

"Simon."

He sighed, ducking his head. "I didn't mean that. I worry what will happen when he wakes up, that's all."

With her free hand, Mother reached over and pressed her palm to his cheek. She was gentle, but her hand tugged enough to get him to turn to face her. "You worry too much," she said with little room for argument.

Simon still tried. "I know. Father wouldn't have been—"

"You are not your father, Simon."

His heart fell, though he knew she was right. Otherwise, he wouldn't be having this conversation, and he would have thriving businesses galore on top of a well-maintained estate. He would probably be married by this point; his father had been only twenty-four when he married, and Simon was several years past that already. In so many ways, he fell short, and he feared he would never live up to the legacy Lord Calloway had left behind.

"I have work to do." He stood and offered his arm to his mother to lead her back inside.

She shook her head. "I think I will sit a little longer with the flowers."

She might have had more to say, but Simon wasn't willing to hear it. Not today, when he was already dealing with so many other things.

And at the top of his list was Lucy, who was proving to be a mystery he might never solve.

Chapter Ten

Simon wasn't entirely sure why he felt the need to look in on William. Dr. Pritchard had been there a few hours before and laid out the entirety of his care, which Simon had relayed to the staff. But he made his way down the corridor and into his brother's chamber anyway, as if driven there by some emotion he couldn't quite place.

It couldn't possibly be guilt, though it felt disturbingly similar.

As expected, William lay undisturbed, deep asleep beneath the laudanum meant to keep him comfortable while his body fought the fever and healed the unknown wound in his side. At least with the fever, it was always the same, and he would likely remain this way for another day or two until he finally pushed through. With the wound on top of the fever and perhaps contributing to it, this time things might actually be worse.

The first few fevers had been a nightmare. Simon was six years older than his brother and had been old enough that first time William got sick to recognize the danger. William had barely made it through then, and Simon had thought he would become an only son. But his brother eventually recovered and returned to his energetic self.

The second time, Simon had thought for sure his brother would be taken, but William had proven himself stronger than he seemed and recovered in less than a week.

After that, every fever had been enough to cause some anxiety but never anything to truly worry about.

"You're not going to change things up on me, are you?" Simon asked, and his voice seemed to break a tension that had sat heavy in the quiet room.

Outside of William's shallow breaths, the room was completely silent and left Simon a bit on edge as he settled himself in the chair next to the bed. Silence and William had not often existed in the same space, and it felt ominous when they did.

"You have always been constant, Will, and I've always loved that about you. You're not perhaps the paragon of propriety, but you've always been true to who you are. And I have envied that."

William stirred a little, and Simon waited to see if perhaps he would wake long enough to finally have a conversation about Lucy.

He found no such luck.

Simon let out a sigh, sinking a little deeper into his seat. "The one time you decide to do something unexpected, and it has to be this?" he muttered. "I don't even care about the gunshot wound. Can't you just tell me why you chose someone like Lucy? Because I cannot for the life of me understand your choice. She is too quiet for you, William. Too kind. Too—"

"Oh, I am sorry," a gentle voice said from the doorway.

Simon leaped to his feet when he realized it was Lucy standing there with blushed cheeks. *Too beautiful*, he finished silently. "Lucy," he said, then winced when he realized how loudly he had said it. Honestly, how was it he completely forgot how to behave like a normal man whenever she was around? He'd never had this problem with anyone else.

Perhaps if she would stop catching him off guard, he would not be so . . . caught off guard. He ducked his head and cursed his own thoughts for becoming a muddled mess when she was near. He had managed a decently normal conversation at breakfast, but that had been because Olivia was there to balance out the strangeness of Lucy being in the house.

She sent him a quick smile and then said, "I apologize for interrupting," before she turned back to the corridor.

"Wait!" Simon cleared his throat, with no clue what he could say before she thought him a complete fool. "I am not overly fond of one-sided conversations, and William is proving to be a dull companion."

He applauded his own haphazard cleverness when she grinned.

"Oh, on the contrary," she said and approached the bed. Simon noted every single one of her soft steps and hated himself for it. He had no business wondering why she walked so carefully, as if to keep her whereabouts a secret. "You simply have to learn to listen properly."

"I suppose you have become quite adept at speaking to the feverish." Simon frowned. What the devil was that supposed to mean?

If she thought the comment odd, Lucy said nothing about it as she sat at the edge of William's bed and brushed some hair from his forehead. "Only this feverish individual," she said.

Simon resisted the urge to brush at his own hair to understand what the gesture might feel like. Being so busy most of his life, he had never been in a position to be touched so gently by anyone but his mother. "And what does the invalid say?" He felt completely out of his depths with this woman, and standing over her did nothing to help that. He sat again, hoping it would provide him a way to be at the same level as her physically, at least, if not mentally.

Lucy's smile was warm and gentle as she gazed down at her betrothed. "He says he is downright tired of being stuck in this bed, though he does not mind the constant attention."

"I'm sure he doesn't," Simon mumbled to himself.

"And he hopes someone will bring him some food one of these days, even if he has not found the will to be awake enough to eat it. It's the principle of the thing."

Simon's lips twitched in a smile, though he was far too focused on the way Lucy picked up William's hand and held it between her own to fully appreciate the joke. "Is that so?"

"Indeed."

"Is there anything else my brother has told you?"

Lucy grinned at him, and it seemed to push Simon deep into his chair, it hit him with so much force. "He says you worry too much for him and should take a holiday now and then."

"A holiday?" Simon snorted a laugh. "William knows better than to think I am capable of stepping away from my duties long enough for anything resembling a holiday."

"Perhaps he knows better than you in this regard. A man of privilege like yourself should have more than enough time and money to take a break from his duties now and then."

"Would you like to take a walk, Lucy?" Cringing, Simon knew Lucy was far too intelligent not to recognize him changing the subject—anyone would be—but he had to do it. Talking about his free time, or lack thereof, would only make him miserable, and word would inevitably reach his mother, who was concerned enough for his happiness and didn't need to worry further. She had William to look after, anyway. "We have a spectacular pond not far from the house that you might like, and we are having some remarkably fine weather."

Her lips quirked in a little smile. Simon half expected her to decline so she could stay at her intended's side, but she returned William's hand gently to the bed and rose to her feet. "I think that sounds lovely," she said. "I confess I have been wanting to explore more of Calloway Park, but I have not—"

"You've been busy," Simon said, then cursed himself for interrupting. He was already acting the bumbling fool and didn't need to add rudeness to the list of his many faults Lucy was undoubtedly compiling.

Between the two Calloway men, she had certainly managed to snag herself the one with the confidence to rival a duke or beyond. To think, if she had chosen the elder brother, she would have ended up with a cotton-headed baron who tripped over his own feet as he followed her out the door.

Perhaps her choice of husband was for the best.

"Besides," he added since things couldn't get any worse, "Olivia hates walking, so she would hardly want to be your companion."

Lucy gave him a smile that nearly made him stumble again, but she didn't say anything until they'd stepped outside into the sun. "From what I've heard, Lord Calloway, you travel quite often. Where has been your favorite place?"

Simon was so busy concentrating on where he put his feet—he feared he might somehow slip and land face-first in the dirt—that he didn't immediately realize that she was trying to make conversation. And when he deciphered her question, he had no idea how to answer it. "I have been to many great places," he said, gesturing in the direction they should go to find the pond. "I am not sure I could choose a favorite."

He doubted she would think highly of him if he told her he would rather stay home in the country for the rest of his life, particularly this country, considering Calloway Park had always been wilder than most estates. Much of the grounds had remained a refuge for the creatures who had made it their homes. Simon always hated to leave, and having to spend the Season in London because of Parliament was bad enough without adding all of Father's ventures on top of that.

Lucy had agreed to marry William, though, which meant she would be getting herself into a life of hopping from place to place. It sounded exhausting. Unless she was content to remain at home while William did his traveling. Simon couldn't imagine her being content to be left anywhere. He had not been around her long, but she seemed lonely with William being unconscious.

Perhaps that was why he had suggested this walk. She needed the companionship, and he needed a distraction from his failures.

"London is rather fine," Lucy said.

She kept at a slow pace as she followed the narrow trail, her eyes taking in the fields and hills that surrounded Calloway Park, and Simon found it easier than he would have guessed to stay at her side. Usually, when he made the trek to the pond, he walked as quickly as he could so he could put some space between him and his responsibilities. Today, he was perfectly content to hold his arms behind his back and let Lucy take the lead.

Though, perhaps he would do well not to let her take the lead in conversation. "I have never much liked London," he said.

"No?"

Simon couldn't tell if she was simply curious or if there was more to her question. She barely spared him a glance, which rather bothered him. How could he guess her thoughts if he couldn't see her expression? Blast it all, why should he even care what she thought? It wasn't like he could pursue her. He simply wanted to get to know his future sister-in-law, and pretending to be fond of traveling would only make things awkward between them when the family inevitably pointed out his contrary opinions.

"I prefer the wilder parts of the world," he said. "Well, the wilder parts of England, more like." When she had no reaction outside of another glance, he added a bit more. "Truth be told, I would be content to stay at the Park the rest of my life. At least, I do not particularly enjoy traveling when everyone I love is here."

It was at that moment they crested the hill that overlooked Simon's pond, and Lucy stopped dead in her tracks, her eyes going wide as she took in the scene.

Simon had to admit he had timed his confession well. The late-afternoon sunlight glittered across the surface of the water and bathed the oak trees and grasses in gold, leaving the whole space warm and enchanting. The pond had never been more spectacular, despite it being Simon's most favorite place in the world.

Lucy clasped her hands together and held them to her heart as she took in the scene, and her eyes seemed to glow in the sunlight like everything else. As if she belonged here. "It is breathtaking, Simon," she whispered.

He thought his heart might have stopped beating, because she had not said his name before now, and it sounded like music to his ears.

That was going to be a problem.

Chapter Eleven

Lucy had never seen anything more beautiful. She had never imagined anything could look or feel the way this pond looked and felt. It felt like . . . she could hardly put a word to it, but the closest she could think of was *home*. And as much as she had been missing the feel of home before arriving at Calloway Park, the ache of longing settled deeper in her heart. The more in love she fell with this place and the people who lived there, the harder it would be to leave.

Lord Calloway watched her carefully, as if waiting for her to pass judgment, and she did her best to give him a smile. The tears that had built up inside her eyes made that a little difficult, however, and she swiped them away so she could still see the paradise before her.

"It's the most beautiful thing I've ever seen," she told him.

"Are you sure?" he replied, lifting one thick eyebrow and gazing at her as if she might faint at any moment. "Your tears say otherwise."

Taking hold of his arm, Lucy did her best to make him understand. "This place feels familiar," she said. "Like a piece of something I have been missing for a long time."

"It is nothing like London."

Oh, she hardly cared for London. It was simply the most exciting place she'd ever been. She had only been fighting to make conversation before the silence between them made her spill all her secrets before she had prepared the best way to admit to everything and ask for help. "The only part of London I care for is the people. Some people. Only a few people. Or perhaps only Rebecca."

"Your maid?"

Lucy nodded. "She is the only friend I have in this world."

"I see," Lord Calloway said and clasped his hands behind his back, looking for all the world like the most impressive gentleman Lucy had ever had the pleasure of meeting. He *was* a baron, after all, and he had a right to stand there with such majesty as he looked out over his domain. Must he always be so formal around her though? She far preferred him when he teased her and smiled, though those moments seemed to be more of a rarity than commonplace with Lord Calloway.

A pity. She liked him best when they felt on even ground.

"I suppose, with William here, you have no reason to go to London anymore?" he said.

"Oh, he's not—" Lucy swallowed her words as he glanced over at her. She had nearly told him that William wouldn't be taking her anywhere, but she still feared for Lady Calloway's constitution. The woman was barely holding herself together, and Lucy still had to earn the family's trust before Mr. Granger found her.

Had it been long enough that he had already been to the Winthrops' to find her? Perhaps that didn't matter, considering she had not arrived when she was supposed to. They would have no reason to keep their agreement to hire her on.

Lucy needed a distraction before her tears turned into those of fear and hopelessness.

"I can imagine William travels to London fairly often," she said with no idea how correct she might be. Was he the sort of man who would bring a wife to Town with him? Or would she be forced to remain in the country on her own, wondering when he would return? Not that it mattered; Lucy was in no position to do either.

Lord Calloway turned his gaze back to the glittering pond, his lips pursed together as if in disapproval. "He travels many places," he said.

"Yes, it seems him coming home with a fiancée in tow has caused quite a stir," Lucy replied with a frown. For some reason, Lord Calloway's mood seemed to have taken a turn for the worse, and she had no idea why. What was so wrong with traveling when Lord Calloway himself did it so often?

"My brother is not inclined to stay in one place for long," he agreed.

"Perhaps he will take his poor wife along with him on occasion."

"I would certainly not call you poor, Miss Staley."

Lucy felt the formality as much as she heard it, already missing her name on his lips. It left a dull ache that settled next to the churning ball of guilt in her chest.

Lord Calloway, on the other hand, carried on with no idea how much she hated his use of her false name. "My brother has two thousand pounds a year."

Lucy squeaked. She had known the Calloway estate was well off, but she would never have guessed a second son would receive so much. Lord Calloway was looking at her again now, and she fumbled for an excuse to cover her surprise. Surely, as William's betrothed, she would know such a thing already. She was rather surprised he was not married already, being the brother of a baron and with such a sum to entice any woman to accept his hand.

"I thought I saw a fox up ahead," she said and pointed as vaguely as she could. "Perhaps I was mistaken."

Squinting in the sunlight, Lord Calloway searched the wild grasses and smiled a little. "Clever creatures, foxes."

"Indeed," Lucy replied, though it was not a thing she knew. Her father had never been one for hunting. Still, this seemed to be a topic that brought a bit of happiness into Lord Calloway's eyes, and she far preferred him in a good mood.

She wondered if William had the same tendency to rock back and forth in temperament or if it was solely a Simon trait.

"We have quite a few out here on the Calloway lands," he said, "and they always seem to sneak up on me when I least expect it. Then they're gone in a flash, leaving me wondering whether I saw them at all." He lifted one corner of his lips, and his eyes seemed to twinkle in the afternoon light. What lovely eyes; they were neither green nor brown but entirely warm and gentle. In this light, they almost looked gold. She'd never seen anything like them, and she felt herself becoming lost in those eyes. She likely wouldn't come out the same, if she made it out at all.

Lucy shivered.

"You're cold," he said immediately and looked around as if hoping to find something to remedy the situation.

The summer air was hardly chilly, but Lucy wrapped her fingers around her arms if only to give herself a reason to go back to the house instead of continuing the awkward conversation. Thus far, Simon Calloway had been easy to talk to, but something about their little walk had made everything feel forced, as if she thought she needed to try harder to be someone he would like.

She did need to try, if she wanted his help, but the idea of being disingenuous made her stomach churn.

Perhaps the awkwardness between them was for the best. She would be leaving him behind just as she would the rest of the family, so there was no point in getting attached.

"We should return to the house anyway," she said with a timid smile. "I believe your mother said she would be having guests over for dinner tonight, and I should hate to make you late."

"Of course." Lord Calloway offered his arm but refused to make eye contact with her, which hurt more than she thought it would. He hadn't had that problem before, so why should he now? She wanted another look at his fascinating eyes.

She feared she had not been as adept at keeping her secret as she hoped and Lord Calloway had begun to suspect her deception. Would it be better if she came right out and told him everything? Taking hold of his arm, she breathed in deep and tried to weigh her options. Even if she did decide to speak the truth now, how did she go about telling a wealthy and powerful man that she had been lying to his entire family since the moment she met them?

She would begin with the problem: Mr. Granger. If she started with the danger he presented, maybe that would overpower any ill feelings Lord Calloway would rightfully have toward her.

"Sir," she began as they walked back toward the house.

"Are you back to that again? I thought we were making progress."

When he threw her a crooked grin, Lucy felt like stomping her foot and demanding he explain himself. Why was he so confusing? Did he trust her or not? How was she supposed to act around him if one moment he was teasing her and the next he seemed suspicious of her?

"I don't think you have earned your name yet, sir," she replied through gritted teeth.

He pulled her a fraction of an inch closer as they walked, and the movement made her look up at him again so he could wink. "You used it not ten minutes ago, Lucy."

Had she? Oh bother. She needed to take better care to avoid using a man's Christian name when she had no business even knowing it in the first place. "That was because you showed me such an exquisite pond," she argued. "You were deserving of it then, I suppose."

"So if we turned around and went back?" He stopped so suddenly that he nearly pulled Lucy off her feet.

Struggling out of his hold, she considered glaring at him but thought better of it. This man held her fate in his hands, whether or not he knew it, and she would do well to do everything in her power to keep him in a good mood for as long as possible. For the sake of his family and the sanctity of her reputation. "Have you never heard of too much of a good thing?" she asked.

He chuckled a bit. "Hardly. I could sit by that pond for hours if I were able."

"Are you not? These are your lands, aren't they?"

Lord Calloway shook his head and looked around them with a sort of longing in his eyes. "I hardly have time to explore my lands anymore," he said wistfully.

A spark of pity entered Lucy's chest, and she watched Lord Calloway's expression fall into a deeper sadness than she would have expected from a man who had so much in his life. "No time to walk your grounds," she said, "and no time for a holiday. Poor, poor Simon."

His eyes jumped back to hers, and he seemed torn between laughing and complaining. "I am not sure I approve of the use of my name in this instance," he said. "Am I to hear my name on your lips only when you are either overjoyed or oversaddened?"

Clasping her hands in front of her, Lucy could not prevent herself from speaking her mind, as always seemed to happen around this man. "With my life, it is generally one or the other, my lord. Especially the latter."

He frowned, stepping closer as he looked down at her. "Are you often saddened, Lucy? Surely not now that you have William. My brother is a lot of things, but he is not one to make his wife miserable."

Maybe that was true, but Lucy would never know. Neither would she be able to keep her secret if Lord Calloway continued to remind her of her lie. Brushing away a tear that escaped, she flashed a smile and then hurried back toward the house.

Lord Calloway caught up to her with only a few strides and took hold of her arm. She flinched as her mind flashed back to her memories of Mr. Granger and the number of times he had caught her in some corridor or another and begged her to accept him, but she silently told herself that Lord Calloway was not Jonathan Granger. His hold was nothing if not gentle, while Mr. Granger's grip had always been overly firm.

"I've upset you," Lord Calloway said and released her, further solidifying the differences between the two men. "What did I say? Has my brother—"

"Of course not," Lucy whispered. William had hardly been conscious long enough to make her miserable. That was part of the problem. "I simply do not want to delay dinner."

"Lucy." Keeping his movements gentle, he slowly turned her to face him and nudged her chin up until she looked at him. "What is the matter?"

William's chivalry was what had convinced Lucy to reluctantly remain at his side, but somehow Simon outshined his brother in this regard. Looking up into his eyes, she saw nothing but kindness and concern, and she couldn't remember the last time someone had looked at her that way. He reminded her so much of her father that seeing this side of him hurt far more than it should.

It was not something she was likely to find again.

"Lucy!"

Olivia's voice made them both jump, and Lucy realized how close she and Lord Calloway had been standing in the dying sunlight when she took a step away from him and was instantly chilled. She turned and was more than grateful to see Olivia hurrying toward them.

Lord Calloway took two more steps away from Lucy and cleared his throat as his sister approached.

"Mother has been looking all over for you two," Olivia said, glancing between the two of them. "Our guests will be arriving at any moment. Simon, you need to play host."

Lucy didn't trust herself to look back at Lord Calloway to see if he was as red in the face as she felt. Surely not; he had no reason to be embarrassed by a conversation with his future sister-in-law. "We were on our way back," she told Olivia, then latched on to the girl's arm before her brother could offer his own again. "I hope we haven't held things up."

"I'll tell Mother it was my fault," Lord Calloway said, striding away as if he couldn't wait to be out of Lucy's company.

"What's bothering him?" Olivia asked.

Lucy shrugged.

Clearly Olivia wasn't all that concerned, because she smiled at Lucy and tugged her forward. "Come, we must hurry. It's a pity there won't be any eligible gentlemen in attendance tonight, isn't it? Though, I suppose that does not matter to you! You're already happily engaged and don't need to find yourself a handsome husband."

Lucy wouldn't have disagreed even if Olivia knew the truth. After playing this charade as long as she had, even if it was only for a couple of days, her chances of ever finding a husband were slim, and she would forever be a governess. That was probably for the best, as she had little to offer a man, but she didn't much fancy the lonely part of her future life.

It made being a part of the Calloway family taste that much sweeter, but everything thereafter would be bitter.

Chapter Twelve

Simon had never much liked the Thatchers. His neighbors were from new money, elevated to wealth by Mr. Thatcher's business ventures, and the man had always made a point of lording his success over Simon's head. Father had done well for himself, but never as well as Thatcher, and the man took a good deal of pride in that.

Then there was the fact that he credited himself for all his success, ignoring the fact that he had stewards and men of business and a literal partner helping him with all his endeavors. But no, according to Mr. Thatcher, every penny came because of his own merits, and it drove Simon mad.

As he leaned his shoulder against the fireplace mantel and pretended to listen to Mr. Thatcher tell the family of his latest acquisition, Simon looked over the room and grew increasingly more frustrated because Lucy was nowhere to be found. According to Mother, she had been nervous about meeting anyone beyond the family until William was awake and they could officially announce their impending marriage. While the sentiment was logical, it didn't sit easy in Simon's stomach. Surely she didn't need her betrothed at her side to meet a few neighbors.

Still, he envied her. She had a legitimate reason to avoid the evening with the Thatchers, but Simon was trapped. Even if he came up with some way to make his excuses and take a tray in his room, his mother kept sending him piercing looks that told him under no circumstances was he allowed to leave her alone with this dreadful couple.

For a woman who was always so sweet-tempered, she truly had a talent for instilling fear in her children. Simon remained rooted to the spot, trapped by his mother's silent command.

"Calloway, m'boy." Thatcher waved his arm in Simon's direction, as if making sure he was paying attention. "I hear you lost your sugar farm." Where the devil had he heard that? He'd only just decided to sell. "A pity, considering mine has at least doubled its capital since I acquired it."

Simon forced a smile. "How fortunate for you." He made a mental note to check with North and ensure his man of business hadn't been spreading information around. Simon needed to remain in high standing among the other Lords of Parliament if he wanted to have any hope of being a valued voice, and he didn't need anyone knowing about his failing business.

As Mr. Thatcher launched into what was likely to be an exhausting recounting of all his thriving enterprises, Simon readied himself for an excruciating evening. He couldn't imagine anything that could make tonight better, and he prayed the butler, Porter, announced dinner sooner rather than later. For now, he would simply have to try to distract himself and hope Thatcher didn't try to pull him into conversation again, though that would also leave his mother to endure the man alone, which was not a better alternative.

Simon wasn't certain he had the stamina to assist his mother this time, so distraction would have to be his course of action. And what better way to distract himself than thinking about Lucy?

He wasn't sure why he'd shown her his pond, but he was immensely glad he had. Not only had she appreciated it and seemed to lose some of the invisible weight on her shoulders—weight from what, he hardly knew—but he had gotten the chance to learn a little more about his future sister-in-law.

She had acted somewhat strangely on their walk back to the house though. Simon couldn't make sense of it. He had replayed the conversation many times without any insight as to what had upset her. She truly was a mystery—one he was itching to solve.

Porter appeared at the doorway to the sitting room, and Simon perked up. Finally time for dinner and a respite—however brief—from Thatcher's endless yammering. But he was to be momentarily disappointed in his excitement because Porter merely carried in a calling card on a platter.

It was late enough into the evening that it was hardly the time for unannounced callers, so Simon took the card with interest. They had many neighbors, but most people had lived in Downingham long enough to know the routine lifestyle of the Calloways, so this card must be from someone from outside the village. Simon hoped it was someone intriguing.

The instant he saw the name on the card, he grinned. "Show him in, Porter," he said, hardly caring about the questioning look his mother shot him.

If anyone could liven up the evening, Nicholas Forester could.

Forester swept into the room with the swagger of a man who had everything in the world, even though that was hardly the truth. There was nothing noble about the man, and he was far from wealthy, but Simon had never met anyone with the same level of confidence as his old friend from his Eton days.

"Calloway!" Forester said with gusto, crossing the room and clapping Simon on the back. "If it isn't my favorite peer."

Simon scoffed. "I wouldn't let Lord Harstone hear you say that."

Forester made a face of disgust. "Rowland is far too busy with his babies to care what I say about him. And he would probably agree with my choice."

And he probably wouldn't mind that Forester never called him by his title. Lord Alvaro Rowland, Viscount Harstone, had only recently inherited his title from a distant uncle and had come to England from Spain to claim his birthright. Simon and Forester had befriended him during his first Season in England, and he was the humblest man Simon had ever known. Forester was probably right in his assessment of Lord Harstone being busy, but the comparison between the viscount and Simon only reminded Simon that he had not had the chance to see his friends in a long time. Forester was dead wrong in thinking Simon should be a favorite when Simon had hardly had the time to be a friend to anyone.

Lucy had agreed to be his friend though. That had to count for something.

"How many children is he up to now?" Simon asked, if only to pull his thoughts away from the woman upstairs.

"Three daughters," Forester said with a laugh. "With his wife and sister-in-law in the mix, the man is positively surrounded by women, and he couldn't be happier."

Simon's stomach twisted in his gut. "You've been to see him recently?" Oh, to be a man of no title, free to roam the country however he pleased. He had always envied Forester for that, just like he had often envied William for being a second son and having no responsibilities except for himself.

Forester, however, shook his head. "Haven't seen him since our last romp in London," he muttered, only now seeming to realize there were others in the room. He took them all in with his keen eyes, likely deciding whom he wished to greet first. "Though, I plan to spend time with him in the fall, if he'll have me. I have business with one of his neighbors. Ah, Lady Calloway, you are stunning, as always." Forester would never make a fool of himself in front of a beautiful woman. Not like Simon had with Lucy.

He watched his friend plant a kiss on his mother's hand, wondering how people like Forester and William managed to get through life without a care in the world. They were always so charming and free, and Simon felt like he was suffocating, because he never had a moment to himself. Shouldn't it have been the other way around? He was a wealthy lord and had everything he could possibly want. Even Lucy had pointed out the fact that he should have ample free time. So why did he feel trapped by his life?

Mother introduced Forester to the Thatchers, who eyed him with interest. If Simon recalled right, they had two young daughters at home and were likely appraising the man as a possible future match for one of the girls when they were out.

If that was their intent, they were looking in the wrong place. Forester had been searching for a wife for more than two years now and apparently had the highest of standards, considering he hadn't yet found a woman who came up to snuff. The daughter of a merchant would hardly suit him if a marquess's daughter wasn't enough.

Unfortunately, Olivia seemed to be as in love with Forester as she always had been, though she was doing a good job of hiding it as she sat quietly off to the side, waiting to be acknowledged, the poor girl. Forester would never do anything to intentionally hurt her, but neither was he interested in courting her.

And Simon was perfectly okay with that, mostly because he definitely wasn't ready for his baby sister to be grown up.

"What brings you to Oxfordshire?" he asked his friend.

Forester shrugged. "I happened to be in the area after hearing of a man selling a particularly fine piece of horseflesh. Turns out it was merely a cow."

Simon bit back a laugh when he caught the confusion in Mr. Thatcher's expression. "How unfortunate," he said, knowing Forester's story was entirely false. Nearly everything about Nick Forester was false—exactly as he wanted it.

"I considered buying it anyway," Forester said. "I've always wondered why more people don't ride cows when they are far more comfortable than horses. Just perhaps a bit slower."

"Are you staying for dinner, Mr. Forester?" Mother asked, changing the subject.

Forester grinned at her, a bit of mischief in his expression. "I was hoping I could stay longer than that, Lady C., if it wouldn't be imposing."

As expected, Mother waved his comment away. "You are hardly an imposition, Nicholas."

Though he smiled, Forester sent a pained look toward Simon, which made Simon chuckle. Forester hated when people called him Nicholas, and Simon hadn't spent any energy to indicate as much to his mother. He liked seeing his unflappable friend squirm now and then.

"What say you, Calloway?" Forester asked Simon. "As head of the family, you have the final say. Are you going to send me away?"

Though tempted to play along with the man's jokes, Simon was still too bothered by his earlier conversation with Lucy to do so. "Stay as long as you'd like," he said and breathed a sigh of relief when the butler returned, this time to at last announce dinner.

To no one's surprise, Olivia bounced up and attached herself to Forester's arm. "It's been so long since you last visited," she said with a smile that made Simon's stomach twist. As long as Forester behaved himself, though, his stay here could pass in peace.

"Ah, but there are so many people to see!" Forester replied as he led Olivia through the doors to the dining room.

Apparently they were going to ignore any rules of formality tonight, and Simon groaned a little, knowing the Thatchers would surely judge him for letting that happen.

"I had to ignore seven different invitations to come see you lovely Calloways," Forester continued. "The Duke of Westermoor is very put out with me, I'll have you know."

Simon scoffed as he took his seat at the table's head. "I don't believe the Duke of Westermoor even knows you exist, unless you've been pursuing his daughter, in which case you are having delusions of grandeur."

"I am always having delusions." Forester laughed. "And his daughter was married in February, to Lord Bartlett."

Was she? Simon was out of touch, apparently, and he needed to pay more attention to the other peers the next time he was in Town. Easier said than done, considering half his time in London was usually spent dealing with his many inherited businesses. Bartlett was a good man, though, and was a solid match for the duke's daughter in terms of rank. Simon would never have guessed their personalities to mix, however, and he was curious to know how the stoic earl handled the exuberant Lady Elizabeth.

None of that mattered though. Not when Simon had several strong personalities right in front of him to deal with.

Dinner, as to be expected, was a noisy affair, dominated primarily by Forester's endless stories, stories that got progressively more ridiculous as the evening went on. Simon suspected that was because Mr. Thatcher seemed to be hanging on every word as if he truly believed a near-dandy like Nick Forester would ever spend two years in the American wilderness fighting wolves. And each time Thatcher attempted to make a comment, Forester spoke right over him and sent a grin in Simon's direction.

The man could be exhausting, but he understood people in a way Simon never had. He must have noticed how little the family wanted to interact with the Thatchers, so he was doing what he could to keep that interaction to a minimum.

Simon tried to be a dutiful friend and pay attention to Forester's tales, but his eyes kept straying to the empty chair that should have been Lucy's, had she been willing to join them. She was probably up in her room enjoying a book and blessed silence, and he envied her for that.

Perhaps dinner wouldn't have been so tedious had she attended. He wasn't sure why he thought that, but something about William's beloved made it easier for Simon to breathe. That made little sense, considering he turned into a bumbling fool who tripped over his words when he was around her, but it was the truth all the same. He preferred the fool to the stoic baron he usually played.

"What a delightful adventure that must have been! You were so brave." Olivia's high-pitched remark made Simon wince. She was clearly trying to appeal to Forester's vanity. Perhaps it was a good thing Father wasn't here to witness her attempts at wooing eligible gentlemen, bold as they were. Hopefully she would grow out of that before her Season.

Though he knew Forester had never once given his sister any particular attention, Simon still sent a scowl in his friend's direction.

Forester chuckled and gave him an expression that seemed to say, "Will you relax?"

Simon hadn't been relaxed since the day his father died, and he highly doubted he would find any peace for years to come, if ever.

Finally, after what felt like hours, the ladies retreated to the drawing room and left the men to share a bit of port and talk freely, though Simon imagined the conversation would hardly change. Forester enjoyed the sound of his own voice a bit too much.

As Forester lifted his glass to his mouth, Thatcher perked up as if eager to finally get a chance to make himself look good. "Calloway, m'boy, did you know—"

"I nearly forgot!" Forester said loudly. "I haven't told you about the woman I saved in Hyde Park last Thursday. You will not believe how mad the place was, and if I hadn't been there . . ."

Thatcher huffed in annoyance, but he seemed to recognize his defeat and dropped himself into a chair at the other end of the room, staring into his glass.

Simon wrapped his arm around Forester's shoulders and breathed a sigh of relief. "I owe you one," he muttered, not loudly enough for Thatcher to hear.

Forester chuckled. "It took only three words out of the man's mouth before I pitied you for your unfortunate array of neighbors. Has he no shame?"

"None. You didn't really save someone in the park, did you?"

"And risk becoming even more of a spectacle of Town? Of course not."

Simon frowned as he tried to make sense of that. "You make yourself a spectacle," he pointed out.

Forester shrugged. "I can control my own words, but there is little else I can control. I use what I have and hope it serves me well in dampening whatever else people might decide about me."

Here was some of the sincere Forester back, the part of the man Simon had first grown to love. "How long do you plan to stay, truly?" he asked quietly so as not to be overheard. "You are welcome as long as you'd like."

"I give you my thanks, old friend. Town was becoming rather suffocating, and I can't bring myself to go back home now that my parents are both gone." A sadness filled his expression, even though his parents had died many years ago, when he was still a schoolboy.

Simon counted himself lucky. He still had his mother and sister, and now that William was nearly married . . .

William. Forester would have to find out eventually, though Lucy wouldn't like it. She had been quite adamant that no one but family know her as William's fiancée until William woke, but Forester was like another brother to Simon. He couldn't very well tell his friend that he had a random woman hiding upstairs like some scandalous secret.

"By the way," he said as the pair of them led the way into the drawing room a little while later, "William is engaged."

"What?" Forester's question was loud enough that everyone looked in their direction, and Simon was tempted to smack the man. He had meant to break this news gently. "When?"

Simon sighed. He and Forester took their places by the windows, letting the others return to their own conversations before he said anything. "That is the question," he muttered.

Forester pulled his eyebrows together in consternation, apparently as thrown by this revelation as Simon had been. "To whom?" he asked.

"Lucy."

"Who the devil is Lucy?"

"William's intended."

Forester narrowed his eyes. "I gathered as much from your own words, Calloway. Care to elaborate?"

"I would if I could." Folding his arms, Simon could barely stop himself from pacing. That would only make his mother nervous, and he had done that plenty of times of late and didn't need to add to her anxiety for him.

But even after he had let things sink in, he hardly understood the circumstances of William's engagement any better than he had when Lucy first arrived, so he wasn't sure how to explain them. "Miss Staley came to us yesterday morning with a fevered William in tow."

Forester glanced around the room, as if just realizing William was not there. That shouldn't have surprised him, though; William was hardly ever in Oxfordshire. "Where is he?"

"Upstairs. He is recovering, I hope."

"I saw your brother in London not two weeks ago, Calloway," Forester said, leaning in, his brow wrinkled with concern. "He was as he always is. That is, I daresay not a lady passed by who did not catch his fancy. Are you sure he is engaged?"

"I thought it strange as well, but Lucy wouldn't lie." Did he actually believe that? He wasn't sure. He knew nothing about the woman.

Forester must have realized as much too. He put his arm around Simon's shoulders and lowered his voice even more. "You met her yesterday, Calloway. How well could you possibly understand her character?"

He made a good point, and it only reaffirmed thoughts Simon had been having since he returned home. He hadn't given much weight to those thoughts, chalking it up to a strange form of jealousy or something like it, but the idea didn't sit well in his gut. Had he opened his home to someone more sinister than she appeared?

But what reason could she have to lie? Besides, it was the innkeeper who had told them he was sending Mrs. Calloway with William, and that man wouldn't have gained anything by concocting something so ridiculous, especially because he was wrong about the exact relationship. It had to be true, no matter how perplexing it might be.

"Well," Simon muttered, "tomorrow you can meet her for yourself, and perhaps you will decide she is not as honest as I hope her to be." He glanced at Mr. and Mrs. Thatcher as they dominated a conversation with Mother and Olivia. "She has asked us not to tell anyone of the betrothal until William is recovered."

For some reason, that seemed to catch Forester's interest, like a dog picking up on a scent. "Has she? Isn't that interesting?"

Simon didn't get a chance to ask what he meant by that. Mother waved Forester over just then, pulling him into a game of cards with the Thatchers, and Simon considered the possibilities of tomorrow. He couldn't decide what outcome he preferred, whether Forester uncovered some scheme or whether the engagement was true. Surely honesty was the best conclusion.

But if it weren't . . . it would mean Lucy was unattached, and Simon couldn't believe how appealing that idea was, considering how little he knew the woman. He reminded himself rather forcefully that a lie would also mean she had some reason for abusing his family, but he couldn't begin to imagine what she would gain from doing so. Pretending to be engaged to the brother of a baron would only bring her to ruin.

He simply hoped Forester would be able to bring some sort of resolution to the situation, because not knowing was making Simon's head spin. He couldn't afford to be distracted, and a smirk from Mr. Thatcher as he loudly challenged Forester to a wager on the game told Simon his neighbor would look for any reason to tear him down even more than he already had in order to make himself appear better.

Simon had to stay focused on keeping his father's businesses alive, and that meant he had to do everything in his power to ignore Lucy. No matter how beautiful and intriguing she was.

Chapter Thirteen

When Lucy stepped into the breakfast room, she was almost eager for some company. She hadn't realized how attached she had already grown to the warmth of the Calloway family's presence, and spending the evening in her chamber had helped her realize how little she wanted to be alone.

But when she found herself face-to-face with an utter stranger sitting at the table, one who locked eyes with her the instant she entered the room, she regretted ever leaving her room and quickly considered how easily she could slip away without saying a word. A familiar discomfort settled in her gut as he rose to greet her, and she felt as if she were back in the Grangers' home again.

The man at the table dressed well enough that he would look at home among the *beau monde*, but with his blond hair and blue eyes, he held no resemblance to the Calloway family, which meant he likely wasn't a relation. Or if he was, he was likely quite a distant one. Then again, he settled back in his chair perfectly comfortably, which meant he was rather accustomed to being at Calloway Park on his own, and that meant . . .

She had no idea what that meant, and nausea burned in her gut. The twinkle in his eyes made it seem as if he were laughing at her, and Lucy definitely didn't like that. "You must be the mysterious Miss Staley," the man said, and his lips twisted into a smug grin that set her even more on edge.

She took a deep breath and told herself to hold her ground, just like she had so many times against Jonathan Granger. She had nothing to hide from this stranger. Nothing, of course, beyond her entire identity.

Oh goodness, what if he knew Mr. Granger?

"I wouldn't call myself mysterious," she said carefully. She made her way slowly to the sideboard to find something to eat, though she wasn't sure she had the stomach for it now. She would surely wither away while here at Calloway Park because her guilt for her lies kept her from taking more than what she absolutely required.

She needed to be careful. Whoever this man was, he watched her intently as she picked food that would settle easily in her stomach. It wasn't that she didn't plan to tell the family the truth, but she wanted it to come from her, not from some strange man who seemed to think he knew something he shouldn't.

His smile grew as she sat, and he rested his chin in his hand, far too relaxed for someone who had not even been introduced to her. "I never thought William to be the marrying sort," he said. Nothing in his voice conveyed suspicion, but that didn't mean he didn't feel it.

Or perhaps Lucy had merely become suspicious herself. "Perhaps you do not know William very well, Mr. . . ."

"Nicholas Forester, at your service," he said with a little bow in his chair.

At least he wasn't nobility. It wasn't much, but it made it a little easier for Lucy to breathe as she nibbled at the bit of toast she had put on her plate. "Lucy," she said, unwilling to lie about her name again. She had told enough lies already. "I am not fond of formality."

That made Mr. Forester smile again, this time with one far less arrogant than anything he'd given her before. It was as if there were some sort of unspoken understanding between the two of them, but he was the only one who knew what it was. "You and I have something in common then," he said brightly. "In that case, I would be delighted if you would call me Nick."

A pit settled deep in her stomach. Using the man's Christian name would only make things worse when the truth came to light, but now that he had given her permission, she worried not being familiar with him would only make him question her reasoning for it. With her claim to abhor formality, she would simply have to agree, something that seemed to make him rather pleased as she spoke. "Very well, Nick. I am happy to make your acquaintance. How are you connected to the Calloways?"

"Simon and I were in school together, though he was merely a mister back then and far more agreeable than he is now." He chuckled to himself as if recalling fond memories of his youth. "And I hope you'll forgive me for my comment about William. He and I are not very close, despite my connection to his brother. I was simply surprised to find he had found himself such an astonishingly pretty wife after all this time."

Had he been any other handsome young gentleman, Lucy might have been uncomfortable beneath such praise, but Mr. Forester—Nick—said it without any of the implications that had always come from Mr. Granger's praises. Nick merely meant it as a compliment, rather than something to be repaid with equal attention. Recognizing that, Lucy felt her fear starting to slip away again.

"William is truly a lucky man," she said with a little grin, and she was pleased when Nick matched her smile. "Though, I am not his wife, as I am sure you know."

"I like you," he decided and reclined in his chair.

Maybe Lucy could admit her lies to this fellow, given his cheery mood and easy nature. She could use him to soften the blow to the family, and he seemed the sort who would know how to help her stay in their good graces.

Lady Calloway stepped into the room just then, and she looked far worse than she had yesterday, as if she hadn't slept through the night. Lucy suddenly felt a pang of sympathy for the poor woman, along with a healthy measure of guilt. She hadn't even thought to inquire after William's health this morning, coming straight to breakfast instead.

"How is Mr. Calloway?" she asked now.

Lady Calloway looked up with wide eyes, as if surprised to find anyone else in the room. "Hmm? Oh, the same. Simon is with him now, and he thought I should eat something before . . ." She let out a sigh before sinking into the nearest chair. Goodness, she looked worn to the bone, and Lucy had no idea how to help her.

But she did know the truth would do no one any good right now, so she clamped her mouth shut. Rebecca would be elated that she was doing so well at living with her guilt.

Hopping from his chair, Nick filled a plate with food, then gestured to a footman who stood nearby. "Take this upstairs to Lady Calloway's chamber," he directed, and then he waved the other footman over. "If you could accompany Her Ladyship upstairs, we would be most grateful."

Lady Calloway smiled wearily as she took the footman's offered arm. "You are a good man, Mr. Forester. I am glad Simon found you all those years ago."

"You mean you are lucky your oldest isn't a total bore. Otherwise, I would hardly tolerate him."

Though Lucy couldn't see Nick's face as he watched Lady Calloway leave with a quiet laugh, she could see the tension in his shoulders. He held himself stiffly, his jaw tight, and he seemed to be lost in thought as he stood motionless. It was so unlike the man she had seen thus far that she wondered if there was more to him than what he presented.

But the moment soon ended, and he grinned when he returned to his seat. "She worries too much," he declared.

"How could you say such a thing?" Lucy replied. "She is clearly suffering."

Nick sighed. "I know it. And I wish she wouldn't. William will pull through as he always does, and everything will go back to normal. What Lady C. needs is some light in her life, which is exactly why I am so very glad you are here, Lucy."

"Me?" She swallowed. "I am not that important."

"You are William's betrothed, which makes you that important."

"And if I weren't?"

"If you weren't his betrothed?" He sat up a little straighter, interest and a healthy dose of suspicion in his eyes.

Lucy had let her guard down a little too far, and she squirmed in her chair. Nick clearly cared about this family, and he would tell them the truth as soon as he learned it, likely without giving her a chance to explain why she had lied in the first place. She had thought he would be helpful, but he might very well prove the opposite.

She scrambled to cover her tracks. "Being engaged to William can't be my only redeeming quality, can it?"

Nick's smile slid up on one side, more mischievous than Lucy would have liked. "Perhaps we should compile a list of your qualities to see whether you measure up."

Why was she still sitting here? She would do better to go back up to her room and try to convince Rebecca to help her find a way to break the news to Lady Calloway without risking her health. Then Lucy could figure out what she would do now that she had nothing and nowhere to go. But Nick's bright gaze held her in place, and she had a feeling he was not one to give up easily.

Sitting up straight, she called on every lesson of poise she had given the Granger girls. "I suppose if you feel it is necessary, you may tell me all of my good qualities."

He laughed. "Well, you are certainly spirited."

"That is a good thing?"

"To some, yes. And you are clever and graceful and quite beautiful."

Lucy waited for the flush of heat to rise to her face at his compliments, but it never came. Flattery from Mr. Granger had always made her nervous, and nearly anything Lord Calloway said made her blush. Why was it so easy to take a compliment from Mr. Forester without becoming embarrassed by it? Could it be that he didn't mean a word of what he said?

"I do not see how any of these things would help Lady Calloway," she said. "And beyond your consideration of my beauty, which is rather subjective an opinion, you cannot know whether I truly possess those other traits. You hardly know me at all."

He acknowledged that comment with a nod. "True. So perhaps I should rectify that. Where are you from, Lucy?"

"Not far from London."

"Is your father a gentleman?"

Her eyes went wide. "I hardly think that is an appropriate question."

"He is not, then."

"My father is dead, Mr. Forester."

He winced, properly censured for his bold question. "My apologies, Miss Staley."

"Lucy."

"Nick."

"Apology accepted. Am I allowed to ask my own questions?"

His grin returning, Nick leaned in his chair and rested one elbow on the chair's arm, fully at ease now. "You can ask what you wish, but know that my answers may not be what you want to hear."

What was that supposed to mean? My, but Nick was a strange man. As much as she wanted to ask the same questions he had asked her, she chose a different option, curious to see what his answer would be. "How did you sleep last night?"

His lips rose in that crooked smile again. "Poorly," he said, though his energy belied his answer. "I fear I was woken by the most atrocious-sounding bird I had ever heard this morning, and I had to get out of bed to shoot it dead and bring it to Cook for tonight's supper."

What utter nonsense! Lucy put her hand over her mouth to mask her smile, determined to play the man's game. "I do hope it wasn't that little wren Olivia is so fond of," she said as seriously as she could. "She said it sings such lovely songs to her each morning."

Nick's eyes practically danced. "Oh, I *really* like you," he said with a laugh. "Where is Miss Calloway, anyway? I usually can't get her to leave my side when I visit."

"She is likely mourning the death of her fowl friend," Lucy replied.

A stifled laugh behind her made her jump, and she turned in alarm to find Lord Calloway standing in the doorway and looking at her with a curious expression. She wished he wouldn't hide his happiness like that; he was far more handsome without the practiced sobriety he usually carried in his countenance. She had learned that morning, after prying as much servant talk from Rebecca as she could, that Lord Calloway hadn't always been so serious. As a younger man, he had found a good deal of joy in life, and she had seen glimpses of that man when they'd gone out to the lovely little pond and when he'd bantered with Olivia about their race.

Why did he fight so hard to be something he wasn't?

"Forester," he said as he entered the room and began loading up a plate. "I hope you haven't frightened off our Lucy with your tall tales."

Our Lucy. She shivered at the thought, knowing she had little time left to enjoy being one of them, and she had only just arrived.

Nick tossed a bite of toast into his mouth, grinning as he watched Lord Calloway. "Tall tales? I don't know what you're talking about, Calloway."

"I am surprised you're even awake," Lord Calloway said next. He sounded perfectly serious, but Lucy was sure he was teasing his friend. It wasn't exactly easy to tell, though, and he was far too stiff for someone who clearly enjoyed humor as much as Nick did.

"He had a run-in with a horrid songbird this morning," Lucy said.

To her surprise, Lord Calloway chose the seat directly next to her, even though he probably should have sat at the head of the table. Or anywhere else, for that matter. Empty chairs were in ample supply. "Do not believe a word the man says," he told her, raising one eyebrow. "He is prone to uttering only lies, unlike us proper people."

Any appetite that might have grown over the last few minutes disappeared in an instant, and Lucy swallowed as she glanced at those in the room. Out of the three of them, she was the only true liar. Even Nick had probably told some bit of truth about the bird waking him up.

"How long are you planning to stay at Calloway Park, Mr. Forester?" Lucy asked, hoping to dispel the tension that had risen inside her.

Nick studied her before he answered. "That depends entirely on how many lady callers the family receives."

Lord Calloway grunted. "Still wife hunting?" He clearly didn't like the idea, if his scowl was any indication.

Nick didn't seem to mind his friend's gruff question, however, and he merely smiled, though it wasn't as broad as it had been earlier. "Always, my friend." He let out a dramatic sigh, and Lucy sensed a bit of genuine hidden misery in the gesture. "Though, it seems William already claimed the loveliest lady within a day's ride, or I might have staked my claim when I first laid eyes on the almost-Mrs. Calloway here."

Though she wasn't brave enough to look at Lord Calloway after what he'd said about lies, Lucy thought she felt him tense beside her. Goodness, their chairs were much closer than she had realized. Her arm was only a breath away from brushing against his.

"This coming from the eternal bachelor?" Lord Calloway said, ice in his words.

Nick wasn't the least bit cowed. In fact, he seemed to sit up a little taller. "I will hardly take criticism from an heirless baron of nine and twenty who spends as little time in Town as he can muster and hasn't the least interest in settling down."

"Then, perhaps you should stop letting young ladies believe you are in love with them before turning around and breaking off engagements."

Lucy was certain the tension in the room had grown thick enough that it was practically visible. Nick's expression hardened, but there was an underlying layer of pain beneath his anger. Were these two truly friends? Because it seemed there was a good deal of unrest between them.

Clearing her throat, she did her best not to flinch when both glares turned to her. "Why is it men are always determined to find fault with one another?" she asked. "It is a wonder the two of you became amiable in the first place."

Nick chuckled, but it was forced, and it made Lucy nervous because it reminded her of Jonathan Granger. Not because Nick was anything like Mr. Granger but because of the insincerity of it. It made her wonder whether or not his comment about choosing her if she'd been unattached was true; he had said it with such ease. If she had not been "engaged" to William, would Nick have taken an interest in her?

She liked what little she knew about the man, but she did not know whether she could trust Nick Forester. Perhaps she had been right to doubt and he wouldn't be an ally after all. She would have to return to her original plan of appealing to the Calloways once she knew they liked her enough to forgive her lies.

If they ever did forgive her.

"Ah, well, Lord Calloway here took pity on me when we were boys, though I am sure he has regretted it ever since," Nick said, though there wasn't the same energy in his words as he'd had before. Lord Calloway had truly hit a nerve with his comment about broken engagements. "You see, I was quite an unfortunate boy, raised by gypsies, with no knowledge of my true parentage until I was nearly grown."

Lord Calloway groaned a little, and Lucy chanced a glance in his direction to find him pinching the bridge of his nose. His antagonism had disappeared, replaced by light frustration. "You were raised in Derbyshire," he said with a strained voice. "Your mother and father brought you up in a loving, happy home, and you should consider yourself lucky."

Nick's expression softened, graced with his warmest smile yet. Lucy hadn't realized a man could have so many different smiles. "True," he admitted with a little shrug that seemed more out of relief than nonchalance. It seemed he was glad for the change in tension, just like Lucy was. "You and I shared that fortune, Calloway. And what of you, Lucy? Should your almost-brother-in-law be counting you among us lucky ones?"

Try as she might, Lucy couldn't hold back the tears that built up in her eyes, though she had no desire to have these people pity her. That would only make things worse when she told them the truth. "My mother died when I was very young," she said. "I had only my father, but we loved each other very much until he also passed, five years ago."

The table grew quiet, and Lucy refused to look up from her plate.

"Are you alone in the world, Lucy?" Lord Calloway asked quietly.

"Hardly," Nick replied. It sounded like he was trying to lighten the mood once more, but Lucy was pretty sure it wasn't working, even when he kept talking. "She has a fiancé with a weak constitution who spends half his life in a fever."

If only that were true. If only Lucy weren't entirely alone, perhaps the ache of losing her father wouldn't still hurt this much. She would have thought after five years she could bear the loss better, but it felt as if he had only just left her, and she felt more alone in this moment than she ever had.

But then a hand took hers underneath the table, and she turned in surprise to meet Lord Calloway's gaze. "You're practically a Calloway now," he said gently. He gave her a little smile that settled inside Lucy like a rock because she desperately wanted his words to be true. "You'll never have to be alone again."

Of all the lies spoken at the table this morning, that was the worst, and Lucy couldn't find the strength to remain there with these people whose kindness she didn't deserve. Unable to find any words to make her excuse, she pulled her hand free and fled from the room, wishing her lies could be left behind her.

Chapter Fourteen

Why was Lucy always running away from him?

"You're in for it now," Forester said with a laugh, though Simon hardly thought this was a laughing matter. If he had known about her parents . . . if he had known, he probably would still have said the wrong thing. For some reason, he always said the wrong thing around Lucy.

Without gracing Forester with a response, Simon hurried out after Lucy and caught her by the arm before she reached the stairs. He felt her stiffen beneath him, as she had done yesterday, and he let go immediately. She never seemed to mind when Mother or Olivia touched her, which meant she was either afraid of Simon or of men in general. He didn't like either implication.

Blast it all, if he could only convince her to trust him, he could know how to help her relax. He knew too well how it felt to carry the weight of the world on one's shoulders, and someone like Lucy should never know that burden.

"I've upset you," he said. *Again.* And he hated it. Why was he so awful at talking to this woman? He had never had this problem before, even with people he disliked.

Perhaps that was the problem. There was so much to like about Lucy that it made him nervous to speak to her, knowing she was everything he wished he could be, even with the tension she carried. She was confident, kind, attentive. She even had Forester teaming up with her, and Simon had been trying to make jokes with the man for years with no success.

"Lucy," he said a little more forcefully because she refused to even look in his direction. "How can I make it better?"

"I am well, my lord."

"You're clearly not. I'm sorry about your parents. If I had known, I wouldn't have let Forester—"

"You could not have known because I didn't tell you. How could I expect that of you?" She turned to him finally, tears glistening in her eyes and a sort of pleading expression that made his heart ache for her.

He had never been a very affectionate person, but he wanted so badly to take her in his arms and dry her tears. He was quite certain that level of intimacy was hardly proper. Lucy may have been almost family, but she was William's to comfort. Not his.

Tucking his arms behind his back before he did anything to cross a line, Simon fought for something to say that might help. "William will wake soon," he mumbled.

Lucy's head fell to her chest, and she muttered something he barely heard. He must have heard wrong, because it sounded like she said, "I pray he doesn't."

Simon was saved from wondering what that might mean by a knock on the front door that made them both jump, and then Lucy ran up the stairs and disappeared.

Groaning, he rubbed his temples with his thumb and middle finger and tried to distract himself with thoughts of all the work he needed to be doing instead of standing in a corridor. He had a shipping manifest to look over and a colt to sell and half a dozen tenant farmers who deserved to see more of him than a few minutes every month or so. But there were too many questions running through his mind for him to concentrate.

Had Forester really seen William only a couple of weeks ago? What did Lucy think of her future husband's flirtatious nature? William had never been a cad, as far as Simon knew, but he had broken a good number of hearts over the years by being overly friendly. At least, that was what many of the rumors said. He was certainly Simon's opposite in that regard, as in many others.

Simon had never been close enough to a woman to break her heart.

Whoever was at the door knocked again. Where was Porter? Had all the footmen taken a holiday? Sighing, Simon decided to open the door himself rather than hunt down the butler to do the simple task.

He found himself face-to-face with an unfamiliar gentleman, though he only guessed at the gentleman part. The man wore more than fashionable attire, his collar points touching his cheeks, and he wore a confident gaze to go with it. But there was something about him that immediately put Simon on edge. He could hardly judge a man's character based on the way he dressed, so there had to be something about his expression that made Simon dislike him from the start.

"Yes?" He was grateful Mother was not there to witness his utter lack of politeness.

The man frowned a little, taking Simon in. He must have recognized he was not speaking to a servant, and he faltered over his words. Simon hoped the man had merely been caught off guard, because otherwise his first words would have been entirely uncouth.

"I'm looking for a governess."

Simon waited in vain for elaboration. "A governess?"

"Indeed."

"And you thought you would steal mine?"

The man perked up, peering behind Simon, as if he might see deep into the house. "Do you have one?"

What in the world? "No."

"Blast."

Unless he had forgotten some long-ago discussion with William or Forester, this was the strangest conversation Simon had ever had, and he and this unwelcome visitor had exchanged only a few words. The man was acting as if all of this was commonplace. As if he often went around knocking on doors and asking about staff availability.

Clearing his throat, the presumptuous dandy finally decided to explain, though it hardly helped Simon make sense of anything. "She left London a few days back, and no one has seen or heard from her since."

"So you are looking for a particular governess?" Why would he be looking in a place like this? Few people within twenty miles of Calloway Park even employed staff beyond housekeepers and men of all work.

The man nodded. "Miss Hayes. You haven't seen her, have you? Eyes dark as coal? Hair nearly black? A spirited temperament with a tendency to speak out of place?"

An uneasy tension settled between Simon's shoulders. It wasn't as if there weren't other women with similar coloring, but combined with the time line of when the missing Miss Hayes disappeared, he couldn't help but wonder. Lucy had said her surname was Staley. But she had hesitated, and that hadn't bothered Simon until now.

"How do you know this governess?" he asked, though his words stuck a little in his throat. He didn't want to imagine the worst—he didn't even know what the worst could be—but he was dangerously close to thinking rather uncharitable thoughts about his future sister-in-law. What if these two were part of a scheme, preying on helpless invalids and their families in order to gain . . . something?

Lucy had hardly eaten anything since coming to Calloway Park, and she certainly hadn't asked for anything besides. Cook had even approached him last night in concern for the quality of the food, thinking Lucy was entirely dissatisfied, and Simon had had to assure her everything was as delicious as ever. Lucy hadn't even tried to spread the word about her upcoming marriage—the opposite, in fact—so Simon forced himself to stop jumping to radical conclusions. If she was there to gain something, she was doing a very poor job of it.

The man at the door took a look around the house, his eyes growing wider with every passing moment. It was as if he were only now realizing where he was. But then he puffed out his chest, looking for all the world like a man who thought he was better than everyone around him.

"Miss Hayes and I were practically engaged before she disappeared."

Did she *know that?* Simon forced himself to keep his mouth shut before any sort of insult came out. He was never one to be anything but kind, but this as yet unnamed man seemed to bring out the worst in him.

"Engaged, you say?" he said instead.

The man nodded vigorously. "Indeed. I am high enough in status and especially wealthy, so I cannot imagine why she is so afraid of the tender feelings she harbors toward me. If she had but remained in London . . ."

Another mark against Lucy was the fact that this missing governess had come from London, just like she had. But people left Town every day, so he could hardly fault her for coincidence. He reminded himself again to stop making conjectures and focus on the task at hand.

Namely, ridding himself of this tedious fop and getting back to work.

"Calloway!" Forester's clear voice echoed through the entry hall, preceding him by only a moment. He came to rest at Simon's side, looking out to the doorstep, where the strange man still stood, seeing as Simon hadn't bothered to let him in. "Who's this well-dressed specimen?"

While the stranger stood a little taller, Simon forced back a laugh. Forester spent enough time in Society to recognize a dandy when he saw one, and Simon knew for a fact that Forester cared little for them. There was more to a man than the clothes on his back, and Forester had been known to subtly knock vain men down a peg or two without them realizing he had done it. That tongue of his was used for more than spinning falsehoods.

"Mr. Jonathan Granger, at your service," the man said, offering a bow. Then he frowned. "Did you—did you say Calloway?" His eyes flitted about the entryway again, this time with a different gleam in his gaze. Envy. Desire. *Greed.* "I had no idea—you're Calloway?"

Simon had just about reached his limit, even with Forester here. "There's usually a *Lord* before that, but yes."

Forester coughed, though it sounded suspiciously like a laugh. He knew too well how little Simon cared for titles and prestige. If Simon could have gone his whole life without using his birthright to intimidate someone or get his way, he would have died happy. But England put a good deal of stock in the power of nobility, and his name had saved a business on more than one occasion when Simon had first taken over after the death of his father.

"This man has lost his governess," Simon said to his friend.

Granger's eyes went wide, a bit of color popping up in his face. "Not my . . . that is to say . . ."

"I understand," Forester said with mock solemnity. "I too would be lost without my governess. How would I know how to be a proper member of Society if I did not have her there to show me the way? How unfortunate for you, Mr. Granger, to lose such a valuable asset to your life. Might we be of assistance?"

He must have pushed the jest just a little too far, because Granger shifted his stance, growing more angry than embarrassed. "And you are?"

If he were being proper, Simon would have made the introductions, but he simply stood there at the door and let Forester take the lead, knowing it would be far more entertaining if he did. Anyone who dressed as carefully as Granger would be well enough acquainted with London Society to know exactly who stood before him.

Forester offered a little bow. "Mr. Nick Forester," he said as pompously as he could. "I imagine you've heard of me."

Simon might have been offended that Granger's reaction this time around was far stronger than it had been when learning Simon's identity, if not for his increasing desire for anonymity and a quiet life in the country for the rest of his days. He didn't care what people thought of him, as long as they never thought him a detriment to his father's legacy.

Nicholas Forester, on the other hand . . .

Granger took a step back, turning pale. "F-Forester? The same Forester who captained a navy vessel at Trafalgar?"

"The very same." Forester smirked. That battle had happened a decade ago, and he had never once set foot on a ship, let alone captained one at twenty. No one else seemed to know that though.

"Who owns half of Wales?" Granger continued.

"You've got it."

"Who is closely connected with the royal family?"

"Ah, I do love my evening chats with Prinny. Most entertaining."

Granger nearly choked on his next exclamation, his eyes nearly popping out of his head. "You single-handedly saved an entire village from a terrible fire last month!"

"Did I? I mean, yes, I did." Forester met Simon's questioning glance and shrugged minutely. Apparently that rumor was a new one. "Now that we have that settled," he said, resting his arm on the doorframe and looming over Granger, "I seem to recall you were searching for a governess."

Still in awe, Granger took a moment to answer. He had apparently forgotten all about Simon and focused entirely on Forester. "I should like to find her and ensure she is safe. The family she was to work for is most anxious."

"As are you, as you have said," Simon muttered.

"Truly. So you have not come across a governess wandering around?"

Simon clenched his hands into fists. "Not recently."

"She is not here?"

"That is what Lord Calloway said," Forester threw in. He had lost his humor and was now eyeing Granger with something closer to suspicion. Forester, for all his stories, was always inclined to trust those he came into contact with, so if he was beginning to question Granger's motives, it had to mean Simon wasn't acting out of jealousy.

There was that thought of jealousy again. But for what? Even if Granger was talking about Lucy, Simon had no reason to be jealous of anything.

"She was supposed to arrive at the home of a family friend on Tuesday last," the man said without even a glance in Simon's direction. "But she never turned up. She was under the employ of my brother until recently, and I confess I miss having her around. She is a lively little thing, and my life was better for it."

Forester grimaced, clearly feeling the same about Granger as Simon did. "Does the lady return your regard?"

"Undoubtedly. If I had but made the depth of my feelings known sooner, she would not have felt the need to seek new employment."

"Did she know of your affection, then?" Forester asked. A valid question.

Granger nodded, though he seemed a little more unsure of this response. "She knew of it, but not its extent. Blast it all, if I had just . . . I am desperate to find her. Miss Hayes is everything a man could want in a wife." There was a sort of hunger in his eyes that made Simon uneasy, and he knew how often men felt entitled to do as they pleased with women. Was the fop in front of him among the breed of so-called gentlemen who saw women as possessions rather than as equals?

Assuming, by some chance, that Mr. Granger was speaking of Lucy—at this point, Simon had no idea what to believe—the poor girl had been through enough over the last few days and didn't need to deal with the pressure of facing an old beau now that she was engaged and nearly settled.

Was she engaged though?

Simon shuddered. It was time to send the impeccably dressed Mr. Granger on his way before Simon thought too deeply about William's fiancée or her potential lies. "If I do happen to come across someone who fits your provided description, how might I alert you?" Assuming he chose to do anything of the sort. Most likely, Miss Hayes had disappeared on purpose, whoever she was.

Mr. Granger bowed. "I will be staying at the inn in town, as I am sure she couldn't have gone far. I am trying to track her down in every way I know how, and she traveled this direction. Your assistance would be most appreciated, and I am sure if she knew my intention to wed her despite her low circumstances, she would come out of hiding rather quickly. Miss Hayes is an intelligent woman, and she would not waste an opportunity such as this. My lord, Mr. Forester, thank you for your time."

Simon met the man's final bow with a nod, then closed the door, not caring about social niceties anymore. He needed to think.

"What the devil?" Forester said with a little laugh.

Simon figured he had best get right to the point—he did not need some long, elaborate story out of Forester—but before he could speak, movement down the entry hall caught his eye.

The maid who stood there paled and bowed low. Was that Lucy's maid? "Beg pardon, my lord," she squeaked, turning on her heel and disappearing.

Simon didn't have the energy to wonder about that strange reaction. "Do you believe Lucy?" he asked Forester.

"Do I believe her about what?"

"Everything. William, the engagement, how she came to be here."

Furrowing his brow, Forester glanced toward the stairs, as if he knew exactly where Lucy had gone. "I only met her this morning, I'll remind you. I hardly know anything about the woman."

"As do I. But she has been here long enough that I should know more about her, shouldn't I?"

Forester snorted a small laugh but held the bulk of it back, something Simon appreciated. "You, my friend, are not an easy person to get to know, and you still surprise me after all these years. If you think you can learn everything about someone like Lucy in two days, you are in need of education. Why so much suspicion of your future sister-in-law? You think she is the woman the charming Mr. Granger is hunting? I thought you said her name was Staley."

"*She* said her name was Staley. What if that was a lie?"

"Why would she lie?"

"You tell me."

After all, Forester hardly ever spoke the truth anymore.

Thinking that over for a moment, Forester looked around the grand entryway and shrugged. "You've never known how it is to live without money, and I thank Providence I am not in such dire straits to yet consider myself poor." He grimaced a little, making Simon wonder if Forester was closer to poverty than he'd thought. "I am not saying Lucy is lying about anything, but if she were . . . perhaps she merely wants somewhere to belong. In fact, that could be the very reason she agreed to William's proposal."

"So you think the engagement is real?"

Forester let out a heavy sigh. "I am more prone to lies than anyone you know, Calloway, so I am not the person you should be asking that. Why can't you ask her?"

Because that would be disastrous if he were wrong. She would take offense to the question, and rightly so, and that would ruin any hope he had of becoming her friend. Ignoring Forester's question, Simon started to pace, working through his thoughts out loud. "You said yourself you saw William only two weeks ago. And he was not engaged then?"

Taking a seat at the base of the stairs, Forester stretched out one long leg and leaned back on his elbow, seeming to settle in for a long conversation. "Believe it or not, I do not make it my regular business to inquire about your brother's marital status. I have my own to worry about, you know."

Sighing, Simon pinched the bridge of his nose and wished he could go back to bed for the rest of the day. Technically, he needed to worry about his own status if he ever wanted an heir, but he hardly had time to breathe, let alone court someone. "I'm so tired, Nick."

"You never call me Nick." Forester looked utterly disarmed by the use of his name, and he seemed to watch Simon as if waiting for him to fall apart.

Maybe he would if he stood still for too long. Maybe he would crumble into a thousand pieces if he didn't find something to hold himself together. "My world is entirely upside down now," he muttered. "Calling you by your preferred name is hardly the most shocking thing that has happened of late."

Forester chuckled, though still a little unnerved, if his expression was to be believed. "Perhaps. Are you going to spend the day working?"

"When do I not?"

"Ah, see, that is exactly the point I was going to make. If you live your life subject to your father's legacy, you're going to spend it all in exhaustion. I hardly think he meant that to be your life, Simon."

That was where Forester was wrong. Father had spent hours with Simon over the years, showing him ledgers and introducing him to contacts and teaching him the finer points of owning an estate and being a decent man. Simon had been taught since birth to fill his role as a peer of the realm and someone others could rely on. Father had lived the perfect example and never once showed a moment of weakness, even when he'd fallen ill.

If Simon couldn't even keep up, what did that say about him?

"I am sure I can devise some way of getting you to relax this afternoon," Forester said with a smirk.

Simon resisted the urge to sigh. "I doubt that."

"We'll see."

"I'll be in the study," Simon muttered and walked away, knowing Forester would want to continue this conversation. But he couldn't do it this morning. This morning, he had to decide what to do about Lucy.

Chapter Fifteen

It had taken a good deal of persuasion to convince Lady Calloway, who had not gone to her room as suggested, to leave William's side and get some decent rest, but Lucy finally had the room to herself. Well, to her and the maid who kept a dutiful watch over her ailing charge. Lucy didn't particularly want to be in William's room, but it was better than her own, where Rebecca had a tendency to find her and repeat the need to keep their secret.

Their lie.

After her morning with the lighthearted Mr. Forester, who seemed to have a propensity for lying, Lucy had decided she would do better to clear the air and admit to everything before she became just like him. Particularly because Lady Calloway would have Nick to lighten her load, Lucy hoped she would come out of her admission with no more guilt than she already felt.

More than anything, she wanted to come clean to Simon, who deserved a far simpler life than the one he had been thrown into. He didn't need his brother's false fiancée creating complications with his family.

She would figure out what to do about Mr. Granger on her own, and she had high hopes that he had moved on by this point. He would have been only a few hours behind them at most, and he had likely already arrived at the Winthrops', found her missing, and returned home. That was her hope, as was the notion that the Winthrops might still accept her employment after her delayed arrival. She had been too afraid to write to them in case they passed on her current location to Mr. Granger.

"Lucy!"

Lucy jumped as Olivia came barging into the room as if she had entirely forgotten her ailing brother. "We're going shopping!" She practically wriggled with excitement as she took hold of Lucy's hands.

Lucy couldn't think of anything she wanted to do less. "We are?" As much as she loved Olivia's company, her secrets were piling up so quickly she worried she might burst with them. "You should go without me," she said, hoping she didn't sound rude. It would give her a chance to really think through how she would admit the truth, something she should have done the minute Rebecca had started the deceit. "I don't need any—"

"You are wearing my dress, Lucy." Olivia pierced her with a look of mock disdain. "You need your own clothing, dearest, and you deserve something amusing to take your mind off poor William here."

William hadn't stirred in the slightest, the only indication that he was alive being the slow rise and fall of his chest.

Lucy shook her head. If only Olivia knew how impossible this idea was. "I couldn't possibly afford—"

"Don't you know William is wealthy?" Mr. Forester—Nick—came into the room next, warming the room with his easy smile. "Surely that would have been the first thing he told you to recommend himself. William Calloway has never been the modest sort. Not like his dull older brother."

Lucy had never thought of Simon as dull. He was quiet at times and had a good deal on his mind, she imagined, but there was a quick wit behind those hazel eyes of his, and a goodness of heart she admired about him.

"Come, Lucy," Nick said, taking her hand. "A day out, away from your beloved's sick bed, will do you good; I am sure of it. Besides, Miss Calloway and I could hardly go on our own, could we?"

Lucy could tell Olivia wouldn't mind in the slightest, but Nick seemed to be of a good sort, like Simon, and would not implicate the girl in any way regardless of his connection with the family.

When had she started thinking of Lord Calloway as Simon? It must have happened that morning, when he tried to apologize for bringing her to tears. She had longed to fall into his arms and feel like he would keep her safe from the sadness of her past, but she knew that would never happen. Not when he thought she was to marry his brother. And once he learned the truth? He would hate her, and she would never get to see that concerned look in his eyes that made her feel like she mattered to someone.

But at least he would be free of her.

She was in an impossible situation, and she knew it. She couldn't very well let Nick and Olivia go off alone, though surely there was a maid or footman who could accompany them for propriety's sake—Olivia would be hurt if Lucy suggested that route—but neither could she spend any of William's money, no matter how rich he was purported to be. She had no right to anything of his, and that included his family.

She would have to stand her ground and remain behind, lest something go wrong. "Perhaps I should wait until William—"

Her words stopped immediately upon Simon entering the room, and at first she wasn't sure why she couldn't look away from him. There was something . . . different . . . about him. She couldn't quite place it, but it was like he had a sort of determination in his eyes that she hadn't seen before. She had seen confidence and humor, weariness and uncertainty, but this was a new look for Lord Calloway, and she found she liked it very much. It made him look powerful. Like the sort of man who would never feel belittled by someone who had their own aspirations and dreams because another's success could never devalue his own. Where had this come from?

It hardly mattered, because he looked at Lucy in a way no one had ever looked at her before, like he could see right through her. A large part of her wanted him to see the truth as they stood there gazing at each other. Then everything would be out in the open, and she wouldn't have to hide anymore. But another part hoped he would see only the good parts of her. The parts that hadn't lied to him. She wanted him to see her as someone worth knowing.

She had never thought much about marriage since the death of her father, and at twenty-two, she was well on her way to becoming a spinster. Besides, no respectable man wanted to marry a penniless governess, and when the truth came to light about her sham engagement to William, she would likely be ruined anyway and never have a single prospect for the rest of her life. Despite girlish fantasies in her youth, she had come to accept that she would forever be alone, so she had rarely looked at a man and wondered whether she found him attractive. There was little point in getting distracted.

But Simon? Simon was assuredly attractive, and he had so much to recommend himself. His dark hair and strong jaw had given him that commanding appearance of a baron she'd seen in him a few times, but his eyes were always so soft, with laugh lines at the edges that spoke of easier days, before his father had died. He noticed when she was upset, even when she tried to hide it, and he tried to make things right when he made a misstep . . . or thought he did. And with this new determination in Simon's eyes, Lucy had to wonder whether she could ever find a man to rival him.

She doubted it.

It didn't matter that she had known him for only a couple of days and knew very little about him. It didn't matter that she would have loved to spend her whole life learning what made him happy. Lord Simon Calloway was so far beyond her reach that she refused to acknowledge the pounding of her heart as he stepped closer.

"What better way to get to know you, Lucy, than a romp in the village?" he said, and the way he said it left little room for argument, as if he knew Lucy would keep protesting. "It has been a stressful few days, and surely you would like to have a distraction from the weight you are carrying. We all deserve some time away, don't you think?"

It was almost a challenge, and Lucy could feel her defenses rising. Did he suspect her? Though she felt she had done a decent job avoiding the truth despite her aversion to doing so, she hardly expected someone as intelligent as Lord Calloway to remain in the dark indefinitely. But something about his words felt like the perfect opportunity to turn the tables on him. "Do you include yourself in that, Lord Nothing-at-All? I seem to recall you saying you had no time for anything."

He almost smiled, but he seemed to be fighting it for some reason. Lucy wished he wouldn't. She wanted to see that smile of his as often as possible before she no longer had the chance. "That is not what I said."

"But is she wrong?" Nick threw in, reminding Lucy that the two of them were not the only ones in the room.

Olivia felt the need to do the same, looping her arm through Lucy's. "Are we going shopping or not?" she demanded. "Mr. Forester promised to buy me a new pair of gloves."

"I most certainly did not," Nick replied calmly. "But an excellent try, Miss Calloway. I admire your conviction."

"Please do not encourage her," Simon replied. His unbreakable stance had softened, leaving him looking weary again. Lucy didn't like it. "And whether or not we go will be determined by William's beloved. I believe she needs the distraction more than anyone, and we cannot abandon her to only Mother for company, seeing as she is finally napping, and hopefully for a good deal of time."

All three pairs of eyes turned to Lucy, and her face started to burn. She was hardly skilled at deflecting so many people at once. How was she supposed to say no when Olivia looked so eager for her to say yes and Nick was such an easygoing fellow and Simon gazed at her like he wanted to know everything about her even though that was entirely impossible?

He had no reason to care about her beyond believing her to be William's future wife. If he was not close to his brother, he would hardly want to be close to her.

Lucy sighed, knowing she was outnumbered. Perhaps, away from the house and Lady Calloway, she would finally work up the courage to tell the truth. "I haven't any money on me," she admitted. At least that part wasn't a lie.

"Simon can pay for it," Olivia said without hesitation, and she latched on to Nick's arm as well, marching them both out of the room with Simon right behind them. "We are wasting precious time!"

As they walked together to Lucy's chamber so Lucy could change into something better suited for the trip to town, Olivia talked nonstop about how excited she was for her upcoming Season. Lucy had little to offer the conversation, not having had her own debut, so she kept her mouth shut and let Olivia do the talking.

It was for that reason she was able to notice the absolute terror in Rebecca's eyes when the maid arrived to help her dress.

"Rebecca?" she whispered while Olivia kept chatting.

"It's Mr. Granger. He's here."

* * *

In the carriage, Lucy found herself seated right next to Simon since Olivia had engaged Nick in conversation and seemed unlikely to stop talking anytime soon. And though Lucy had no inclination to talk, with those two filling the silence with their animated voices, she didn't much care for the awkward silence between her and the man at her side either.

It didn't help that she kept falling into him.

Unlike the public coach, the Calloway conveyance was well sprung and in good condition, and yet each little bump sent Lucy nearly toppling over. She might have found her inability to stay in her own seat quite amusing if Simon didn't seem to be growing increasingly irritated each time their shoulders collided. She had never seen a man clench his jaw quite so tightly, and she feared the muscle near his ear might snap from the force.

"I am sorry," she whispered after the sixth or seventh time she bumped into him. "I am not usually so . . ."

"Bouncy?" he suggested, the word coming out in a growl.

"Yes."

"Hmm."

Perhaps if she planted her foot against the side . . . Lucy tried it, concentrating on staying in one place as she looked out the window. This countryside was truly beautiful, and it reminded her so much of home. How much time did she have left to enjoy it? A day? Less?

Since they were going into town, chances were high she would run into Mr. Granger, and all of this guilt she carried would have been for nothing. She hardly thought she had made herself well-enough liked by the Calloways for them to step in and help her should anything happen, and the thought of Simon stepping aside to make way for Mr. Granger made her stomach twist into knots. She liked to think he was too good a man to let anything bad happen to her, but if he discovered the truth first? There was no telling what might happen.

She simply had to hope she avoided Mr. Granger entirely.

"Where did you spend your childhood, Lucy?"

Lucy turned, unsure whether she had imagined Simon's question, because he was most assuredly staring out his own window. "Sir?"

"It was a simple question," he said without a glance in her direction.

If he was trying to make conversation to pass the time, he was doing a very poor job of it. If Olivia and Nick weren't deep in an argument about some particular dance, Lucy might have tried to bring them into the conversation as well, just to serve as a buffer between her and Simon's sudden moodiness.

"Surrey," she said. "How long has your family lived here in Oxfordshire? It is strange, is it not, that your title does not carry its own unique name with it?"

Simon shrugged. "My family has been on this estate since its inception, when the King named the area a park and entrusted the first Calloway to care for it. Though, the royal family quickly forgot about us, hence the Calloway title remaining such a low rank." He turned this time, leaning in so quickly that it caught her by surprise. "You have said you do not enjoy London, but you must have been presented and had a Season for you to know you dislike it." He spoke quietly now, likely so they would not be overheard, but it made the conversation suddenly feel too intimate.

Lucy shivered as she tried to think of an answer that wouldn't make Simon suspicious. She had done well to keep little known about herself, but he was asking questions that dug beneath the surface level. She had to be careful. Why couldn't they keep discussing the history of his family? That was far more interesting than her own past.

"My father died before I turned seventeen," she said. "Though, I can't imagine he would have parted with me easily. I went to London to find work when I had nothing else." That and she was hardly of the upper class. She had barely been able to consider herself the daughter of a gentleman, and people like her did not meet the Queen and rub shoulders with nobility.

Usually, Lucy thought as another bump in the road knocked her into Simon's arm.

He put a hand on her arm near her elbow, though he didn't seem to realize he had done it. He was deep in thought, as if her answer hadn't been something he'd expected. "He was a good father, then?" he asked.

Lucy fought back the tears that always seemed to appear when she thought too hard about her father. "The best. What of yours? I have heard only good things about the late Lord Calloway." In truth, she had heard very little about the man, but his children proved his good nature simply by behaving the way they did. They had to have learned it from somewhere.

Simon's gaze softened, his irritation making way for a sadness that made Lucy's heart ache for him. "He was an incredible man," he said quietly, and his eyes slid over to where his hand rested on her arm. His touch seemed to confuse him more than anything, and his eyebrows pulled low. "His illness was a burden on all of us, and I will forever be struggling to fill his shoes and live up to his name."

"Don't sell yourself short, Calloway," Nick said.

Both Lucy and Simon jumped and moved apart. They had done it again, shifting closer without either of them realizing it.

Nick seemed to find their position amusing, but Olivia was looking between them with concern, as if she saw more than she was supposed to. But there was nothing to see. They were simply having a conversation that didn't need to be shared between the four of them, and Lucy slid as far to her side of the bench as she could to prove that Olivia had no reason to fear.

"You know Father was proud of you, Simon," Olivia said, still frowning. "He said so all the time."

Simon shrugged. "Before I took on the mantle of baron, perhaps he was."

"You're an excellent baron," Nick said with a scoff. "The number of people who talk about you in London would astound you, my friend. And I mean that in a good way. You're one of the few who actually takes his seat in Lords seriously, from what I hear."

Simon seemed to squirm beneath that praise, and Lucy couldn't understand why he wouldn't believe his friend. From what she had seen of him, which was admittedly very little, Lord Simon Calloway was an impressive man for a multitude of reasons. A man she would have liked to know better under different circumstances.

Although, without the current circumstances, she likely never would have met Simon, and a shudder ran through her at the thought. He unnerved her and seemed on the verge of discovering her lies, and yet she wanted him to know her. Every part of her. It was a dangerous game to play, and she knew she could not win. If she continued to get to know the man as she would like to, she would eventually spill her secrets and ruin any friendship that might build between them.

Perhaps he would help her once he knew the truth about Mr. Granger, but she could not imagine him keeping her in his good graces beyond his protection. That almost seemed worse than anything Mr. Granger might do, which made no sense at all.

"Perhaps you're right," Simon eventually said to Forester, but his agreement had hardly lifted his mood. "It's everything else I worry about."

"Everything else?" Lucy asked before she realized it was not her place to ask such a question.

Nick chuckled. "Calloway is a man of many talents and assets," he said with a grin. "He owns every business in England."

Simon grunted. "Your lies do not become you, Forester. I don't know why you insist on spewing nonsense."

"And I've never understood how you became such a grump," Nick shot back. "You were always so happy in school."

"Life changes a man. You should know that."

"Only if you let it."

Both men fell silent, and Lucy wanted to slap Simon across the face and knock some sense into him. She might have done it, if striking a peer weren't a punishable crime. But she had to find some way to break him out of this self-deprecating nonsense before he went his whole life thinking he wasn't worth anything.

Olivia had told her a little about the businesses the last Lord Calloway had acquired over the years, but Lucy hadn't realized until this moment how much that inheritance weighed on Simon. No wonder he found it so difficult to smile. But what could she do? She knew nothing about the responsibilities of a lord, and she had given him absolutely no reason to trust her yet.

Besides, the carriage came to a stop, which meant they had reached the village and Lucy was out of time. Her panic returned tenfold, though she did her best to hide it.

"We will be at the modiste," Olivia said as soon as Nick had helped her out of the carriage, and she slipped her arm through Lucy's, almost as if she knew Lucy was considering how easily she could run. That didn't stop Lucy from planting her feet, however, hoping to delay as long as possible. "You men are not allowed to come with us," Olivia added.

To Lucy's surprise, Simon immediately argued against that pronouncement. "You expect me to leave you on your own?" he said with some alarm. "Don't be absurd." And for some reason, he looked right at Lucy.

Her cheeks burned hot, and she ducked her head before anyone noticed her blush. She had no reason to blush because the likes of Lord Calloway looked in her direction. She was being ridiculous, and she needed to stay focused.

"I hardly think you want to spend your day in a dressmaker's shop, Calloway," Nick said with laughter in his voice. "Come, I have a mind to convince you to purchase me a new watch fob."

Simon seemed as reluctant to leave this spot as Lucy was, even though Nick had put a hand on his arm. He just stood there, his eyes locked on her, yet another new expression on his face that kept her transfixed. He was searching for something, and though Lucy had no idea what he was trying to find in her eyes, she was tempted to let him have it. The man had so much in his life, but she had a feeling he had nothing of what he truly needed.

She hardly had anything to give him, but she wished she did. She wished she could help him see what she had seen that first time they'd met in the library: a man of power, conviction, and strength. The kind of man who looked after his family and would stop at nothing to see them taken care of.

The kind of man who would lead to Lucy's ruin if he chose. It had never been a matter of *if* she would fall to the truth but *when*.

"Come along, Lucy," Olivia said, giving her a little tug that pulled Lucy's eyes away from the one man she had no business staring at. "We'll have you a new wardrobe in no time. Mrs. Bradley is a wonder with fabric and thread, and I can just picture you in a divine emerald-green gown. All the men will be in love with you and make William jealous, no doubt, and . . ."

Lucy stopped listening, letting her thoughts still. She would have to put all her effort into not blurting out her secret halfway through being measured and fitted. With Granger in town, if she told the truth now and ended up being left behind in Downingham, her chances of being found were so much greater than they were at Calloway Park. She wanted the family to know she had knowingly spent the last few days lying to them in the hopes of using their influence—anything less would feel just as dishonest as the lie in the first place—but her fear kept her silent.

At least Olivia was close enough in size that she would be able to wear the dresses that would be made for Lucy after she was gone. That was the only reason Lucy allowed the dressmaker to do her work.

Olivia spent the entire time at the modiste talking, telling Lucy about when she and her brothers were young and how she couldn't wait for the next Season, when she would finally be presented to the Queen, and how she had never realized how much she would enjoy having a sister until she met

Lucy. Lucy did her best to remain calm, but the longer the day went on, the harder it became to keep her emotions in check.

Olivia was exactly how she would have hoped a sister would be. She was kind and enthusiastic with her praise, and she often put her hand on Lucy's or hugged her from the side or played with her hair and talked her through different styles she should try. Maybe if Mama had lived longer, Lucy would have had a little sister like Olivia, and it felt like her heart cracked a little more with each touch and compliment.

How could she give this up? How could she continue on when she deserved none of it?

Chapter Sixteen

Eventually, after enough time that Lucy couldn't be sure how long they had even been with the dressmaker, Olivia proclaimed that she was absolutely famished and wanted nothing more than to meet the men for tea at the local inn and tea shop. She took Lucy by the hand, told the modiste to send the bill for the dresses to Calloway Park, then pulled her out into the sunlit street.

"Strangely sunny lately, isn't it?" Olivia said as she pulled a mute Lucy through town.

Lucy would have felt far better if the sky had been pouring rain, seeing as that was how she felt inside. Besides, she was too busy searching the street for a familiar face. She hadn't expected Mr. Granger to discover her in a dress shop, but if Rebecca was right about him being in town, he could be anywhere.

Olivia and Nick must have agreed on a time to meet while they were talking; he and Simon arrived at the tearoom nearly the same time as the ladies did. Lucy prepared herself, knowing her time as William's fiancée was quickly coming to an end. With Mr. Granger so close, she wasn't sure if she would have a choice in when the truth came out.

"Have you managed to squander your brother's fortune yet?" Nick asked as they settled at a table.

Olivia giggled. "Hardly. Besides, I haven't ordered any gowns for the Season next year, and those will certainly cost a pretty penny. I can't very well show up in London in anything but the latest fashions, can I?"

"Certainly not. Just this year I witnessed a new debutante get thrown out of a dinner party because her dress was in vogue two years ago."

Olivia gasped.

"You'd best start practicing your flirting now, Miss Calloway, or you'll find yourself without any proper suitors, whether your gowns are in fashion or not."

Lucy thought she might explode from her secret building up inside her, so she tried to distract herself with the conversation at hand, pretending all of this was real. If she were a part of this family, she could go to London for the Season and watch Olivia flirt with all the eligible gentlemen. She could experience the balls and musicales and the theater instead of remaining at home with children who were not even her own. She could wear pretty gowns and have fancy hair and dance the night away until her feet ached, and then she could go back home with a man who loved her, whom she could call her own and keep forever.

Why was Simon looking at her that way?

He hadn't even touched his tea, and despite the fact that Nick was giving Olivia detailed advice on how to catch a husband, Simon's hazel eyes were fixed on Lucy with that searching look again, only now there was a hint of something else in there as well. Something familiar, as if he were mirroring her, aching for something he could never have.

Lucy swallowed and lifted her teacup to her lips, except her hands were shaking so badly that she quickly set the cup back down on the table before anyone noticed.

But Simon noticed. The vulnerability that had been in his expression a moment before vanished, and his gaze flicked down to her fingers before she hid her hands beneath the table. "I must have missed when you told Mother and Olivia this," he said, and his voice came out somewhat cold. "How long have you known William?"

A chill ran through Lucy as the other two grew quiet, and she shifted in her seat to hide her shudder. So he *did* suspect her? But why? What had she done wrong? "It feels like I only just met him," she said softly. If she spoke too loudly, he would hear the tremor in her voice and only grow even more suspicious.

Olivia let out a sigh. "That sounds so romantic. What made you fall for him?"

She hadn't fallen for him, and there was no way to answer that question without another lie. Her heart racing, Lucy was too tired to pretend she could keep deceiving these people. But when she tried to admit to her lies, the words stuck in her throat as she looked up and caught the familiar profile of Mr. Granger speaking to the proprietor of the tearoom. Even without seeing his full face, she knew it was him, and suddenly she couldn't breathe.

"Lucy?" Olivia asked.

Swallowing, Lucy did her best to remain calm. Perhaps Mr. Granger wouldn't notice her sitting among the Calloways. The wonderful, gentle, kind Calloways, who were the only people standing between her and her ruin.

"His kindness," she said, though she'd nearly forgotten Olivia's question.

Simon didn't like that answer, proven by his scowl. "Why did William not tell us he was getting married?" he growled.

"Because William never tells you anything." Nick laughed.

"But surely he would have said something about this."

Olivia scoffed. "William rarely tells you things, Simon, like Mr. Forester said."

Mr. Granger shook the proprietor's hand and turned, but his eyes were on the floor as he made his way toward the door. Lucy held her breath.

"Besides," Olivia continued, "isn't it all the more fun to have the surprise? Lucy is amazing, and he wanted us to know her before they wed." She tucked her arm through Lucy's in a sort of embrace from the side. "I can't wait to have you as my sister."

And something broke inside Lucy. Tears welled up in her eyes because she wanted this so badly. She wanted to be a sister to Olivia. To be a friend to Nick. To help look after Lady Calloway when her worry for her children overwhelmed her. She wanted to live at Calloway Park and for once have the chance to dictate her own day-to-day and be her own person rather than a fixture in someone else's household.

She didn't want to be alone and afraid anymore.

"Lucy, whatever is the matter?" Olivia pulled her closer, though Lucy refused to meet her gaze.

"I am not going to marry William," she said. There. The truth was out. Let them do with it what they would. They could find the best way to break the news to their mother, and Lucy would send for Rebecca and see if she could find a coach here in town without ever having to go back to the house she had come to love.

The table was silent, the only sounds those of the conversations happening around them. Lucy wished she were brave enough to look up at their expressions, but she kept her gaze on the table, waiting.

It was Olivia who spoke first, far louder than Lucy expected. "Oh tush, you mustn't think Simon means anything by his questions. Right, Simon?"

Whether or not Simon responded, Lucy didn't know. He certainly didn't speak, and she didn't have the courage to look up at him.

"See? William chose you out of any woman he could have had, and I refuse to let you question that decision," Olivia said.

Finally, Lucy forced herself to meet Olivia's eyes, if only to confirm what she'd just heard. "That isn't what I meant." But she couldn't bring herself to say more than that. She'd gotten lucky with Mr. Granger today, but she doubted that luck would last. Whether or not she wanted to lie to the Calloways, she needed them. She was never going to survive on her own.

"Are you referring to the fever?" Nick guessed, though his expression was more of confusion than Olivia's. He had his eyes on the door, where Mr. Granger had disappeared. "William always recovers. And if he doesn't, well . . ."

"Then, you are free," Simon muttered, and Lucy wasn't sure she was meant to hear it.

Olivia took hold of both of Lucy's hands with her eyebrows pulled low in determination. "*When* William wakes, which he will do soon, he will be as in love with you as ever, and you two will have the most wonderful wedding. I promise."

When William woke, he would destroy this little scheme of hers with a word. "What if he decides he would rather not marry me because I am utterly unworthy?" Lucy asked.

"Unworthy?" Olivia gasped. "How could you say such a thing?"

"Unless there is something you haven't told us," Simon said. His eyes seemed to search every inch of her, as if he knew exactly how unworthy she was of someone like William. "Unless you are not who you say you are."

"Calloway," Nick said, and it was as much of a warning as it was censure. They were starting to draw attention to their corner of the tearoom.

"Don't be ridiculous," Olivia threw in, and she seemed as shocked by Simon's behavior as Nick was apparently disgusted by it. "You are perfectly lovely, Lucy, and I am sure you are perfect for William."

Lucy would have embraced the girl if she weren't still terrified of the very real threat that had only just left the building. She could tell them that truth, but she still didn't know how they would respond. It would be safer if she pretended nothing was wrong, and then she could suggest they return to Calloway Park as soon as possible. Breaking the news there would at least give her some distance from Mr. Granger. "Thank you, Olivia," she breathed, "though I am not sure Lord Nothing-at-All would agree with you. He seems to disapprove of me." *For good reason.*

Simon clenched his jaw as well as his fists, and for a peer, he certainly had a lot of muscle. The fabric of his jacket strained against his shoulders as he held his ground against Lucy, unwilling to yield. "I never said I disapprove," he said, his voice low. "I simply do not understand why William would choose you. My brother is a lot of things, but he is no fool."

"Simon!" Olivia said at the same time Nick muttered, "Bad form."

Lucy felt the sting of his insult as if he had slapped her in the face. Had she really thought she might like this man? "Are you implying he was forced into something?" she asked.

"Of course he isn't," Nick said.

But Simon offered a little shrug, his eyes locked on Lucy's across the table. "I am not implying anything," he said carefully. "Merely trying to understand how he ended up with—"

Lucy shot to her feet, unwilling to listen to any more. She would not take his implications, whether he admitted them or not. "You think the only reason your brother could possibly want to marry someone like me is because he didn't have a choice," she surmised. "I am glad you think so highly of me, my lord, and I am infinitely more so knowing your brother is far slower to judge than you. Excuse me."

Knowing the whole room was looking at her now, Lucy ran for the door, desperate to get out into the open air where she could breathe again. The door opened right as she reached it, and she stumbled to a halt but still collided with the person entering. "I am so sorry," she whispered to the man and tried to skirt around him before she burst into tears for the whole room to see.

"Miss Hayes?"

Under other circumstances, Lucy might have welcomed a familiar voice. But not now. And not this voice. "Mr. Granger," she gasped, looking up into Jonathan Granger's surprised face as he stared at her open-mouthed. The unsettled feeling that had followed her for five years returned in full force, leaving her breathless as she looked up into the man's searching face. Why had he come back inside? "Please, if you will let me pass, I need—"

"You're unwell. Let me get you some—"

"I just want to be outside."

"Allow me." He took her by the arm and shuffled her through the door he had just entered, and she had no idea whether anyone had seen their little exchange or the way he practically dragged her with him.

"Miss Hayes, you are trembling." Mr. Granger tightened his hand around Lucy's elbow, and she flinched. He didn't even seem to notice the way she tried to pull away; he never did. "What happened to you?" he asked. "You never arrived in Lowbury, and my brother was worried, as was I."

If it had been up to him, she never would have arrived in Lowbury anyway. Lucy tried again to pull free, but his grip held strong. "Please," she said, "I should go back inside. My friends—"

"I wasn't aware you had friends in Oxfordshire."

If she were being honest, Lucy wasn't so sure she did. At the very least, she soon wouldn't, and she and Rebecca would have nothing and nowhere to go. But even that was preferable to spending a life with the man in front of her.

"Lucy!" Olivia appeared at the door, and she immediately pulled Lucy away from Mr. Granger to wrap her arms around her. "Oh, Lucy, I'm so sorry about Simon. I don't know what's gotten into him. He's not usually . . ." She must have only now noticed Mr. Granger standing there.

When Olivia loosened her arms, Lucy glanced back at Mr. Granger and was surprised to see nothing but gentle confusion in his expression. She had expected him to be angry with Olivia for interrupting his moment with Lucy.

Knowing she would need to introduce the pair until she could have a chance to explain the situation, Lucy took a slow breath and tried to sound unaffected. "Olivia, this is Mr. Jonathan Granger. A . . . friend . . . from London. Mr. Granger, this is Miss Olivia Calloway."

Mr. Granger bowed to match Olivia's curtsy, though his eyes remained drawn to Lucy. "And how do you know Miss Hayes?" he asked.

Lucy stiffened.

"Miss *Staley* is nearly a Calloway now," Olivia said and grabbed Lucy's hand. She seemed to think Mr. Granger was mistaken, though Lucy had no idea why she'd gained the girl's trust so easily. "Lucy recently became engaged to marry my brother, William."

Mr. Granger's face went so pale that he looked as if he might faint, ridiculous as that would be. "Calloway," he repeated, and it seemed he had a good deal of thoughts running through his head as he glanced between Lucy and Olivia. "Miss Calloway, might I have a moment to speak with Miss . . . with your brother's fiancée for a moment? Privately?"

Olivia bit her lip and looked at Lucy, who silently begged her to stay, but Olivia nodded and slipped back inside the inn, leaving them alone once more. It wouldn't last long, and Mr. Granger would not waste his opportunity created by Olivia's slip in leaving them alone.

Lucy braced herself for anger, but it didn't come.

"Engaged," Mr. Granger said thoughtfully, and he straightened the cuff of his jacket as he considered that. "I saw you not five days ago, *Lucy*."

It wasn't exactly an accusation, but he certainly wasn't happy about the news. She had expected him to turn on her; she wasn't entirely sure how to react to this measured, calm response to what he had just learned. Perhaps she didn't know the man as well as she'd thought.

"It was an accident," she whispered, tears filling up her eyes again.

He frowned a little at that, grabbing her arm again. "An accident that you became engaged?"

Lucy could see no way she could win, but she would try. "Yes," she whispered. "It all happened so fast." If nothing else, perhaps she could keep the man at bay long enough for someone a bit stronger than Olivia to come rescue her.

As if reading her thoughts, Mr. Granger glanced around them, then tugged her around the side of the building, bringing her down an alley away from the main street so they wouldn't be seen. "You are not engaged, Miss Hayes."

"I—"

"You can't be. You wouldn't be. Not when you and I have an understanding."

Was he absolutely mad? As he pressed her up against the wall, Lucy bit back tears. He *was* mad, and Rebecca had been right to be wary of the man. But what was she to do? She could scream for help, but she feared what he would do to her then. His grip was already tight enough on her wrist that she would likely bruise.

"I saw you, you know," he said. He spoke so calmly, as if he had no idea how frightened she was. "In the dress shop. I almost didn't recognize you because you looked so . . . happy, even with those tears of yours. I've never seen you that way." Then his eyes dropped to her arm he held between them. He released her slowly, taking a step back. "Forgive me, Miss Hayes. I merely . . . Do you have any idea what this nonsense will do to you?"

Lucy had no idea how to react to the sudden shift in the man, and she stood frozen, staring at him, because it was like he was another person. He sounded like he actually cared about what happened to her.

He took a careful breath. "I can't imagine how you convinced the man to go along with this, but . . . with you and I having a previous understanding, when the truth gets out about the engagement you have concocted with Calloway, and you know it will, you will be ruined. Did you not stop to think about that?"

Lucy had hardly thought about anything else, but she couldn't tell him that *he* was the reason she had carried on the ruse this long. "We have no understanding, Mr. Granger."

He scoffed. "Of course we do. Half of London knows about it."

What on earth had he been telling people? "What are you going to do?" she asked, her voice shaking.

He frowned. "What am *I* going to do? Miss Hayes, I have never been shy about my intentions. The question is what are *you* going to do?"

Then he leaned forward and kissed her.

Lucy had never been kissed. She had never really *thought* about being kissed. The life of a governess didn't exactly lead to dreams of romance, and she liked to think she was a practical sort. But she hadn't expected to feel so . . . unmoved. Servants at the Granger house had sometimes talked about being kissed when she was around, though they had never included her in their conversations. But the girls had spoken of fire and stars and being warm all over.

Mr. Granger's kiss felt . . . wet.

And it was over before she could push him away, leaving her stunned and frozen in place.

"I will give you three days to see to your affairs with that family," he said, running a hand through his hair as if the kiss had entirely unraveled him. "Make your peace with them and end your engagement before I am forced to end it for you. I would hate for Mr. Calloway to be on the wrong end of a pistol again so soon after the first time."

Lucy's heart stuttered. "What?"

"Lucy?" Nick appeared at the corner, heading right for them.

But Mr. Granger wasn't quite done. "And, Lucy?" He narrowed his eyes. "End it quietly. I love you, darling, but the last thing you or I need is you causing a scandal surrounding the Calloways. For their sake and yours, keep this between us."

And then he was gone, disappearing in the other direction and leaving Lucy reeling as she stood pressed up against the wall. She was so disoriented that she could hardly make sense of anything that had just happened, but she knew one thing: Mr. Granger had threatened the Calloway family, and she was the only thing standing between them and something horrible.

"Lucy, what's the matter?" Nick took her hand, though he stared in the direction Mr. Granger had gone. "Did he hurt you?"

Yes. She wanted to say yes. But she feared what Nick would do, and she feared even more what Mr. Granger would do if she complicated things further. Though Mr. Granger seemed to believe her engagement was real, he also seemed to know something about William that she didn't, and he wasn't afraid to do whatever it took to remove any obstacles in his way.

Rebecca had spoken truth when they'd first arrived: what Jonathan Granger wanted, he got.

So Lucy shook her head and forced her hands to stop shaking. "No," she said, her voice thin. "No, he thought I was someone else. We were only talking."

Nick watched her with an expression that clearly said he didn't believe her, but thankfully, he said nothing about it as he offered her his arm. "We're heading back now."

As she climbed into the carriage alongside Nick, Lucy did her best to pretend nothing had changed. Her plan was entirely the same, and she would continue to act as though she were a part of this family for as long as she could. Now that she had a deadline—now that the truth threatened more than just herself—she had no idea how she could do otherwise. Three days was all she had, and she would simply have to make the most of it.

Chapter Seventeen

Lucy was lying about her relationship with William—Simon knew that much, and while that was a massive piece of the puzzle that was Lucy Hayes, he had no idea where it was fit. That was supposed to be the easiest part, but there was a considerably large obstacle in placing Simon's new puzzle piece:

He didn't know exactly what the lie was.

He had thought perhaps William had forced her into the engagement or even the other way around, but the hurt in Lucy's eyes when he'd said as much had disproved that theory and given Simon a piercing pain somewhere in his gut when he saw it.

Then he considered the fact that William and Lucy's engagement was not a love match, as he had originally thought. But what would William gain from marrying a governess? Lucy's gain was obvious, but she couldn't possess anything William would want if not her heart. There was no convenience in the match.

But then she had kissed Mr. Granger! After a whispered argument with Forester, Simon had finally forced himself to go outside and apologize to Lucy for the things he had said, and he'd found her in the middle of an embrace with the dandified imbecile.

Kissed Mr. Granger was putting it wrong, he reminded himself. *He* had kissed *her*. And like a fool, Simon hadn't been able to look away from the exchange. Unless he was out of practice when it came to kisses—definitely true—Lucy had not returned the gesture.

But neither had she fought against it.

Too riled up with a million different emotions, Simon had gone back inside to send Forester to retrieve her. And the intimate moment he'd witnessed had been repeating in his mind ever since.

Which left him utterly nonplussed about the girl currently out on a ride with Olivia and Forester. A ride that should have been his. It had been bad enough being forced to sit next to her in the carriage and endure the heat that sprouted from every touch as she bounced around in her seat, but now . . . now he was utterly out of sorts because of the beautiful woman who had come out of nowhere.

None of them had said a word on the drive back to the Park, and none of them had protested when Simon had said he would be working in the study the rest of the afternoon. Not even Forester, whose sole purpose in coming to Oxfordshire was to spend more time with him.

What an utter boor he had become.

The only other conclusion Simon had come to, and it was the one he hated most, was the thought that perhaps the engagement wasn't even real in the first place. That thought kept popping up in the back of his mind until he wanted to knock his head against the wall to get it out. Why would she lie about something like that? Perhaps she hoped to force William into a marriage.

But no, she had made her thoughts on that idea clear, and though he knew little about the woman, he could tell she truly hated the idea of anyone being forced to do anything. With the death of her father, she had lived a life of little choice and wouldn't wish that on someone else. Simon empathized with that completely.

Was she after the Calloway fortune, then? Simon would pay her off, happily, if it meant he could be rid of the questions that made him dizzy as he sat in his study pretending to do something useful. He had a whole stack of correspondence from his man of business, Mr. North, and many of his contacts around the country, but he knew he would never be able to focus.

Not with Lucy on his mind.

How in the world had Father loved his wife, raised his family, seen to his estate and other holdings, and run so many thriving businesses?

The answer to that question remained elusive, so Simon asked it out loud. "How did you balance it all?"

"I do believe you are rather young to begin talking to yourself, Simon."

Simon jumped to his feet as his mother stepped into the room, and he couldn't figure out why it was so strange to see her in the study until she touched a finger to the chair in front of the desk. The chair that Simon had only kept because his father had been the one to put it there when this was his study. No one ever sat in it, plush as it was, and North had utterly refused to touch the thing, though he had never explained why. He had always taken the much harder and plainer chair farther back in the room.

Simon realized now it was Mother's chair.

And she had not been in this room since the death of her husband.

"Mama," Simon said, though he didn't have the words to smooth the sorrowed expression on her face.

She did smile a little, though she kept her gaze on the chair, where her fingers rested. "You haven't called me Mama in years," she said.

Probably not since he had taken over as baron, though it had never been a conscious decision. Simon had simply grown up, though he had not realized how much it might have hurt his mother to lose that little part of her first child.

"Did you know I used to spend hours in this chair?" she said, and her smile grew at the memory.

Simon furrowed his brow. Had she come to talk about a chair? "Why?"

"Because your father wanted the company, and I was happy to give it to him. I know nothing of business or trade, but I think it comforted him to have me there. It helped him think, having someone with whom he could talk things through."

Suddenly the room felt suffocating. Simon glanced around, trying to figure out what had changed, but everything looked the same as it always had. Father's books were on the shelves, and his desk sat near the window to get a little more light. The rug was worn in a distinct path that he must have paced as he thought, and Mother's chair remained in its place.

But Simon now felt like he was an intruder in a space he had spent hours in each day without issue, and that terrified him.

Mother placed a hand on his cheek, and he did his best not to recoil from her touch. "My sweet boy," she whispered.

He had no desire for a repeat of their garden conversation the other day, so he took hold of her hand and changed the subject. "You look tired, Mama." He should have noticed sooner; her nap that morning didn't seem to have done her much good. "You're spending too much time looking after William." Something Simon should have been doing. "You need to rest so you don't fall ill yourself."

He wasn't sure he could handle losing another parent so soon. Not now.

Though she smiled, it did nothing to hide the exhaustion in her eyes. "I will rest when I know both my boys are taken care of," she said, and then she headed for the door with weary steps. She paused in the doorway, however, and cast a sweeping glance over the room before her eyes landed on Simon again. "You are not your father, Simon."

His heart sank. Why would she feel the need to tell him that yet again? Would he never live up to the man?

Chapter Eighteen

Lucy had only two days left before Mr. Granger did something she would feel guilty about for the rest of her life. At the very best, she could picture quite easily how much he would enjoy marching up to Calloway Park's door and proclaiming her engaged to *him* for everyone to hear, making her engagement to William a terrible scandal. And she wouldn't have the strength to argue because he would be only half wrong. While she was not and hopefully never would be in an understanding with Granger, neither was she engaged to William. That lie alone was enough to ruin her.

He would probably call it mercy, but Lucy would hate him for it for the rest of her lonely life.

At worst, he would drag the Calloway name through the mud, maybe even shoot William. He would never get away with it, but that wouldn't change the fact that William's inevitable death would be on her head.

No, she would have to tell the family she couldn't marry William, then slip away quietly before any of them truly realized what she had done to them. After Olivia's reaction to her weak attempt at telling the truth at tea yesterday, even if Lucy directly said she had never been engaged to William, it would take a miracle for the family to believe her. She wanted to be the one to tell them, but more and more it was looking like Mr. Granger might be the one to get them to believe it, unless Lucy could leave before he got the chance. She hated that thought.

Lucy was just glad she had decided not to tell Rebecca of yesterday's encounter. The maid surely would have panicked and done something even more drastic than lying about Lucy's relationship with William, though Lucy couldn't fathom what could possibly be worse.

"You seem to be gathering quite a lot of wool," Olivia said, breaking Lucy out of her thoughts. "What has you so deep in thought this afternoon?"

"I wasn't thinking about anything in particular," Lucy said, and it alarmed her to realize how easily the lie came.

Lady Calloway, who had reluctantly agreed to join the young ladies for a spell while they embroidered, smiled at Lucy, though she looked ready to fall asleep where she sat.

Lucy had been trying for almost an hour to think of a way to convince her to take a nap without it being offensive.

"I treasure those moments when my thoughts are calm," Lady Calloway said. "It is such a rarity nowadays, and too often I find myself overcome with worry for my family."

Reaching across the sofa they shared, Olivia put a hand on her mother's arm. "You needn't worry about us. Simon takes care of us."

Lucy didn't miss the flash of pain that crossed Lady Calloway's face, and she had to agree with the dowager baroness. Simon spent a good deal too much time thinking about everyone but himself.

Though she hadn't seen him since they'd parted ways after their journey to the village yesterday—he had taken dinner with a tenant he was visiting—Lucy couldn't help but worry about the man. Even despite his insulting words, she felt herself drawn to him. To help him swim when he was clearly drowning.

Funny, considering Lucy had never swam before in her life and was probably the least qualified person to help a man of his status and accomplishment.

But that didn't mean she didn't want to try, and she also wanted to try to apologize to him, if her tongue let her. He was only trying to protect his family, and if he suspected there was more to Lucy than she said, all the better. The last thing she wanted to do was hurt this family, and perhaps Simon could be the one to help her. After all, he was the only one who seemed to suspect she might not be what the others believed, and he was the only one with the power to thwart whatever plans Mr. Granger had made.

"I am rather tired," she said abruptly, and both ladies looked up at her. "I think I will go lie down for a little bit, if you don't mind."

"Of course not, dear," Lady Calloway replied. "You have had a trying few days, and your poor William is still under the weather."

"Under the weather" was far too generous for the man who hadn't woken in days, but Lucy would not counter the woman's optimism.

Excusing herself, she very nearly did go up to her room to lie down, perhaps write out what she would say to the family when she told them. But with so little time left here at the Park, she was not about to waste a moment of it.

Nick had gone shooting that morning with a couple of the footmen, but Simon, she knew, had remained behind to work. According to his mother and sister, the man spent far too much of his time working, and Lucy would do what she could to rectify that before she left.

He also deserved to live a bit.

Though she hadn't exactly seen the whole house—it was rather massive—Lucy knew the general area of Simon's study. It wasn't too far from the drawing room, from what she guessed, but it still felt like it took her ages to arrive. Probably because she was terrified. She and Simon hadn't exactly parted on good terms yesterday, and he had no reason to expect or welcome her company. But she would try to give it to him all the same—get him in a good mood before she told him the truth. If he were to help her fix the mess she'd gotten into, he couldn't be in a rage.

Simon's study, unfortunately, was empty and looked like it hadn't been used all day. Lucy took a moment to look around and decided this room was the first to give her any insight into the late Lord Calloway. This room felt like him, or at least how she imagined a successful, business-driven baron would feel. It certainly wasn't the sort of room she would expect Simon to be comfortable in. He was softer, more prone to be outside than surrounded by walls.

Chances were high that he wasn't even at home. He had plenty to keep him busy beyond the Park's grounds, but something told Lucy she simply had to keep looking. Where would he go when he was on his own?

The library was her next guess, and she walked with a determination in her step. She was probably mad for even trying to approach the man, but she wanted to prove to him—and maybe to herself—that she wanted to repay what kindness she had been shown by this family. Though he had insulted her and questioned her, Simon had also taken her to his pond and made jokes with her.

He had seen her as a person worth talking to, and that alone deserved some form or repayment, however little it might be. Besides, the sooner she told him about Mr. Granger and his threats, the better he could protect his family.

To her relief, Simon was indeed in the library, surrounded by papers and books and with an absolute mess of hair atop his head. One hand sat stuffed into it, and she imagined he had been running his hands through it in frustration for some time now. He was usually so well put together, and Lucy grinned at how human he looked in that moment. This was the Simon she had first met, and she was glad to see him back again.

Lucy cleared her throat, and Simon nearly jumped out of his chair when he looked up and saw her. "Lucy! Sorry, I didn't mean to shout. Um, did you need something? I believe my mother is—or Olivia might . . ." He pursed his lips together, apparently choosing not to finish his half-formed sentences.

Lucy bit back a smile. He had been too confident and smug of late, and it was nice to have him closer to her level again. This was the Simon she had come to care for. "I didn't mean to interrupt," she said. Another lie.

Simon sank back into his chair and managed a little smile, though it was nothing like the one she'd hoped for. "I welcome the interruption, actually." He gestured to a nearby chair.

The frustration had returned to his eyes, and Lucy watched him carefully as she sat. She still carried some fear of the man, so she would take her leave at the first sign of that frustration turning on her. This would be a delicate process. "Are you well this afternoon, my lord?"

He tried a few times to find the words, his mouth opening and closing with each attempt. "I fear my mind has stopped working entirely, so a change of company is exactly what I need."

"But you are alone, Lord Calloway."

"Exactly." And he gave her an actual smile that brought a bubble of warmth into her chest, no matter how small it was. At least he did not seem to hate her after yesterday. "I am surprised you would agree to stay," he said, his eyebrows pulling low. "Lucy, what I said yesterday, I didn't mean—"

"You don't have to explain."

He grimaced. "The only explanation is that I am a fool, so if I can keep that fact to myself, that is a relief." He leaned forward. "I truly am sorry."

Lucy believed him, and the room around them seemed to sink into a comfortable warmth, despite overcast skies. Simon's smile had a way of bringing her peace. Nothing had done that since before her father's death. Nothing except the man before her and everything connected to him.

"There is nothing to be sorry for, my lord," she said, and despite this being the perfect moment for her to admit the truth, she couldn't bring herself to do it. She wasn't ready to be rid of that peace and return to feeling lost and forgotten and afraid.

"Lucy," he said, reaching across the table as if to take her hand but stopping short. "Is there nothing I can do to make you call me Simon? Truly?"

A grin threatened to ruin her response, but she forced it down. "Nothing at all," she said as calmly as she could.

Simon laughed.

Just like before, Lucy treasured and loved that laugh, and not only because she was the one who had brought it on—she had not made anyone laugh since her father—but also because Simon laughed so seldom that it seemed a monumental feat to bring it on.

How could she bring more stress into his life when he was already struggling so much? It seemed, as from the beginning, she would have to fix her own problems. For now, she wanted to fix Simon's.

"What is it you're working on, Simon?"

Goodness, his smile warmed the entire room, and Lucy couldn't look away. It reminded her of the smile William had given her back at the inn, only she hadn't gotten the same spark in her chest when William smiled. When Simon smiled, she thought she might catch fire.

"I fear it will only bore you," he said, much to Lucy's disappointment. But then he continued. "My father was fond of business and trade, as you have heard. But I can't figure out why on earth he would purchase a tailor's shop in Liverpool."

Lucy shifted her chair closer so she could look down at the paper he pointed to. She knew next to nothing about business, but a tailor's shop? That intrigued her. "My father was a tailor," she said with a smile. "Perhaps yours found an interest in the profession as well, though I didn't know barons often purchased shops and trades like this."

"They don't. My father was unconventional in many ways—this, in particular—and if he hadn't been so profitable, as well as attentive to his seat in Lords, he probably would have been shunned by the upper ten thousand. There are few acceptable professions for a gentleman to begin with, and most of Society would agree that a baron who spends his time among the working class is an insult to his station."

He sat forward so he was looking at the same page as her, his frown far less appealing than his smile. For a moment there, he had actually been happy. "From what I understand in this letter—which is far less than I'd like, mind you—the tailor in question is in need of supplies and has sent me a request to purchase them. I would have thought he purchased such things himself."

Lucy considered that. "Unless your father took it upon himself to be a patron," she suggested. "Perhaps the tailor has been struggling, and the late Lord Calloway was a benevolent supporter."

Simon frowned even more. "From the income I have seen in my accounts, Mr. Pike is hardly struggling."

"Ah." Lucy was pretty sure she knew exactly what the situation was, though she had no idea how to explain it to a man who had been born to a fortune rather than having to build it up through his own efforts. Running his father's businesses had given him a good understanding of how to raise capital through a trade, but some things could come only through experience. But what reason would he have to listen to anything she said?

"I believe," she began slowly, "the tailor is right." She searched the many papers strewn about and found one that listed the general income from the shop, as well as what money came into Simon's coffers each month. The two were not dissimilar. "I could be wrong, but I think I understand what is happening."

Simon leaned back in his chair, his eyes fixed on her. "Then, that makes one of us. If you enlighten me, Lucy, I will be most in your debt."

It was by far the other way around, but Lucy wouldn't say so, not unless she admitted the truth about herself. One problem at a time. "I believe all profits beyond Mr. Pike's salary are sent to you, as the owner."

"That is the point of purchasing the shop, is it not? To generate income? The man is paid a considerable amount, from what I can tell."

"Enough to care for his family, yes, but not enough to purchase tools and fabric. Expenses that are usually taken from the excess profits . . . my lord," she added because she didn't want him to think she was being condescending. She bit her lip; she hardly expected a man who'd inherited land and fortune to understand the fine details of running one business, let alone several.

Simon sighed and ran his hands through his hair again, making it stand up straight, and Lucy couldn't help but grin at the picture he presented. She definitely liked him much better this way, when he wasn't being the intimidating baron she had seen the last couple of days. This was simply a man who was trying his best with something he wasn't born to do.

"I believe you are right," he said with a deeper frown. Did he really mean that? "How did you know something like that?"

Lucy raised an eyebrow. "Do you ask because I am a woman? Merely a governess?"

"I ask because I've spent the last three years trying to learn all of this, and I still feel like it is all a language I will never understand. You made it sound so simple."

Warming at the praise, Lucy ducked her head a little. She had never felt so valued before. "I used to spend hours at my father's side when he worked. He wasn't necessarily teaching me his trade, as he hoped I would one day make a good match for myself and not have to rely on an occupation to survive. But

I think he simply appreciated the company. It helped him concentrate, having someone else there with him, someone who understood him and offered silent support when he needed it."

When she looked back up at Simon, he was gaping at her with an expression that made her squirm. He seemed to be looking at her in a new way, like he hadn't truly seen her before now. And his gaze was not in the least unpleasant.

"What is it?" Lucy asked when a shiver ran through her, breaking her eye contact with him.

He shook his head. "I am merely frustrated that it took someone far more intelligent than I am to help me understand such a small thing. How did I not realize?"

"Because you are not a businessman, Simon. And I mean that in the kindest of ways."

"Then, what am I?" he asked, though Lucy wasn't sure if he really wanted an answer.

She gave him one anyway. "You're a man who runs an estate and has tenants to look after. You have a family to care for and a good deal of pressure from your late father, though I cannot imagine he expected you to understand all of this without first being taught. Does he not have a steward or man of business he worked with?"

Simon shrugged. "I am afraid Mr. North has lost patience with me over the last few years. He explains only when he must."

"Can you not let him handle this sort of thing?"

He looked at her like she had just said something incomprehensible. "My father handled all of this."

Lucy stopped herself from telling him that he was not his father, choosing instead to change the topic. He would surely take her words the wrong way, thinking it a failing that he was his own person instead of a copy of the late Lord Calloway. Though she couldn't say she knew much about his father, she did know Simon would do better to take on his life in his own way rather than trying to mirror someone he could never fully mirror. Not exactly, anyway. She got to her feet and held her hand out to him. "Lord Calloway, you are coming with me."

He looked up, his thick eyebrows low but his hazel eyes sparkling with interest. "That sounded very much like an order, Lucy."

"Perhaps it was."

"I am not accustomed to taking orders."

"And I am not accustomed to giving orders to anyone older than fifteen, yet here we are."

To her surprise, Simon stood and slid his hand into hers. For a moment, she couldn't concentrate on anything but their fingers pressed together, but then he said, "And where are we going?"

She shook off the strange feeling in her stomach and grinned at the man who looked far too nervous for someone who held so much power. All she held was his hand. "Somewhere without papers to scowl at. Come."

Only when they were outside did she realize how intimate the gesture of holding his hand really was. Locked together as they were, her skirts brushed his boots and she could smell the soap he used. Hardly appropriate, even if she had been his sister-in-law or close to it. She attempted to release him—he could hardly want that prolonged contact—but he held fast to her fingers and watched her with an intense look as they walked, as if he were desperate for whatever reprieve she could give him. How long had he been staring at those pages?

It didn't take him long before he realized where she was leading him, and he picked up the pace, practically pulling her along with him in his hurry to get to the place she was starting to suspect was his only sanctuary.

Simon's pond was just as it had been when he brought Lucy there the other day, only the sun hid behind a layer of gray clouds and left the place feeling somewhat melancholy—tainted by the weight he carried on his shoulders. When they reached the nearest shore, he plopped himself down in the grass, pulling Lucy with him, and didn't even seem to notice how close together they sat.

Neither did he seem to realize he still held on to her hand, something she was keenly aware of because her hand fit so well inside his. Lucy hadn't intended to sit beside a smooth-surfaced pond, shoulder to shoulder with a baron who held her hand without reservation, but she had no inclination to change her situation.

After several minutes, Simon finally let out a small sigh, his shoulders dropping with his breath. "I used to come here all the time as a boy," he said, almost reverently. "Will always thought I was boring because I would just sit here. For hours. He never understood how much I needed to sort through my thoughts without distractions. How much I needed some peace."

"I can imagine your life has little peace in it," Lucy replied. And here she was, threatening to destroy what little he had.

He turned to meet her gaze, and both of them froze. Lucy didn't know why he'd became so still, but she realized how close their faces were to one another, and the experience was not altogether unpleasant. After a moment that felt like an eternity, his eyes—which were much more golden than Lucy had realized, even without the sun—slid down to their hands clasped between them, and he loosened his grip.

But he didn't let go entirely.

Lucy knew one of them would have to break the silence that had settled between them after her comment. She feared what he might say about their current position, so she said the first thing that came to her mind. "Your hands are rough."

She bit her lip. That was hardly a normal thing to say, and to a lord no less, and she had to fight a laugh when Simon pulled his eyebrows together in confusion.

But then he said, "Yours are not," which was equally ridiculous. He cleared his throat and stretched out his fingers, giving Lucy a chance to stroke the calluses in his palms, which she did without hesitation. "Odd for a gentleman of rank, isn't it?"

Not that she had had much chance to feel how rough or soft a man's hands were, but Mr. Granger had held her hands on multiple occasions. His skin had been perfectly smooth, like he hadn't worked a day in his life, and she imagined many men of the *ton* had similar appendages. When their lives were lived out in Parliament sessions and ballrooms, they had no reason to have rough hands.

So why did Simon?

"Most people don't notice beneath my gloves," he said, as if that answered her unspoken question.

"But you're not wearing gloves now."

Simon mirrored her movements, running his fingertips across her palm and making her shiver a little. No one had touched her like this, like she was something worth a good deal and needed to be treasured. "Nor are you," he said as he compared the size of his hand to hers.

Lucy had never thought her hands to be small until this moment, when they were pressed up against his. Her hands were tiny.

And then she realized what the two of them had just said, and she snorted out a laugh because they both sounded absolutely ridiculous, saying such insignificant things as if they meant something.

To her delight, Simon joined in her laughter and seemed to relax even more. It was as if laughter were a medicine he'd badly needed, and he came back to life as they sat there in the grass beside the pond. Eventually, he lay back and put his hands behind his head as he closed his eyes, laughter still in his expression.

"Now you see why I do not particularly enjoy social gatherings," he said with a self-deprecating grin.

"I didn't know that about you. But I can imagine how awkward you must make every interaction if all you can talk about is a person's gloves or lack thereof."

He chuckled. "Whereas you are likely the center of attention wherever you go, with your skills at commanding a man's focus like you do."

Lucy's face burned with heat, as she was unsure what his comment might have meant. She had never commanded anything, but she liked thinking she had managed to capture attention from someone far better than Mr. Granger. Clearing her throat of a sudden swelling of fear, she tried to sound perfectly unaffected. "I haven't been to a social function in my life, sir, and I resent the fact that you think me incapable of being just as awkward as you."

Simon opened his eyes at that and leaned up on one elbow, turning to face her fully now that he was a little farther away. "You've never gone out in Society?"

Lucy shrugged a shoulder. "I was a governess for the last five years, and before that I was only a child, the daughter of a tailor. I've never had a reason to go out."

"But surely you have gone places with William." His thick eyebrows pulled together, his expression making Lucy nervous. "He must have courted you."

Sighing, she tried to find the best way to explain. She didn't want to lie to Simon any more than she already had, particularly in a place that was so special to him. Neither did she want to ruin this place for him by admitting the truth or speaking of Mr. Granger. "I have always lived an unconventional life, and nothing has changed."

"Ordinary lives are for ordinary people, Lucy. I may not know you well yet, but you are certainly extraordinary. Anyone can see that."

Heat filled Lucy's face yet again when she realized he was perfectly serious. No one had ever called her extraordinary before. Not even Mr. Granger. That man was determined to marry her, and he had never even told her she was anything but pretty. How was this man, who thought she was his future sister-in-law, far more romantic than the one who planned to make her his wife in truth, whether she wanted it or not?

That question reminded her that she had only two days before she would have to give Simon up. Not that he had been hers to begin with, but a part of her wished she could keep him forever. She wished she could tell him everything without him immediately using his limited time and energy to help her fix something beyond his responsibility. "You have to call me extraordinary because that is how you would treat your future sister-in-law," she said, hoping she sounded casual and unhurt by the thought. "You need not say that out of obligation."

Clenching his jaw, Simon looked away, but not before Lucy caught the flash of anger in his eyes. "I say that because it is true." He paused, then said, "Thank you, by the way."

"For what?"

"For making me come out here. It doesn't change the amount of work I have to do, but I can breathe again."

He was thinking about his work again, and that was the opposite of what Lucy wanted. Forget telling the truth; she wanted to spend the next day and a half learning about this man and committing every detail to memory. She would keep him in her heart next to Olivia and the rest of his family as a treasured piece of a life she could have only in fantasy, and she would leave Downingham and hope Mr. Granger followed her and left the Calloways alone.

For now, she would do what she could to make Simon's life a happier one.

To do that, she needed to keep him distracted, and she needed to do it without touching him. Touching him again would only distract *her*, and that was the last thing she needed.

As he seemed to ready himself to return home to his stress, Lucy searched for something—anything—to keep him out here a little longer. He was so much more pleasant when he was out here, and it was practically the only time he truly smiled.

The only thing she could see in the nearby vicinity were rocks along the edge of the pond. Rocks and weeds. "Can you skip stones, my lord?"

He raised an eyebrow. "Not when you call me that, no."

Lucy groaned. "Simon."

At least he smiled again, though he seemed more confused by the question than anything. "Of course I can."

"Well, I cannot. Will you teach me?"

The look he gave her, apart from sending blazing heat into her cheeks, told Lucy that Simon Calloway had no idea what to make of her, and she rather liked that. Mr. Granger had always acted as though he understood everything she could possibly want, and the fact that Simon had to work to know her and was still trying made her like him all the more.

"You want to skip stones?" he asked, a measure of incredulity in his voice.

"That is what I said."

She thought he would deny her attempt at distraction and return to the house, but then he shrugged and rose to his feet before offering his hand to help her up. "I thought everyone learned to skip stones as a child," he said.

"Not everyone grows up in a life of leisure," she replied. "Our lands struggled too much to give us an adequate income, so I worked alongside my father from the day I was old enough to use a needle and thread, using any free time I had to study everything I needed to know to be a proper lady should I catch the eye of a suitor later in life. And I didn't have a pond to practice skipping stones on. But I heard other children talk about it, and it sounded amusing."

Though he winced with appreciated sympathy and apology for forgetting their very different positions in life, Lucy hadn't intended to make him pity her. They were out here to help him, so she bent down and picked up the roundest pebble she could find.

"Not that one," Simon said immediately, and he wrapped his hand around hers, holding onto her while he searched for a better rock. When he found one, he replaced the one in her palm with an exceptionally flat one. "The thinner the stone, the easier it skims the water."

Grabbing a similar stone, he turned with his left side facing the pond and tossed the rock across the water. It skipped three times before it slid beneath the surface.

Well, that didn't look so difficult. Mimicking his stance, Lucy did the same motion and threw her own rock, only hers went straight into the water with a *plunk*.

Simon chuckled as he picked up another stone. "Hold it like this," he said, demonstrating the way he curled his finger around the edge. "Use your wrist and throw it as flat as you can."

Her second attempt was worse than the first, and she couldn't help but laugh. "Perhaps I am not meant to skip them," she said with a grin.

"Try one more time." This time, instead of demonstrating, he stepped behind her and put a hand on her elbow. "Get a little closer to the water." He guided her directly to the edge of the water, and though it was a bit muddy in that spot, he didn't seem to mind in the least. She would have expected him to at least grimace at the state of his boots, but he didn't give them a passing glance.

The differences between him and Mr. Granger were growing by the minute. Even if Lucy had no reason to compare the two of them. It wasn't as if Simon wanted to marry her.

"Keep your movement low," he instructed as he guided her through the action, though she was a bit distracted by his soft voice in her ear. "Think of it as the rock flying from your fingers, not falling, and aim for the far shore."

With Simon standing so close that she could smell him again—he smelled clean, masculine—Lucy tried one more time to skip her rock, throwing it exactly as he instructed.

But just as she threw it, her foot slipped in the mud, and she shrieked as she tumbled right into Simon's arms.

"Careful!" He slid his arms beneath hers, and though she felt as if he could easily hold her up, there was something tense about him.

"You're slipping too, aren't you?" she whispered.

He grunted a little. "Yes. Perhaps if I . . ."

His hold shifted, and Lucy tried to get herself steady on her feet. But she couldn't get a solid foothold. "Wait," she said as much to herself as to him since she was on the verge of laughing. Of course she would be the reason they got themselves in this predicament. It seemed she was as prone to small problems as she was to big ones. "Maybe if I turn around."

She did, gripping Simon's strong arms as she moved as slowly as she could. Once they faced each other, she figured she would be able to hold onto him until she could get back to sturdy ground, and then she could help him do the same. How, she wasn't sure, but she would do her best.

But when she finally managed to turn without falling, she found herself pressed up against the man with his arms wrapped securely around her. She had a clear view of his cravat from where she stood and knew instinctively that if she lifted her head a few inches, her nose would brush his chin.

Perhaps he had realized the same thing, because suddenly he seemed to be holding his breath.

Lucy needed to be anywhere but where she was, and she swallowed as her fingers pressed against the solid muscle of his chest. Honestly, how was the man so strong? Was he a pugilist on the weekends? Did he spend his mornings wrestling lions?

"Um . . ." Lucy tested her foothold, hoping something had changed over the last several seconds, but she slid yet again and had to wrap her arms around Simon's torso to keep herself from falling. "I should . . ." She had no idea what she should do, but she couldn't very well stay where she was.

She felt Simon swallow, his heart racing in her ear. "I am going to—"

What he was going to do Lucy never found out because as soon as he moved even the slightest bit, their feet slid out from under them, and they tumbled into the pond.

Cold water hit Lucy like a slap to the face, and though she told herself she'd needed that, she quickly became focused on the fact that the pond was much deeper than she had anticipated and her feet could not reach the bottom without submerging her head in the water. Panicking, she fought to rise to the surface but seemed to be sinking deeper and deeper with the weight of her skirts and the fact that she had never learned to swim. She had never needed to.

An arm went around her back, and suddenly she was rising with impressive speed until her face hit blessed air. Coughing and spluttering, she breathed as quickly as she could and clung to the body that held her up, as if he might let her go.

"Easy," Simon's soft voice said, and his gentle fingers brushed the hair out of her eyes. "Breathe normally. I have you."

Lucy wrapped her arms around his neck and buried her face in his shoulder as she cried, though she didn't even know why she was crying. And then she laughed because Simon was standing perfectly still while keeping both their heads above the water, which meant the pond wasn't nearly as deep as she'd imagined. How dramatic she was!

"Lucy?" Fear colored his words, and he must have thought her absolutely mad for crying and laughing at the same time.

"I'm sorry," she replied shakily. "I thought—You must think me ridiculous."

The circle of his arms around her tightened along with his jaw, which was right in front of her eyes and somewhat stubbled with hair. "You should never feel ridiculous for being afraid. I take it you can't swim."

"Never tried," she corrected. She had no reason to hold to him so tightly—she knew he would not let her sink again—but she did anyway. She never wanted to let go. "Like I said, I did not have a pond where I grew up, and swimming has never been a very ladylike pastime."

It may have been her imagination, but Simon seemed to pull her even closer. "Something tells me you would be marvelous at it if you tried," he said, his voice husky and low.

Lucy wanted to see his expression, to know what his eyes would tell her in that moment. She pulled away a little, her arms aching as she relaxed a bit, and heat spread through her cheeks when she met Simon's gaze. This was a new expression again, but it was one she wouldn't mind seeing often. He seemed to look at her like someone recalling a beautiful dream.

"You have a leaf in your hair," she whispered and reached up to grab it, clutching it in her fingers as if it were something important she couldn't afford to lose.

Simon didn't even look at it, his eyes fixed on her. "You are entirely beautiful," he said. Then something shifted in his expression, which grew so dark that

Lucy almost wondered if a sudden storm had blown in. "William is a lucky man, Miss Staley," he added.

Lucy's heart sank. How had she forgotten everything she had done? He was never going to forgive her. "Don't say that," she whispered with a wince.

He narrowed his eyes. "Whyever not?"

"What do we have here?"

Lucy jumped at the unexpected voice and would have slid back under the water if Simon hadn't kept a firm hold of her. Nick stood with his shoulder leaning against a tree, and his eyes glittered with amusement as he took in the sight. Lucy thought she might be sick; she was far closer to Simon than she had a right to be, particularly for someone who was, to anyone's knowledge, engaged to his brother. How long had Nick been standing there anyway?

Folding his arms, he leveled them with a look that seemed to say a lot more than Lucy could understand, and she felt Simon tense beside her.

"We slipped in the mud," Lucy said.

"I'm sure you did," Nick replied.

"Watch your tone," Simon growled, and he started making his way back toward the pond's edge.

As he laughed, Nick reached out and took hold of Lucy's hand, helping her scramble out of the pond and back onto dry land. Somehow he managed to avoid the dangerous mud, even though he stood almost exactly where Simon and Lucy had been standing. "I don't know what you're talking about, Simon," he said before his eyes traveled over Lucy and her dripping clothes. "Did you know Simon once fell into a fountain at Lady Adley's garden party?"

"I did nothing of the sort!"

Lucy might have laughed at the look of horror on Simon's face as he extricated himself from the pond, but she was overcome with a fit of shivers that fully distracted her. The water hadn't been all that cold while she was in it, but now that she was out in the air, she mourned the hidden sun and the loss of Simon's warmth.

Mostly the sun, she told herself. She would have been warm next to anyone, and it wasn't Simon himself she missed, just . . . just the way he had held her like he would never let anything bad happen to her.

"I'd best get you back to the house," Nick said, and he put his arm around Lucy, pulling her to his side.

The gesture was nearly as intimate as it had been with Simon in the pond, so why didn't Lucy feel the same level of heat? She had to draw even closer to Nick to stop her teeth from chattering.

"Are you coming, Simon?"

Lucy glanced back and realized Simon had collapsed onto his back, and he was lying on the shore with his thick hair plastered to his forehead and his arm over his face.

"No," he said, barely audible. "Not yet. Go on without me."

And Lucy wondered if he was as undone by the afternoon as she was.

Chapter Nineteen

Simon had never been more of a fool in his life, and he was really starting to think he was incapable of reading a sheet of paper and comprehending any of it. After two disastrous days in a row with Lucy—frankly, every day with her had been a disaster—he had to buckle down and get to work.

But the entire morning as well as all of last night when he should have been sleeping were filled with thoughts of Lucy Hayes.

She was Lucy *Hayes*, not Staley—he was sure of it now—assuming her name was even Lucy to begin with. He hadn't wanted to consider it, and at the pond he had told himself every reason he should believe her story. She hadn't given him any real reason to think otherwise, so he had been determined to stop thinking the worst of her.

That look in her eyes, though, when Simon had told her William was lucky to have her . . . she had looked at him like . . . well, like he had never been more wrong about something in his life. Either she had some other monstrous secret that would somehow ruin William through their marriage, or . . .

Or they weren't engaged to begin with.

And she had winced when he'd called her Miss Staley. As someone who was a terrible liar, he had recognized the signs of being caught in a lie. Considering that plus the fact that the illustrious Mr. Granger had called her Hayes, Simon couldn't deny his family had been duped.

He had been duped.

He only wished he knew why she would lie in the first place or how the whole thing had begun. Had she drugged William with something? Forced him into the rain so he would catch fever? But to know that would work would require her to know William quite well. Simon's brother had never been keen to talk of his susceptibility to fevers, and he wouldn't tell a stranger.

So that made Lucy an opportunist, perhaps. She'd found a man ill with fever and decided to capitalize on his incapacitation. And yet that explanation didn't sit well either. She would still need to know William to know he was worth exploiting, and she had been surprised when Simon had told her of William's income, no matter how much she had tried to cover her tracks. Besides, Simon had seen the note from the innkeeper after he'd asked Mother for it; Lucy had been at William's side *before* he'd taken ill. He would have known exactly who she was.

So who was she? Why was she here? And what part had William played in all of this?

There was no way Simon would get any work done today with so many questions running through his head.

He was too much a coward to ask Lucy herself. If he ended up being wrong, his suspicion would completely ruin their friendship, something he had come to treasure more than he'd like. She was the only person who had gotten him to relax in weeks, and confronting her with any of this would likely lead to disaster. He wasn't sure he had the strength to deal with that. Until William woke and could offer the answers to all these mysteries, Simon would have to occupy his time with something else and pretend all was well.

"I hate to say it, old friend, but your sister may actually beat you in a race." Forester let himself into Simon's chambers, where he had been trying—and failing—to get work done, and he dropped himself onto the bed with a deep sigh. "She certainly left me in the dust this morning."

Simon was still a bit too distracted by Lucy to really pay attention to his friend, but he did his best. "Is that the truth or another one of your stories?"

Forester chuckled. "I tell tales only when they are to my benefit. No point in wasting creativity if there is nothing to gain."

As telling as that statement was when it came to Forester's strange inclination to lie, Simon could hardly focus on that when he felt like his mind had been scrambled. How had his life come to this? "Did you ever see your life going in a different direction than it has?"

"Ah, I see we've gotten to the root of the melancholy."

A restless energy pushed Simon up from his desk, and he started to pace the room. At least Forester seemed to have caught on that the situation was more serious than he'd thought; he sat up and frowned as he watched Simon make his rounds. The man had a nasty habit of playing the fool a little too well, but at least he could be sober when it mattered.

"I always knew I would be Lord Calloway."

Forester nodded. "Because you were born to it."

"But I wasn't born to be a businessman." That had made itself clear, especially this last week. How many more of Father's ventures would Simon have to sell because he was incapable of doing the job as well as the last Lord Calloway?

"The curse of being your father's son," Forester said with a shrug.

Far from making Simon feel better, that comment made his anxiety rise. "Then, why couldn't William—"

"William has never taken responsibility for a thing in his life. Do you honestly think he could help your father's endeavors thrive? He would run them to the ground."

Simon grunted. "So would I, apparently."

Rising, Forester placed himself in Simon's path and narrowed his eyes at him, fixing him with a stare that made his heart pound a little harder. Simon hadn't seen this much conviction in his friend's face in years, and it was enough to pull his full attention.

"One sugar farm is nothing when one considers the scope of what you accomplish on a weekly basis, Calloway."

Simon's eyebrows rose high. The sale hadn't even been finalized yet. "How did you know—"

"You don't spend your every moment at the heart of the *ton* without learning a few things."

As concerning as it was to think people in London already knew about him selling the farm less than a week ago, Simon was more fixated on the way his friend spoke about Society. Though Forester was a gentleman in all ways, his estate wasn't remotely livable, which led to him either staying in London or spending his time with friends across the country. He had no sanctuary like the pond, but that had never seemed to bother him. Simon would have fallen apart without a place to go, but Forester seemed to thrive.

"I don't know how you stand being around Society day in and day out," Simon said, shaking his head.

Forester smirked. "By necessity, my friend. Purely by necessity. You don't think I envy your little hamlet here? But a man needs a partner in life, and I am not going to find her in the countryside."

How was Nick Forester still single? As far as Simon knew, he was one of the most sought-after men outside of the peerage, and he could have had his pick of a wife. Simon envied him that, just as Forester apparently envied Simon his home. Perhaps, if he had the time, Simon might have met Lucy under different circumstances, and things would have been different.

There he went, thinking about Lucy again.

Forester didn't help matters when he said, "Speaking of women in the countryside, we should talk about Lucy."

Simon groaned. "Why would we need to do that?"

"Because you were alone with her yesterday. Or you would have been, if I hadn't followed you. And Olivia mentioned finding the two of you along that same path the other day. Unchaperoned, I should add."

A sense of foreboding settled in Simon's gut as he considered that. Whenever trapped in London, he was always careful to avoid any situation that might compromise himself or a lady. But here at home? He didn't usually given much thought to Society's rules.

"Calloway, she is to be your sister-in-law."

It was too much to hope Forester had said that as a reason to think nothing untoward had happened. "I know that," Simon said slowly.

"Do you?"

"Nothing happened, Forester." Simon couldn't fully believe himself, however. At the pond yesterday, something had nearly happened, stopped only by Forester. Simon had temporarily lost his mind when he fell into that water. "How long were you there?" he asked warily.

For once, Forester didn't smile. "Long enough. Have you discovered something about our Lucy, or is your brother going to have to call you out when he rises from his deathbed?"

"Nothing happened," Simon repeated. "I haven't compromised Miss Staley, and I have no plans to."

"Good, because you're a decent fellow, Calloway, and I would hate to think less of you." Thankfully, he smiled a little at that. "I wanted this conversation less than you did, you know."

Simon had a hard time believing that. "Then, why bring it up?"

"Because you're one of my closest friends, and if someone else had discovered you—"

"On my own grounds?"

Forester shrugged. "Experience has taught me that no one is safe from the prying eyes of the world. I only wish to see you content in life, and the extent to which you like Lucy could get you into trouble."

Simon's stomach twisted. "Who said I like her?"

One eyebrow lifting, Forester made it clear without speaking that it would take a fool not to see the way Simon's eyes were drawn to her whenever they were in the same room. "We all like Lucy," he said simply.

Desperate to get out of the house and do something before his thoughts ran away from him, Simon grabbed Forester by the shoulder and led him out into the corridor and straight for the front door. "You're coming with me," he said with as much strength as he could muster. He needed Forester to listen to him.

"Er, why?" Forester followed close behind him, though he seemed wary.

"Because I'm not leaving you in this house with my sister."

Forester scoffed. "You can't honestly think I would—"

"She fancies herself in love with you, and you have been wife hunting for more than two years. That is not a combination I am comfortable with."

Thankfully, Forester didn't argue, and the pair of them headed out into the sunshine. Today was a lot brighter than yesterday had been, which was nothing short of ridiculous. Why couldn't the English weather mimic Simon's mood like it usually did? Why couldn't it have been sunny and warm at the pond yesterday so Lucy wouldn't have been so keen to get out of the water and return to the house and he could have learned the truth? Why couldn't Forester have waited five more minutes before announcing himself?

Simon growled to himself as he walked. At what point had he become such a terrible person that he *wanted* to act on his attraction to someone completely outside the boundaries of propriety? His own brother's betrothed! He was a cad for even entertaining thoughts of something more with the woman. But he had come so close to learning something important about her, and now he feared he never would.

Especially because Forester was right. Simon should not be alone with her, no matter how innocent the intention.

But thinking that only made him want to be alone with her even more.

Simon growled again and picked up his pace. He needed to get over this attraction, and fast.

"Where are we going?" Forester asked. He had fallen a bit behind, but Simon knew he would follow. He was a good friend, even if he wouldn't like what Simon said next.

"The east field."

"Blast it all, Calloway, not again."

There were only two controllable circumstances under which Simon didn't feel weighed down by his responsibilities. One was when he was riding, when he could push Hermes to full speed and let the wind in his hair brush him clean of all stress. He never felt freer than when he rode without holding back.

The other was when he worked the fields with his tenants.

He knew he was entirely unique in this—at least, he had never heard of other members of nobility condescending to manual labor—but Simon had been assisting the tenant farmers for years, even before Father died. Down to his shirtsleeves, with a scythe in his hand and nothing but fields of grain in all directions, he could focus on his hands instead of his thoughts.

He could spend hours out here if he had the time.

Forester, on the other hand, had worked for about ten minutes before jumping into a conversation with farmer Wilson's wife. From the bits and pieces Simon had picked up over the breeze, Forester was telling her a story about how he'd led a few men from the village near where he grew up and helped save the crops of a nearby tenant from something nasty. Simon hadn't caught what it was they'd saved it from, but Forester had gotten rather animated.

Simon had ignored his friend for the most part, focusing on the work rather than his growing worries that Forester would never take life seriously again. That would only add to Simon's stress, and the whole point of coming to the field was to empty his mind. But his arms were starting to ache, and it was time to return home before his mother got after him for missing a meal yet again.

He hadn't been able to work up the courage to go down to dinner last night after the pond incident.

"Finally done, are you?" Forester said when Simon joined him. "We missed tea, and I'm half-starved."

"You'll survive another twenty minutes until we reach the Park," Simon said before Mrs. Wilson could invite them in. He knew his tenants well; he knew they often struggled to feed anyone but themselves, and he would never put more strain on their finances if he could help it, which was just another reminder that he needed to keep his inherited businesses afloat—so he could continue offering a low rent to his tenants. He already charged far less than most.

He did, however, accept the cup of water Mrs. Wilson offered him. "Thank you kindly."

"You don't have to keep doin' this, m'lord," she said, and she seemed nervous as she watched him drink. She kept wringing her hands and glancing out to the field, where her husband still worked in the hot sun. "Mr. Wilson can manage."

Smiling as warmly as he could, Simon pressed the cup back into her hand and sandwiched her fingers between his hands. "I do it because I want to, Mrs. Wilson. Never fear. Thank you for allowing me to spend time on your farm when I need it."

Not bothering to put on his waistcoat and jacket, as he planned to wash and change anyway, he simply carried both items and led the way back to the big house with Forester on his heels.

"Have you worked out your woes, then?"

Simon frowned. "What are you talking about?"

"Please. You've been this way since we were boys. Even Rowland knows about it."

Lord Harstone, as the newest addition to their little group of friends, had known Simon for only a decade, and they hadn't spent any considerable amount of time together in the countryside. For Harstone to know how often Simon used his hands to work through stress, Simon was doing a poorer job of hiding it than he'd hoped. Higher in rank than Simon, Harstone had managed to find himself a wife, have beautiful children, and build the life Simon craved, and it was doubtful he had any stress to work through.

"Whenever you're frustrated," Forester continued, "you always try to solve it by making something or destroying something. At some point, you have to get it into your thick skull that your hands have nothing to do with your head."

He whacked Simon on the back of the head, as if he needed a demonstration.

Forester was right again, of course, but so far Simon hadn't found anything else to lessen his stress. He couldn't give up his father's businesses without giving up his father's trust, he couldn't stop being a baron without dying, and his family would always need him to look after them because they deserved the very best of lives.

"Treasure your easiness of life, Forester," Simon said with a sigh. They had nearly reached Calloway Park again, which meant he was nearly back to the heaviness of his life. "You have no idea how good you have it."

Forester stopped in the middle of the pathway, a strange look on his face when Simon looked back. It made him wonder what was going through his friend's head, which was an odd thing indeed. Forester usually said everything that was on his mind and was perfectly transparent, almost to a fault. "Ease," he murmured, then slowly shook his head.

Simon might have responded if a little squeak hadn't pulled his attention back to the house. He knew that squeak. Heat flooded his face when he realized Lucy and Olivia were only a few paces away, because while Olivia had seen Simon work the fields plenty of times, Lucy had not. And she had noticed—to Simon's horror—that he was in quite the state of undress.

Her eyes took him in, her lips twisting in the smallest of smiles and making him both nauseated and proud.

Apparently the hard labor had done the trick, because Simon had quite forgotten about Lucy and the chance that he might run into her. Anything he might have said stuck in his throat.

"Miss Calloway," Forester said, breaking the sudden silence. "How fortuitous, running into you. Might I have a word with you?"

Simon had no idea what Forester might want to talk to Olivia about, but he couldn't bring himself to worry about the pair of them walking several yards away, out of earshot. Not when Lucy had turned slightly pink as she continued to look him over. Unless he were mistaken—highly likely—she appreciated what she saw, even if she was absolutely seeing too much.

Focus, man. Clearing his throat, Simon shifted the jacket and waistcoat in his hands so that they hid some of the more exposed parts of his torso. True, he still wore a shirt, but he had sweat a good deal in the sun, and he was not used to anyone paying him such particular attention. "Good morning, Lucy." It was still morning, wasn't it? *Barely.*

She dipped into a slight curtsy. "Good morning, Lord Calloway."

Hmm, she was back to that? It was probably for the best if she wasn't really to be his sister-in-law. He still had no actual proof of that though. The moment he found any proof that she *wasn't* engaged to William was the moment he would have to cut her out of his life. As much as he needed to do that anyway, his brother's fiancée or otherwise, he couldn't find it in himself to *want* it. With the way the tightness in his chest eased at the mere sight of her, he was realizing she was the only thing that was keeping him from falling apart. Funny, considering that he felt like every second he spent with her unraveled him that much more.

"Er, how is William this morning?" he asked.

She wrapped her shawl a little tighter around herself. Why was she wearing a shawl? It was blasted hot out today, and Simon was still sweating after that work in the field. "I confess I have not yet been to see him this morning," she said quietly. "I slept later than I planned, and Olivia begged me to walk with her while it was still . . . cool." She frowned and glanced up at the cloudless sky.

Simon almost laughed at the suspicious look on her face. "Olivia wanted to go walking?"

"That is what she told me."

And Lucy hadn't even been to see William yet. What was Simon to make of that? Was she starting to slip up in her game of pretend?

"Are you well this morning, my lord?"

Though the question was innocent enough, there was a new spark of amusement in Lucy's eyes as she looked him over again. He knew what she was really asking, and he decided to indulge her, no matter how strange it made him seem. "Sometimes I help the nearest tenants with their fields," he said. "When I have some time."

She made a face of confusion. "Why?"

It was a valid question, but Simon bristled at the tone she used. "Because I am no better than the men who have to labor for their bread. I may have been born to privilege, but I am merely a man, the same as them."

Lucy smiled, sending a bolt of lightning through him because it was a smile without any hesitation to it. She wore no mask of pretend—not that she had really done so before—and she wasn't laughing at him or mocking him for adding yet another oddity to his repertoire. She offered that smile solely for him.

"What a lovely thought," she said. "If only more men were like you, Simon."

And Simon knew he had to get to the bottom of things once and for all. He refused to spend any more time wondering if she was going to betray him and his family. He refused to go any longer wondering whether she truly was engaged or whether she was more available than she'd led him to believe. No matter the risk to their friendship, he couldn't live any longer in uncertainty.

But he would need to be delicate about this. The family was already hanging by a thread, and it would be best to get her away from the house and any potential prying ears.

He cleared his throat. "Have you been to William's estate yet?"

Her smile dropped immediately, something Simon did not much like. It was only proof that he was on the right track.

She shuffled her feet, no longer meeting his eyes. "No, not yet."

"Would you like me to show it to you? It's not far, and perhaps it would make you feel more at home to know what will be yours."

"I would like that," she replied, though her expression said the opposite. She looked like she was going to be sick. "Only, I should check on William before I am gone for any length of time. I should have done that first thing in the morning. I should . . . excuse me, Lord Calloway."

She picked up her skirts and hurried back to the house, leaving Simon with a stone settling in his stomach. Whatever he learned at William's house would be the end of it all, and at this point, he still couldn't decide which outcome he wanted more. Either she was lying about her relationship and was entirely unattached, or she would truly marry William and forever be off-limits to Simon as his sister-in-law.

Forester and Olivia returned to his side a moment later, both of them looking for Lucy.

"Did she go back inside?" Forester asked, a little wrinkle forming between his eyebrows. That only made its appearance when he was judgmental of something or someone.

“Oh, thank goodness,” Olivia breathed. “I was not looking forward to our walk, though I was sure Lucy needed it. It was the only reason I asked her. Do you think she will return, or . . . ?”

Simon tried to smile. “Your afternoon is free, dear sister.”

Olivia bounced with excitement. “I’m going to go practice for our race! I’ve not forgotten, Simon. I will beat you.”

Simon hardly cared about the race now, but he knew Olivia did, so he forced a better smile. “Not a chance.”

As soon as she was gone, Forester wrapped his arm around Simon’s shoulders. “Back to work for you, I suppose? Honestly, I don’t even know why I still bother to visit you. You’re always working. I’ll have to go beg a footman to join me for a rousing game of billiards or something.”

“Actually . . .”

Forester’s eyebrows shot high.

“You’ll still need to find a footman, but I am not going to work. I’m going to take Lucy to Penworth.”

That seemed even less plausible to Forester than Simon not working. “William’s estate?” he asked with a scoff. “But he hasn’t lived there for years. Are the servants even there?”

“I suspect not. He keeps them in London, as you know.”

“Exactly, so why . . . ? Ah.” Forester grimaced a little as the two of them started walking for the house. “Am I to understand you still suspect the future Mrs. Calloway to be hiding something?”

“I suspect there are many things we don’t know about her.” Her true name, among other things. “But if William was bringing her home as his wife-to-be, he would have sent his servants ahead to prepare the house. He would not be one to wait long for the wedding to take place.”

“You mean to find the truth, once and for all.”

“If the house is empty, Lucy is not who she says she is.”

“And if the servants are there and waiting for her?”

Simon wasn’t sure how to answer that question, and Forester didn’t seem surprised in the least. No matter how much Simon pretended nothing had happened at the pond, Forester had seen what he’d seen.

When they reached the corridor that separated the guest rooms from the family wing, Forester paused and put his hand on Simon’s shoulder. “Be careful,” he said, perfectly serious. “No matter what the truth may be, there is a real person behind those captivating dark eyes. Why are you so determined to see her ruined?”

Yet again, Simon had no response, and he felt like a boulder had settled between his shoulders, threatening to knock him down and keep him pinned to the ground. He didn't understand why he was so desperate to prove that the engagement was false, and guilt wormed its way into his stomach as he considered the consequences of bringing Lucy to Penworth under false pretenses. Maybe it was a bad idea; she had done little to deserve his distrust.

Forester frowned. Whatever he saw in Simon's expression, he didn't like it. "I urge you to be delicate, Simon, whatever you do."

Whatever he did, Simon feared he would be the one to lose the most.

Chapter Twenty

It felt like an eternity since Lucy had been in this room, even though she and Rebecca had come to check on William before going to bed last night. The last two days had passed in a blur, and all she could think about was Mr. Granger's unwelcome kiss and her moment with Simon in the pond.

How had time flown by so quickly? Tomorrow was her last day. After that, Mr. Granger would take her down to London so they could be married. That or he would inflict harm on the Calloways. Were those her only options? She had felt so much at home here at Calloway Park that she knew she would never find the same feeling anywhere else, but no matter what happened, she would have to say goodbye to this dream of a life unless she wanted the family to get hurt.

That choice was easy.

William was sleeping far more peacefully than he had yet, and he had moved a few times, as if trying to wake from beneath the laudanum. He would likely wake in the morning and right all the wrongs Lucy had inflicted, except for those she had done to herself. The Calloways would be all right, if rather hurt, but Lucy would be lost.

No, better to get the hard part over with. She would have to tell Simon everything when he came to fetch her for their excursion. Better for him to hear it from her lips than to discover her lies from the likes of Mr. Granger.

Someone knocked gently on the door, and she turned in her chair beside the bed, expecting to see Simon come to fetch her for their little jaunt over to William's estate. Instead, she found herself smiling at Nick as he stepped into the room.

"May I join you?"

She would even miss Nick, and she hoped at least he would still consider her a friend after all of this. He seemed to be of a good, forgiving sort. She nodded at him, knowing this would probably be one of their last conversations.

"Could you fetch more water?" Nick asked the maid who sat in the corner.

The girl glanced at Lucy since she had only just brought up a fresh pitcher when Lucy arrived, but she dipped in a curtsy and went to do as requested.

Lucy thought it strange to send the girl away, but she wasn't sure how to approach the breach in conduct. William was hardly able to chaperone, so they were basically alone in the room with a closed door behind them. "I thought you said you were never very close to William," she said, nerves pooling in her belly.

Nick sat on the edge of the bed so he was rather close to Lucy, and he looked William over before giving her another smile. At least it was a friendly smile, not one that indicated any other intentions. "I'm not. I thought perhaps *you* could use a friend."

Despite the impropriety of their current situation, she loved to hear him call her that. She had never had a true friend, not even when she was a girl. It had always just been her father and her. Rebecca was the closest thing, and Lucy was somewhat put out with the maid at the moment. All of this had started because of her.

"That is very kind of you," she said, though her heart ached a bit. That feeling would likely not go away until she had been away from this place for several years at least. "But I will not be here for long."

"That is precisely my worry."

And with that, Lucy was completely on her guard. Not because of what he'd said but because of the look he gave her. The look that said he knew the truth and had for a long time. There was wariness in his expression, too, and she knew instinctively that were it to come down to a choice between helping her or helping the Calloways, she would not come out the victor in Nick's eyes.

"Nick," she whispered, not sure what she could say.

He glanced at William. "Does he know?"

Maybe there was still a chance he didn't know her secret. Maybe he was talking about something else. Lucy slowly stood, noting Nick following her movement with keen eyes. "Does he know what?" She held her breath.

With a brief smile, Nick shook his head. "Does William know his family thinks you are to be married?"

So that was that. And though Lucy's gut told her to run, Nick grabbed her hand before she could get far.

"I mean you no harm," he said, but he held her tightly enough that she couldn't pull herself free. That didn't stop her from trying. "I only wish to understand."

"Understand?"

Nodding, he rose to his feet and stood over her to block the way to the door. "Yes, Lucy. I need to know why. I need to know why you are perpetuating this story. Why let them think you are to be Mrs. Calloway? Are you hoping for a fortune? Connections? To ruin the Calloway name?"

Lucy felt like she was being stared down by the sun itself, and tears filled her eyes. She couldn't look at him, knowing she had betrayed him too. "I didn't mean for any of this to happen," she whimpered, and her strength gave out, sending her down toward the floor. "I don't want to hurt them."

Nick caught her by the elbows and returned her to the chair, though he sat close enough that he could hold her down if he so chose. "Tell me," he said. Gently. Like a friend would.

So she did. She told him everything, starting from her meeting William at the inn and the misunderstanding he had created, though she left out the reason for it. She told him about arriving at the Park and being overwhelmed by the family's excitement and worry and Rebecca being the first to claim Lucy was William's fiancée. The one thing she didn't mention was Mr. Granger. He'd told her to keep that part to herself, and she still feared his threat to the family.

"I never meant to let it get this far." She swallowed and tried to figure out what Nick's expression meant, but she couldn't. The man was suddenly a closed book, and she wondered if this was the man most of England saw when they met Nick Forester. Did anyone really know him?

"I'm going to tell them," she continued when he offered no commentary on her story. "I'm going to tell them the truth. Today. Before it goes on any longer. And then I'll leave and stop pretending I deserve this family's kindness. I've already let it go on too long, and—"

"Don't you say a word." Nick grabbed both of her hands, and he waited until he had Lucy's full attention. "Miss—what was your name?"

She smiled a little. "Call me Lucy."

"Lucy. You said the reason you haven't told the Calloways the truth is because you fear for Lady Calloway?"

"Yes, partially, but—"

"She always wears herself down when she has children to worry over," Nick said, frowning. It was the first time Lucy had seen him truly affected by something. Though he wasn't meeting her gaze, she could still see the anxiety in the man's eyes. "Lady C. has a good deal to worry about right now, what with William still fevered and Simon cracking under the pressure of his role."

"Simon?" Lucy's heart beat an erratic rhythm in her chest as soon as she heard the man's name. "What's wrong with Simon?"

For some reason, that question made Nick smile, changing his entire countenance. All his worry had been replaced by something closer to amusement. "Calloway finds himself with too much to do and not enough time to do it," he said, his words light. "You seem to be the only person able to convince him to take a break now and then, even if swimming in the pond is rather . . . unconventional."

Lucy had been doing everything she could to forget the events at the pond, but Nick's words brought her memory right to the forefront—particularly Simon holding her close and protecting her from drowning. She had felt so safe, just as she had from the moment she'd arrived at Calloway Park. But in Simon's arms, the feeling had been magnified tenfold.

Rising back to his feet, Nick looked even more amused than before. He must have seen the blush that spread across Lucy's face, as there was little she could do to hide it. But what did he think her redness meant? Lucy didn't even know why she felt warm all over at the thought of being in Simon's arms.

Then again, perhaps that was just another of her lies. She had her suspicions of how she truly felt about the baron, even if she refused to acknowledge them. Leaving would be easier if she never admitted how deeply she was starting to care for all things Calloway.

"How did you know?" she asked. "That I am not really engaged to William, I mean."

Folding his arms, Nick smiled a little. "You said so. At the inn in Downingham. You even mentioned something that first morning we met. And maybe the others didn't believe you, but I know a liar when I see one, and a liar you are not—outside of playing this role you've fallen into, of course. My whole life is a lie, Lucy, for the same reasons your current situation is, I would imagine. There is still something you're hiding, but . . . I am sure you have your reasons for not telling me." He shrugged. "I recognized a person trapped because it is what I see every day in the mirror, and that is not a life I wish on anyone."

Before Lucy could comment on that revelation, Nick chuckled, as if recalling some joke he had only now understood. "As I was saying, I do not think you should tell the Calloways the truth just yet. This may turn out better than I'd hoped."

That didn't make any sense. "But surely I can't—"

"If you tell Lady Calloway that her son is likely to leave again as soon as he is strong enough, she is going to wither away to nothing. William leaving is inevitable, but she'll start to improve as soon as he wakes. A little strength will soften the blow to her. Besides, this is far too entertaining to stop it all now, and there's something I would like to figure out before you go throwing the truth into the mix."

Well, Lucy didn't like the sound of that, and she jumped to her feet once more, hoping to give herself some confidence when she argued with this man, who seemed to think he was always in the right. "I am glad my painful circumstances, as well as the health of that lovely woman, are amusing to you, sir," she snapped.

To her dismay, that comment only amused him more, so that his eyes glittered with mirth. "I deserve that," he said, "but that isn't what I meant. I have every concern for Lady Calloway, and as for you . . . well, I didn't mean what you think I did."

"What else could you possibly have meant?"

But he moved for the door, speaking as he went. "You will figure it out soon enough, I imagine."

"Nicholas Forester, you get back here and explain yourself!"

But he was already gone.

Lucy groaned, unsure of how she was to proceed. She had been quite determined to tell Simon the truth, but Nick had some reason she shouldn't. That man was a habitual liar, so she probably would do better not to listen to a word he said, but . . . he knew she was still hiding something, and unless she wanted him to get mixed up with Mr. Granger and be in danger like the Calloways, she should appease him however she could.

After the maid returned to look after William, Lucy trudged back to her own room to change for her excursion with Simon. Whatever Nick thought, he knew nothing of Lucy's dwindling time line, and though she was torn, she began to prepare herself to tell Simon the truth.

Rebecca was waiting for her there, and though Lucy was usually glad for the familiar face, her mounting frustration only grew at the sight of the maid. She couldn't forget she was only in this mess because of Rebecca. Assuming she had managed to avoid Mr. Granger, she could have been a few days into her employment with the Winthrop family by now—a family she should have written to as soon as Mr. Granger had found her.

It wasn't like she could explain her situation though. *My sincerest apologies, Mr. Winthrop. I have been detained due to a powerful and wealthy family believing me engaged to their son who is currently laid up with fever and uncertain to wake, all while avoiding your friend Jonathan Granger so he does not carry me off. You might even go along with his plan and help him, so I'm too afraid to arrive in the first place.* No, whatever she said in a letter to the Winthrops would have been another lie, and Lucy had done that enough.

Now she was without employment or recommendation, and her best chance at a future was a man who was forcing her into a marriage by threatening the only people she cared about.

"You don't look well, Miss Lucy," Rebecca said as she helped Lucy into a sturdier dress for the short trip to William's estate. She had started calling Lucy that yesterday, and Lucy hated it. It made her feel more important than she was. "Is something wrong?"

What a stupid question. "Everything is wrong," Lucy said on a sigh, flopping into the nearest chair. "Rebecca, I can't keep doing this. I can't keep lying."

"But you can't tell the truth, miss!"

"Of course I can. And I should!"

Rebecca was hardly done arguing, and she even put her hands on her hips to further her point. "But, Lucy, Mr. Granger—"

"Mr. Granger already knows I'm here."

That had been the wrong thing to say, and Lucy knew it. She had purposefully been keeping her encounter with him in Downingham a secret from Rebecca, knowing she would react exactly as she did: the maid turned frightfully pale and sank onto the bed. "He knows?" she whispered. "You saw him?"

Lucy swallowed. "Yes, I spoke to him."

"And?" When Lucy didn't answer, Rebecca turned ashen. "Lucy, he is going to take you like he took—" But she stopped herself midsentence, biting the inside of her lips.

Lucy's stomach twisted. "Rebecca?"

The maid's head dropped. "A few years ago, before you came, Mr. Granger fancied one of the kitchen girls. And what Mr. Granger wants . . ."

"He gets," Lucy finished, pressing her hands to her stomach. "What happened to her?"

Tears pooled in Rebecca's eyes. "She thought he loved her. And when she became with child, the Grangers wouldn't listen when she said who the father was. They turned her out without a reference, thinking she was lying because he said he had never met her before."

"That's horrible. And you're sure it was Mr.—"

"The way he looks at all of us," Rebecca whispered. "We were just glad none of us caught his fancy like Dottie. Until . . ."

Lucy swallowed. "Until me. But five years, and he never did anything to me. He never—" Well, he had kissed her in the street two days ago. And his eyes had taken on a hungry look she'd never seen before, like he had gotten a taste of something he desperately wanted more of.

Rebecca shook her head. "One of the stableboys saw a man lurking about the Park last night and chased him off. What if it was Mr. Granger?"

Shuddering, Lucy pulled on the half boots Olivia had loaned her. Surely Mr. Granger wouldn't think to keep such a close eye on her, would he? Not when the Calloways had so many servants about. He had said he would give her three days to admit the truth, and she still had another day after today before he followed through.

"I am going to tell Lord Calloway the truth about the engagement," Lucy said, though she wasn't feeling as confident about that decision now. Learning what she had about Mr. Granger had made her realize that she was dealing with more than a lovesick fool. The man was truly dangerous, and his threats to the Calloway family were therefore just as real.

But the thought of Simon's expression as soon as she told him reminded her how badly he needed someone to remind him to slow down now and then.

What would he do without someone to help him breathe a little? The truth would only add to his stress, and even Nick could see he was on the verge of falling apart.

"Once I tell the truth," Lucy muttered, "it won't matter if Mr. Granger is lurking about, because we will no longer be here. We will be on our way elsewhere."

Poor Rebecca had given up her place at the Granger household, but Lucy finally understood why. Where would she go now? Where would *Lucy* go?

The maid grabbed her hand. "I'm begging you, Lucy. Don't tell him. But if you do, at least wait until you've gone out, in case Granger is around looking for you."

They would hardly be gone long enough for that logic to make sense, but Lucy nodded. "I will consider it," she said. It was as much as her guilt-ridden stomach could handle.

She found Simon in the entryway with Olivia in her riding habit, both of them bickering as they had the other morning at breakfast. But they both smiled as well, and Lucy had never seen Olivia looking so pleased with herself.

At the sight of Lucy on the stairs, Olivia bounded over and took her hands. "You'll never guess!"

Lucy could guess rather easily, based on the exasperated smile Simon wore. "You are to have your race?"

Olivia jumped up, her excitement too much for her to hold still. "He agreed to race me tomorrow. Is that not wonderful? I need to go tell Mr. Forester!" And off she went, leaving Lucy and Simon alone.

Lucy couldn't help but grin at the man, despite all the thoughts rolling around in her head. "I am glad you finally set a time for your race," she said. "Your sister has talked of little else since I arrived."

Clearing his throat, Simon looked more uncomfortable than happy, his countenance much changed from a moment ago. "It was long overdue," he said. "Though, I fear she may actually beat me this time."

"I suppose it would be good for you to come in second for once," Lucy joked. It was so easy to make jests with this man that she couldn't help herself. "I imagine you are used to being the first in everything."

"Not everything." He pierced her with a look of such longing that something sparked to life in her chest, warm and heavy. What did he mean by that?

"Simon, I—"

"I owe you my gratitude."

That caught her so off guard that she took a step back, something that seemed to frustrate Simon as his eyes tracked her movement. "For what?"

He ducked his head. "The housekeeper told me you've been looking after my mother and making sure she rests. I am ashamed to admit I have neglected her care."

"But you have seen to everything else, my lord," Lucy argued, though she winced when he made a face at the title. "Surely no one could expect you to remember every small detail when you already have so much to worry about."

"My mother's health is not a small detail." He reached out and took hold of her hand, momentarily freezing her in place when she realized he was again not wearing gloves. Though she wore her own, she could still feel the warmth of his fingers around hers. "I offer you my thanks, Lucy. For that and for being such a dear friend to Olivia at a time when she badly needs one."

Lucy had no idea what to say to that, knowing she was moments away from telling the man she had been lying to him and his family from the start. That she had put them in danger simply by being there.

Simon, it seemed, had more to say, however, and he stepped closer, making up the space she'd put between them. "I have not been good at showing it, but I am glad you'll be joining my family. You've been so good to all of us. Even Forester. He seems to be less his usual ridiculous self when you're around, which is a miracle unto itself."

Simon was gazing at Lucy so intently that she found it difficult to breathe. It was as if his eyes had stolen the air right out of her lungs.

"And what of you?" she whispered. "Have I been good to you?" He would say no, and it would give her the perfect chance to explain why.

"Me?" Somehow he managed to move even closer so that they were only inches apart, with their hands still clasped together. "I couldn't say."

Under no circumstances should Lucy have been disappointed by that response, but she was. She wanted to think she had been a boon to Simon when he'd so badly needed one. Pulling away, she ignored the way he seemed to lean toward her again, because clearly he had no reason to want to be around her outside of thinking they were soon to be related.

If she didn't tell him the truth now, she might lose her nerve. "Simon—"

"I have a confession." He spoke so loudly and quickly that he seemed to surprise even himself, turning red and clasping his hands behind his back.

"Oh?" Lucy hadn't known how to react to this man from the beginning, and she feared she would never fully understand him. That didn't stop her from wanting to try.

He nodded. "Yes, I . . . that is to say, I have an admission."

"About?"

"My reasons for you being here. I mean, for my meeting you here to take you to Penworth. That is, I have to admit to my motivation for wanting to . . ."

"What is it?" Lucy couldn't help but be both nervous and intrigued. She had wondered why he would be so intent on taking her to a house that didn't belong to her.

The words seemed right on the tip of his tongue, stuck there in a way that made her nerves grow. "I, well, I thought perhaps you were not being entirely truthful." He grimaced, as if bracing himself for her anger and hurt.

And Lucy *was* hurt, but only because she knew she could no longer keep her secrets. She had thought perhaps Simon suspected her, but now she knew for sure, and her dream was over.

"Lord Calloway . . ."

He rushed forward so quickly that her hands were in his again before she could react. "Please forgive me, Lucy. You do not deserve such treatment when you have given few reasons for my suspicions, and I feel awful. I hope you will still allow me to take you to William's estate and give you a tour of your future home, as I am sure you need the distraction as much as I do. No pretenses. No expectations. Just . . ." He swallowed. "Just you and me . . . and a chaperone."

Though shocked by his stream of repentant words, Lucy nearly laughed at that last bit. They hadn't intentionally had a chaperone during her entire stay, so she wasn't sure why he'd decided they should have one now.

But that thought disappeared as she looked into the man's hopeful eyes, and she realized what he had said. He wanted to spend time with her. He wanted to bring her to William's estate, essentially alone, and spend an afternoon with her for no reason other than to give her a glimpse at what he thought would be her happy future.

And Lucy wanted to say yes. "We can bring my maid," she said, grinning when a smile lit up Simon's handsome face.

Bringing Rebecca would mean it would be next to impossible to tell Simon her secret, but perhaps Lucy had known that before she made the suggestion. Perhaps she wanted a little longer with this man before she had to let him go. Couldn't she be selfish for one day more?

As if he just realized he still held her hands, Simon cleared his throat and released her. "My apologies," he said, then rushed over to direct the butler to send for Rebecca. That taken care of, he returned to her side and offered his arm. "The carriage is waiting out front, and your maid can join us as soon as she is ready. The sky is lovely. That is, the weather today is quite pleasant, if you would like to wait outside."

Sliding her arm through his, Lucy pretended a shiver of delight didn't run through her at the contact. It recalled to mind again the moment at the pond yesterday, when he had looked at her with such tenderness.

"I would like that, thank you," she said. "I confess I am rather fond of the grounds here."

Simon brightened the instant they stepped out into the sun, his eyes sparkling as he gazed at the sky. "I know I said this before, but I have never been happier than when I'm home. These lands are a comfort I have found nowhere else in the world."

Lucy had always thought anywhere would be better than wherever she was, but after spending several days here with the Calloways, she had definitely started to understand his position. If she lived here, in such a beautiful place, she wouldn't want to leave. She already didn't want to leave.

"You belong at the Park," Lucy agreed. Simon was a part of this place; she couldn't picture Calloway Park without him, even if he spent most of his time in London or traveling elsewhere.

They had reached the waiting coach, and now that they were within view of the driver, Simon pulled his arm free. Lucy felt his absence more acutely than she would have liked, under the circumstances, though she forced herself not to think about what her disappointment might mean. Nothing could happen between her and Simon, even if she wished it to. They were too far apart in station, and Simon would undoubtedly hate her once she told him the truth.

She clung to the smallest hope that he would forgive her, even if they did not continue their tentative friendship.

"What are you so deep in thought about?"

Lucy glanced over at Simon, smiling at the curious look he gave her. If she pretended they had simply met in passing, while traveling perhaps, and were not from such different worlds, she could imagine him giving her this look quite often.

"I am contemplating what will become of us when William wakes," she said truthfully.

Simon frowned, as if he hadn't even considered the idea, and though he opened his mouth to say something, a different voice cut through the small space between them.

"I am ready, miss!" Rebecca slid to a stop at Lucy's side and dipped into an unsteady curtsy, her chest heaving as if she had run the length of the house. She probably had, now that Lucy thought about it, and she seemed all too pleased to interrupt their conversation. "You must be so excited to see your future home, Miss Lucy," she added for good measure.

Lucy groaned at the same time Simon raised an eyebrow. It was odd enough to have a maid be so outspoken and obvious, but calling her Miss Lucy was another reason for Simon to return to those suspicions he had only just relinquished. Lucy had only wanted a few more moments with the man before she admitted the truth, and she had just condemned herself to an afternoon of lying through her teeth as she tried to skirt around Rebecca's unwavering insistence that she do so.

"Well, I suppose we should . . . ," Simon said, but though he offered his hand to assist Lucy and Rebecca into the carriage, he hadn't stopped frowning yet. Lucy longed to smooth out the wrinkle that had formed between his eyebrows. "Shall we?" he added.

"Yes, my lord!" Rebecca said, far too loudly for someone who should have remained silent. "Miss Lucy is most eager."

The wrinkle on Simon's brow deepened, driving Lucy mad. "Yes, you've said."

"Yes," Lucy agreed, trying to send Rebecca a look of warning. It might have succeeded if the maid had looked her direction.

Instead, Rebecca grabbed hold of Simon's waiting hand and hopped into the carriage.

Lucy did not move as quickly, knowing the journey was going to be agonizing. Why on earth had she suggested Rebecca as their chaperone? It could have been anyone, and she had chosen the one person who wanted her to keep up the lie. Well, one of two. If Nick had come with them, who knows what might have—

"Might I join you, Calloway?"

Simon and Lucy turned back toward the house in tandem right as the confusing Mr. Forester himself reached the bottom of the stairs. Though Simon's expression hadn't changed, Lucy had the sudden urge to slap Nick across the face. He stood there with far too much mischief in his eyes, and undoubtedly he had concocted some scheme he wished to put into play.

Whatever plan he had come up with, Lucy wasn't keen to see it play out. "Surely you have better things to do with your day," she said, trying to sound as if their excursion would be utterly dull.

Unfortunately, her attempt backfired, leaving Nick biting back a laugh and Simon looking far too dejected. "We don't have to go, Lucy," Simon said quietly. The sunlight in his soul had been dimmed by the cloud cover of disappointment, leaving him gray and lifeless.

It broke Lucy's heart, and she quickly put her hand on his arm and gave it a squeeze. "Of course we should go," she said, though she feared her smile was as false as Nick's was amused. "I would like to see Penworth, if you're still willing to show me. I only meant I can't imagine Nick would find much entertainment in it."

"On the contrary," Nick said without hesitation. "This little jaunt of yours promises far more entertainment than anything I could find here."

Simon's eyes had slid to where Lucy's hand rested, and it seemed to take him a great deal of effort to lift his gaze to his friend. "I believe Lucy is right, Forester. Touring William's estate is far from your usual pursuits."

"Exactly why it sounds so amusing." Nick stepped around the pair of them and peered into the carriage, where Rebecca sat waiting. "You are Lucy's lady's maid, are you not?"

"I am, sir."

"If you don't mind, I have a question for you, the answer to which would be most thrilling for the drive over. May I?" He gestured to the seat next to her, then hopped inside, even though he should have waited until Lucy was in the coach before alighting. Then again, Nick had never seemed one for following the rules, so Lucy shouldn't have been surprised that he would disregard so many standards of conduct. "Tell me," he said as soon as he was situated. "What is the most difficult part of being a lady's maid?"

"Sometimes I wonder why I put up with him," Simon muttered.

Lucy would have responded if she hadn't looked up into the man's face and realized the cloud had gone, replaced by a small smile of genuine friendship. Simon liked Nick's oddities, and Nick was good for him. Maybe if Lucy charged Nick with looking after his friend when she was gone, Simon would be okay.

She would discuss the matter with him after they returned from Penworth. For now, Lucy would simply have to hold herself together and pray she could survive the next few hours. When Simon helped her into the carriage and settled beside her close enough that their knees brushed, she knew that would take all her courage and concentration.

Chapter Twenty-One

If not for Forester and the maid's endless conversation during the short drive to Penworth, Simon was sure the coach would have remained silent. Lucy kept her eyes out the window, as did he, and neither seemed inclined to continue the conversation they had been having before the others joined them. Perhaps they should have left the maid behind, as Forester served enough as a chaperone to keep Simon and Lucy from being alone.

Honestly, he wouldn't have even thought one necessary if Forester hadn't confronted him that morning. He and Lucy hadn't had one before now—though they were hardly ever on their own—and Simon had only wanted to get to know his future sister-in-law better. But the longer he knew Lucy, the more difficult he found it to keep his imaginations and hopes to himself. And if Forester's assertions were correct, Simon was not being subtle about how he was starting to feel.

She is to marry William, he reminded himself for the thousandth time. The words hadn't done him much good, however, and he hated that he even had to tell himself anything of the sort. He shouldn't have even looked at Lucy with any sort of intention, but ignoring her was next to impossible.

She got under his skin. Despite his lingering misgivings about her, something about her forced him to reconsider bachelorhood. He had feared perhaps it was simply jealousy—not for her specifically but for William's life in general. William had always had freedom and joy in a way Simon could only dream of. He had only responsibility for himself, and he had lived his life well with that knowledge. And now he was settling down. He had found himself a wife and would soon have children running about to spoil and laugh with and watch grow.

Simon wanted all of that. He always had.

The problem was he was starting to want all of that with Lucy. The one woman he couldn't have.

If he really thought about his feelings toward her, his aversion to her marrying William had nothing to do with general envy. He had to admit that he loved the way she challenged him. The way she saw his struggles and didn't belittle him for them but found ways to help him. He loved her mind and her kindness and the way she had him questioning his whole life like no one else ever had. He had never met anyone like her.

She wasn't right for William. Or, rather, William wasn't right for her. She needed someone who would see her potential and pull it out of her instead of keeping her in her place. Her place was on equal footing with whichever man was lucky enough to be hers.

Like Mother had been with Father.

He could feel Lucy next to him, even if he refused to look at her. This road was less maintained than the one to Downingham, and she had been struck with the same inability to remain planted in her seat as before. She fought it like she had the last time, but every once in a while, she bounced against Simon, each touch more agonizing than the last.

It was good that Forester had come. The maid—Rebecca?—would have been enough to maintain propriety, but Forester sitting across from them, occasionally glancing over, kept Simon from pulling Lucy into his arms to keep her steady. Such a show of familiarity would have pushed their odd relationship into something wholly different from what they shared now, and he would have had no explanation for it. As her future brother-in-law, he could not hold the woman in his arms like he had at the pond without certain implications.

And that was a line he refused to cross again. He would not have his brother return to the living only to discover Simon had overstepped his duty as host. It would not be fair to William or to Lucy.

"Do you think the house will be open, Simon?" Forester asked.

Simon pulled his gaze away from the window, making sure to keep Lucy just out of view. Not easily done. It helped that his friend's question confused him; they had already discussed this. "I suppose that depends on when William planned to return home."

Forester nodded. "What was the plan, Lucy?"

Why did that question evoke such heat into her face? "Oh," she squeaked, "well, I'm not entirely sure."

"Mr. Calloway did all the planning," Rebecca offered with a brief smile, though she refused to make eye contact with anyone.

"Did he now?" Forester asked. Why the devil was he so interested? "From my understanding, William planned to stay at the Park only a few days, seeing as he brought so little with him and left his valet in London. Is that what he told you, Lucy?"

Now Lucy was pale, and Simon glanced between her and Forester, trying to understand the silent conversation they seemed to be having between the two of them. Had he missed something?

"When did you plan to be married?" Forester asked. He hadn't bothered to wait for an answer to the last question, though Simon didn't care about that. He wanted an answer to this one, because it would help him know how much time he would get with Lucy. As her friend, of course. Nothing more.

As the carriage slid into a hole in the road, Lucy slid directly against Simon, practically falling into his lap. "Oh, I am so sorry!" she said, still in that frightened squeak. She tried to right herself but in doing so fell against Simon's shoulder just as he turned his head in her direction to see how he might assist her.

Suddenly they were only inches apart, and he wondered what it would be like to kiss someone like Lucy. No, he wondered what it would be like to kiss *Lucy*.

"Ah, Penworth! As forlorn as always."

At Forester's words, Lucy pulled away so quickly that her head hit the side of the carriage, and Simon winced with her. He hadn't meant to make her so uncomfortable, but he really shouldn't have expected anything less. The day he didn't make a fool of himself in front of this woman would be a fine day indeed.

"Forgive me," he muttered, though he wasn't sure what, specifically, he was apologizing for. Making her come here? His inability to act rationally around her? Nearly pressing his lips to hers and hoping it wasn't the biggest mistake of his life? He slipped out of the carriage as soon as the door opened, then let Forester assist the women out, knowing he needed to avoid contact with Lucy as much as possible. He was not nearly in control of himself today, which happened far too often in her presence than he would have liked.

"It really is rather forlorn, isn't it?" Lucy's voice held far less disappointment than it did curiosity. Simon couldn't help but look back at her and see her expression. She looked up at Penworth and its ivy-covered walls with a melancholy expression, but it was as if she felt sadness for someone other than herself. Perhaps she hadn't internalized that this house would soon be hers.

She'd never answered the question about her marriage date.

And Simon was too much a coward to repeat it.

"William Calloway is so rarely at home that he cares little for his estate," Forester explained, offering his arm to Lucy as the maid trailed behind them on the short walk to the front door. "He pays a steward to look after his lands and maintain his income, but that is about all this house is good for."

"Until now," Simon offered, feeling rather useless as he followed Rebecca.

Forester glanced back but didn't acknowledge the addition. Nor did Lucy.

"It doesn't look like anyone is here, does it?" she said, peering through the nearest window.

Forester shrugged. "Like you confirmed, William planned for only a few days here in Oxfordshire, and the Park is far more comfortable for such a short visit."

Thinking back on the conversation in the carriage, Simon tried to remember what Lucy had said about William's plans. *Had* she said anything?

The look in Forester's eyes as he turned back to Simon didn't ease his uncertainty, and Simon feared he was the butt of some joke he hadn't heard. It wouldn't be the first time. "Simon," Forester said, "I suppose you'd better open up the house if we are to let the lovely Lucy see her future here. Then again, perhaps we—"

His words stopped when the door opened, revealing William's laughably young butler, Mason, in the entryway.

"Lord Calloway!" Mason said, clearly surprised by the sight of visitors. "Mr. Forester." But then his eyes landed on Lucy, and recognition set in. "And the future Mrs. Calloway!" He bowed low before opening the door wider to let them all inside.

Whatever confusion Simon was feeling, he wasn't the only one. For once, Forester was speechless, and even Lucy looked ready to run for half a second before she plastered on a smile and stepped into the house. Even the maid frowned at the reception, and she seemed to have far more answers than Lucy did.

"Forgive our unpreparedness, miss," Mason said once everyone was inside. "We didn't expect you for a couple of days yet. Mrs. Hughsley!"

The old housekeeper had been coming up the entry hall, but at the sight of guests she shuffled her feet faster until she arrived at the little gathering. "Lord Calloway," she said, though slightly out of breath, and she sank into a curtsy as low as her geriatric legs would allow. Mrs. Hughsley was practically as old as the house itself. "And Mr. Forester, I didn't expect to see you away from Town."

Forester flashed the woman a smile. "And miss coming to see you? My dear Mrs. Hughsley, you are always my favorite part of coming to see the Calloways, and you know it."

Miraculously, the housekeeper blushed a deep red at the flattery, though Simon had been sure she was no longer capable of such a thing. Then her eyes fell on Lucy, and though she wasn't as confident as Mason had been, she still said, "And you must be William's beloved. We've been so eager to meet you, Miss . . . ?"

Simon frowned. They didn't know her name? But he held his breath, waiting to see which name Lucy chose to give. Staley or Hayes? He had almost forgotten the confusion between the two.

"Lucy," Lucy said, grasping the woman's hand as Simon's disappointment left him feeling empty. "It is so lovely to meet you, Mrs. Hughsley."

"But where's William?" Mason asked, as if he only just realized the party was missing someone. "I mean, Mr. Calloway."

Simon suppressed a groan. Honestly, why had William employed a man so inexperienced? He looked no older than the two footmen who lined up with two maids and the cook, completing the whole of the Penworth staff. Simon had tried to tell his brother that he needed a proper butler who had worked in a household for longer than a decade, but Will had ignored him.

"I am afraid Mr. Calloway caught fever on the journey here," Lucy said, and she seemed pleased by the concern of the staff. "From what I saw this morning, though, he seems nearly recovered."

That would explain why she had been thinking about the future of her relationship with Simon. If William was to wake soon, things would change. The marriage would take place—when, Simon feared he would not know until the day arrived, despite the absurdity of that happening—and Lucy would leave. And Simon would be alone with his fears again, with no one to explain why he needed to purchase supplies for tradesmen who could not afford such purchases themselves.

No one to give him reasons to smile when he could find none himself.

"Lord Calloway, you're looking awfully pale," Mrs. Hughsley said with some alarm, clearly worried about the state of his health. "Shall I have Cook bring up some tea? Oh, forgive me, miss. I suppose that's a question I should be asking you now, isn't it? It has just been so long that William—Mr. Calloway—was on his own. You've no idea how excited we were when he told us he was getting himself a wife! I've never seen the boy more giddy, and he left before he even told us your name. I suppose that's what happens when a man falls in love in a matter of days, isn't it?"

Simon had mostly given up his conjectures about Lucy's engagement to William, choosing instead to trust what Lucy told him. But now he couldn't even fall back on his suspicions. Everything she had told him and his family from the beginning was true, apart from her name, and from the sound of things, the engagement had come on so suddenly that it had caught her by surprise as well. No wonder she had a difficult time explaining how things had come about.

"Perhaps we will take tea later," Lucy said quietly. "I don't want to be away from William for too long, but I would like to look around the house, if it isn't too much trouble."

This would be hers. She and William would live out their days here and have lots of little dark-haired children, and Simon would be forever resentful that his brother had found the perfect woman.

"Shall I give you the tour?" Mrs. Hughsley asked.

Lucy replied with some hesitation. "On the contrary . . ."

Simon opened his eyes when a hand touched his arm, and he was surprised to see Lucy right in front of him, her expression one of concern. There was a question in her eyes, too, and it was as if he could understand every word.

"I am well," he assured her, though when they had reached a point where he could read her thoughts, he had no idea. "Truly."

"I don't believe you," she whispered so no one else heard. Then, louder, she said, "Lord Calloway can give us the tour. I am sure he knows the house well enough, and I don't want to take you from your duties after surprising you with my visit."

"Of course," Mrs. Hughsley said, and then she and Mr. Mason both directed the servants to return to their work.

Lucy's hand still rested on Simon's arm, and he wished she would never remove it. Her touch offered a calm he had found nowhere else, and he knew that knowledge would lead to his downfall. How could he ever find anyone to compare?

Forester cleared his throat, and Lucy slipped away from Simon, leaving him feeling empty. "Mrs. Hughsley," Forester said, though his eyes roved Simon's face. "While I acknowledge the fact that Lucy holds more sway than I do, I find I am positively famished. Would it be presumptuous of me to take tea apart from the others? And Lucy's maid, here, looks rather parched and could use a spot of tea as well, if I am not mistaken. It isn't easy looking after a woman like Lucy, and she deserves a respite."

While Rebecca looked ready to argue, her eyes wide, the ever-eager Mrs. Hughsley gestured for both of them to follow her down to the kitchen. Simon stared after them, trying to understand why Forester would be so eager to accompany them to the house, only to spend the whole time in the kitchen, stuffing his face with biscuits.

"Can you manage on your own, then?" Mason asked, his eyes jumping between Simon and Lucy as if he weren't sure who to concede authority to.

Simon managed only a nod, too jumbled up by the unexpected reception to find his words.

Lucy did not have the same problem. "What an odd pair they are," she said as soon as the butler had wandered off to see to his duties.

At least it was a neutral topic, one that didn't involve him. Simon needed that until he could get his bearings. "Mrs. Hughsley has been a fixture of this house for years. Possibly since the day it was built. I tried to convince William to pension her off, but he has always been insistent that it is she who chooses to stay."

"She does seem happy to be here," Lucy agreed. "And am I mistaken in thinking the butler is—"

"Barely out of leading strings?" Simon offered a wry smile. "Mason was William's valet before he moved to Penworth. I believe he promoted him when he took himself off to London and made his townhouse his more permanent residence."

"They seem lovely."

So why didn't Lucy seem happy to meet them?

Gesturing to the nearest room, Simon figured he could still give her the tour, even if he was so full of questions that he could barely concentrate. The one at the forefront was why Forester would make such a fuss about Simon being alone with Lucy before purposefully ensuring that very thing happened. What was he about? Simon needed to think about something else. "Why did you want me to show you around the house? Mrs. Hughsley could have—"

"Mrs. Hughsley didn't look like she was about to panic."

Simon grimaced. "I was not about to panic."

Raising an eyebrow, Lucy stepped through the open door to the parlor. "You still are."

"I'm not—"

"I know you well enough by now, Simon, to know when you don't want to be in a situation."

Though his chest swelled with an uncomfortable warmth, given the circumstances, Simon couldn't bring himself to agree with her, no matter how much he wanted to. "We barely know each other, Lucy."

They moved onto the kitchen area next, not bothering to step into William's study. Neither of them seemed keen on exploring it, and they each merely peered inside.

"Then, tell me about yourself," Lucy said when they reached the kitchen. She smiled at Cook and the kitchen girl as they served Forester and Rebecca but didn't linger in this room either. It seemed this was to be a rather quick tour.

Simon was grateful for that part. This conversation wasn't exactly one that would make him feel any better about the situation, and the sooner he could get it over with, the better. "What would you like to know?"

They took the stairs up to the first floor, which contained more rooms Simon thought Lucy would enjoy, like the library and like the sitting room that looked out over the grounds.

"When you were a boy, what was your dream?"

That question stopped Simon in his tracks. "What?"

Smiling a little as she glanced back at him, she continued into the library, forcing Simon to follow if he wanted clarification. "You know. Did you hope to be wealthy or own an entire county's worth of land?"

"You think my dream would be something so monetary?" The thought rankled.

She still smiled, though, as she ran her fingers along the spines of books on one of the shelves. This library was not as impressive as the one at the Park, but Simon had to admit William had collected more books than he would have expected. Or perhaps they had simply been here from when their great-uncle had been owner of Penworth.

"I do not think so poorly of you," Lucy assured him. "I was merely offering up examples."

That didn't mean the question was an easy one to answer, though Simon did his best. "I always wanted to be a baron."

She raised an eyebrow.

"Truly. For as long as I can remember, I've wanted nothing more than to fill my father's shoes in his role as Lord Calloway."

"But not when it comes to his businesses."

If this was how he made amends for suspecting her, Simon would endure it, even if he would rather have been talking about anything else. Lucy had already learned more about Simon's reluctance with Father's businesses than he would have liked, and he was hardly in a state to defend himself now.

"I have always wanted to make my father proud," he said, even if that didn't necessarily answer her question.

She was intelligent enough to recognize he was deflecting, and that made her grin. It was a far better sight than her nervous frown, so he couldn't begrudge the reason for it too much.

"Have you ever stopped to think you have already made him proud?" she asked. "You have a flourishing estate with happy tenants, which is not something every gentleman can claim. Your mother and sister have good lives, and Olivia will never wonder whether you will sell her off to the highest bidder. You clearly want her happiness more than anything."

When had she gotten closer? No, that was him. Simon had been so desperate to listen to what she had to say that he didn't even realize he'd moved farther into the room until he was right in front of her, close enough that she reached out and put a warm hand on his chest, over his heart.

"Simon Calloway, you have a good heart, and that is not something to take lightly. I know little about your father, but I know he would be proud of the man you have become, whether or not you keep his businesses thriving."

"Oh, begging your pardon, sir."

One of the maids must have come into the room, and as Lucy pulled back to a respectable distance, Simon cursed his luck. He was desperate to hear more words of praise from her lips, and he couldn't deny how much he liked being close to her. But he had to be careful not to cross any lines he shouldn't. He was still dangerously close to betraying his brother and turning this friendship with Lucy into nothing more than a scandal. William would wake any day now, and Simon would have to watch him marry Lucy. As much as he hated it, he needed to admit the impossibility that was a future with Lucy. Preferably before he lost his heart entirely.

No wonder Forester had warned him about being alone with her. Why, then, had he made it happen now? Simon feared he would never understand that man.

"Shall we continue?" he said, gesturing for the door while the maid pretended to dust books while glancing between them.

He took Lucy through the portrait hall, which was rather small and unexceptional, given most of the family portraits were at the Park, and showed her the window that looked over the grounds. Then they moved on to the guest chambers and the family wing, and when they reached the room that would be Lucy's, Simon paused in the corridor.

She glanced back. "Are you not coming in?"

He cleared his throat. "I hardly think I need to join you in your room, Lucy. What would the staff think?" That was hardly the problem, and he knew it.

Though she seemed to consider his point, she raised one dark eyebrow and sent him a look that seemed to issue a challenge. "Are you afraid of entering a woman's unoccupied room during a house tour, Simon?"

"That's not—"

"Or are you afraid of me?"

He was terrified of her. "I'm not afraid—"

"Clearly you're afraid of something in this room."

Growling, he stomped inside and ignored the smirk on her face. He had been inside Olivia's room before, and he had seen his mother's chamber before she moved into a different room after Father died. But the chamber next to Simon's was empty now, and he had been avoiding it since taking his father's place. It had felt strange to think of stepping into the place that would be his wife's room, assuming he ever found someone to marry.

But this? This was the room of William's wife. *Lucy.* Someone Simon would never have as more than a dream.

"I don't see why it was so necessary that I come in here," he muttered, but then he started looking around the room and realizing how . . . impersonal it all felt.

Everything was gray and brown, and all of it plain. Had William really never thought to update the furnishings?

"It doesn't feel like a place anyone could be comfortable in, does it?" Lucy asked. She ran her hand across the duvet and seemed to be imagining herself in this place. "Do you know why I wanted you to come in here?"

Simon didn't bother answering, seeing as he had already given his opinion on the matter.

Lucy sent him a grimace. "I didn't want to be in here on my own. I've never been able to imagine myself being someone's wife, especially not in a place like this. It feels like a completely different life from mine, like some sort of dream that will never come true. And this room is a testament to everything I am not."

Simon had no idea what to say to that. "You can make it your own."

"Can I?"

What reason did she have to think otherwise? "Of course you can."

Sighing, Lucy moved over to the door connecting this room to William's, and she gazed at it as if planning to go into the other room. Simon had struggled to follow her into this one; under no circumstances would he go any farther. At least the door to this room was wide open; he couldn't say the same for the other.

Thankfully, Lucy merely put her hand on the door and touched her forehead to the wood. She looked miserable, and Simon hated that, but there was nothing he could do to comfort her. Not when they were in this particular room having this particular conversation. No matter how much he wanted to step forward and put his arm around her, he had to stay where he was.

"Simon," Lucy said, and her voice caught on the word, threatening to break through his already weak resolve. But then she asked a question that made his heart seem to stop. "What if I've made a huge mistake?"

Chapter Twenty-Two

Lucy was walking a dangerous line, and she knew it. But being in this room and thinking about what her life might have been if things had been different was making her consider the value of being honest. Right here. Right now. Nick and Rebecca were too far away to stop her.

Simon had been so calm after they'd started their tour, and he had spoken of difficult subjects she knew he would rather not touch. Perhaps it was ridiculous to think, but she thought maybe the man even had some tender feelings for her, with the way he watched her and seemed to hate every minute of being in this house.

She had never had anyone be jealous over her. She had no idea what to make of that possibility.

"Mistake?" he said at last. "What do you mean? I doubt you have ever made a mistake in your life, Miss Hayes."

"I've made plenty. I—" Lucy stopped, and her stomach dropped when Simon narrowed his eyes. She had never told him her real name. Where had he learned her name?

The impressive and intimidating baron was back, a stiffness in his movements as he stepped forward. Lucy had nowhere to go unless she went into William's chamber, and that seemed like a terrible idea right now. So she pressed herself up against the door as he approached like an animal who had cornered his prey.

She should have known better than to think Simon was stupid enough to miss her hints at subterfuge. She shouldn't have brought it up at all, and now she was going to pay for that mistake. She would be admitting the truth whether she wanted to or not, and he was not in the calm and peaceful mood she had hoped for when the moment came.

"How do you know that name?" she whispered, working up the courage to explain everything.

Simon shook his head, now close enough that she could smell hints of his soap. "I've been trying to forget about what I witnessed in Downingham, but it seems there was more to your interaction with Mr. Granger than you would care to admit."

Mr. Granger? Suddenly dizzy, Lucy was tempted to sink to the floor. How much had he seen and heard?

"That's right," Simon continued. "I know your little secret."

Was her name the only secret he thought he knew? Lucy prayed so. She wasn't ready for him to know the rest. It was too dangerous. "What secret is that?"

Her question seemed only to irritate Simon more, bringing him even closer than before. Lucy hadn't thought that was possible. "You are having a secret dalliance with Mr. Granger." He said it as a matter of fact.

Unable to stop herself, Lucy snorted a laugh as relief shot through her. "Dalliance? With *Mr. Granger*?" If only he knew. That was the last thing in the world she wanted. "I used a false name so I could *avoid* Mr. Granger, and you think I am involved with him?"

"He claimed you were madly in love with each other." Simon was so frustrated that he put his hands on the door on either side of Lucy's head, as if it gave him a sense of stability.

Lucy groaned. It was bad enough knowing she would have to admit her lies, but having to defend herself against the villainy of Jonathan Granger felt like torture. But she didn't know if she could trust Simon to act rationally if she told him his family was in danger. He would get himself hurt, and she would never be able to live with the guilt if that happened. "He also claims a fashion sense to rival Brummel himself."

Simon clenched his jaw, clearly not appreciating how lightly she took his accusation. "He kissed you."

"He caught me by surprise."

"You didn't fight him."

"He didn't give me a chance to! It meant nothing."

"A kiss is never nothing."

Why wouldn't he let this go? If only she had been brave enough to grow angry with Mr. Granger before he'd disappeared from that side street, Simon would have seen how little she wanted that man's attention. And perhaps Mr. Granger wouldn't have had the chance to make his threats.

But that would be worse, Lucy decided. At least this way she had an idea of his plans so she could keep the Calloways safe.

"I promise," she whispered, praying Simon believed her. "I have no understanding with Mr. Granger."

Simon leaned closer. "That isn't what I saw. Even now, simply speaking of him, you can't hide your reaction to the man. You're drawn to him."

He was going to make her say it. Tears pooling in her eyes, Lucy shook her head. "No."

"I've had enough of your lies, Lucy. Please, tell me the truth. Are you and Mr. Granger—"

"I'm terrified of Mr. Granger," Lucy gasped.

Stiffening, Simon stared at her for a long moment, as if that was so far from what he'd expected that he had no idea how to respond to her admission. But then his arms snaked around her and pulled her up against his chest in an embrace like she'd never felt before, like he could keep the entire world at bay simply by holding her.

"Tell me," he begged.

Lucy gripped the front of his jacket, her tears falling thick and fast. This was exactly how she'd hoped he would react, but she didn't deserve this level of kindness. Tucking herself deeper into his embrace, she fought her sobs and tried to focus on how it felt to be held by this incredible man. It would never happen again, and like a fool, she wanted as much as she could get before she had to give him up.

"Lucy," Simon said, his voice strained.

She took a shuddering breath. She didn't want to burden him with this, but she didn't have the strength to keep it to herself anymore. "I worked for his brother," she admitted. "For the last five years, Mr. Granger has . . ."

Simon's hold tightened as he growled, "What has he done?"

Lucy's tears intensified. "Nothing. Yet. But he is determined to marry me, and the man is relentless. He followed me from London."

Swearing under his breath, Simon seemed to shift where he stood, as if he was looking around for some way to help her. "No wonder you gave a false name," he muttered. "Does William know?"

For once, Lucy could give an honest answer, and she pulled away enough to see Simon's face when she said this part. She wanted him to see her honesty so he would know she meant it when she told him the whole truth later. "Yes, he knows. To an extent. Mr. Granger was at the inn where we stopped because of the storm."

Simon winced and let go of her, using the distance to clench his hands into fists and mutter insults to himself as he paced a bit. "Is that why he engaged himself to you?" he asked.

Lucy swallowed, unwilling to speak anything but the truth. "It is why he pretended I was his wife," she whispered, knowing how horrible that sounded.

Engaged or no, pretending to be William's wife went far beyond the bounds of propriety. "I didn't like it, but William thought it would be safer."

He pondered that, his eyebrows pulling downward. "You could have had Granger thrown from the inn."

"He hasn't technically done anything wrong."

Simon was back at her side so suddenly that she gasped, though he didn't seem to notice as he took up her hands in his. "He made you afraid for your safety and reputation," he muttered, and his eyes seemed to pierce hers with an intensity she'd never seen before. His finger brushed her cheek. "He brought these tears to your eyes. Is that not enough?"

Lucy could hardly breathe as she gazed into Simon's eyes. Since her father's death, no one had cared for her the way Simon seemed to, and her heart ached knowing she would have to leave him. She could never tell him of Mr. Granger's threat to his family, not without adding to the burdens he already carried, and it was the only way to keep him safe.

Simon shifted even closer, near enough for Lucy to breathe in the clean scent of his soap again. His eyes flickered between hers, like he was searching for something he couldn't quite see but desperately wanted to. Every second pulled him closer, until his breath brushed her lips. "Why did you not tell me before?" he whispered.

Because you're going to hate me when you learn the truth, and I could not bear to see you hurt. But Lucy couldn't say that out loud, so she said the next best thing. "I have already imposed on your family so much." She twisted out of his hold and scurried for the door before she let herself linger, but his next words made her pause.

"You *are* family, Lucy."

If only that were true.

Chapter Twenty-Three

If Simon could have guessed what would push him past the breaking point, he would have put his money on Father's businesses. Or Olivia having so many suitors he wouldn't know how to keep them away. Or a frost killing all his tenants' crops and causing a famine.

Never would he have thought a woman would be his undoing.

Not just any woman. His brother's betrothed. His future sister-in-law. The one person he could never have unless he considered the horrible notion that William might one day succumb to his fevers completely and leave her a widow.

That thought alone convinced him he was already losing his mind. He didn't want William to die! He would never want that, no matter the opportunities it would present. He was happy that his brother was happy.

But as soon as William woke, Simon would be having a conversation with the man. A stern one. For one, Lucy was absolutely terrified of Mr. Granger, which meant William had done little to ensure her safety. For another, who in his right mind would invent a marriage as a means of protection? Creating a ruse like that could only create trouble.

The worst part was how grateful Simon was for Lucy's fear. He hated that he was glad he had had a reason to pull her into his arms, where she fit so perfectly. Hated that he hadn't been able to think of a reason to let her go. Hated knowing that if she hadn't stepped away, he might have become the worst sort of cad imaginable. But for all of the reasons that made it even harder to keep his distance, he was glad she had had a valid reason for lying about her name. Glad that her character was every bit as wholesome as he'd hoped. Glad that all his suspicions had been for naught, because she had done nothing but good for his family.

But more than anything, he hated that the ache in his chest as they finished their tour—now with Mrs. Hughsley in the lead and Forester and Rebecca behind—was a clear indication that he was desperate to go back to that room and finish what he'd nearly started. What sort of man did that make him?

He was going to wring Forester's neck for leaving him alone with the intoxicating woman.

"I do hope Mr. Calloway will be well enough to come home soon," Mrs. Hughsley said loudly, breaking Simon out of a dangerous line of imaginings. "It will be ever so nice to have him here again, where he belongs."

Lucy put her hand on the old woman's arm and gave her a smile that made Simon want to step between the two so he could feel the warmth that gesture likely brought to the housekeeper. Lucy was always so kind to people, no matter their station. She was treating Mrs. Hughsley just as she treated Mother.

Simon had never seen a highborn lady act that way, and Lucy's actions proved that one's status meant little when it came to the things that mattered most.

"I am certain William will be whole any day now," Lucy said. "Then you will have him back."

"And we will be ever so glad to have you join him, miss."

Though her cheeks turned a bright red, Lucy seemed more pleased by the comment than embarrassed. "You have been wonderful today, Mrs. Hughsley. I can see why William was so keen on keeping you."

Mrs. Hughsley seemed truly touched, pressing her fingers to her mouth as if holding back tears. "Must you be going back to the Park so soon?"

Lucy turned now to Simon, who felt like he'd been punched in the gut when their eyes met. It took everything in him not to let his eyes stray to her mouth, or he would start imagining what it would feel like to kiss those lips of hers. No surprises, no distractions, just . . . every reason for him to be the worst brother in the history of the world. What was he thinking? He wasn't. Clearly.

Simon nearly slapped himself, choosing instead to bite his tongue before he let his mind wander any further. He had given himself far too many liberties upstairs, and he would not do so again, no matter how much he wanted to.

Lucy must have seen something in his face—intense pain, perhaps?—because she turned back to the housekeeper and nodded. "I should return Lord Calloway to his work, and I would hate to leave William on his own for too long."

That sounded like the truth, so why did Lucy say it with a touch of fear? William was hardly feverish today, and she would know that because she had been sitting right at his side before coming to his estate. He was out of danger now, so why would she fear to leave him?

Simon had thought he would get answers by coming to Penworth, but even though he had gotten a few, he had never been more uncertain of things in his life.

"We look forward to seeing you soon," Mrs. Hughsley said with emotion choking her words.

Mason opened the door for them and seemed to be fighting his own overwhelming gratitude for Lucy.

Either she had endeared herself to the staff as easily as she had done at the Park, or none of these people had expected William to ever settle down. Perhaps it was both.

Lucy pulled Rebecca into conversation the moment they were outside, and though Simon was tempted to hurry forward and attempt to hear what they said, he could not ignore the amused glint in Forester's eyes.

"Whatever you're thinking," Simon growled, "you're wrong."

Forester clasped his hands behind his back as they walked toward the waiting carriage. "I didn't say a word."

"Which is a first for you, I am sure."

"I was merely wondering how your tour was. It seemed to take a good deal of time to examine the chambers upstairs. Did anything of note happen?"

Though he considered telling his friend everything that had transpired, Simon had little desire to be laughed at. If he told Forester how close he had come to kissing Lucy, his friend wouldn't let him forget it. He would be forced to consider why he was so desperate to be near the woman when she was promised to William.

"Whatever happened to your lecture about being careful around Lucy?" Simon asked. "You practically threw us together." Better yet, why had Lucy even allowed his nearness?

Shrugging, Forester seemed to be admiring the landscape. "You told me you had no intentions toward the woman, so I assumed it would not matter. I only wanted to look after Lucy's maid. You didn't answer my question though. Anything of note upstairs?"

"Lucy's name is Hayes, not Staley," Simon muttered, though he hardly cared if she lied about her name. From what little he knew of Mr. Granger, her reasons for doing so made perfect sense now. It was the only part of their tour he would admit to.

Forester chuckled. "I wish I could have witnessed the conversation that came of that discovery."

Simon was immensely grateful his friend had witnessed nothing. He wasn't sure why he didn't tell Forester about Granger's fear-inducing actions, but he imagined it had something to do with his desire to help Lucy. He didn't want anyone else to receive her gratitude when he chased Granger out of town. But he would say a little about the subject, if only to excuse some of Lucy's odd behavior. "She said she used the false name to keep Granger off her scent."

Forester chuckled. "I've done the same thing many times. Well done, Lucy."

He said it loudly enough that Lucy glanced back, her face bright red, though she couldn't have heard the rest of their conversation. Her eyes searched Simon's, and he tried to tell silently her that he hadn't said a word about their shared moment.

Not that anything had happened. The ache in his chest throbbed most uncomfortably, and he worried it would not stop until he had put considerable distance between his future sister-in-law and himself.

As before, Forester helped Rebecca inside the carriage and climbed in after her, leaving Simon and Lucy momentarily alone. Unsure of what he might say to her, Simon offered his hand, which she took with a smile that left him dizzy.

She paused with her foot on the step, however, and looked back at him. "Thank you, Simon."

"For what?" he choked out. He did his best to sound normal despite the very real distraction that was Lucy's hand resting in his. She wore gloves, but he could feel her warmth anyway. This was the opposite of distance. Did she not understand that he needed to be as far from her as possible?

Lucy smiled. "For bringing me here and showing me William's home."

William's home. Why not *her* home?

"And for understanding," she added. She leaned over and touched only a whisper of a kiss to his cheek, but it was still enough to make his heart try to pound out of his chest.

Once again, they were forced to sit beside each other, something Forester seemed to find amusing. Simon kept his eyes on the window again as the coach rolled forward. Knowing she was only a few inches away would help nothing, but he hoped he would be able to hold himself together as long as he ignored her as much as possible.

"Simon, may I say something?" Lucy spoke quietly, keeping her volume below that of Forester and Rebecca, who yet again chatted away like they were the best of friends.

Suppressing a groan, Simon looked Lucy's way only long enough to discern whether she was looking at him. She was, and he felt exposed under her dark gaze. "Of course," he said, though he wanted to deny her the chance to further destroy him.

She shifted a little closer, which Simon only knew because he swore he could feel every inch between them as it disappeared. "I am not sure you will like this comment, so I am still trying to decide whether I should speak it or keep it to myself."

"When have you ever kept something to yourself?" Simon grimaced as soon as the words left his mouth, and he glanced over at Lucy in time to see the hurt in her eyes. "Lucy, I didn't mean—"

"You know nothing about me, Simon."

And it was probably better if it stayed that way. "At this point, you know everything about me," he grumbled.

"I know you are unhappy."

A ringing entered Simon's ears, drowning out the sounds of the road and the other conversation, leaving only Lucy. "I am happy," he argued.

She made a face of disbelief. "You're miserable. Trust me; I've been miserable for five years. I know it when I see it."

Though he opened his mouth to argue, Simon couldn't find any words to use for his defense. Was he miserable? He couldn't call himself overjoyed by his life, but neither did he hate the day-to-day. He wished to focus on what she'd said of her own misery. If she truly had been living under the gaze of Mr. Granger for the last five years, he wanted to pummel the man for doing anything to hurt her. What kind of man professed love but only evoked terror?

"See? I knew you wouldn't be able to argue." She sounded a little too proud of herself, so Simon sat up a little straighter. Perhaps he would use his anger toward Granger to his advantage, as something told him this was about to turn into an argument.

"What reason have I to be miserable?" he said, keeping his voice low. "I have a loving mother, a wonderful sister, and an estate that has always done well. My tenants are happy, and my father's businesses are thriving. Most of them, anyway. My life is perfectly idyllic."

Lucy smirked. "Idyllic for whom, Simon? Because I know it isn't utopia for you, or you would actually smile once in a while."

That comment seemed to slap him across the face. "I smile."

"Hardly. And I know your mother notices as easily as I do."

That was exactly what Simon didn't need, and he squirmed in his seat. It seemed to be taking an exceedingly long time to return to the Park, and he was glad Forester and Rebecca were still deep in conversation. "What do you know of my family, Miss Hayes?" Maybe he could end this conversation before she dug too deep.

But Lucy simply smiled, making him squirm even more because she was too beautiful for him to be anything but nervous around her. "More than you, I am starting to think," she said, keeping her voice too soft for the others to hear. "Otherwise, you would have raced your sister long before now, and you wouldn't try so hard to be your father. They don't need your father, Simon. They need you."

She spoke with such conviction that Simon almost believed her. Almost. His father had been the best of men, with a good heart and a solid head on his shoulders. Simon was only a fraction of him and would never live up to the legacy he had left behind.

"You are speaking nonsense," he muttered, knowing full well that she would argue. "You have no idea what my family needs."

"I know what they do not need. They do not need the man who rides his horse like he can escape his life if only he goes fast enough. They do not need the one who works himself to the bone trying to run businesses he would do better to sell. They do not need a shadow of the man they knew before he lost his father far too young. They need the man who works the fields so he can understand those who care for them. Who would see to his sister's every happiness and who takes in a friend who does not have the heart to be alone. They need Simon."

If he hadn't been in love with Lucy before, he certainly was now, and that was a terrible state to be in when there was nothing he could do about it.

This woman was going to be the death of him, but he was done trying to stop it. Let him meet his end at the hands of a woman he could never have.

"You seem to have such a high opinion of me," he said and forced a smile, though he managed to lift only half his mouth, so it probably looked lopsided. "You are the only one."

Reaching over, Lucy hesitated just a moment before she took hold of his hand and gripped it tight. "Sometimes you are so blinded by your insecurities that you can't see your own value, so you have to let others see it for you."

Simon might have done something he would regret if the carriage hadn't come to a stop just then. But that didn't keep him from locking his eyes on Lucy and taking her in for as long as he could. No one had ever looked at him the way she did. No one had ever given him reason to think he was worth something more than his title and his money. No one had made him feel like he could live a life he was actually proud of.

But Lucy did. No matter what agony his future would be without her, he was better for knowing her.

"What is Miss Calloway doing?" Forester said, breaking their connection.

Simon looked over just as Olivia flung the carriage door open, her eyes wide as she gasped, "You must come quick!"

Simon climbed out first so he could assist Lucy, and then he forced himself to forget the last few hours so he could focus on the immediate need. Olivia was crying. "What's happened?" he demanded as he hurried toward the house, leaving Forester to assist the maid. Lucy was right on his heels, for which he was grateful. He needed her confidence in him so he could know what to do. "Olivia!"

"It's William."

Simon stopped dead—Lucy did the same—and looked back at his teary sister. She smiled. They were tears of joy, which meant William was healed and whole again. Awake. "He's awake," he said, if only to confirm what he already knew.

He turned to Lucy, who had gone a little pale as she stared at the house, and he fought his first instinct to take her hand. They would have to face this alone. They would have to face everything alone from here on out, and something told him neither of them would handle that very well.

"Come," Simon said gently, and he offered his arm when he saw her trembling. She looked as if she might collapse. As much as it would hurt him, he would see to it that she made it up to her beloved in one piece. "William will be exceedingly glad to see you."

Lucy hesitated, her eyebrows close together as she looked at his arm. "He will be something," she replied.

Whatever that meant, Simon said a silent prayer that they would both survive this and come out the other side intact.

Chapter Twenty-Four

If Simon hadn't been guiding Lucy's every step—and quite possibly holding her just tight enough to prevent her from slipping away—she would have turned tail and run. Instead, she was moving ever closer to William's bedchamber and her ultimate downfall.

After the way Simon had held her at Penworth, she had almost told him everything in the carriage. With Nick there, perhaps together they might have kept Simon from doing something reckless. But she had taken the path of the coward and told Simon he wasn't happy, as if she had any right to tell the man how he felt.

Now she was half a corridor away from the whole family collectively learning the truth about her deception and throwing her from the house because she hadn't admitted to everything herself.

Olivia was ahead of them and slipped into the room, leaving Simon and Lucy alone once more. Nick must have remained downstairs to give the family some privacy. Now was her chance, and she would have to take it.

"Simon," she said and pulled him to a stop.

He released her arm enough to turn to face her. "Lucy."

Tell him the truth, Lucy told herself. "Things are going to change," she said instead. It wasn't another lie, at least.

Simon gave her a gentle smile. "I will always value your friendship," he said.

Friendship. If nothing else, Lucy now knew where she stood with this wonderful, beautiful man. Their closeness at William's had been nothing more than a demonstration of his goodness and desire to protect her, just as it had been at the pond. She was reaching for something, but no matter how far she leaned in to it, she would undoubtedly fall flat on her face because he would not be there to catch her. Not in the way she wanted.

"Shall we go see how our invalid fares?" he asked.

It took everything in her to keep her tears at bay, but Lucy nodded. There was little point in delaying the inevitable now.

Lady Calloway stretched out her hand as soon as they entered, which Lucy took with some measure of hesitation, and pulled her into a tight side hug. "Isn't this wonderful?" Lady Calloway whispered, looking more alive than she had all week. "We are finally all together as we should be."

Goodness, the truth would cut this woman deep.

Lucy swallowed, unable to bring herself to look at the bed just yet. She would savor this feeling of having a family who cared for her and welcomed her.

She would lose it all the moment she acknowledged William.

Unfortunately, Olivia felt the need to hasten that moment. "Look, William. It's Lucy!"

"Your fiancée," Simon offered, as if he thought William might need the clarification. He wasn't wrong.

Fighting a grimace, Lucy finally lifted her eyes to the bed. Her gaze was met with one of blue, and for a moment William seemed to panic as they stared at one another. But then recognition set in, and his eyebrows pulled low over an expression of relief.

"My fiancée," he repeated.

Lucy offered a smile that she hoped conveyed her deep regret for what had happened without tipping off the rest of the family. "I am so glad to see you well again," she said softly.

His eyes, still dulled from his fever, searched the room. Whatever he was looking for, he brightened a little and attempted to sit up a little higher. "I know you're all happy to see me, but I was wondering if I could have a moment alone with . . . my betrothed." He shot Lucy a look that told her to stay silent.

She had no desire to disobey.

"Of course, dear," Lady Calloway said, though she seemed as reluctant to leave as Lucy was for the others to stay. "Olivia, let's leave the young couple alone, shall we?"

For some reason, she glossed right over Simon as she shuffled Olivia out of the room, and he seemed to be considering that as an invitation to remain. He met Lucy's eyes and almost seemed to be asking her if she wanted him to stay.

Yes, she might have said if it wouldn't have meant Simon learning the truth in the worst way. *Please never leave.*

But then Simon turned his gaze to William, and his expression immediately hardened. "You and I will have a talk later, Will," he said, and then he turned on his heel and left, closing the door behind him.

But not all the way. He left the door a fraction of an inch open, which made Lucy breathe a little easier. She had no reason to fear William, but now that they were not pretending—now that William was actually awake—being alone with him at his sickbed could not be seen as innocent as it had before.

The time had come to begin clearing the air, and Lucy couldn't even find her voice.

But William could. "I am sorry."

Lucy searched his face for any sign that he might not mean what he said. She found nothing but sympathy, and that made her feel worse. If William truly was a good man, like she suspected, she could not push all blame onto him.

"Will you sit?" William asked when she remained silent.

She eyed the chair, unsure whether that would be the best course of action.

"There can hardly be more scandal than there already is, can there? I would come to you if I thought I could stand. Please sit, and we can figure out what to do now."

Lucy only agreed to his request because her legs trembled beneath her. Even talking to Nick, she hadn't felt the full scope of her situation, but now everything was right in front of her. *William* was right in front of her, looking so much like Simon but so different as well.

William was thinner, and not only because of his recent illness. He didn't have the muscle his brother had gained by working the fields. His face was sharper as well, and his eyes were brighter, and he had the mouth of someone who used it often. Whether that was for good or bad, Lucy couldn't say, but it was not a mouth she imagined kissing. She felt nothing as she looked over this man. Even after pretending to be his betrothed for several days, she could only think about how he wasn't Simon.

"I don't mean to be indelicate," William said, and he watched her carefully as he spoke. "But how exactly did my family come to think you are my fiancée? Why would you—"

"The innkeeper," Lucy said. She didn't want to hear his accusation any more than she wanted to admit to her part in things. "When you fell ill, he sent a message ahead to your family and informed them you and your wife would be arriving shortly. I only intended to see you home safely before continuing on my way, but then your mother greeted me."

William's lips curled in a tired smile. "And she overwhelmed you." It was not a question.

Lucy's smile was only slightly wider than his. "The whole family welcomed me in before I could get a word out to explain the mistake, and it was my maid who said I was your fiancée, thinking I should use your family to hide from the acquaintance I was eager to get away from when we met at the inn. And I couldn't . . . I didn't want to . . . your family is wonderful, William. Mr. Calloway, I mean."

And before she knew it, she couldn't hold her words back. "Your mother is the kindest woman I have ever known, with such a gentle heart, and I haven't known that kind of love since I was a child. And Olivia is the sister I have always wanted, and I cannot express how fond I am of that sweet girl, who never once questioned my worth. And Simon . . ."

"Simon?" William repeated the name with a raised eyebrow, perhaps a little too intrigued for Lucy's liking. The last thing she needed right now was someone guessing her feelings for a man she could never have.

"Lord Calloway has been a gracious host." She tried to sound aloof. "He insisted I use his Christian name, considering he thinks we are soon to be related."

William's other eyebrow joined the first, rising high on his forehead. "I never would have thought my high-and-mighty brother would stoop to such familiarity," he muttered. "He has always thought himself above everyone else, with his title and his fortune and those ridiculous little hobbies he calls businesses."

It felt like a fist had closed around Lucy's heart as she listened, but no matter how much it hurt to hear such things being said about Simon, she suddenly understood the brothers a little more. "Have you ever wanted to work with Lord Calloway's businesses?" she asked, even though it was hardly her place to ask such a thing.

William managed a small shrug, though he grimaced with the effort. "Running a shipyard is hardly a profession for a gentleman." He shifted where he sat against the headboard, likely trying to get more comfortable.

"That didn't stop your father," Lucy pointed out.

"Father also had a barony to keep up his social standing. Besides, I hardly want for funds." He turned slightly red as he met Lucy's gaze. "Forgive me. I should never talk about money or business in front of a woman. That is not your place."

Simon hadn't had the same opinion, and Lucy loved him for it. He had welcomed her thoughts on the subject and had listened to her. He had made her feel like an equal.

"So what are we to do?" Lucy asked quietly, deciding it would be best to move on to another subject. "I have tried so many times to tell your family the truth, but I fear it may be too late to salvage whatever reputation I have left."

Grimacing, William nodded. "I take full blame for what has happened. You didn't want my lie, but I pushed you into it. I'm afraid I've ruined any hope you had for a future." He seemed genuinely sorry about that. "No man will want you if he learns about this deception."

Lucy scowled. "I do not appreciate your bluntness, sir."

"Being blunt is necessary. I have put you into an impossible situation, and for that I owe you the humblest of apologies. I would imagine word has already spread."

Sighing, Lucy smoothed the skirt of the dress that would only be hers for a short time longer. "Yes. I tried to stop it, but the servants—"

"The servants never know when to keep their mouths closed." William grunted as he rubbed his stubbled cheek. "And what of the man at the inn?"

Lucy shuddered. "He knows I am here at the Park. He is the only reason I haven't been brave enough to leave."

"That does present a problem," William agreed, even if he didn't know the extent of Mr. Granger's plans. "And if he knows you and I are not actually engaged, he could become dangerous."

He was already dangerous. "Is the only solution to save our reputations for us to be married in truth?" The thought made Lucy sick to her stomach. No matter how much she loved the Calloway family, she imagined she would not particularly love being married to the man before her.

William grimaced. "I am not worried for myself. I have survived worse. But you . . . Miss Hayes, if I could, I would marry you in a heartbeat if it meant saving you from utter ruin."

Lucy believed him, and she had a pretty good guess for why he couldn't. "But you are already engaged." She had guessed that much when she'd found his servants preparing the house and welcoming her with open arms. "By the way, your staff are going to be very confused when they meet the real future Mrs. Calloway."

"Future— You went to Penworth?"

Lucy didn't particularly appreciate how like an accusation his question sounded. The visit to the house was hardly her fault, though she supposed she hadn't put up much of a fight. "Si—Lord Calloway insisted on it."

"You could have resisted."

"Surely you know your brother well enough to know he generally gets his way." That was perhaps a bit harsh, but Lucy was getting more frustrated by the moment. She had hoped to have a solution to her predicament, even if that solution was to leave the house in the dead of night and never look back. But the longer she spoke to William, the more she understood Simon's irritation with him, especially if he always gave up so easily.

He did, however, seem to be running low on energy, sinking a little deeper into the pillows at his back. "Martine is not the *future* Mrs. Calloway," he said with a grunt. "She *is* Mrs. Calloway."

Lucy couldn't hold back her gasp of shock. "You're already married?"

He shrugged a shoulder. "I was hoping to ease my family into the idea of me being a husband," he said. "We're not long married, you see, and I do not doubt my family will judge the circumstances, considering we went to Scotland. Her father, er, didn't approve." He touched a place on his ribs and winced. "Blasted man had better aim than I expected, and I hardly grazed his arm."

Lucy's jaw dropped. "You were in a duel with her father?"

He chuckled. "He didn't like the idea of an Englishman taking fancy to his only daughter," he said with a grin. "We married without his permission, and the man called me out for it before retreating back to Paris."

"She's French?"

He offered up a wistful smile. "Now you see why I must tell them gently. I've been lying low since the duel to avoid drawing more attention to myself until everything dies down in London. But I had only so many friends willing to hide me before I decided to come up here, where it was safer. Martine planned to join me in a few days, once I had broken the news to my family. I never dreamed that journey would be so dangerous, and look where that has gotten us."

Lucy was ready for this conversation to be over. It had only made things worse, and she needed to figure out how to tell the family the whole truth. "What am I to do?" she mourned, though she hardly expected William to have an answer. He was nearly as useless as Simon seemed to think he was. "With no family or station to protect me, I will be lost forever, and you will live out your days with your pretty French wife, happy as can be."

"I am sure there is some occupation for you here at the Park." William recoiled when she glared at him. "Or perhaps not. I will do whatever is in my power to help you, Miss Hayes. I promise."

"What could you possibly do?" It was an empty promise at best.

"I don't know. Martine is set to arrive any day now, but until then, I will play the dutiful fiancé until I can figure out how to make this right."

Lucy was grateful he was at least trying, but she also knew continuing the charade would only make things worse, because it was no longer merely a misunderstanding. "I fear there is no saving me," she muttered and headed for the door. Maybe Nick would have a better solution.

She found the family out in the corridor, far enough away to allow for privacy but near enough to resume their happy reunion with William as soon as he was free. The ladies hurried back into the room, but—to add to Lucy's anxiety—Simon lingered with Nick, who had come upstairs. Nick, she could tell, had similar thoughts to her and wanted to talk about the ruse, but Simon?

He seemed to think he knew exactly what hurt ached in Lucy's chest, and she was pretty sure he wanted to fix it. This wasn't something he could fix. But as soon as the truth came out, she would have to leave, and he would never think of her again.

Mr. Granger was right. This was never going to last, and in her efforts to protect the Calloways, Lucy had only ensured the break would be even more painful than before.

She wasn't sure she would survive.

"Nick, I have a favor to ask you," she said, hoping she sounded unconcerned.

"Of course." He gave her a little bow.

"Lord Calloway, I believe your mother would appreciate your company with the rest of the family."

Simon's eyebrows pulled low at the title she addressed him with, and he glanced once at Nick. She probably should have called Nick by his surname as well, but it was too late now. "Do you need anything, Lucy?" he asked quietly.

She needed everyone to stop looking at her like she was anything more than a liar. "No, I am perfectly well. Thank you. Mr. Forester?" Reaching out, she took the arm he offered her. "If you could accompany me to the drawing room . . ."

"Forester."

Nick paused and glanced back at his friend. "Yes?"

Simon seemed to chew on his words as he glanced between Nick and Lucy. Eventually, he wrinkled his nose and spoke quickly, as if worried he might lose his courage to speak if he took too long. "I hope I don't need to remind you that this one"—he nodded toward Lucy—"has already been claimed. You will have to do your wife hunting elsewhere."

Nick actually cringed. The comment must have hit a nerve. "I am insulted you even have to say as much." There was no hint of jest in his voice; Lucy was pretty sure he had just spoken the truth.

Simon grunted, threw another glance in Lucy's direction, and then he disappeared into William's room, shutting the door behind him.

Lucy hadn't realized how tense Nick was until he suddenly relaxed. For all his outward appearances of being unconcerned with life, she had a feeling he cared about a good number of things.

"Why are you so desperate to find a wife?" she asked him. Their friendship, though new, felt strong enough for her to ask such a question without risking their easy relationship.

Nick shrugged as he led her toward the drawing room. It would be better if they were alone while they talked. "It's complicated but necessary. I have no future without someone at my side. Simon thinks I have little regard for the women I pursue, but the fact that I have not married yet only proves how determined I am to find a good match. I will not subject anyone to a life of anything but complete happiness, and my wife, whoever she may be, deserves my utter devotion."

Lucy nudged him a bit with her shoulder, hoping a little humor would restore him to his happy self. "I would marry you, Nick Forester, if I weren't already promised to poor William."

He smiled, though it was small. "I can see us being dear friends, Lucy, but we would be far too ridiculous a married pair, and I fear I would never love you as I should."

"You believe in love, then?"

"Believe in—" He stopped in the middle of the corridor, his eyes wide. "Lucy, are you telling me you are a skeptic? A woman of your beauty and wit, and you think marriages are only business deals and mutually beneficial arrangements?"

That was exactly what she had been starting to think after the way Mr. Granger approached marriage, but she'd had enough hope left in her to think she might be wrong. But how could she put that into words for Nick to understand? "Hardly. My mother and father were blissfully in love, and I always hoped I would find something even half as pure as what they shared. I simply fear I have lost my chance at ever finding such a match myself."

"Never fear, my darling friend. You have the Calloways half in love with you already. *All* of them, to be clear."

A bit of a nervous flutter entered her stomach at those words, though she had no idea what he meant by them. "Is this another one of your stories?" she asked warily.

"I tell tales only when they are to my advantage."

She couldn't for the life of her figure out how this could benefit him at all. "Nicholas Forester, you had better explain yourself this instant."

He winced. "Using my full name against me? You injure me, Lucy." But then his teasing expression faded as he glanced back the way they'd come. "But now that William is awake," he muttered, leaving it at that.

Lucy sighed. "I have to tell them. You know I do."

"Yes," he agreed, though he didn't seem to like the idea. Nick was always so confident, but that confidence had disappeared when Lucy needed it most. "I'm worried about Lady Calloway," he said. "Yes, William is awake, but I've never seen her this weary. She isn't strong enough yet."

Lucy had been afraid of that, and it didn't help to have Nick confirm her suspicions. "Will she ever be?"

The fact that he didn't have an immediate response brought tears to her eyes, and she sank onto the sofa the moment they reached the drawing room. "Nick, I don't know how to fix this. William can't help me, and anything I say will injure Lady Calloway, and the last thing I want to do is hurt *him*. Them, I mean. I don't want to hurt *them*."

Sitting beside her, Nick took hold of both her hands and offered a gentle smile. "Speaking of Simon," he said, as if he knew where Lucy's thoughts had strayed. "I sense you are worried about his reaction most of all. You shouldn't be. He cares for you, Lucy."

She did her best to ignore the heat that spread through her at those words. "He cares for his future sister-in-law," she argued. "He's going to hate me, Nick."

"He won't. I know he won't. Give him a chance."

Lucy prayed he was right.

"I would tell him myself if I thought he would believe me," Nick said with a frown. "I'm afraid, with the way I've acted these past couple of years, this is all going to have to come from you. Trust me, Lucy; tell Simon the truth in the morning. I will be right behind you with all the support you need, and everything will work out."

Knowing she would fall apart if she didn't believe him, Lucy decided to listen to the man and hope he wasn't lying as usual. The only way she was going to survive all of this was knowing there was a chance that Simon Calloway could find it in his heart to forgive her.

Chapter Twenty-Five

Though it was probably too early for a morning visit, Simon had been waiting far too long for a conversation with his brother, and he let himself into the bedchamber without bothering to knock. He found William sitting at the edge of his bed, fully dressed and glaring at the floor.

If Simon had to guess, William hadn't been sitting there a moment ago. "You need to take things slowly," he said, perhaps a little too harshly, all things considered. "Do you really think you should be up and walking?"

William didn't even glance up. "I have been stuck in this blasted room for who knows how long, Si. I will not spend my life confined to my bed."

"You can't even stand on your own," Simon guessed.

William sighed. "I feel like I haven't eaten in days. Broth only goes so far. How bad was it, really? Mother won't tell me."

That question softened Simon's mood a little, and he sank slowly onto the bed next to William. As angry as he was with his brother for the whole Lucy situation, he had to remind himself that William had been in danger of never waking this time. All things considered, he should have been overjoyed to be having this conversation in the first place.

"Dr. Pritchard thinks you've had worse," he said quietly. "But I wasn't very optimistic." No matter what he had told Lucy about William always pulling through, the fever this time had lasted longer than Simon was comfortable with.

William rolled his neck around, stretching the soreness that always lingered after his fevers. "This is what I get for being chivalrous," he grumbled.

Simon frowned. "Care to explain how you ended up shot? And why you thought it was a good idea to ride through a storm? You should have taken your carriage, especially being wounded like that!"

William grunted. "It doesn't matter why I was shot. I made it through. Besides, I needed my carriage for . . . something else."

Simon narrowed his eyes. William was hiding something from him, and he didn't like it. Was it something Lucy knew about? Maybe she would tell him.

He cursed under his breath. Was he really considering using Lucy to spy on her own betrothed? The notion was absurd, and she would never do it.

He needed to change the subject, but he had only one thought running through his mind. Now was as good a time as any to try to find out the truth. "You got engaged."

William gave him an odd look. "I did."

Simon was fairly certain there was no lie in that answer. "Lucy's lovely."

"Is she? I mean, yes, she is. Of course she is." William nodded to emphasize his point, even if he had slipped up with something.

Simon had no idea what that slip meant, and he had the sudden fear this conversation would only make things worse. He decided to keep probing anyway. "I didn't think you had plans to marry."

William laughed a little. "I didn't. Not soon, anyway. But when you find someone like her, you can't let her go. Love is funny that way."

"I will have to believe you," Simon mumbled.

"Simon, have you never been in love?"

How had the conversation suddenly turned onto him? "I am not you, Brother."

"You need to spend more time in London before you're too old to attract a young wife and too bitter to entice a sweet one."

Laughing without any real amusement, Simon shook his head. "I hardly have time to dally about Town like you. Father's business ventures are—"

"Why do you keep those?"

"What?"

It was William's turn to laugh again, though he sounded as bitter as Simon felt. "I hardly think Father expected you to spend all your days with your nose pressed to paper. You're a peer; I expect that keeps you busy enough."

Simon scoffed. "Father was as much a baron as I am now, and he found the time to start these businesses and make them flourish."

William put his arm around Simon's shoulders, though he grimaced as he did so. The gesture must have felt as strange to him as it did to Simon. "Father also *enjoyed* the work. You need a wife, Simon. Not a life of exhaustion."

Simon considered that for only a moment before shaking his head as he pulled away from his brother's touch. "I doubt I will ever marry. The title and everything with it will go to you and your many progeny."

"Not marry? Simon, the man who has dreamed of nothing but his future wife and children all his life? You have either changed drastically since I saw you last, or you think you have a good reason for pretending you can't have your pick of women."

If he had his pick, he would choose . . . But Simon didn't let himself finish that thought. "I am better on my own," he said, though he didn't believe it. He had been lighter and freer the last few days than he'd ever been since Father's death, and it definitely wasn't because Forester was visiting.

"I have no desire to be a baron, Simon," William said, fully serious. "You need to get yourself an heir."

Simon refused to think about that. "Come. Let's get you down to breakfast, as I assume you're too stubborn to call for a tray."

William grimaced. "I was never meant to be trapped in one place, Simon. Not like . . ." He shut his mouth before he finished, but they both knew what he had been about to say. *Not like you.*

Simon had never minded the fact that his future was tied to Calloway Park. Only that the many businesses his father had started so often called him away beyond the duties of Parliament. Without those, he would happily remain in this part of the country when he wasn't needed at Lords. William was the one who liked to travel, who liked to be pulled this way and that.

Simon wanted stability. Contentment. Something more fulfilling than filling his coffers with money he didn't need.

"Help me up, will you?" William kept his arm around Simon's shoulders, and when they stood, he was far lighter than Simon liked. This fever had taken a lot out of William. Though his brother protested, Simon maintained his hold on him the entire journey to the breakfast room, where he would ensure his brother ate as much as possible to gain back his strength.

The breakfast room wasn't empty, as Simon had expected. Olivia was there, probably eager for their race that morning, but he was surprised to find Forester with a plate of food as well. He was generally the sort to stay up into the long hours of the night and sleep late into the morning. Then there was Lucy, who looked almost sick as she sat beside Forester and refused to look up when Simon and William entered the room.

"Ah, the invalid has risen," Forester said a little too loudly. "We were wondering how long it would take you to join us. Are you going to watch the great race with us?"

William lifted an eyebrow. "Race?"

"Simon has finally agreed to race me on horseback," Olivia proclaimed with a wide smile.

"Again?" Pulling away from Simon, William used the backs of the chairs to maneuver himself around the room and into the chair next to Lucy's. Simon tried not to let jealousy rise up in his throat, but he failed miserably. He had thought the ache he felt for Lucy was bad before, but now that William was back to charm her with his smiles, Simon was tempted to lock himself in his study and never leave.

The time for dreaming was over.

"Hurry and eat," Olivia said, hopping up and grabbing his hand. "I cannot wait to gloat over my victory."

Seeing the way William watched Lucy push her food around her plate, Simon was more than ready to get to their race as well. Anything to distract himself from the love he shouldn't have. *She is not yours to love*, he told himself yet again, and his stomach soured at the thought. Hopefully she and William would be married soon, and then she would leave his house and be a distant memory.

"I am ready when you are," Simon declared. He feared any food he ate wouldn't sit well with him as long as Lucy was nearby.

"Are you sure you're up for this?" Forester asked, though it wasn't clear who exactly he was asking because his eyes drifted from Simon to William to Lucy. She still hadn't lifted her eyes, and Simon refused to wonder why. "You don't look well."

Clenching his jaw, Simon offered his arm to Olivia, who bounced on the balls of her feet with excitement. "If you care to watch, William, Forester can help you outside." He led Olivia out to the stables before anyone could reply. He hardly cared if they were spectators or not. He longed to feel the wind in his hair and let his horse run free. He longed to be anywhere but here.

By the time both horses were saddled and walked out to the south pasture, Forester, William, and Lucy had all gathered at the edge of the field. Someone had brought a chair for William, and Simon guessed that had been Lucy's idea. She was already caring for her future husband.

A chill wind picked up, tugging at Simon's coat and pushing his hair from his forehead, and he wished it was Lucy's warm fingers doing it instead. But that would never happen.

Sensing Simon's agitation, Hermes stamped his feet a little, and Simon grimaced. "Sorry, my friend," he muttered to the horse and rubbed his nose. "I hope you are in the mood to run."

"Cordelia is going to beat him," Olivia said beside him. She had already mounted and was patting her animal's neck with fondness.

When Simon had set up the race for today, he had considered letting his sister win. She had been working so hard to get as fast as him, and she deserved some happiness in her life. But he wasn't sure he could do it now. Not today. More than ever, he needed to fly across the field without looking back.

"Don't listen to her, Hermes," he told the horse in front of him. "You will always be the best."

"He's a magnificent animal."

Simon jumped when Lucy appeared at his side, though he was the only one startled. Hermes seemed eager to meet the woman and even pulled away from Simon's hold on the reins so she could pat his cheek. "Yes, he is," Simon said. Why had she come over to him after putting so much effort into ignoring him in the breakfast room? He glanced back toward William and Forester, who shared concerned expressions, as if they knew something he did not. "Lucy, I should get ready to—"

"Simon, wait." Lucy put her hand on his arm, which held him in place more effectively than if she'd used force. Her touch was enough to immobilize him entirely. "I have to tell you something."

Simon could tell Olivia was getting impatient, and he had to clear his throat before any words reached his lips. Lucy was too close for him to concentrate. "Can it wait?"

"No. I wish it could, but I can't hold this in any longer."

When she started crying, Simon dropped the reins and put his hands on Lucy's shoulders. What the devil had happened? "Lucy, what is the matter? What can I do? Is it Granger?"

She pressed a hand over her mouth and her tears intensified the moment her eyes met his. "I've tried to tell you so many times," she said, her voice broken and weak.

Simon thought he might fall apart as he fought to understand. "What is it, Lucy? Please tell me. Has William—"

"No. No, this has nothing to do with William. At least, not directly. Simon, I . . ."

He couldn't stop himself from running his thumb across her cheek to dry her tears, but that only seemed to make things worse, and he had never felt so foolish. He had no idea how to fix whatever had hurt her, and that was driving him mad. "Lucy," he begged. "I will not leave your side until you tell me what is the matter."

Taking a shaky breath, she grasped his hand at her cheek and shut her eyes tightly. "I never had an understanding with William. I hadn't even met him before Mr. Granger appeared at the inn. All of it was a lie to serve my own benefit."

The world stilled around him. Simon felt frozen as a haze filled his mind, leaving him senseless. He had heard the words she said, but he wasn't sure he understood them.

"I was going to wait until after the race," Lucy said, wrapping her fingers more tightly around his. "But I couldn't bear to keep lying to you, Simon. I couldn't—"

He tore his hand free, staring at her as if he'd never seen her before. "You lied," he repeated. After everything he had done to befriend her. After the torture he had gone through in knowing he'd been in love with his brother's intended. After he had practically begged her to confide in him at Penworth yesterday. She had lied to him, as if she'd thought he would throw her out onto the street if she had told him the truth. Did she really think so little of him? Clearly she did. His heart had just shattered into a thousand pieces knowing she had chosen lies over trusting him, and he was too weary to try to catch them before they fell at his feet.

"Simon."

He mounted his horse in one swift movement and kicked Hermes forward, ignoring Olivia's shout as he flew across the field toward a building storm. He didn't know where he was going; he just knew he needed to get as far away as he possibly could.

Chapter Twenty-Six

Lucy had known heartbreak before. Losing her father had been more painful than she'd thought she could bear, and she would always have a hole in her heart where he'd once been. But watching Simon disappear into a flash of lightning had torn her apart. She'd never seen pain like she'd seen in his eyes when she'd admitted who she really was—or who she wasn't—and though she didn't blame him for being angry, she wished he had given her a chance to explain.

She sank to the ground in sobs, too miserable to keep standing and staring at the place she'd last seen him.

"Lucy!" Olivia dropped to her knees at Lucy's side and grabbed her hands, only making the pain worse because she didn't deserve such tenderness. "Lucy, what did he say to you?"

Lucy shook her head. "I'm sorry, Olivia," she whispered. "Your race . . . I didn't mean . . ."

"We can race another time. But what happened? What did Simon—"

"It was my fault." Lucy tried to take in a breath, but she couldn't manage it. "I told him . . . I'm not . . ."

A heavy hand rested on Lucy's shoulder, and she looked up to find Nick crouched on her other side. "Lucy was never engaged to William," he said, his eyes locking on Olivia. "It was a deception created by her maid to keep her safe, nothing more."

As Olivia's jaw dropped, Lucy tried to find a way to apologize without it sounding trite and insincere. But how could she possibly do such a thing? She had lied from the beginning, so Olivia had no reason to believe anything she said now.

Olivia sat back on her heels, putting some distance between them. "Lucy, is that true?" Before Lucy could say a word, she let out a heavy sigh. "You tried to tell us. So many times. Oh, Lucy, I am so sorry. I should have listened to you."

When Olivia wrapped her arms around her in a tight embrace, Lucy thought for a moment she was in a dream. Maybe none of this was real and she could have a second chance at telling Simon how guilty she'd felt the whole time she'd been here with his family. But Olivia felt too real and Nick's hand still kept a warm pressure on her shoulder and she knew Simon's reaction had been genuine.

"You don't hate me?" she whispered.

Olivia pulled Lucy even closer. "How could I hate you? We're practically sisters, are we not? You don't have to be engaged to my brother for that. Wait." Letting go, Olivia looked over at William, who had struggled out of his chair and managed to walk over to them, and she narrowed her eyes. "What did you have to do with all of this?"

William shrugged. "If I tell you, will you promise not to tell Mother?"

"I will promise no such thing."

"I told the innkeeper Lucy was my wife so she could stay in my room."

"William!"

He held his hands up, as if surrendering to his younger sister. "Easy," he complained. "It seemed like a good idea at the time, and I fully intended to sleep in the stables."

Olivia glanced between her brother and Lucy, still trying to figure out what had happened. "But everyone knows you don't have a wife," she said after a moment. "Why would the innkeeper believe—"

Nick cut her off with a laugh. "Little Calloway," he said and clicked his tongue with judgment. "Do you have a secret you'd like to share with your sister?"

Though William scowled at the nickname, he had turned quite red and half turned back toward his chair, as if he knew he would need to make an escape. "I . . . may, in fact, have a wife," he said, then winced. "But how did you know that, Forester? My servants don't even know we went to Gretna Green. No one knows."

Still chuckling, Forester helped Lucy to her feet—she wasn't feeling quite as broken as she'd been a moment ago, thanks to Olivia—then shook his head at William. "My dear man, at some point, you will have to learn that nothing stays a secret in London. I may not have known which poor fellow was at the mercy of that enraged Frenchman for marrying his daughter, but I can piece things together easily enough. It's nice to see you survived the duel."

"Duel!" Olivia shrieked as William edged closer to his chair, but she was not alone. Another voice had joined hers, and all of them turned to find Lady Calloway a few paces away.

Lucy wanted to rush toward the woman in case she collapsed, but she decided perhaps she should let one of the others do that, considering she had no real ties to the family. Olivia did the honors, grabbing hold of her mother's arm as the woman stared at William.

William sank right back into his chair, knowing it would be foolish to attempt to run. "I am perfectly well, Mother," he said, though his voice had dropped to an almost inaudible level.

Lady Calloway looked from her son to Lucy, likely piecing things together just as Nick had. "So you are not engaged to my son," she guessed.

Lucy shook her head and gripped Nick's hand, preparing herself for the worst.

To her utter surprise, Lady Calloway smiled and approached Lucy with an outstretched hand. "I must confess I am relieved."

She must have heard wrong, because Lucy thought she had heard the woman say she was *relieved.* Was she truly that beneath William's station? She'd thought Lady Calloway liked her, but clearly she'd only been pretending for her son's sake.

"Oh, my dear." Still smiling, Lady Calloway pressed her palm to Lucy's cheek. "Don't look so dreary. I would absolutely love to have you in my family, but you deserve so much better than William."

"Excuse me?" William was back on his feet, though he wavered. "Mother, what do you—"

"Hush, William." Lady Calloway cut him off with a glare that frightened even Lucy. "As it seems you have married a poor girl under questionable circumstances and could have killed her father because of it, you will accept knowing you have a good deal of growing up to do and amends to make. I only hope this wife of yours has a far more sensible mind than you do and will keep you from making any more foolish decisions. If your father could see you now . . . I can only imagine what Simon thinks of— But where is Simon?"

All of them turned in the direction of the approaching storm, and the ache in Lucy's chest returned. Wherever Simon was, she hoped he would return. At the very least, she hoped he was safe.

Chapter Twenty-Seven

"Lucy, you need to sit down a moment," Nick said.

Lucy couldn't sit. If she sat, her mind arrived at terrible conclusions. As long as she was moving, and as long as she had a view out the window to the rain-soaked grounds, things were still uncertain.

"Lucy." This time, instead of just insisting, Nick took her by the hand and led her to the sofa, forcing her down onto the cushion. "You're making me dizzy, pacing like that."

"We should go after him," she said, craning her neck to look out the window again. "Nick, it's been hours. What if he's injured?"

His hands wrapped around hers, and he waited until she looked at him before he said anything. "Simon Calloway is no fool. He would have sought out shelter before the storm hit with full force. There are plenty of tenant cottages in that direction, and he knows these lands better than anyone. He could probably ride them blindfolded and be perfectly safe."

Pressing a hand to her forehead, Lucy groaned. "You're laying it on a bit thick," she said, though she was grateful for the positivity. All she could think about was Simon being thrown from his horse after a clap of thunder and lying in a ditch somewhere, injured and frozen. "Oh, Nick, you should have seen his face when I told him. He was so hurt."

"He was confused."

"He hates me, just as I thought he would."

Nick huffed out a sigh, almost angry as he commanded her attention with a tug on her hands. "Lucy Hayes, you are impossible to hate." He turned to the other side of the room, where Lady Calloway and Olivia had taken up sewing to pass the time; William had gone to bed an hour ago, too exhausted to continue the vigil with his family. "Lady C., I could use your assistance."

Lady Calloway offered a smile, though she was clearly just as worried about Simon as Lucy, because she couldn't hold the gesture for long. "I understand why you did what you did," she told Lucy.

Lucy had explained everything to her and Olivia a few hours before, with the help of Nick. Now all of them knew about Mr. Granger, except for the threats he had made to the family. She'd still kept that part to herself, hoping she could find a way to make things right without adding more to their burdens.

"Simon will come around," Lady Calloway said. "I know he will."

"If he's alive," Lucy muttered under her breath. The storm had been raging for several hours now, and there had been no sign of Simon or his horse. If something happened to him, she would never forgive herself.

"We'll give him another half hour," Nick said, though he seemed reluctant to give in to Lucy's nerves. "If he isn't back by then, I'll—"

"Simon!" Lucy was out the door before Nick could finish speaking, and she nearly tripped on her own dress as she darted down the corridor and outside. The rain still came down in buckets, but she hardly cared, running with all speed to the stables, where she'd seen a horse and rider appear.

She stepped into the stables at the same time Simon told the stablemaster to take good care of his horse, and she could barely breathe as she stood there, waiting.

When he finally did turn, he froze, his eyes locked on hers beneath waterlogged hair that dripped into his face. Everything about him was soaked, and though he breathed heavily, he didn't shiver or give any indication that he was particularly cold. Lucy hoped that meant he would not meet the same fate his brother had only days before; she wasn't sure she would survive waiting by his bedside for him to wake.

"Where have you been?" she asked when he still didn't move.

He swallowed but said nothing.

"I was worried about you," she told him, though she wanted to tell him far more than that. She had feared for his life, and she would have been utterly devastated if he hadn't returned. But how could she tell him such things when she saw nothing but coldness in his gaze?

Eventually, he took a single step closer, his gaze dropping to the ground as he did. "Why should you care?"

The question hit Lucy hard, as if he'd swung a blow with his fist at the same time. "What?"

"You are not connected to me in any way, Miss Hayes. So why should you care for my fate?"

It was worse than she'd feared, and she had no idea how to react to such a question. "How could you ask that?" she whispered.

He looked up, nothing but exhaustion in his face. "I'm tired, Lucy. I need to—"

Lucy blocked his path toward the door. She refused to end her relationship with him like this, with him unwilling to even listen to her. She would tell him the whole truth about Mr. Granger if it would stop him looking at her like this. Putting her hand on his cheek, she ignored the way he froze again and focused entirely on what she said to him. She had to make him understand. "You could have gotten yourself killed out in a storm like that. Have you no sense?"

He laughed, the sound falling dead at their feet. "None whatsoever. It is one of my many failings, no doubt."

"What is wrong with you, Simon?"

"Oh, now you will use my name? How fortunate for me." He tried again to move past her, but this time she grabbed his arm, holding him there with every bit of strength she had. He could easily pull away, but she would do her best to keep him there until she'd said what she wanted to say.

"I know what I did was wrong," she said. Her voice broke, but she didn't care. She needed him to know how overcome with emotion she was. "I can't tell you how sorry I am for lying to you like I did, and my reasons will never justify doing it. I know that."

"What could you possibly have hoped to gain from it?" he asked, and his mask of anger split in two, revealing the misery that plagued him. "Our money? A chance to ensnare a wealthy husband and a well-connected family?"

Did he really think so little of her? "Of course not!"

"You could have told me from the beginning about Granger. I would have helped you."

Lucy's heart was breaking, but what could she do? No excuse would change the fact that she had lied. "All of this started with a lie," she said. "Would you have believed me if I had told you then?"

The fact that he couldn't immediately say yes said far more than any response he might have given, and he clenched his jaw. "You're right," he said, his countenance growing darker. "I have no way of knowing if anything you've said to me is true. For all I know, you and Granger have concocted some sort of scheme to ruin my family. To ruin *me*."

Lucy's stomach dropped. "No, that isn't—"

"Well, unfortunately for you, I am stronger than you seem to think, and I am perfectly capable of protecting my family."

"Simon."

"Did you stop to think for one moment what this was going to do to my family? To you? Did you even consider how *you* would come out of something like this?"

Even in his anger, he was thinking of her. Lucy stumbled backward, realizing she could never deserve this man before her. She wanted him to have the best life he could possibly have, and that couldn't include her. Not with Mr. Granger and his very real threats nearby. Even if Simon forgave her, there was no way he could love her after all of this. The best thing she could do for him now was to leave and let him find someone who would deserve every smile. Every laugh. Every kiss.

"I'm sorry," she said, stepping away from him in anguish. She shut her eyes when she reached the opposite wall, pressing herself against it as if she might disappear into the wood. "I should never have come into your life. I've done nothing but hurt you, and you deserve so much better than me. You are all that is good in this world, Simon Calloway. You deserve everything."

When she was met with nothing but silence, she knew he was gone, and she let the tears fall from her eyes as she pictured her life without him. It was miserable. But then she opened her eyes, and she realized the man still stood there, staring at her with an expression she couldn't put a name to. Like he wished he could be anywhere else but couldn't find the strength to move because everything he wanted was right in front of him.

"Simon," she breathed.

He moved so quickly that in the space of a breath his lips collided with hers in a fierce kiss that seemed to stop her heart in her chest, leaving her senseless. Though his hands were cold at her neck, his lips were warm, and they explored hers with an urgency she'd never felt before. Kissing Simon was like bringing the sun back, and she was desperate to stay in that spot, so when he pulled away the slightest bit, she followed him, wrapping her arms around his neck and threading her fingers into his hair.

"No," he said suddenly, pushing her away and gasping for air. Shaking his head, he moved several paces away from her, as if he needed the distance to breathe again. "You lied to me. To my family. How can I ever trust you when all I've known are lies?"

As much as she wanted to tell him that she would never lie again, she had no way of promising in a way that he would believe. And there was nothing she could do to fix that. Her heart already ached for him, and though he was only a few feet away, she knew she would miss him for the rest of her life.

"You can't," she whispered, tears pooling in her eyes. That, at least, was the truth. Though she had never been anyone but herself, he could never trust her, and that—knowing she might have had a chance if only she had told him the truth from the beginning—hurt worse than his hatred.

She took one step toward him, one final hope in her heart of making things right, but he held up a hand and closed his eyes. "Go, Miss Hayes," he said. "Leave. Please." Then he stepped out into the rain and disappeared into the darkness, leaving Lucy heartbroken and alone.

Chapter Twenty-Eight

Lucy wasn't sure why she went up to her room to pack. It wasn't like she had anything to call hers except a crumpled little leaf—the one she had pulled out of Simon's hair in the pond. Beyond that, everything she had was borrowed, including the family who might have accepted her if things had been different.

When she'd finally stopped crying enough to go back to the house, Nick had been waiting for her at the door, and she didn't have to say a word for him to recognize what had happened. He had pulled her into an embrace and, for once, said nothing. Even he had no idea how to repair her shattered relationship with Simon.

Thankfully, he had let her go up to her room alone, though she knew it wouldn't last. Olivia would probably try to convince her to stay, as would Lady Calloway, but Simon's order had been final. She was no longer welcome at Calloway Park, a verdict she fully deserved.

"What happened?" Rebecca asked when Lucy stepped into her chamber.

Lucy broke into sobs again, but she managed to tell her friend everything that had happened with Simon before her exhaustion had her curling up on the bed without undressing. "I ruined everything," she said through her tears. "Now he'll never speak to me again."

Rebecca rubbed soothing circles on her back, and Lucy had never been more grateful that the maid had come with her to Oxfordshire. After everything she had gone through, at least she still had a friend. "What will you do now?" Rebecca asked.

Lucy took a deep breath and held it in her lungs until her crying subsided. Her tears would be back, but she could hold them at bay for a little while. "It's time we left Calloway Park," she said, sitting up slowly. "Mr. Granger may arrive at any moment to expose me, but I have nothing to fear from him if I'm gone."

"Where will you go?"

"It doesn't matter. Anywhere that is far from here. Mr. Granger can do nothing to me if he doesn't know where to look," she told Rebecca, taking a long look at the room that had been hers for a short while. "I'll leave in the morning, as early as I can. All of this will simply be a beautiful dream. And you—"

"I want to go with you."

Lucy frowned at her friend. "I don't know where I'll go," she warned again.

"I'm sure we'll find somewhere to start over," Rebecca said, sounding so convinced that Lucy almost smiled.

"I'm sure we will," she agreed. She pulled Rebecca into an embrace that was long overdue. "I'm glad I've had you here with me. I wouldn't have made it this far without you."

"You might have become friends with the Calloways differently without me," Rebecca argued with a sad little laugh. "It's my fault you're in this mess with Lord Calloway, and I'm right sorry about it."

"I don't blame you." She really didn't. She had grown so much during her time at Calloway Park that she almost thought she should thank Rebecca. She would have been content to remain a governess for the rest of her life, but now she knew there was so much more out there. She would never find herself a baron or his brother; perhaps she would find a kind tradesman to marry if she did not remain alone, but at least she knew what love felt like.

Yes, she had fallen in love with Simon. There was no way to argue that.

Now she knew why her father had always wanted to stay close to where Mother was buried. Leaving Calloway Park was going to be more difficult than anything she'd done.

"You should get some rest," she told Rebecca. "The sooner we can leave in the morning, the sooner we can put all of this behind us." She just wanted to fall asleep and wake up in the next phase of her life, whatever that would look like.

"I'll see you in the morning, Lucy." Giving her one last embrace, Rebecca slipped away and left her on her own.

Before Lucy had found the energy to undress—she would have to send this gown back to Olivia as soon as she procured her own—and go to bed, a soft knock sounded on the door. For a brief moment, she thought perhaps Simon had come to reconcile, but she tossed that ridiculous notion aside and rose to see who had come to offer pity. Most likely Olivia or Nick.

To her surprise, William stood on the other side of the door. He already looked better than he had this morning, his face less gaunt and his eyes a little brighter. He was coming back to life, and Lucy felt like she was dying.

"I saw Simon," he said with a frown. "He refused to talk to me, but from the looks of things . . ."

Lucy bit back her tears before they resurfaced. "He wants me to leave. I can't say I blame him."

"Might we sit?"

"What? Here?" Lucy glanced behind her. Surely he did not intend to enter her bedchamber.

But William shrugged. "I'm not sure I have the energy to go somewhere else. We'll leave the door open, and my family will hardly think anything of it."

Perhaps he was right. Besides, Lucy wasn't sure she had the energy either. Sitting on the edge of the bed, she waited until William joined her.

"I know we don't know each other, Lucy," he said. "But I know as well as my family does that you had no intention of hurting anyone. You cannot blame yourself for the way Simon reacted."

William was wrong, but Lucy kept that thought to herself. "I shouldn't have lied to begin with," she said. "I shouldn't have agreed to your offer back at the inn. I could have found some other way to stay away from Mr. Granger. For someone who claims to value honesty, I knew better than to deceive anyone, and I shudder to think what my father would think of me were he alive."

For some reason, William laughed a little, shaking his head as he leaned his arms on his knees. "My father was never proud of me. I never gave him a reason to be. I've always been glad to be the second son, to have no responsibility, and I don't even care for the estate that was handed to me. I've always thought only of myself. If anyone should be ashamed of how he acted, it is me."

"Perhaps we both have some growing to do."

Meeting her eyes, William seemed to search her for something, his eyes piercing. He looked a good deal like his brother, but he lacked the warmth Simon had always had in his gaze. "Is there anything I can do to make things right?" he asked quietly. "If I am to become a better man, I would like to start with you."

Lucy managed a smile. Perhaps there was more to William than she'd thought, and she put her hand on his arm. "Look after your family, William. Especially Simon. He needs you. He may seem confident from the outside, but I fear he is drowning. You have a good head on your shoulders, and I imagine you could do great things if you tried. Show him what you're made of, William Calloway."

William shook his head again, as if amazed as he looked her over. "Simon is a fool," he said, but he added a smile to show he didn't really mean it. "He would have to be, to let someone like you go."

As much as Lucy wanted to hear that, she refused to let herself hope again. Simon had made his choice, and it wasn't her. "It's time for me to go, William. Promise me you will make an effort to be a part of your family, and I will rest easy."

"Where will you go?"

She had no idea. "I may return home," she said with a shrug. "Go back to the place I grew up and hope I can find somewhere to go from there. A fresh start will be good, I think."

Nodding, William struggled back up to his feet. "I wish you all the good fortune in the world, Lucy. It may not mean much, but you are always welcome at Penworth. My wife would love to meet you, I am sure."

She had no intention of being anywhere close to Calloway Park, but she was grateful for the invitation all the same. "Thank you."

As soon as William was gone, Lucy climbed into bed still dressed, but a restlessness settled over her, and she knew she would not be able to sleep well. She lasted as long as she could, lying there for several hours, but eventually she gave up and rose again. It was still rather dark, but one last walk around the grounds would hopefully soothe her heartache and clear her head of negative thoughts. Her father had raised her to be resilient, and she would make it through whatever she faced in her uncertain future.

"Lucy? Where are you going?"

She had made it to the entryway before anyone found her, but she couldn't be frustrated by Nick stopping her. He had proven himself to be a dear friend. "I need to get some fresh air," she told him.

Nick approached slowly, as if afraid he might frighten her off. "It's early. Too early." It looked like he hadn't slept at all either, and she felt terrible for being the reason. "Perhaps I could—"

"Simon needs you more than I do," Lucy argued. She glanced at the flickering light coming through the closed door to the parlor Nick had come from, knowing Simon was likely inside. Yet another person who hadn't slept because of Lucy. "How . . . how is he?"

Nick let out a frustrated sigh. "He won't listen to me. Calloway has always had a level head, but he refuses to see reason. He's . . ."

"He's hurting," Lucy guessed.

"Yes," Nick agreed. "But he doesn't have to be. He's more angry at himself than anything. You're still here, and he will realize here is exactly where you should be. Everything *will* work out, Lucy."

As an ache throbbed in her chest, she folded her arms and wished she wasn't so close to tears. She wanted to seem strong so Nick wouldn't try to change her mind. "I am leaving this morning," she said. "I don't want to hurt him further, and it will be best for everyone if I am not here to remind him—everyone—of what I did. I hope to be gone before Mr. Granger thinks to come for me here."

"Lucy." Nick held his arms open, and she fell into his embrace again without hesitation. Though being in Nick's arms was nothing like she'd felt when Simon had held her at the pond, she knew he cared for her just as she did for him. "Where will you go?"

It was the same question William and Rebecca had asked her, but Nick truly wanted an answer. His concern for her future was clear in his voice and the way he held her against him.

"I don't know," she admitted. "I have no one. Nowhere. Nothing."

She wasn't sure how long she stood there in Nick's arms, but when he finally pulled away, a determined glint had entered his eyes. "I will go with you," he said. "I must return to London as it is to answer a summons from my benefactor, and I will rest much easier knowing you are not on your own. Will you allow me to escort you?"

Tears of relief filled Lucy's eyes, along with a good deal of guilt. "Nick, as grateful as I am for your offer, I couldn't trespass on your hospitality."

"Good, because I have nothing to give you. I was going to suggest appealing to my benefactor to help find you a position somewhere far from Granger's reach."

Lucy snorted a laugh. "That is even worse. I do not know your benefactor!"

As a smile spread across Nick's face, she realized how much of his usual exuberance had been missing. The poor man was probably struggling to remain his light-tempered self when surrounded by so much misery. "There's the Lucy I know and love," he muttered and brushed a tear from her cheek with the back of his finger. "Trust me; Mr. Mackenzie has a soft spot for strong-willed ladies. He will not hesitate to do what he can to assist you, and he knows a good deal of good people far from London. Please. For my own sanity."

"Very well." An enormous weight seemed to lift from her shoulders, and she took a slow breath, as if she hadn't been able to breathe deeply for days. Maybe she hadn't. "I suppose I will go take my walk now."

Nick grimaced, glancing at the closed door that separated them from Simon. "Couldn't you at least take that maid of yours with you? I can't like the idea of you being out there on your own."

"I need only a few moments to myself," she assured him. "A chance to see the grounds one last time. Besides, only someone truly touched in the head would be awake this early." She grinned when Nick chuckled. "Go. Look after Simon, and I will come inside shortly."

He clasped her hand briefly, then stepped back, walking backward in the direction of the parlor. "I will see to the travel arrangements once the rest of the world is awake. Don't stay out too long, Lucy."

"Thank you, Nick. Thank you for being my friend."

Lucy stepped out into the cool morning and breathed the air damp from the rain, feeling almost at peace for the first time since her admission. She would still ache from missing this place—even in the darkness the grounds were beautiful and wild—but her future was not looking so bleak. She would survive once she woke from this dream, and perhaps she would even be better for it.

A gentle wind blew through the leaves of the nearby trees, and Lucy closed her eyes, letting the coolness of the breeze dry her tears. *Yes*, she decided. She was at peace. Ready to move on and let her past disappear behind her.

"Good morning, Miss Hayes."

Lucy shrieked, though the sound was cut off when she recognized Mr. Granger's voice. She could barely make out the man's silhouette in the thick darkness, but he was far closer than she'd expected. Where had he come from?

"Mr. Granger," she said, her heart still racing from being startled. "What are you doing here?"

He chuckled, the sound low and far more menacing than she'd ever heard him. "I told you three days, did I not? Well? Have you made your peace? It is time for us to be on our way."

Chapter Twenty-Nine

Was it possible for a man to sleep when his heart was broken? Simon doubted it; he hadn't slept a minute since the moment Forester had finally let him go upstairs to his chamber to get a couple of hours' sleep. He had simply lain awake, staring at the ceiling and wondering how he could have been so completely foolish.

That and reliving the kiss that would haunt him for the rest of his life.

And now that the sun was up, much to his irritation, he would have to face his family and see the damage Lucy had done. Her lies had likely broken them, but they would have him to put them back together again.

He had no one.

Groaning, he opted not to call his valet and chose to dress himself today. He had no reason to look presentable, as he had no reason to leave the house, except perhaps to go work a field or twenty. Anything to keep him away from Lucy until he could figure out what to do with her.

Any ideas he had come up with so far had involved kissing her again, which was the exact opposite of what he needed to do. Lucy had thought the worst of him, that he couldn't be trusted, and that was something he needed to fix before he ruined other relationships or brought more businesses to failure.

One thing at a time. First, he had to make sure his family had endured the blow. They hadn't known about her false name ahead of time, and he could only imagine how his mother had taken the news.

It was late enough that he found his mother and sister in the sitting room, both of them working on their embroidery and perfectly content with life. He had to wonder, with how calmly they sat, if they had even learned the truth, but he knew from experience that it was easy to hide behind a wall of indifference when one was suffering. Besides, Forester had said the family did know the full truth.

It was the one thing Simon had heard him say last night. The rest had been nonsense—lies designed to manipulate him into being blinded by the woman who had split his heart in two. He didn't know how Forester had fallen under Lucy's spell, but Simon refused to yield.

For his family's sake.

Perhaps Lucy had trusted Forester. He hadn't been nearly as surprised by the truth as he should have been, which only made Simon feel worse. He was no better to her than a man who spoke only falsehoods.

Taking a steeling breath, he forced himself into the drawing room, ready to fix things. "Good mor—" He stopped halfway through the word when he realized there was a third woman in the room, one he had never seen before. Despite that, she looked just as comfortably situated as Olivia or Mother, and she was dressed finely enough that she couldn't be a neighbor. In fact, the jeweled ring on her finger put her as wife to someone rather well off, and no one within thirty miles could boast of that level of wealth outside of the Thatchers. As the woman was neither one of the Misses Thatcher, Simon was at a loss.

"Simon, dear, I was wondering when you would wake." Mother offered a small but somewhat strained smile as she waved him inward. "You are usually up so much earlier."

He remained where he was. "Mother," he acknowledged.

Olivia wasn't looking at him. In fact, she seemed rather put out with him, her needle moving a tad too aggressively through her fabric for Simon to want to get anywhere close to her. Just what had he done to get on her bad side? He hadn't even realized she *had* a bad side. It couldn't be because of their failed race yesterday, could it? That hadn't been his fault.

He cleared his throat, hoping that would be enough for someone to acknowledge that an introduction was required.

The strange woman smiled, resting her needle and thread on her lap with utmost delicacy. "He will learn soon enough," she said to the room in general, her accent decidedly French.

Mother sighed, all outward signs of happiness disappearing. "Simon," she said heavily, "have you met William's wife?"

"William isn't married," Simon said. Nor was he engaged, as Simon had learned yesterday.

Heat flared through his face as he again recalled confronting Lucy in the stables. Particularly the latter half of the conversation. The part that hadn't been conversation at all. Blast it all, would he ever get the feel of her lips out of his head? Or the way she challenged him with only a look, telling him he could be more than what he'd limited himself to?

Letting out another sigh, Mother lowered her own sewing and gestured to the stranger on the settee, who stood gracefully. "This is Martine. Martine Calloway. She arrived early this morning, much to our surprise."

Calloway? But they didn't have any relatives in France. Simon opened his mouth to say so when a hand clapped on his shoulder, making him jump.

"You're blocking the door," William said brightly. He seemed to have fully recovered overnight, and he pushed Simon deeper into the room so he could get inside as well. Then, to Simon's consternation, William stepped right up to the mysterious Calloway woman and planted a kiss on her lips.

Oh.

He didn't have the energy to deal with this new development. Simon turned right around and left the room. If William was already married to someone else, that somehow made all of this even worse, and he was desperate to find some reason to leave the county and give himself some space from the topsy-turvy world his life had become.

He made it only a dozen steps down the corridor before William caught up to him, sliding to a halt in front of him and blocking his path.

"Get out of my way," Simon growled.

William shook his head. "Not until you hear what I have to say."

Simon had no idea what to believe anymore, and no matter what William told him, he had no way to know if he could trust him. Even his mother and sister seemed privy to whatever nonsense was happening around him, and Simon wanted to run. To ride his horse as far as he would go and then keep running.

But he couldn't go to the stables now. Not when it would only remind him of that kiss with Lucy. An involuntary shudder ran through him at the memory. First the library, then his pond, now riding—Lucy had tainted everything he loved.

"I am not in the mood, Will," he said.

Narrowing his eyes, William looked far stronger than he likely was. Simon had always been able to beat him in a wrestling match, but after this latest fever, he knew it would be perfectly easy to knock his brother down and get away. He had endured enough unrest the last several days, however, so he kept his fists at his side and clenched his jaw tight.

"You were the one who said you wanted to talk when I recovered," William pointed out, relaxing a bit as he stood there. Did he really think Simon might have hurt him? Perhaps they didn't know each other at all. "So let's talk."

Simon knew he would regret this. "About what?"

"About Lucy."

Simon reconsidered his decision not to fight, but his mother would surely find them if he laid a finger on William. She had always had a knack for turning up at the worst moments.

Groaning, he shook his head. "I don't want to talk about Lucy." He wanted to forget he had ever known her, though that would be impossible with how deeply she was now etched into his heart. He had no idea how she had managed that in such a short space of time, but she had likely taken up permanent residence in his soul. And yet he hadn't been enough for her.

Where was she, anyway? Simon looked in the direction of the staircase, as if he might find her on her way down. She was usually among the first ones up, but she hadn't been in the room with Olivia and Mother and that woman who was apparently the new Mrs. Calloway. What had been Lucy's reaction to meeting her? Had she known ahead of time that William was already married?

"I would imagine she's gone, Simon."

Simon's heart seemed to turn to stone inside his chest at those words. "What?"

"She told me she would be leaving this morning, after the imbecilic way you reacted to her admitting the truth."

But he hadn't even had the chance to see her one more time. The thought of never seeing her again . . . Simon ran a hand through his hair, suddenly dizzy. Where would she have gone?

"Ah, Forester," William said, though Simon barely heard him through his jumbled thoughts. "Perhaps you can help me convince my brother how much of an idiot he was to let Lucy leave."

"Leave? But she agreed to travel with me later today."

Perking up at Forester's words, Simon reached out and grabbed his friend's arm. "She's still here?" His relief was minimal, knowing he was hardly in a state to convince her he was more than the measure she'd taken of him, but at least this meant he had a chance to fix things. How could he have been such a fool to react so poorly last night? He should have spent all that time fighting for a future together, not wallowing in misery because he had so much to prove about himself.

Lucy's maid appeared on the stairs just then, and Simon let out all the breath in his lungs at once. Apparently he'd been holding it. If Rebecca was here, Lucy would be too. "Thank the heavens," he breathed.

Forester, however, tensed as the maid approached. "Rebecca, what's the matter?"

In truth, the young woman looked rather harried now that Simon looked at her more closely. "Begging your pardons, sirs," she said with a quick curtsy, "but have any of you seen Lucy? She dressed without my help this morning, and no one has seen her."

The maid's words echoed in the entryway, bouncing around in Simon's head and leaving him disoriented. She wouldn't have just left, would she? Of all the times to listen to him, she wouldn't have picked last night in the stables, when he'd been overcome with confusion and heartbreak. Would she?

"What are you saying?" Forester asked.

Tears filled Rebecca's eyes. "I'm saying I've searched the whole house over, and I can't find her."

Forester turned, meeting Simon's gaze, and something in his friend's expression brought Simon back to reality, like his mind had been floating overhead but had just been tugged back into place. Simon had never seen Nick Forester afraid before, and he very much did not like the sight.

"She went for a walk early this morning," Forester said, his fear leaving his voice weak.

Simon cursed loudly, hardly caring that a woman heard him. "Jed mentioned one of his stableboys saw someone wandering the edge of the grounds the other night," he growled. Why hadn't Simon done something about that the moment he was told? Without knowing who or why, there hadn't been much he could do about the trespasser without catching him. He might have realized it was Granger after Lucy had admitted her fear, but William had woken, and— Simon's stomach twisted itself into a knot.

"Granger," Forester realized at the same time Simon did.

Cursing once more, Simon buzzed with adrenaline and terror. The cad had been determined to marry Lucy. If he'd snatched her from the grounds . . .

"I will go ask if any of the servants out of doors might have seen anything," William said, dashing off.

"We don't know where they would have gone," Forester said.

"London," the maid guessed. "He doesn't have a home anywhere else."

Forester nodded. "I'll send a man to the village, just in case, but someone should take the road to London without delay. And you." He pointed to Rebecca. "You need to tell us everything you know about Mr. Granger."

As the maid quickly filled them in on the man's disgusting exploits, Simon could barely breathe.

"What if we're too late?" he asked as Forester followed him to the stables. What if he had lost Lucy forever? "Forester, I can't lose her."

"Then, ride, Simon," Forester said, the urgency in his voice enough to push Simon forward without another moment's hesitation. "Ride as fast as you can."

Chapter Thirty

All things considered, Lucy's situation could have been worse.

True, Mr. Granger had dragged her into his waiting carriage. Yes, he would stop at nothing to see that their marriage took place as soon as possible; he had an illegal special license to assist in his endeavors. And yes, he had told Lucy in no uncertain terms that he was her best and only option, especially now that they were alone together in a coach on its way to London. The moment they arrived in the bustling metropolis and were seen, she would have little choice.

But he hadn't hurt her. He had apologized for the rough manner in getting her to the coach in the first place. He'd promised her a comfortable life with everything she could want or need. He could have had his way with her in the coach, and he had kept to his side. That was something.

Near the start of their journey, she had asked him why he was so determined to marry her. She was a governess with no money to her name, and her beauty was nothing compared to anyone he could find in London. With his thriving merchant business, he could have married into the aristocracy if he found someone in need of his fortune to rescue a failing estate. So why had he chosen her?

"I have loved you from the moment I saw you," he'd said, as if that justified everything.

The sentiment was sweet, she supposed, but Lucy wished he would ignore his strange infatuation and choose better for himself. She wished she had never learned about the kitchen girl Dottie, because maybe then she could have seen a glimpse of a good man.

As it was, she saw nothing but misery for the rest of her life.

He had fallen asleep two hours ago, and she was grateful for the reprieve. He had waxed long about their future together and the half-dozen children they would have, telling her how eager he was to present her to his brother's family again, only this time as his bride. Now that he snored lightly on his side of the coach, Lucy could stop pretending to be strong and let the tears fall. She hadn't wanted him to think she had given in. She'd wanted to seem ready to fight him as soon as she had an opening, even if she knew she had no chance.

Yesterday, she had been accepted and loved by a mother, a sister, and a friend, and even William had been good to her.

Yesterday, she had had Simon.

"Enough," she chided under her breath. She had lied to all of them, Simon more than anyone, and she deserved to feel their loss. She needed to be reminded how far beneath that family she was. Their world was not her world.

Mr. Granger would give her a roof over her head. She knew that much.

Whether he could make her even a little bit happy was doubtful.

"Your happiness is not dependent on anyone else," she told herself, and her voice sounded incredibly loud in the silent coach.

She hoped Mr. Granger would soften in his manners. Perhaps, in his love, he would be kind to her. If nothing else, being married to a decently wealthy merchant might give her an opportunity to make friends in London, a luxury she hadn't had before. She might even find herself in the same circles as Olivia when the girl made her debut.

The thought of seeing Olivia again was both a comfort and a sting. The girl had told Lucy she forgave her for the lies, but would that last? Would Simon even let them be friends? And what of Nick? He would be in London as well, but eventually he would find himself a wife and would be far too busy with her to consider time spent with someone like Lucy.

There were too many uncertainties in her future, and that made her stomach churn. So she focused on the one thing she could control right now, and that was looking at the man across from her and trying to picture him as her husband. She would have to get used to the concept eventually.

"But can I get used to you?" Lucy asked aloud, frowning at him. He had always made her tense and uncomfortable.

She already knew the man's family, and while the Grangers had been kind to her, there had never been a sense of love. The Calloways had welcomed her with open arms, no questions asked, and they had accepted Lucy as she was.

The Grangers would expect her to be more.

As she considered the idea that her pupils would soon be her nieces, the coach suddenly slowed. One glance out the windows told Lucy they were nowhere near a stopping point, and when the driver shouted something with obvious fear in his voice, her heart pounded out an irregular rhythm.

A highwayman, perhaps?

"Mr. Granger!" she hissed, desperately searching for something to use to protect herself. "Mr. Granger, wake up!"

He woke only when she kicked him, which she found absurd, and even then he seemed in a daze as he looked at her. "There already?"

Another shout from the driver pulled his eyes to the window, though he still seemed bewildered.

"We're under attack," Lucy snapped, and then she groaned when Mr. Granger pressed himself into the corner of the coach in fear. Had she really been so afraid of this man?

She was not about to be set upon by a highwayman with nothing but a cowardly fop for protection. She would go down fighting.

Gathering up her skirts, she took several deep breaths to convince herself this was not a terrible idea, and then she grabbed hold of the door handle with her other hand. She could still hear voices outside, and the coach swayed beneath restless horses. Footsteps drew nearer, just out of sight.

Lucy tensed. The door was heavy enough to do some damage if she timed it right. Holding her breath, she waited a few more seconds and then shoved the door open with all her might.

It collided with something large and heavy, and a cry of pain and surprise told Lucy she had found her mark. The man outside fell to the ground in a heap.

She might have cheered if she weren't still very much in danger. What had happened to the driver? She had to make sure he was all right, as he was her only valuable ally.

"Blast it all, Lucy!"

She had one foot out the door when she froze at the familiar voice. It was so familiar, in fact, that she was pretty sure she had imagined it. What other explanation could there be?

"How the devil did you get so strong?" the same voice asked.

Trembling, Lucy climbed to the ground and poked her head around the door to find none other than Simon Calloway sitting in the dirt, testing his nose as if wondering if it might be broken.

"Oh my goodness," she breathed. "My lord, I am so sorry. If I had known . . ." She dropped to her knees at his side and fumbled for some way to make things better. "I thought you were—but that's ridiculous. My lord, if you can ever forgive me for—but why should you? You must hate me. And now I've gone and . . . my lord, please say something."

Pinching the bridge of his nose, which by some miracle hadn't started bleeding, he eyed her sideways. "Call me that one more time," he growled, "and I'll make you *walk* back to Calloway Park."

"Back to—" Lucy fell back on her heels, bewildered.

"You belong with our family, Lucy."

As much as she wanted to hear that, it was utterly impossible. Simon should have known that by now. "But I can't marry William. Your brother—"

"Has a ridiculous French wife. I know."

"But how—"

"Have you ever thought of being a lady?"

Just how hard had she hit Simon in the head? He was speaking nonsense. She couldn't become a lady on a whim!

"I don't understand," she admitted.

He dropped his hand and turned to stare at her, his gaze so intense that it seemed to burn like the sun, which currently sat behind a thick layer of clouds. "Neither do I," he said, but he sounded surer of himself than he ever had. "But I am madly in love with you and couldn't watch you lose your freedom to a pathetic lout like Granger. No offense intended," he added, despite him most likely definitely intending offense. He narrowed his eyes at Mr. Granger, who had poked his head out the door, probably trying to figure out what was going on and why Lucy hadn't been robbed yet.

She was still a little lost, though she was pretty sure Simon just told her he loved her. Then she thought back on his first question, and she suddenly felt faint. "You want me to be Lady Calloway?" she whispered, even though that was awfully presumptive of her. He'd never actually said those words. He was simply here to rescue her, nothing more.

But Simon smiled and tucked some of her hair behind her ear since it had come loose from its coiffure sometime during the night. His fingers lingered at her cheek, barely touching her and sending shivers through her. "I want you to be by my side and force me to take leisure time, and I want to be the one who makes you so happy that you forget you were ever otherwise."

Lucy leaned into his touch, which seemed to dissolve any remaining hesitation he might have had. Determination filled his hazel eyes as he looked at her.

"And I never want to have to say goodbye to you."

He captured her mouth with his without warning, pulling her into a kiss every bit as breath-stealing as the last one had been. Lucy fell into that kiss but got only a moment of it before something jerked her back.

"What is the meaning of this?" Mr. Granger demanded, dragging Lucy to her feet. "Miss Hayes, you can't—"

"I believe she can do whatever she wants," Simon said. He hadn't moved, sitting there on the ground with his chest heaving, but he smiled up at Lucy as if he had never been happier. "You had best let go of her, Granger."

Lucy tried to tug her arm free, but Mr. Granger held fast. "Please," she added, hoping if she sounded small, he would listen to her. She hoped Mr. Granger would never hurt her, but she knew he would not let her spurn him without putting up a fight. She needed to coax him into letting her go. "We can discuss this."

"There is nothing to discuss, Miss Hayes. You have already agreed to be my wife."

Before Lucy could say anything, Simon barked out a laugh. "Did she ever say those words?"

"What?" Mr. Granger made a face of disgust, as if Simon's question were utterly offensive.

Simon sat up straighter, and he had never looked more unburdened than he did in that moment. He seemed perfectly content to be sitting in the dirt and arguing with a man so far beneath him in every way. "Lucy never says something she doesn't mean," he said, giving her a little half smile that made her heart pick up its pace. Did that mean he had forgiven her?

"Simon," she whispered, hoping he understood just how much his argument meant to her.

He grinned, his smile so full that it practically brought the sun out with it. "And when you drag a woman across the country against her will," he continued, "I am of the opinion that that hardly counts as an agreement."

Mr. Granger tightened his hold on Lucy's arm ever so slightly. Not enough to cause her pain but enough to tell her he was not going to give her up easily. "Lucy, we should be on our way."

"What if I say no?" she replied. Fighting him would only make him angry, but she did not want to just stand there and let these men argue over her.

Eyes going wide, Mr. Granger gaped at her before he recovered. "We have a long way to go, my darling."

"I believe the lady said no," Simon offered from his place on the ground. He must have realized it would take more than that to persuade Mr. Granger, however, because he rose to his feet and took a step closer. Compared to Mr. Granger, he was huge and far more impressive. "I don't think you should need more than that, do you?"

Paling, Mr. Granger took in Simon's large shoulders and seemed to realize he was outmatched, both in argument and physicality. His grip loosened, but he hadn't let go yet.

Simon narrowed his eyes. "Mr. Forester is right behind me," he said, lifting one eyebrow. "Perhaps you would care to explain to him why you think you have any right to dictate a woman's life for her."

For some reason, that did it. Mr. Granger practically shoved Lucy away, sweat beading on his brow as he took her in for one more moment.

Simon decided to add one more argument, drawing a pistol from his jacket and pointing it right between Granger's eyes. "I trust this warning is unnecessary," he growled, "but I'm going to give it anyway. If you set foot anywhere near Lucy Hayes, it will be the last thing you do. And if I catch word of you mistreating any woman, of any status, you'll be looking down my barrel once more."

"You can't threaten me," Mr. Granger spat. He had gone cross-eyed as he stared at the gun. "I'll tell everyone you do business with that you stole my fiancée away from me at gunpoint, and you'll lose everything."

Simon simply smirked. "Who will believe you over me? I know all about your illegal dealings, and you're lucky I have only threatened your life and not your trade. I trust you won't give me a reason to change that."

Glancing once more at Lucy, Mr. Granger seemed to debate whether it would be worth keeping up the fight. It couldn't have been easy to give up something he had been trying to get for five years.

Simon realized the same thing and stepped forward enough to touch the point of his pistol to the man's forehead. He cocked the weapon. "Shall I tell Forester you were noncompliant with my requests? Or perhaps you would like to tell him yourself?"

Turning frightfully pale, Mr. Granger stumbled back to the coach, slipping inside with a shout to the confused driver. The horses soon leaped into a run, carrying him off.

"Thank goodness," Simon breathed, dropping the gun at his feet as if it had burned him. "I had no desire to use that."

Lucy told herself to ignore the fact that she was now standing in the middle of the road with only Simon and a single horse. There were more important matters to discuss.

"You saved me," she whispered.

As Simon's eyes jumped to hers, his body seemed to tense. "I did," he agreed. "Though, that was far easier than I expected. I was ready for a fight."

Lucy wouldn't have minded seeing that, though perhaps avoiding a true confrontation was the preferable outcome. "Nick isn't really coming, is he?" she asked.

Simon seemed drawn to her, pulled close by an unseen power, until he wrapped an arm around her waist and held her against him. "I have no idea," he said, his voice husky. "That man is impossible to keep track of."

Lucy shivered despite the warmth of Simon's hold. For the first time, there were no lies keeping them at a respectable distance. "Why would Mr. Granger be afraid of him?"

"Because he believes everything he hears." Simon rested his forehead against Lucy's and breathed her in.

"How did you know about Mr. Granger's illegal dealings?"

"I didn't. I guessed, and it seems I was right."

Grinning, Lucy pressed her hands to his chest. Was there anywhere in the world she would like better than being right here? She could think of one place. "Simon?"

"Hmm?"

"How are we going to get home?"

Oh, that was a lovely word. *Home.*

Without pulling away, Simon turned and looked at his horse where he grazed. "He can hold us both."

"We won't be able to go very quickly."

"I'm planning on it. Lucy, I am sorry for the way I reacted. Whatever your reasons, I know you never meant any harm, and I never should have gotten angry with you. I wasn't . . . I couldn't bear the thought that you didn't trust me. That I wasn't enough for you."

Lucy blinked tears from her eyes as she ran her palm over the scruff on his cheek. "You are everything I could want and more. I thought you hated me."

"I could never hate you. You are more important to me than anything."

More beautiful words had never been spoken, and Lucy slid her hands up and around Simon's neck. If he could humble himself enough to apologize, she should too. But what came out of her mouth was entirely the opposite. "I would say I regret what I did, but then I would never have gotten to know you the way I did, and that would have been a shame."

He laughed, the sound far warmer than the sun that shone down on them. "I love you, Lucy Hayes." He sealed that comment with a kiss, this one gentle and full of so many promises that Lucy wouldn't be able to put words to them if she tried.

Chapter Thirty-One

SIMON SAT IN HIS FAVORITE armchair in the library, a fire burning in the grate and rain pattering against the window. He was quite cozy, and somehow he had managed to ignore the fact that he had a pile of letters and notices sitting on the desk in his study, waiting for him to deal with whatever new problems had arisen. That itself—avoiding responsibility—was a new experience, and one he was most grateful for.

For the first time since before his father's death, Simon just wanted to have a few hours of peace.

Unfortunately, he had been reading the same page in his book for at least half an hour and had taken in none of it, and he blamed that entirely on Lucy.

By the time they'd made it back to the Park, Simon had had to walk and lead Hermes beside him. Lucy had tried to walk alongside him, but given the fact that she had hardly slept the night before and had had to endure an entire morning in the company of Jonathan Granger, she was understandably exhausted. So she had ridden in silence, and Simon had talked more than he'd talked in years.

He'd told her about his childhood and how devoted he had always been to his father. He'd told her about the years he spent at Father's side, learning to be a good estate owner and knowing how best to use his voice at Lords when he eventually took on the mantel of Lord Calloway. He'd told her about when his father had gotten sick and the days leading up to his death. How Simon had felt the weight of his responsibility even before his father was gone.

By the time they'd made it back home, Lucy was half asleep, and Simon's voice was nearly gone. Lucy had gone straight to bed, and Simon had been greeted by a particularly anxious Forester, who in his own exhaustion, had revealed he had known Lucy's secret all along but recognized her need to do what she had done, even if he hadn't known the reason for it at first.

Simon wasn't surprised in the least.

The man was an enigma, and his tall tales were a little misguided, but he had a good heart, and he could always see good hearts in those around him. Simon prayed Forester could find a wife who would soften his sharper edges and convince him that the only man worth knowing was the real one. Maybe then he would stop hiding behind his masks and lies and finally tell Simon why he had taken on the role of the deceiver to begin with.

But he was glad Lucy had had someone to confide in. Otherwise, she might have run before Simon could fall in love with her.

"Oh, I'm sorry."

Simon glanced up, surprised to see William in the doorway. He was pretty sure he'd never seen his brother in the library before. "Will."

William made a face of discomfort. Despite everything turning out relatively well, there was still a lot of tension between the two of them.

"I didn't mean to interrupt," William said, and he took a step back toward the door.

Simon was tempted to let him go, but he swallowed his pride and shook his head. "Stay," he said, shutting his book. "I can't focus anyway."

"I came to get a book of poetry for Martine," William explained as he drew deeper into the room. "She says it helps with her English, but I think she just really likes poetry."

Cringing, Simon debated opening up this particular topic, but he knew they would need to talk about it eventually. "About your wife . . ."

William sighed. "I know you think poorly of me."

"I didn't say that."

"You didn't have to. It's written all over your face."

This was going to be harder than he thought, but Simon was determined to really talk to his brother. It had been too long since he had. "Will you sit?"

William eyed him warily but did as requested. When he moved stiffly, wincing and touching a hand to his rib cage, Simon suddenly remembered what the physician had told him days ago.

"We need to talk about how you were wounded."

Paling, William glanced at the slightly open door before he spoke. "I hoped you would forget about that."

"You were nearly on your deathbed. Of course I wasn't going to forget about it. What happened?"

William was clearly reluctant to elaborate, glancing at the door again, as if considering the value of leaving before he got himself into more trouble, but then he sighed. "Marrying a girl without her father's permission can stir some . . . unwelcome feelings. When we returned from Scotland, he wasn't pleased."

Simon gritted his teeth. "Will, you idiot."

"I was smitten."

There was no point in trying to convince William he had made a mistake in getting married. The deed was already done. Simon would just have to move on and hope his brother did right by the girl. "Tell me about her."

"About Martine?" William's eyebrows rose high, as if this was the last thing he had expected. And when Simon said nothing, he took a slow breath. "Oh. Well. She's French."

"I know that part."

"And beautiful."

Simon knew that, too, but he wouldn't admit that out loud. Just in case. Lucy had been sleeping late this morning, but there was always the chance she would appear and hear something she could misconstrue. William's wife was far from homely, but no one would ever compare to Lucy.

"She . . ." William waved a hand around. "There's just something about her, isn't there?"

Simon had never heard anything more ridiculous in his life, and he had to fight a grin. "Do you know anything about your wife, Will?"

"Of course I do!" But he didn't exactly speak with confidence. "She is a divine dancer. And she . . . er . . . speaks two languages, possibly three, though perhaps that was only musical terms, not Italian . . ."

While William struggled to describe the woman he had pledged his life to, Simon considered the one he hoped to wed. Lucy had grown up with little more than a loving father and a desire to be good. She was true to her word and often said things she shouldn't, and she had an honest heart, even if she had been forced to lie. If he thought back on it, she really hadn't lied at all. She simply hadn't corrected others' lies. In fact, she had even tried to do just that, but none of them had believed her.

She understood business but knew the value of leisure as well, and she had the most stunning dark eyes that always seemed to be hiding something amusing just beneath the surface. She cared for the people around her, no matter their station. And she was the person who made Simon's heart pound with renewed vigor. She made him want to be better, and she made him believe he was more than what he had been given.

"I love her, Simon," William said, breaking him out of his thoughts. "I've loved her from the moment I first laid eyes on her. Is that not enough?"

Lucy had nothing to offer Simon. No title, no fortune, not a connection to speak of. In the eyes of the *ton*, she was hardly worth noticing.

But Simon loved her. He would do anything to be with her. A week ago, he would have called William a fool, but today he smiled.

"Yes," he said. "That is enough. If you're happy. Try Burns."

William frowned. "What?"

Simon pointed to a book behind William's head. "Poetry. I think she'll like it."

"Oh." He grabbed the book in question and flipped through the pages with his thumb. He made to stand, but he must have thought better of it and instead met Simon's gaze. "It wasn't her fault, you know. Lucy's. I was the one who suggested she pretend to be my wife, and I don't think she was thrilled about the idea from the start. If I hadn't—"

"If you hadn't done what you did, she would have fallen into the hands of that lout Granger. And I never would have met her. So I suppose I should thank you."

Laughing, William did stand this time, and he tucked the book under his arm as he headed for the door. "Simon, thanking me," he muttered. "I never thought I'd see the day."

When he opened the door, Lucy was standing there, as if she'd been about to come in, and Simon's heart lurched in the most ridiculous way. It wasn't like he had gone long without seeing her. Perhaps a part of him had wondered if yesterday had been nothing more than a dream.

"You're in luck," William said to Lucy with a grin. "He's in a good mood today."

Simon might have scowled at his brother if Lucy hadn't laughed and filled the room with light. Oh, how he loved that laugh, which was so much lighter than anything he'd ever heard. If he had known how much her secrets had muted her over the last week, he would have begged her to tell him everything days ago. She looked so much more alive now, her eyes bright and a smile playing at her lips. Lips that were looking mighty tempting . . .

"William," Simon growled.

"Leaving," he replied, and he shut the door behind him.

Simon forced himself not to run to her, but he still moved with laughable speed across the room until he was face-to-face with her. "You look well-rested." He clapped a hand to his face. That was the first thing he said to her after such an eventful afternoon yesterday? What an imbecile.

Fighting another laugh, Lucy glanced behind her. "Aren't you afraid of the scandal that might come if we're discovered here alone?"

Simon moved in closer, though he worried what might happen if he touched her, so he kept an appropriate distance. Perhaps this was only a dream. "I suppose I would be forced to marry you," he said with a wavering voice. He cleared his throat, hoping that would help.

Lucy cocked her head. "Are you afraid of me, Simon?"

His stomach dipped. "Immensely."

"Why?" Her suppressed grin only touched half her mouth, and it was driving Simon mad.

"You make me nervous," he admitted. The vulnerability felt good to admit. "I never know how to act around you."

"This coming from the man who chased down a coach to propose to me just yesterday?"

Technically, she hadn't given him an answer to that proposal, which was part of the reason he hesitated now. Lucy never said anything she didn't mean. Did that mean she didn't want to marry him?

She crossed the distance between them and put a hand on his chest, sending shivers throughout his entire body. "Why weren't you afraid yesterday?" she asked, probably thinking it was an easy question to answer.

It wasn't. The answer was terrifying.

"I had already lost you," he said quietly, "so the risk wasn't there. Now I fear I will scare you off again."

Moving in closer, Lucy didn't stop until she was close enough that her skirts brushed his knees. "You didn't scare me off."

"I did, and you know it."

"I lied to you about everything, so perhaps we can call it even?" She asked the question in jest, but Simon could feel the real fear behind her words. She worried he wouldn't forgive her for her deceit.

He would have thought his proposal yesterday would have eased her worries, but perhaps he needed to be a little clearer. Swallowing his nerves, he took both her hands, enveloping them in each of his and holding them to his chest. "Lucy Hayes, I don't blame you for anything that happened, and I never will. Do you believe me?" He punctuated that question with a brief kiss because he hoped it would convince her but also because he really wanted to kiss her.

She smiled against his lips. "I might need more convincing. I told a good many lies."

Simon kissed her again. "So does Forester."

"Do you kiss him too?"

"He has never let me." As soon as those words left his mouth, Simon made a face of alarm, his eyes wide as his face burned hot. "Oh heavens, that sounded—"

Lucy cut him off, grabbing his jacket and pulling him in for a kiss that stole his breath. For a moment, he forgot what they were even talking about, but when his fingers got tangled in her hair, he reluctantly fell back into reality as he tried to free himself.

Laughing, Lucy undid the pins holding her hair up.

Seeing her long hair down like that nearly undid Simon.

If she knew how easily she affected him, she didn't acknowledge it. She simply continued to pull her dark hair free until it hung down her back. "Yes, by the way."

Simon had been about to lean in for another kiss, but her words stopped him in his tracks. "What?"

She grinned. "I know you didn't technically ask me to marry you, but you did ask if I wanted to be Lady Calloway, and—"

"Yes?" Simon whispered. Was she in earnest? But this was Lucy, and she never said anything she didn't intend to follow through with. He had learned that much about her, at least. "You mean . . ."

Biting her lip in the most tempting manner—not that that was her intent, most likely—Lucy slowly slid her arms around Simon's neck and stretched up on her toes until their noses brushed. "I am only a governess, Simon. The daughter of a tailor. I will never be like the women of Society."

"For which we are all grateful."

She laughed a little. "There is nothing I can give you except my heart, and I fear I lost it to you long ago anyway. Do you want it?"

"Want it?" Simon was already planning a business trip to London to give himself a good reason to go to Town to obtain a special license. Three weeks seemed an awfully long time to wait for a wedding. He hadn't known this woman for three days before he was head-over-heels in love with her. "Lucy Hayes, I have never met a woman like you, and I doubt I ever will again. You are everything I could want in a partner, no matter how unorthodox our match will be. I have never walked within Society's guidelines, and I am of the opinion that my life would be far better if I lived it my way. With you at my side. I would give up everything I have if it meant I could keep you."

And though he expected her to reward that answer with a kiss, she leaned back so their eyes could meet. "Speaking of that," she said on a breath. "Have you ever thought of letting William handle some of the businesses?"

Simon very nearly laughed. "He would destroy them."

"He might surprise you."

"He ruins everything he touches," Simon argued. "Besides, he never stays in one place for long."

"Because he's bored. With the money his inheritance brings in, he has nothing to do but travel and find entertainment." Lucy smiled just then, the kind of smile that brought back the fluttering in his stomach that always seemed to crop up whenever she was around. "Now he has a wife," she said, and suddenly her fingers were rising, leaving his neck and ending up in his hair.

Chills ran down Simon's back as she ran her hand across his scalp. She was surely messing up his hair, but who was he to complain? He would gladly let her do it because he had a feeling he wouldn't be messing it up himself when she was around. She made him calm. Grounded. *Happy.*

"And now he has a reason to stay home," she added, "giving him even more free time. Plenty of it, in fact."

Her idea wasn't a bad one. Nor was it great.

She had one more argument up her sleeve, one she gave with the softest of kisses. "And letting him take on those responsibilities would leave more free time for you, to do whatever you'd like. You wouldn't have to leave home so often."

Simon swallowed. "What if—"

"If he fails, then it is his failure. Not yours." Lucy brushed her thumb down his lips, sending his heart spasming. "Your father would be proud of you no matter what happens, and maybe William needs a chance to prove himself too. Sometimes you have to have a little faith in people. It worked out with me, didn't it? But whatever you decide, I will be by your side, helping you through it. I would even travel with you, if you wanted me to."

"You'll marry me?" Simon asked. He had to say the words.

Lucy grinned. "Of course."

He pulled her in again, kissing her until he couldn't breathe. He had a feeling life was going to be wonderful with Lucy at his side, and it would only get better with every moment they were together.

He wasn't sure how long they'd been in the library, taking advantage of this rare moment alone, but eventually Lucy pulled away and grinned at him with a bit of mischief in her eyes. Whatever she was thinking, he already wanted to agree.

"I've always been curious about something," she said as she started gathering up her hair to return it to its proper state. Simon traced every motion with his eyes, wondering if he would be able to convince her to keep it down always once they were married. Society standards were overrated.

"What is that, my love?" he asked to distract himself from her tempting hair.

Lucy laughed when she caught his expression, though he had no idea what he looked like. "Since the first day I arrived at Calloway Park, there has been the question of who is the better rider. I confess I'm most interested to know who would win if you had a true race with your sister. I owe it to Olivia to reschedule the event, seeing as I caused a disruption."

Simon's stomach twisted a little. Technically, the disruption had been because of him. If he had remained rational, he would have immediately realized his good fortune in learning Lucy was unattached to William. He wouldn't have been soaked to the bone by that blasted storm. He would have been able to kiss Lucy so much sooner.

Yes, a kiss was a good idea.

His lips were practically on hers again before she lifted her hand to his mouth to stop him, and he groaned against her fingers. She was right, though, and they needed to be cautious. Society could overlook her station, but only if he went about this the right way. A true courtship would benefit them both.

Lucy only smiled as he took a step back with what he felt was a Herculean level of restraint. "Olivia deserves a chance, just like William. Let them show you who they are and what they can do."

"You have a good deal of faith in my family. Why?"

Lucy's expression shifted into one of quiet contemplation, and she took hold of Simon's hands, as if he offered the strength she required to respond. He couldn't remember being needed in quite that way before, and he loved it. "They had faith in me," she said, and tears pooled in her eyes. Happy tears, he hoped. "They took me in without question and treated me like one of their own when I didn't deserve their kindness. They were exactly what I needed, even if I didn't know it."

"And you were what we needed," Simon replied. "Especially me."

She shook her head, and she seemed to be memorizing his features. "I don't understand why you would want someone like me when you could have anyone."

Did she truly have no idea how much she meant to him? He kissed the tip of her nose, then her cheek, and then he pressed a kiss below her ear before he forced himself back once more. "Give me a lifetime," he said, "and I'll make sure you never doubt my love for you, Lucy. Will you give me that?"

She ran her hands through his hair again, and Simon had a feeling they would be in the library for a while yet. "A lifetime?" she whispered. "I'll give you forever, Simon Calloway."

Epilogue

Sometimes, when Lucy walked the path to the pond on her own, she got the inexplicable feeling that if she closed her eyes, she would open them again to find herself walking down a London street among the dirt and the putrid smell that always seemed to permeate the poorer parts of the city. Her fear would bubble up, her shoulders tense, and every inch of her turn to ice.

But no matter how many times she thought she might wake from the dream that her life had become, she always found herself with the most incredible sight at the end of the path, just as she did today.

Yes, the pond was breathtaking, especially in the winter as it was right now, but it was Simon who truly stole the air from her lungs.

She wasn't sure how long he had been out here today, but given the fact that the pond was frozen over and her breath came out in puffs of mist, it had probably been too long. He sat in a frozen patch of dirt cleared of snow, his eyes fixed on the ice in front of him and his eyebrows pulled low in concentration.

Settling at his side, Lucy tucked her blanket around both their shoulders and smiled when he immediately leaned into her. "I hope you remember what we talked about," she said, keeping her voice quiet so as not to disturb the peace of the place.

Simon looped her arm through his, but his thoughtful expression didn't change. "I am not thinking about work," he replied. He had made a promise to her only days after he proposed to her, agreeing to keep his pond free from the stresses of his life. Five months down the road, and he had so far kept that promise.

Lucy frowned, trying to think of what else might cause him to look so concerned. "Tell me," she whispered, brushing a finger down his forehead to smooth out the ridges.

Thankfully, he smiled and leaned closer, touching a kiss to the tip of her nose. "I received a letter from Forester this morning."

"How is Nick?" He had left for London soon after the whole madness with Mr. Granger, returning only long enough to attend their wedding. Though Lucy had written to him more than once, his responses had been few and far between. It seemed his benefactor had caused him some trouble when it came to the money he was due to inherit, leaving him scrambling to provide for himself because his estate hardly brought him enough income to support himself.

When Simon made a face of worry, Lucy's stomach churned. "What is it?" she asked warily. "What happened?"

"He's getting married."

For a moment, Lucy tried to understand why that news would worry him so. Nick had been looking for a wife for years; surely this was a good thing. "Simon?"

Sighing, he reached into his coat pocket and handed her a letter. "He's been searching for so long, and the woman has nothing to her name but a modest dowry. I can't help but wonder if there is more to this than he's telling me. With Forester, it is impossible to know where the truth ends and the lies begin."

Lucy held the letter for a moment, marveling at how thick it was. "Does he always write such long letters?"

Simon chuckled. "Always. Nick Forester writes far more than he speaks, and that's saying something. Read here." He pointed to a line near the beginning of the letter.

> *I never told you, but in order to gain the inheritance I was promised, I was required to be married.*

Lucy raised her eyebrows. "No wonder he was searching so thoroughly. It is good to know he did not choose the first woman who would be willing, putting himself in an unhappy marriage."

"I wouldn't wish that on anyone," Simon said, kissing Lucy's cheek with a sigh. "Thank you, by the way."

Though his lips were cold, his touch filled her with warmth. "For what?"

"For a happy marriage."

Grinning, she pulled him in for a quick but potent kiss on the lips. That was something she would never tire of. "So why the worry for Nick?" she pressed. "You should be glad he finally found someone after all this time."

He sighed. "Here," he said and pointed to another line in the letter.

When I returned to London in the summer, Mr. Mackenzie informed me I had a deadline of six months to be married or I would forfeit my entire inheritance to his granddaughter.

"Oh." Lucy thought she understood now. "You're worried he has settled with his time running out."

Nodding, Simon ran a hand through his hair. "Forester puts on a good face when in Society, but he feels more than most people. A poor marriage will kill the man, but he'd never admit to such a vulnerability now. He would simply lie and say he was perfectly happy, suffering in silence."

Lucy nudged him. "That isn't unlike you, you know."

"We're talking about Nick, my love. Not me." But he offered her a little smile of acknowledgment before he continued. "Until a few years ago, he was one of the most honest, sincere men I knew."

"What changed?"

"I wish I knew. In the middle of the Season, he ended his engagement without explanation and started telling his ridiculous stories until the man I'd grown up with was gone, replaced by the one the world now reveres. Sometimes I see glimpses of the genuine Nick Forester, but I fear this marriage is merely another one of the lies he tells. I worry he is doing it only for the money."

The way Simon was frowning again, Lucy imagined he would sit here in the cold for hours if she let him. Taking his hand, she pulled him to his feet and led him back to the house and the roaring fire in the library.

Only when they were settled on the sofa there, Lucy curled up at his side, did she speak again. "How do you know Nick doesn't love this woman?" she asked. "He told me he wouldn't be married for anything but the deepest love, and I don't believe that was a lie."

As Simon took a slow breath, he lifted his shoulders in a shrug before he met her gaze. "You truly see the good in all people, don't you? Is it any wonder I fell in love with you?"

Her heart beat a little faster. Sometimes, if she let herself overthink things, she wondered if she had made some mistake along the way and never actually told Simon the truth about her. Had he married her because he thought she was something different? Was all of this a lie after all?

Simon's eyebrows pulled together when he saw the look in her eyes. "Stop that," he commanded, some of the impressive baron coming out in the strength of his voice. "I knew exactly who you were when I pledged my life to you, Lucy Calloway. When are you going to trust me?"

"When I forget how thoroughly I lied to you," she whispered back.

Simon's response came in the form of an intense kiss that left her feeling dizzy but wanting more. Everything he felt seemed to be in that kiss. He had been right all those months ago; a kiss was never nothing, and he had proved it time and time again.

"Have you lied to me since?" he asked with a smile.

"Only once," Lucy replied.

That caught him off guard, draining the color from his face as he stared at her.

Though she was terrified, Lucy pushed forward. "This morning," she said. "When I told you I must have eaten a bad piece of cheese."

Concern flooded his expression. "Are you still feeling ill? I can ask Cook to make you a tisane or—"

"Simon." Lucy grinned, glad she was able to stop him from offering up the world to make her feel better. He would do it, too, if she gave him the opportunity. "It wasn't the food that made me sick this morning, and I expect I'll feel the same for some months."

"Months? But what . . ."

Lucy could see the moment he put the pieces together; it was like a new light flickered to life behind his eyes, which slid down to her abdomen with unrestrained hope.

"Lucy."

"Yes?"

"You mean . . . ?"

"Yes."

"You're . . . ?"

"We're having a baby, Simon."

He kissed her again, and though he put his elation into that kiss, he was immeasurably gentle at the same time. Oh, but he was going to make a wonderful father, and Lucy couldn't wait to have her own little family.

Eventually Simon pulled away, though Lucy could feel his heart racing in his chest. "Are you happy?" he asked breathlessly. "I know this wasn't how you thought your life would go."

"More than I could ever say. I never thought I would have this, no matter how much I wanted it. And to think I might have lost this chance thanks to my lies."

Simon shook his head. "Without your lies, I never would have met you. Honestly, I've half a mind to write to Jonathan Granger and thank him for sending you to me."

Lucy hated the fear that rose deep inside her at just the mention of that name. "Please don't. I still worry he is dangerous."

"Did I not tell you?" Simon laughed and grabbed Nick's letter from where it had fallen to the floor during their kiss. "Right here," he said, pointing.

> *Tell your lovely wife that I've recently learned Granger is flat broke and likely to leave Town. It seems many of his business associates have heard of his less-than-reputable dealings and cut ties with the scoundrel, though he has not been able to discern where they got their information. I admit to nothing.*
>
> *Beyond that, he bears a striking resemblance to the fatherless child of one of Huntingdon's kitchen girls. She apparently worked for Granger's brother before and was set upon by Granger, but the family turned her away when she had no proof to the fact. He denies everything, but you know Lady Huntingdon. The countess is not about to let this injustice rest now that she knows of it, and her elusive husband has that way of striking fear into the hearts of cowardly men.*
>
> *I've always wanted to befriend that man, but he ignores me every time. I suppose he is jealous of my infamy, being the recluse that he is. You wouldn't believe the number of people who think it was me, but have you ever thought perhaps Huntingdon could be the notorious Thief of London?*

Lucy looked up. "Thief of London?"

Chuckling, Simon shook his head. "It's been a few years, but for a while there, someone was stealing from anyone in high Society who wronged the less fortunate. Trying to teach them to be more charitable, I suppose. Stop them from using their wealth to harm others."

"I would imagine you were safe?"

He leaned in, teasing Lucy with another soft kiss. "I like to think I'm a good man."

"The best," Lucy corrected. "Even if you are obnoxiously wealthy."

"My wealth counts against me? Then, I renounce it."

"No need to resort to drastic measures, Simon. I don't want to have to call you Nothing-at-All once more."

He gasped. "You wouldn't."

"Wouldn't I?"

"The point is you're safe from Granger. You will always be safe." He kissed her forehead, then her nose, and then the corner of her mouth, taking his time with each one. "We're going to have to tell Olivia about this."

"About the thief? Or about these distracting kisses of yours?"

He chuckled. "About Forester getting married. She'll be heartbroken."

"She's more excited for her first Season than you think," Lucy argued. "And she'll have more suitors than she'll know what to do with."

Simon let out a deep sigh. "That's what I'm worried about. Think she would be angry if I cut her dowry in half? Or even down to a third? Perhaps then she will not be set upon by every fortune hunter out there. Another reason to rid myself of all this obnoxious money."

Lightly smacking his leg, Lucy settled herself into his arms and let herself imagine, for just a moment, what it might have been like if she had been able to enter Society the normal way. If her father had lived, he would have brought her to as many functions as he could, but he had never been anything but poor. Lucy likely would have been overlooked, perhaps even by Simon. As difficult as her life had been, she was grateful it had gotten her here.

Olivia's dowry would get her extra notice, of course, but the girl knew she had no reason to settle for anything less than what she wanted. She would make the right choice when the time came.

"Do you have such little faith in your sister?" Lucy asked quietly. "Olivia is intelligent enough to recognize sincerity when she sees it, and surely there are more men out there like you and Nick. Men who care more about the woman than her station or fortune."

"I truly hope you are right," Simon breathed. "I'm glad she has you though. I might have made a mess of her come-out, but you're wise enough to keep her from making any foolish mistakes."

"Simon, you're saying this to the woman who pretended to be engaged to a baron's brother instead of simply asking for assistance."

"The woman who saved me from myself," he argued, holding her more tightly. "The woman I love more than anything in the world. The woman who is bearing my child." He let out a contented sigh. "My child," he repeated, and though Lucy couldn't see him, she could hear the happiness in his voice as he settled his head atop hers.

She closed her eyes, listening to Simon's steady heartbeat until she fell asleep in his arms and dreamed of the happiness that was still to come.

About the Author

Dana LeCheminant has been telling stories since she was old enough to know what stories were. After spending most of her childhood reading everything she could get her hands on, she eventually realized she could write her own books, and since then she has always had plots brewing and characters clamoring to be next to have their stories told. A lover of all things outdoors, she finds inspiration while hiking the remote Utah backcountry and cruising down rivers. Until her endless imagination runs dry, she will always have another story to tell.

Dana loves connecting with readers and talking books!

Website: lecheminantbooks.com

Facebook: @authordanalecheminant

Instagram: @authordanalecheminant